**He let the desk drop with a thud.
"Did you know that about me?"**

She tried for a nonchalant shrug. "I knew you were strong. Not *that* strong." Who the hell was he? Anger began to slide through her veins.

"Close your eyes. What do you hear?"

She kept her eyes open. "The hum of the heating unit." Other than that, silence echoed through the night.

Shane shook his head. "The elevator has gone up twenty-three times in the last couple hours; gone down twenty-seven times." His hands reached out to grab her forearms. "I need thirty-three steps to walk from here to the elevator." His gaze dropped to her neck. "Your pulse rate increased when I grabbed your arms. I can hear it." The large hands tightened around her biceps. "And you're a liar. When you say this isn't going to happen, you're lying."

He tugged her into masculine hardness, into incredible heat. His lips took hers, firm and determined. While he'd always been passionate, this was new. Intense and dangerous, his hold showed no mercy. Hunger ripped through her veins.

"See what you do to me," he rumbled against her mouth. "From the first second I saw you, you've done this to me."

FORGOTTEN SINS

REBECCA ZANETTI

FOREVER

NEW YORK   BOSTON

Copyright © 2013 by Rebecca Zanetti
Excerpt from *Sweet Revenge* by Rebecca Zanetti copyright © 2013 by Rebecca Zanetti.
All rights reserved. In accordance with the U.S. Copyright Act of 1976, the scanning, uploading, and electronic sharing of any part of this book without the permission of the publisher is unlawful piracy and theft of the author's intellectual property. If you would like to use material from the book (other than for review purposes), prior written permission must be obtained by contacting the publisher at permissions@hbgusa.com. Thank you for your support of the author's rights.

Forever
Hachette Book Group
237 Park Avenue
New York, NY 10017

www.HachetteBookGroup.com

Printed in the United States of America

Originally published as an ebook

First Mass-Market Edition: January 2014
10 9 8 7 6 5 4 3 2 1

OPM

Forever is an imprint of Grand Central Publishing.
The Forever name and logo are trademarks of Hachette Book Group, Inc.

The Hachette Speakers Bureau provides a wide range of authors for speaking events. To find out more, go to www.hachettespeakersbureau.com or call (866) 376-6591.

The publisher is not responsible for websites (or their content) that are not owned by the publisher.

To Vince Rossi: the best godfather, softball coach, cowboy, dentist, and river guide who ever lived. We miss you so very much.

ACKNOWLEDGMENTS

I love the acknowledgments page in a book because thanking people makes me happy; yet it adds some stress in case I've forgotten anyone. If I have, I truly apologize. Many people worked hard to make this book happen, and I am very grateful.

First, a big thank-you to my husband, Big Tone. People ask all the time how an author with a day job and kids gets everything done, and I tell them it's because I'm married to you. You get things done. Even before I sold my first book, when writing just took time away from activities, you encouraged me to give it a shot. Thank you.

To my kids, Gabe and Karly, thank you for the support, for the laughs, and for the fun. You're the best kids on earth, and I love you.

To my talented agent, Caitlin Blasdell, thank you for protecting, guiding, and enhancing my career. The edits you send always make the book so much stronger. You're the calm in a wild industry, and I appreciate you so much! Thank you to Liza Dawson for teaching me to set the scene, to Havis Dawson for his expert editing advice, and to Hannah Bowman for character insights. The Dawson gang truly rocks.

To my amazing editor, Michele Bidelspach, thank you for the fantastic, detailed edits for this book. I think we reached a depth with the characters that readers will love, and that's from your expertise. I've really enjoyed working with you and hope we have many books to come. Thank you to everyone at Grand Central Publishing who has worked so hard on getting this book to readers.

Thank you to Kelly Mueller at Books-n-Kisses for your friendship and support, and thank you to Bonnie Paulson, Tina Jacobson, and Asa Bradley for answering quick questions about grammar and logic...and for your friendship. Also, thank you to Carla Gallway for your hard work.

Thank you to the Lethal Ladies Critique Group for the wisdom and fun, to my FB street team for the encouragement and laughs, and to my local RWA Group, IECRWA, for the support and good times.

And as always, thank you to my constant support system: Gail and Jim English, Debbie and Travis Smith, Stephanie and Donald West, Brandie and Mike Chapman, Jessica and Jonah Namson, and Kathy and Herb Zanetti.

FORGOTTEN SINS

PROLOGUE

Southern Tennessee Hills
Twenty Years Ago

SHANE SETTLED AGAINST the cold block wall, engrossed in the television set across the room but forcing himself periodically to glance outside the darkened window. The second dawn hit, he and his brothers had to flee the computer center. Their current transgression was punishable by beating or confinement. Probably both.

But a night spent watching a marathon of the show featuring a family living in the city was well worth the risk and provided an insight into a world he had only dreamed about. Breaking into the private room housing the television had been almost too easy. It surprised him the soldiers taught them stealth and surveillance but didn't expect them to use the skills.

A boom sounded in the distance—probably from a coal mine hours away. Just to double-check, he lifted his head and used his special hearing to make sure they were safe. A wolf prowled a mile or so away, and prey scattered. No humans breathed nearby. Well, none other than his three brothers while they watched the show. The eighth episode wound down to cheerful music and a happy ending.

"What's a family?" Jory, his youngest brother, asked.

Shane forced a shrug. "I think a family is people who live together."

"So we're family?" Jory's voice cracked.

Shane nodded, his shoulders straightening. "Yeah, we're family."

"What's a mom?" Jory scratched his head.

"I guess it's that lady there." Shane pointed at the woman on the screen.

"She looks..." Matt, the oldest of them all, said thoughtfully, "soft."

They all nodded.

"How come we don't have moms or ladies here?" Jory asked.

Shane shrugged again. He probably didn't deserve a mom, but Jory did. Why didn't Jory get a mom? "Maybe soldiers don't get moms."

"Oh." Jory turned back to the screen. "She looks nice."

Yeah. The soft lady had looked nice.

Nathan jumped up. "It's time to go—sun's out." As the second oldest, Nathan usually kept a close eye on Jory and Shane, while Matt spent his time training them to survive.

Shane stood and reached down to help Jory up.

He yanked back. "I want to stay."

"Now, Jory." Matt slid the door open a sliver to peer outside. "They're already starting hand-to-hand."

Jory stood and brushed off his pants. "Fine."

"Follow me, and don't look guilty." Matt headed into the chilly dawn, followed by Nathan.

Shane waited until Jory was clear before shutting the

door and hustling over to train with Nathan. All around them, boys engaged in mock-fighting. His brother kicked him in the stomach, and he allowed the pain to disappear before punching Nate in the jaw.

The sun angled through the trees when the commander strode onto the practice area followed by two soldiers who pulled behind them a short, dirty man. Grease and debris littered the man's long dark hair and beard. The prisoner's hands were bound behind his back, and he furiously begged in a language Shane hadn't learned yet. The man's bare feet dragged in the dirt, leaving clear tracks. His blood made a swishing sound as it shot through his veins too quickly. Lung tissue crackled as his breath panted out.

Terror had a sound.

"Soldiers." The commander called them to attention.

They quickly moved into formation. The commander was straight and sure, his hair cut in a short buzz. His eyes were a deep, dark black. Shane always tried to concentrate on something else when facing the commander, sure that getting lost in those black depths would mean death. He knew it somehow.

He and the other boys watched impassively as a soldier forced the prisoner to his knees.

"You've been studying anatomy and pressure points for a month now," the commander said. "Today we concentrate on the swiftest and most economical way to break someone's neck."

The live demonstrations always made Shane's head pound. Did the prisoner know he was about to die? Probably. Shane steeled his spine just in case it was his turn. Please don't let it be his turn.

The commander paused and then called out, "Cadet Shane."

As Shane moved forward to stand by the prisoner, Matt began to shift from his place in formation, reaching for the knife sheathed at his calf. Shane subtly shook his head. Even if Matt somehow stabbed the commander so they could run, they didn't have anywhere to go. The commander would always find them.

Matt stood down, his entire body tense. As the oldest of the brothers, he considered it his duty to protect them somehow. Their identical gray eyes met, Matt's hot and desperate. Shane tried to shrug, but his shoulders shook instead. His gut hurt.

Hopefully he wouldn't lose his mind for a few days like Matt had when it had been his turn. Shane understood this was another part of his training—he was old enough to kill now.

He had just turned ten.

CHAPTER
1

Present Day

JOSIE'S HEELS CLICKED in rapid staccato against the well-worn tiles, the smell of bleach making her stomach cramp. Her mind spun. How could this be happening? It must be some sort of trick.

Someone had taped smiling pumpkins along the hospital walls to celebrate the month of October. Something about their jagged teeth against the dim walls creeped her out. Even as an adult, the sense of helplessness she'd felt as a child in the hospital caused her body to tense and brace to flee from the antiseptic smells.

Several nurses converged behind a wide counter, studying charts. Josie ignored them and hurried down the hall. She reached the last room on the left and ran smack into a uniformed police officer. Bouncing back, she struggled to balance herself in the heels she'd worn to work. The call had come in after dinner, and she was still at the office. As usual. A promotion to vice president was up for grabs, and she was going to get it.

The cop steadied her, dark eyes appraising. "You all right, ma'am?"

"Yes." She tugged her handbag strap up her arm, needing to get a grip. She was an adult and in control now. "A Detective Malloy called me to come down. I'm Josie Dean." Her breath hitched on her last name; she'd be changing that soon.

"He's inside with Mr. Dean."

"Major Dean," she said automatically, and then her face heated. "I mean, he used to be a major. He may have been promoted." God. She sounded like an idiot.

A voice over a loudspeaker announced a code blue. The officer straightened, listened, and then relaxed his shoulders as a room on the third floor was named. "You can go right in." He tipped his head toward the open doorway before flashing a smile at a pretty nurse pushing a book cart down the hall.

Yeah. She'd *go right in*. Easier said than done. Josie took a deep breath, steeled herself, and walked inside, her attention instantly captured by the male figure perched against the hospital bed.

For the briefest of seconds, time stopped. Memories flooded through her mind, her body, maybe somewhere deeper until her lungs forgot their job. That quickly, she was helpless with the need to heal him. Coughing, she forced air down her throat and took a good look.

Several bandages were strapped across Shane's muscular torso while a splotchy purple lump rose from his forehead. His long legs were encased in bloody jeans, and he'd crossed his thick boots at the ankles. He sat bare to the waist, his scarred chest and packed abs betraying a life of combat. The new wounds would fit with the rest.

Those scars broke her heart all over again.

His gray eyes lasered in on her, and she fought the urge to run. Pain, need, and familiarity swirled through her brain. Her skin warmed. Damn, he looked good. Dark brown hair swept back from his battered face, and even with the bruises, his rugged features spoke of strength and masculine beauty. Fierce and dangerous like a wolf.

His hair had grown to his shoulders and added a wild new edge to the danger.

She had a lot of layers, and he'd appealed to her on each one by providing security and fulfilling her desperate need to belong. Until he'd abandoned her. She faltered and clutched her handbag strap until the leather cut into her skin.

A throat cleared. "Mrs. Dean?"

"Josie." She shifted her focus to a man in a rumpled brown suit who leaned against a poster depicting the inner ear. The room was small—examination table, smooth counter with sink, one rolling chair for a doctor. Yet she hadn't even noticed the other man until he made a sound. "Detective Malloy?"

"Yes." Shrewd eyes the color of his suit studied her, and he began scribbling in a notebook. "Is this your husband?"

The quiet power of Shane's presence yanked her attention back to him. Even after all this time, he commanded her body's responses. He cocked his head as if awaiting her answer.

She nodded. "This is Shane Dean." This couldn't be happening. The helplessness she'd felt as a frightened and hurting child in the hospital closed in on her. The need to flee made her knees tremble. She focused on the closest person she had to family, struggling to keep her lips firm. It was really him. Really Shane. "They said you have amnesia."

Shane gave a short nod. "I can't remember a damn thing."

The familiar rumble of his voice slammed into her solar plexus. Emotion washed through her edged with a sharp pain. Two years. Two long years since he'd left her. "What happened?"

The detective stopped writing. "We were hoping you might provide an explanation. Where was your husband going today?"

She barked out a laugh. Seriously? "I have absolutely no idea. We're separated."

Shane stilled, the air thickening with tension around him. "We are?"

"I haven't seen you in two years." Her voice shook, and she fought to settle raw nerves. She would not let him affect her. "I didn't even know you were back in the country."

"What country should he have been in?" the detective asked.

Like she'd know. "He's in the marines based out of Pendleton. Call them." Wait a minute. "How did you know to call me if you didn't know he was in the military?" She took a small step back to study her husband. "And what are you doing in Washington State?"

Shane shrugged. The paper on the table crinkled as he moved. "Dunno. Probably coming to visit you from my home in Oregon? I have an Oregon driver's license as well as a card with your name and phone number in my wallet...along with our marriage license. Am I from Oregon?"

Her thoughts began to swirl. "Yes. I mean, I think so."

A muscle in his jaw ticked. "You don't know?"

"No. I didn't know much about you, Shane. We met

in California and married there." Within three weeks of meeting each other—the one and only time in her life she'd taken a risk and been spontaneous. Of course it had ended in disaster. She had been so stupid. What had she been thinking?

The detective cleared his throat. "Your husband isn't wearing dog tags. He was found down by the river, which is miles across the city from your home. To your knowledge, does he know anyone else here in Snowville?"

"No." At least, she didn't think so. More than 100,000 people lived in the eastern Washington town. Shane might know somebody else who lived there.

Her knees began to tremble, and she forced them still with stubborn pride. She dug her nails into her palms to quell the urge to caress his bruises. Her romantic notion of being able to heal him, to show him love was possible, had earned her a broken heart. Rightfully so. It was over. *They* were over. Her body needed to freakin' remember that fact. As did her heart.

Shane's eyes sharpened. "When did you move to Washington?"

"Two years ago."

"When we separated."

"Yes."

He lifted an eyebrow in an expression she remembered well. "Did I know we were separated?"

Warmth flushed through her chest, just under the skin. "Ending our marriage was your choice." In fact, he hadn't bothered to officially end the marriage. He had just disappeared—leaving her alone after making promises he clearly had never intended to keep. Some people didn't get a family, and she should've remembered that before trusting him.

The detective clicked his pen, gaining her attention. "Please explain. Is it some religious type of deal? The separation?"

Josie tilted her head. "Excuse me?"

Malloy straightened his pose against the wall. "The separation instead of a divorce. Is it a religious deal?"

Josie blew out air. "No. We're getting a divorce. I didn't feel right requesting it in absentia, and I wanted to wait until Shane could sign the papers. It just seemed fair..." She'd wanted to face him, to end it right. Of course, there had always been that tiny chance he'd try to win her back—explain why he'd deserted her.

No such luck.

Now she'd had enough of waiting—the papers were ready. As was she.

"That was nice of you, to wait I mean." Irony clanged in Shane's tone and spurred Josie's vertebrae to snap to attention one at a time.

"Yes, it was." More than once she had thought about filing the papers, but she couldn't steel herself to end it one-sided. To divorce a soldier most likely in combat seemed wrong. Even after everything, to hurt him like that would hurt her more. "I sent the divorce papers to your base in Pendleton. You could've mailed signed copies back to me."

"Maybe I don't want a divorce." Shane's jaw set in the way always guaranteed to prod her temper.

She forced anger down. Way down. She would not argue in front of the cop. Her gaze searched Shane's bruised face. "Was he mugged?"

The detective began to write again. "We don't know. If so, the muggers might need medical help, as well." He gestured toward Shane's bloodied knuckles. "He beat the crap out of someone." Scribble. Scribble. "Ah, Mrs. Dean, would you know anyone who'd want to injure or kill your husband?"

Besides her? She'd have to know him to know his enemies—and she didn't. "No. But again, I haven't seen Shane in years. You really should contact the military. Or his brothers."

Shane's head snapped up. "Brothers?"

"Yes. You let it slip once that you had brothers." How could he not remember anything? For a control freak like Shane, it had to be hell. "Though I have no idea who they are."

He exhaled in exasperation, and his gaze wandered over her face in a caress so familiar she almost sighed. "Sounds like I didn't trust you much, blue eyes."

"You don't trust anybody." She'd given him everything she had, and it wasn't enough. Tears pricked the backs of her eyes, and she ruthlessly batted them away. He didn't get to see her cry now. Before he'd left, there was one night when she'd thought they were getting closer, she had thought he was finally letting her in. Then he'd disappeared.

His eyes warmed and a hint of a smile threatened. A tension of a different sort began to heat the room. Josie tugged her jacket closed as her traitorous nipples peaked. She'd forgotten his ability to shift affection into desire. Damn the man.

Shane glanced over his bare right shoulder. "Have I always had the tattoo?"

"Yes." Malloy leaned for a better look. "Nice symbol. What does it mean?"

"Freedom," Shane murmured, rubbing his shoulder. He swiveled his head to meet Josie's gaze, both eyebrows rising. "Right?"

"Yes." She swallowed. "You already had the tat when we met, and you said it meant *freedom*."

"I don't remember getting inked, but I know what the symbol means." Shanc frowned, running his wounded hand through his hair.

The detective cleared his throat. "So, you don't know who'd want to attack your husband, and you haven't seen him in two years. Ah, Mrs. Dean, you've built a life here, right?"

"Yes." A good life with roots. Sure, she was alone, but she was secure.

The detective nodded. "Are you dating anyone?"

Heat rose into her face even as Shane's eyes sharpened to flint. She shook her head. "That's none of your business, Detective."

Shane lifted his chin. "But I believe it is *my* business, angel."

The man always could issue an effective threat with the mildest of words. She opened her mouth to tell him to stuff it when his words hit home. "You remember. You called me 'angel.' " He'd given her the nickname the first day they'd met at a small coffee shop in California.

He shook his head, giving a slight wince and then holding still. "No. No memories. You look like an angel—big blue eyes, wispy blond hair. My angel."

"Not anymore." She wouldn't let him do this to her. It'd taken two years to deal with the past, and she couldn't face the pain again. No matter how lost he looked, or how lonely she was. "We're over."

"Who are you dating, Josie?" As usual, Shane ignored her words and narrowed his focus to what he deemed important.

"We do need to know, Mrs. Dean," Detective Malloy

cut in before she could tell Shane to go to hell. "Just to clear the suspect list, if nothing else."

She sighed. "I'm not dating anybody."

"Someone popped into your mind," Shane said softly. Too softly.

Icy fingers traced her spine, and her heart rate picked up. She shrugged off the sensation. The cop narrowed his eyes. Both men waited.

She took a deep breath, pulling calmness in. "I'm not dating anyone, but I do spend time with Tom Marsh. He's in construction, and the last thing he'd ever do would be to mug somebody. And we're just friends."

"What kind of friends?" Shane kept his focus solely on her as if the cop weren't in the room.

"None of your business." The panic that rushed through her veins ticked her off.

He grabbed a crumpled shirt off the flattened pillow and yanked it over his head, grimacing as he tugged down the worn cotton. He pushed off the bed—toward her. "Does Marsh know you're taken?"

Awareness slammed into her abdomen as Shane's unique scent of heated cedar and rough male washed over her. How could she have forgotten how big he was? How much taller than her own five foot two? She tilted her head to meet his eyes. "Tom knows I'm about to be divorced."

"You sure about that?" Shane grasped her arm, his focus on the detective. "Malloy, you have my contact information while I'm in town. I'll be staying with my wife. Call if you hear anything."

The firm hand around her bicep—so warm, so familiar—sent a wave of thrilling awareness through her veins. The one touch could set her back months, maybe more. The man had always been unreal and larger than life. Wanting him had nearly destroyed her once. Never again. She sucked in a breath. "Did the doctors release you?"

"Yes. I have a concussion, and once it's healed, my memory should be restored. Though"—his voice dropped to a rumble—"you'll need to awaken me every two hours tonight, darlin'."

The twang. That Southern twang that escaped when he was either tired or aroused—an idiosyncrasy he normally managed to camouflage. The mere sound of it ignited memories of heated nights and soft whispers from her brain straight to her core. It was an intimacy most people didn't know about him, and learning about it made her feel special. Her mouth went dry.

A visible tic set up underneath the detective's left eye. "You're not free to leave, Major Dean."

Shane smiled.

The air rushed out of Josie's lungs. She knew that smile. The detective didn't stand a chance.

Neither did she.

Shane lowered his voice to a purely pleasant tone that wouldn't fool anybody with half a brain. "Malloy, I was attacked and have cooperated with you. I unfortunately have no new information, nor am I under arrest. Thus, I'm going home with my wife. Call me if you have questions."

The twang was gone.

Malloy tapped his pen. "I could hold you as a material witness."

"Try me." Somehow the tone became even more pleasant. Josie fought a shiver.

Malloy, to his credit, ignored the threat and turned bloodshot brown eyes on her. "Is there anyone who'd want to hurt you, Mrs. Dean?"

Josie sucked in air. "You think he was injured because of me?"

The detective shrugged. "I don't know. This might've been a random mugging, but we need to explore all possibilities."

She hadn't seen her husband in two years. No way was the mugging connected to her. "Nobody wants to hurt me. Besides, most of my friends don't know I'm married." Next to her, Shane stiffened, and her breath quickened in response.

The detective nodded, his gaze taking in them both. "Are you sure you want him with you?"

No. Though it was time to finish this. "Sure. We need to talk, and I have papers for Shane to sign. Thank you for your concern." Not for one second did she think Shane would stay away at this point.

"Are you sure you're safe? He may be dangerous." The detective appraised them both without expression. Cop face...soldier face. She'd seen it on her husband.

"Shane's dangerous as hell." He'd saved her from an obnoxious jackass the first day they'd met, his combat training obvious. She allowed herself a wry grin. "But he would never hurt me." Physically anyway.

Malloy cleared his throat. "Major Dean, what about your safety?"

Shane blinked twice and then chuckled. "Ah. You mean from the deadly pixie doll standing next to me?"

"Perhaps." Malloy's gaze probed Josie's eyes as he addressed Shane. "You're estranged and she has moved on. Statistically, it's possible *the pixie* hired someone to take care of you." He smiled. "No offense, ma'am."

She coughed out a laugh. "None taken, Detective. Though I assure you, if I wanted Shane dead, I'd do it myself." He'd tried to teach her some dangerous skills during their brief marriage, but she'd never had cause to use them.

The detective's eyes narrowed.

Shane chuckled even deeper. "Let's go, angel."

She allowed him to tug her from the room. They passed the uniformed cop and the many rooms, Shane's large form dwarfing her in a way she'd forgotten, in a way that made her feel safe—protected—and yet so vulnerable. The detective's concern filtered through her thoughts. Shane was dangerous before. What if he was even more so now? Where had he been the last two years? She didn't know him anymore. Heck, she'd never known him.

Maybe she wasn't so safe.

However, as the exit doors came into view, her stride sped up in an effort to escape the hospital. For her first visit, when she was seven, she'd been brought in by a foster parent who had hurt her. The second time, when she'd turned nine, she'd been carried in by a foster parent trying to save her. Different experiences, yet the result had been the same. She'd ultimately ended up alone.

Here she was again, leaving the hospital with someone who would soon leave. He'd abandoned her once. No matter how quickly her heart had leaped when she'd seen him again, or how lost he seemed right now, he wouldn't stay.

Shane wasn't a guy who stuck around.

He paused near the sliding glass exit doors, turning her to face him, tipping her chin up with one knuckle. The breadth of his shoulders, the narrowness of his waist, the strength bunched along his muscles promised power and danger. Warmth and the masculine scent of heated cedar wafted her way. "So, wife. Have you slept with this boyfriend of yours?"

CHAPTER
2

His wife's small bicep tightened in his grasp, and those incredible eyes darkened to violet, betraying her intent to step back. Shane grasped her chin to hold her in place, searching for an answer he wasn't sure he deserved.

She gave him a glare, and a light blush stole cross her fine cheekbones but didn't reach the pert nose he had the oddest urge to kiss. "My sex life is none of your business."

His eyelids lowered. "Ah, darlin'," he breathed out, "we both know that's not true." He raised his hand from her chin to slide his thumb over her full bottom lip and pricked with pleasure as she drew a sharp breath. His brain may not remember her, but his body thrummed with the need to draw the blood of any man who'd dared touch her.

As they paused at the glass doors of the hospital in the day's dusk, Shane cataloged the quiet streetscape. Thirty-five vehicles sat in the lot, and three businesses lined the other street: one selling food, one a pawn shop with possible weapons, and one a mom-and-pop convenience store. There was a good probability the store had a shotgun near the register. A row of apartments stood above the businesses, probably three. Statistically, at least one residence might have a weapon.

How did he know that? Sudden claustrophobia had him struggling to appear normal, even while he tilted his head to hear...something. Anything. But all sounds arrived muffled, as if his head were under water.

So he concentrated on the soft skin beneath his rough hand. Josie had a classic face, well-defined cheekbones, and delicate features. Yet her chin held a stubbornness that intrigued as much as it challenged him.

Josie's teeth ground together. "I don't know how badly you're hurt, but if you don't release me, I'm going to kick your ass."

His quick smile felt rusty, as if the muscles hadn't been used in far too long. Two years maybe—since he left her?

With a shrug, he let go, straightened, and stepped back. Every slight movement dug sharp needles into his skull. Lights flashed behind his eyes from the pain. "I need to know. Are you scared of me?" He didn't know himself. Would he hurt her? The idea that he'd harm such a tiny, defenseless woman was like a punch to the gut. Who the hell was he?

She arched one delicate eyebrow. "If you're asking if you abuse women, the answer is no. If you're asking if you're an asshole, the answer is yes."

He huffed a laugh, barely holding back a wince as his eyes sparked agony. "I appreciate your honesty."

"Anytime." She tossed a thick blond strand over her shoulder and shoved open the exit door to the cool night air. "You might as well come on."

He paused at her statement, taking a moment to appreciate her tight body in the soft gray pantsuit. The woman had an ass he'd love to sink his hands into. The flash of lust rolled through him followed by unease. He'd just scared her, pretty much threatened her about the boyfriend, and now he wanted her naked. After a brief marriage, he'd abandoned her. What if he hadn't had a good reason? Was there a good reason to leave his woman unprotected? Probably not.

Following her out, he quickly caught up to her, his gaze raking the sprawling parking lot. Quiet, peaceful, and nicely lit in the cold evening. Pine and the hint of snow wafted on the breeze. "You're taking me home, angel?" He figured he'd have to cajole to end up at her place. He needed to crawl into a hole until his head stopped pounding, and then he'd figure out who'd jumped him.

Darkness and peace seemed more important than safety right now.

She sighed, yanking keys out of a monstrous purse and striding in pointy shoes toward the center of the lot. "Like it or not, you're my responsibility right now. At least until you sign the papers." She halted and flipped around so abruptly he had to catch her arms to keep from running her over. Her gaze met his. "Unless you're full of shit. Amnesia? Seriously?"

She felt good under his palms. Ignoring the migraine, he stepped into her, truly enjoying the flare of awareness and then irritation filtering across her stunning face. "Have I ever lied to you?" The question held risk, considering he had no clue if he had lied or not.

Anger slammed the irritation out of the way, narrowing her eyes. "No. You just didn't tell me anything."

Oh, but he'd hurt her. The set of her shoulders, the line of her lips, told him he'd caused her pain. What kind of an ass was he to hurt such a soft little thing? "I'm sorry."

She blinked three times and took a step back. "It doesn't matter."

"I think it does. Whatever mistakes I've made, I'm sorry." She was so tiny, her head didn't come close to the bottom of his chin. Maybe he should take off by himself right away—leave her the life she'd built over the last two years.

But he didn't want to. There was warmth buried in the woman, and he was so damn cold. She'd loved him once. Maybe she could explain why.

A humming set up at the base of his skull. He lifted his head to scout the parking lot, its quiet abundance of SUVs providing no answers. Someone was watching, though—of that he was sure.

The headache disappeared, shoved somewhere to be dealt with later. Awareness filtered through his brain that he shouldn't be able to do that. His heartbeat slowed. His breathing calmed. He tucked Josie into his side, ignoring the pain of her shoulder meeting his bruised ribs, hurrying them both deeper into the lot. A cool breeze stung his face, and a van across the street caught his attention. Yep. "Where's your car?"

The woman failed to shrug away his protective arm. "Right here." She pointed a key fob at a black Toyota Highlander, its beep echoing through the silent area as it unlocked the doors.

Adrenaline flooded his system, somehow calming him more. That wasn't natural. Should he be more scared of himself than his attackers? "You should've parked under a light."

"Don't lecture me."

"Then you should be more careful." He had a feeling he'd said those words to her before. Shoving speculation away, he opened the driver's door, and she climbed inside. He followed, grasping her slender waist and lifting her over the center console, setting his own butt in the seat. Doubt tried to crowd his instincts, but his movements were graceful and trained—his muscles worked quickly as if separate from his brain. Pain began to well behind his eyes, and he shoved it away.

Josie tried to bound out of her seat. "Hey—"

"I'm driving." He pressed on the brake pedal and pushed the keyless ignition button. Panic swirled in his abdomen, so he focused hard and fast, surrounding himself with calmness. Interesting trick, that. "Fasten your seat belt."

"No—"

"Now." He lowered his voice to pure command, cutting a gaze at her that even *felt* hard.

She arched her brows in surprise. With a huff, she rolled her eyes and yanked on the belt. Nope. Definitely not afraid of him.

For the first time since he'd regained consciousness, his body felt familiar. Calm, purposeful, alert. A threat existed in the blue van. He chose not to question his certainty of the fact. Not right now anyway. The vehicle sat across from the parking lot's one exit as if waiting patiently, away from any lights. He glanced in the rearview mirror to the entrance on the opposite side. Perfect.

Sure movements had the SUV backed out and maneuvered around the rows of cars toward the exit. Pressing hard against the accelerator, he hit reverse through the entrance with a screech of tires.

"What the—" Josie hissed, clutching both hands at the dash as the attendant at the entrance jumped out of his booth, arms waving in the air.

Shane whipped the Toyota around and into traffic, pressing on the accelerator and zipping around several cars before yanking the wheel and shooting the car into an alley he followed for several blocks.

"What the hell are you doing?" Josie yelled.

He raised an eyebrow, sliding into a one-way street heading away from the hospital. "You have quite the mouth on you, don't you, angel?"

"Oh God, you're crazy. You're concussed. No way should you be driving."

He glanced in the rearview mirror. All clear. Doubt choked in his throat. Maybe he was crazy. Regardless, he didn't feel the threat any longer. "Sorry. I just wanted to play a bit." Realization dawned. He had no intention of telling her about the threat. Interesting. Either he didn't trust her—or instinct dictated he protect her. Regardless, he chose to experiment, to judge her reaction. He cleared his throat. "There were men in a van across from the hospital waiting for one of us. I sensed danger."

Her head turned in slow motion toward him. "What?"

"You heard me." He kept his gaze on the road as they passed quiet storefronts, studying her out of his peripheral vision. The vein in her neck fluttered as her heartbeat sped up. Her breath hitched, and the scent of wild berries wafted from her. What kind of a soldier was he to have this kind of training? Such overdeveloped senses? Dread settled in his gut.

She shook her head. "You're crazy. What van? There was no van."

So, two options there. Either he hadn't let her into his world, or she was lying. The desire for her trust caught him unaware. Well damn. He needed to stick with her until his memory returned.

A voice in the back of his head whispered that was as good of an excuse as any to stay with her. He swung onto a main road, passing a long line of car dealerships. "Which way do I go?"

Her sigh filled the quiet car. She eyed the glove box. "Get on the interstate going east."

Interesting—he could easily read the thoughts scattering across her face. "Is there a weapon in your jockey box, sweetheart?"

She jumped, gaze slashing to him. "Um, yes?"

He raised an eyebrow. "Gun?"

"Yes. Lady Smith. You taught me how to shoot and to always keep a weapon near."

Good. Though he'd appreciate it if she didn't grab a weapon while in his vicinity...at least for now. "Let's leave it there, all right?"

"Fine." She crossed her arms.

He merged onto the interstate, following the signs toward Idaho. "I appreciate you taking me home, angel." The nickname. It affected her if her pinkening cheeks were any indication. His peripheral vision was excellent, as was his night vision—too good. Who or what was he? The world began to close in on him. "I'm not sure what happened to me, but I promise I'll figure it out."

"I'm sure your memory will come back—you're the strongest guy I've ever met." She didn't sound happy about that fact, and her hand trembled as she ran her fingers through silky strands of blond. One small tooth bit into her lip. "Listen. You don't know anybody in town. What happened must've been a mugging." She turned toward him, those soft blue eyes illuminated by outside streetlights. "You can stay with me a few days until your memory returns. Or until we find your brothers."

Hesitation. It wrinkled her forehead. The woman didn't want him staying with her. His heart thumped hard. His wife was kind. Soft. He glanced at her, letting her know his gaze was on her. This time. "I may not know myself right now, sweetheart. But I know I wouldn't have let you go." No way was he that fucking stupid.

Fire flashed in those dangerous eyes. "You left me, *sweetheart.*"

He raised an eyebrow. "Why?"

Her gaze wavered. She shifted in her seat, looking away from him. "Take the next exit."

Doubt pouted her pretty lips. What did she know that she wasn't telling him? Somehow he knew how to get answers from people—no matter the cost. A chill swept down his spine. He wouldn't hurt somebody like Josie, would he? Shaking his head, he signaled and exited, following the road to a quiet street.

She pointed. "Go right and up the hill, and take a left on Newcomer. My house is the fourth on the right." The gentle timbre of her voice caressed his skin, providing comfort and a sense of belonging.

Something told him he hadn't belonged many places. He kept a close watch on the well-kept houses on either side of the street, many of them decorated with huge pumpkins, orange lights, and paper ghosts billowing from trees. He also watched the car lights behind him. More important, he tuned in to his senses. Nothing. No warnings, no fear. Though something was still off with his hearing—almost as if he expected to hear something else. Something beyond the norm. What was he missing?

He pulled into her driveway to eye the white ranch house with cheerful shrubs along the front. The trim was a perfect navy blue. Unease filtered through his mind.

He'd seen the place before. Welcoming. Sweet. Pure. "Your house is pretty."

She started, her gaze cutting into him.

What? Had he never said anything nice to her? With a growl, he pressed the garage door button on the sun visor and drove into the empty space. Neat and tidy, the walls held rakes, shovels, and an assortment of tools with pink handles. The color made something in his chest ache. She shouldn't have to swing a hammer. Ever. "You're going to tell me whatever it is you're keeping from me." He jumped from the vehicle.

Her feet hit the concrete, and her car door slammed shut before she responded. "I'm not telling you squat." She tried to stomp past him.

He shifted his weight, blocking her path. "I didn't give you the option." Not by one inch did he want to intimidate her. But he took a step, forcing the woman to tilt her head to glare at him.

Fury flashed bright red across high cheekbones as her hands went to her hips. "If you think you can show up after two years, with freaking *amnesia* and order me around, you have another think coming."

Okay. Not intimidated. The ball of unease uncoiled in his gut as he relaxed. He bit back the grin that wanted loose. "I'm not leaving until I remember everything."

She inhaled deeply. "Either get out of my way or prepare to be a eunuch."

The woman was something. Indecision filtered through his brain. Surprise filled him with how much he wanted her cooperation. Her willing trust. He stepped to the side, allowing her to open the door and enter a cheerful kitchen with sparkling stainless steel appliances.

He shut the door behind him and locked it. Was he the

good guy or the bad? "Did I teach you to fight?" Instinct whispered that if she was his, even for a little while, he'd have taught her.

"Maybe I taught you," she muttered, shaking off her jacket to drop over an antique carved chair that matched a round table.

He sighed. The warmth of the room caught him by surprise, making him feel like an overgrown bully. Pretty vases and glasses lined the top of the cupboards, the mix eclectic and somehow calming. Girly magnets of flowers and quotations adorned the refrigerator. The house was a home. "Your place is nice."

"Thanks." She eyed the message machine on the uncluttered counter. It blinked with two messages.

"Check your messages, Josie." He kept the command soft while he wanted to push the button himself. Had the boyfriend called? Anger swept through him at the thought. The muscles at the base of his neck began to ache. That headache was coming back and soon. Who the hell would date a married woman? His woman?

Josie whirled around, unease skittering down her spine. As a husband, Shane had been both possessive and protective. She hadn't minded—had even felt sheltered and safe. Well, until he'd deserted her. Then she'd missed the sense of belonging. "This isn't going to work."

Three steps took her to the antique writing desk tucked into the corner. She'd found it at a garage sale the previous spring and had spent hours sanding and staining the piece after refinishing the kitchen table. From day one, she'd determined to create her own family heirlooms. Even if she stayed alone.

She tugged out papers from the desk, throwing them

against the Pottery Barn bowl that held apples on the table. The man was too tempting, and she was still damaged. Protecting her heart was her job, not his. "Sign the papers, and then you need to leave."

He lifted his gaze, those gray eyes that could blaze with passion or freeze with anger. For now, those windows shuttered closed. "No."

Exasperation caught a scream in her throat. It took every ounce of control she had to shove it back down. She'd wanted to do this the right way, the respectful way. A way that demonstrated they'd meant something to each other. Even though their marriage had ended, even though he'd left, enough had been there to end it right. "That's not an option." She tried to keep her chin from tilting as she threw his words back in his face.

A spark flared in his eyes. His gaze swept her body top to bottom, pausing several times on the journey. The air in the room thickened.

The moment slammed a hard awareness into her solar plexus. She'd imagined him in the comfortable home, looking at her like that.

Like he had when they'd lived together.

Her feet stuck to the floor. She couldn't look away from his high cheekbones, straight nose, and the full lips she hadn't touched in two years. His thick hair had grown to his shoulders. Her fingers itched to touch. But she frowned. The military had let him grow his hair that long?

Holding her gaze, he stalked forward as graceful as any jungle cat. Slow and sure—closing the distance between them until she inhaled his scent of heated cedar. A hum began in her abdomen. Heat flushed along her skin.

One of his thick knuckles lifted her chin. She should step back. Away from danger. But something…

something kept her still. Maybe it was curiosity. Maybe it was hope that she could still feel on fire. Her limbs grew heavy. Too heavy to move. Her heart rate picked up.

Slowly, so slowly they both knew she had eons to move away, he lowered his head. His lips brushed hers. Firm, knowing, so hot. Once, twice, and then a third time.

A moan fluttered in her throat.

He stepped into her, one hand clenching her hip and the other angling her chin. Fire. His tongue shot past her lips, taking. One movement and he tugged her against his hard body, forcing her curves to accommodate his larger size, to accept him, to cushion the firm ridge of an erection digging into her skin. Need rippled through her so fast she shivered. Her sex softened. Her nipples pebbled.

The hand on her chin moved and tethered her hair as he destroyed her mouth. The familiar taste of him flayed her heart. His mouth released hers to press wet, open-mouthed kisses along her jaw to her neck.

So fast.

So hard.

So demanding.

She gasped for air, her mind spinning. Her knees weakening. Shane.

He kissed lower, dipping his face in the V of her shirt, pushing the material aside to nuzzle the tops of her breasts. A low hum of male appreciation echoed against her skin. She slid both hands through his thick hair, tugging him closer. Heat filled her. A ringing began in her ears. Her body leaped to life. For the first time in two years, she craved.

Suddenly, he shifted again, cupping her ass and lifting her against him. She gasped as her feet left the ground. Her legs automatically circled his waist.

This was crazy...and she truly didn't care. More. She needed more.

Her body had been asleep for two years and suddenly felt awake. Alive.

The demanding hardness of his cock pressed against her core. His mouth returned to demolish hers, his strong hands working her body against his. Held aloft, she moaned and pressed her thighs against his hips, rubbing against him. Needing. Finally, he lifted his head.

His kiss was harder and more insistent than in their earlier life together. He'd always been so careful—so gentle. Something wild and new cascaded from him now. Excitement flared inside her chest. For once he was treating her as an equal. As a woman and not as something fragile he needed to shield.

Possession. It glittered in his gray eyes along with need. Desire. Promise. She should think. Shouldn't she think?

"Josie. Either tell me where the bedroom is, or I'm taking you on the floor." Low, almost guttural, his voice caressed the raw nerves all but begging for his touch.

Dazed, she opened her mouth to speak. The shrill of the phone made her jump. She shook her head. Reality. Where was reality? The phone rang again.

Shane's eyes narrowed. His grip tightened on her ass, pulling her sex harder against his. She moaned. His dangerous gaze kept her captive.

The phone rang again.

Then her voice telling the caller to leave a message.

Then...Tom. "Hi, beautiful. How about dinner tonight?"

CHAPTER
3

THE AIR CHILLED ten degrees. Maybe more. Tension ripped through the once-peaceful kitchen. This was bad. Disastrous. Josie released Shane's hair and slammed her hands against his chest, trying to unhinge her legs from around his hips.

He held her in place.

"You're hurting me," she whispered. He wasn't, not even close, but the words would make him release her.

"Then stop moving." Not an ounce of give showed on his face.

She blinked several times. Shock kept her body immobile. The Shane she'd known would've set her immediately and safely to her feet.

Tom's voice droned on in the background, detailing late dinner plans. She had to shut off the machine. Josie struggled, fighting to drop to the floor. She'd almost had sex with Shane. Two more seconds and—

"No." Shane's jaw hardened to rock. His eyes darkened to slate.

Panic. Danger. Violence. Josie stilled, her gaze captured by the anger in Shane's. So much. Her lungs compressed.

In all the time they'd spent together, not once had she been afraid of him.

Until now.

The machine clicked off.

The seconds ticked by as her heart rammed against her ribs. His gaze kept hers. No expression showed on his savage features, no glimmer in those eyes. She suppressed a shiver. Who was this man? Slowly, almost gently, Shane lowered her to the floor, holding her shoulders until she'd steadied herself. Then he took two steps back.

A chill ran over her arms, and she rubbed trembling palms against goose bumps. How in the world had she let this happen? She hadn't ever tried to stop him. Even now, her body ached. For Shane. He was different this time. Not in control, not hiding his feelings. She opened her mouth to speak, but nothing came out.

Shane tucked his hands in the pockets of his jeans. So he wouldn't reach for her again? "You're not going to dinner."

Well, no shit. She cleared her throat. "I've built a good life here, Shane." No way was she letting him tear it down. Not again. Never again.

Maybe if she repeated the mantra enough, she'd believe the words.

Regret flashed across his face. "Do you love him?"

She was just getting to know Tom. Recently divorced, he harbored as many wounds as she did and had shown her kindness in the two months they'd known each other. But love? She'd given all she had to Shane. Who was anything but kind. "That's none of your business."

Shane tilted his head. "Do you really believe that?"

"Yes."

A smile flirted with the corners of his lips. "Five more minutes and I would've been inside you. Hard and fast."

Desire slammed below her abdomen even as she lifted her head in challenge. Hard and fast. One of the many ways Shane enjoyed the bedroom. As well as slow and soft. Crazy and fun. Yet always in perfect control.

His smile spread, soft and deadly. "And you would've been screaming my name, begging for more. We both know it."

Was he remembering? Or just so sure of himself? She lifted a shoulder. "The sex was always okay between us, Shane." The lie nearly made her choke. The sex had been incredible.

He laughed. A deep male chuckle. One she hadn't heard in far too long. "Want me to prove it was better than okay, angel?"

Yes.

She sure did. Her breasts ached. Her sex had swollen. Intrigue at this new side of him sent fire through her veins. Hope flared alive, and she quashed it instantly. The man would never truly change, never truly let her in. "Hell, no." Jerky movements had her at the table, where she yanked her cell phone out of her purse and sent a quick text message to Tom. She was too tired for dinner and would call him tomorrow.

Tossing her phone onto the counter, she flung open the refrigerator door and grabbed leftover lasagna. Routine would settle her. Whenever life became too much, she buckled down and got organized. Oddly enough, Shane had taught her that coping mechanism. Taking control of something as silly as color coordinating her closet had given her peace and a new outlook on life more than once. It looked like it was time to pick a new project again.

Cooking was another way she'd learned to soothe herself. The blue glass dish filled her hands. She'd made the lasagna the night before and more than half a pan remained. Shane's favorite. The irony wasn't lost on her.

A chair scraped behind her, and she turned as Shane dropped into it. Even sitting, his bulk overwhelmed the small space. Deep circles lay under his eyes as dark as the bruises covering his skin. "Are you going to feed me now?"

"Yes. Then you can sign the papers and get out." She shoved away sympathy and put the dish in the microwave to set the time, fighting the pleasure of cooking for him again. While married, she'd *felt married* when cooking. Like they were a real family. Warm, healthy food was the only way he'd allowed her to care for him. And she'd loved doing it.

Even now, she'd spend hours at the farmer's market choosing just the right ingredients. The freshest spinach, the home-grown tomatoes. Just last week, she'd spent an hour finding the right oregano plant to grow on the windowsill. In the kitchen, while cooking, for brief moments she allowed herself to pretend they were still together. That he relied on her. That he trusted and needed her.

But he never really had needed her. Until now.

How could she force him out? He had no clue who he was. Unless he was playing her. She grabbed plates and soda as the pasta cooked, taking the dish out and filling two plates before sitting. Beer wasn't her thing, and the kind he liked, Guinness, was too strong for her. So she didn't have any to offer. "You like lasagna. At least you used to."

Shane nodded, taking a big bite and swallowing. "I still do." Pleasure quirked his lip up as he ate.

Warmth filled her in response.

Finally, after clearing his plate, he rubbed his eyes. "Help me fill in the gaps. How did we meet?"

Memories crashed through her with a familiar pang. "We met in a coffee shop." About a million years ago. "Some guy was messing with me, wouldn't leave me alone, and you made him." The guy had thought he was so cool with dark aviator glasses, pretending to be a soldier. He'd been Shane's size but had backed down instantly. "We got married three weeks later." A whirlwind. Fast, explosive, and so damn sexy. Completely opposite of how she planned her life. What had she been thinking?

"I see." Shane's eyes warmed. "How long were we married until we, ah . . ."

"Two months." She sighed as hurt slammed into her abdomen. "Then you just left."

"Without a word?" His gaze narrowed.

She shrugged. "Why are you in Washington?"

"I asked you a question." Quick as that, his voice turned hard.

The tone was new. Her body stilled, while her mind spun. Intrigue kept her gaze fixed on him. So many times she'd tried to push him and make him lose control. Make him stop treating her like glass. Should she try now? "I heard your question."

"I need you to answer it. To help me." His inflection remained the same, but an odd vulnerability darkened his eyes. "I have to know what happened."

For the briefest of seconds, and for the very first time, she saw the boy he might've been before turning into a soldier. Her heart warmed while her shoulders relaxed. No way could she turn away from the plea. "You kissed me good-bye in the morning, said you loved me, and that you'd be back." After the most passionate night of their marriage, one she wasn't ready to remind him about yet. "You didn't come back."

"Why?"

"I don't know." Even now, the words hurt. How many times had she lain awake at night, alone, asking herself that very question? Why hadn't he returned? Had he even thought about her? She'd relived their last week together in her head repeatedly. "The last week—it was bad."

He stiffened. "Bad? How?"

She exhaled. "You were off. Really sad. A week before you left, you found out one of your brothers had died. Your brother, Jory."

"Jory." Shane frowned, rubbing his chest. "How did he die?"

"I don't know." Anger returned in a flash. "Until that week, I didn't even know you had brothers." She struggled to stay seated and not jump away from him. He'd had a whole life, a family, he hadn't shared with her. "Why do you think you're here now after two years?"

"You said you sent the divorce papers to my base. I assume I got them and came up to discuss the issue." His shoulders straightened at the last.

Was he going to fight her on the divorce? Dread pooled in her stomach. "Then where are the papers?"

"I don't know." He took a deep drink of soda. "You're a great cook, Josie."

Pleasure bloomed inside her chest. She'd learned to cook during college . . . hoping to have a family to nurture someday like the moms on television did. Sadness shoved the pleasure away. It hadn't happened. "Thanks."

His eyes narrowed. "Are you a chef?"

"No." Memories flooded in. She'd almost taken the risk and changed her accounting major to cooking during her second year at Cal State. But she hadn't had the courage. Plus, she could control numbers. Organization and hard work counted. She'd never need to rely on one person or an entire system again. "I'm an accountant."

Surprise lifted his eyebrows. "That explains the sexy suit."

Sexy? Not even close. She kicked off the high heels, rubbing her feet on the smooth tiled floor. She'd paid for the tiles with her second paycheck from her new job at the accounting firm's local branch. It had taken an entire weekend of searching for just the right color, a homey beige. "Accounting is safe."

"Ah." Understanding echoed in his low tone. "Safety is important to you. Interesting." He rubbed his chin. "Something tells me I'm not so safe."

"No." She smiled, even as sadness made her chest ache. "You were the only risk I ever took. It backfired."

"I'm sorry."

She shrugged. "I don't want to talk about it."

He studied her, no expression on his hard face. "Okay. You said I have brothers. Plural. Besides Jory, what do you know?"

"Nothing about your brothers." She didn't want to have this conversation. She'd failed as a wife, or she'd know more about him. "But you do have nightmares. At least you used to."

He stilled. "What about?"

Anger flashed through her. "I don't know. You wouldn't tell me." She tossed her napkin atop her plate of half-eaten food. "Even before you woke up one night screaming Jory's name, bad dreams made you a very restless sleeper." She lowered her gaze to her fingers picking at pumpkins on the napkin. "That night, you sounded so broken. I'd never heard you sound like that." A chill skittered across her shoulders. She'd wanted so badly to shield him, to help him. He wouldn't let her.

"I'm sorry." The hoarseness of his voice wrapped around her heart. "You shouldn't have to deal with something like that."

She coughed out irritation. "You should be sorry. Not for exposing me but for shutting me out." For one second, when he'd almost kissed her senseless, she'd thought he'd changed. That he could see the real her. The woman who could be his match.

He pushed back from the table. "You're beautiful, Josie. Soft and delicate. You should be protected."

Ah. There was the rub. She shook her head. "You don't know me, Shane. You never did."

CHAPTER
4

JOSIE CROSSED HER legs, fighting the urge to grind a palm into her eyes. She sat on her bed, a myriad of ledgers spread out before her. After dinner, she'd left Shane to head into the guest shower, saying she had work to do before changing into comfortable sweats, her hair in a ponytail.

But the numbers in the accounts before her weren't adding up. There were problems in several of the accounts she'd taken over a few months ago. Either she'd made a mistake, or the accountant she'd taken over for had screwed up. Not that it was a huge surprise, considering Billy had had to leave for a drug rehabilitation center.

She flipped back open the main manila file for Hall's Funeral Home. The numbers swam before her eyes. She blinked several times, allowing them to right themselves.

Wait a minute.

Scrambling for the accounts payable ledger, she quickly scanned the items. Triumph had her nearly laughing out loud. Of course. Billy had counted the sales of several plots to one family as a lump sum, and not as monthly income. The sale was spread over several months, and the money wouldn't be paid until the fifteenth of each month. But Billy had counted the money before getting paid.

Thank goodness. The problem was an easy fix. Josie took a deep, relaxing breath. Maybe all four troubled accounts had similar mistakes. Drugs had apparently really messed with Billy's brain. Though to be safe, she should double-check all his files, even the ones that seemed all right, especially since competition at the firm was crazy at the moment. She glanced at the other files perched on the bed.

Maybe she should just go to bed and forget about work. It was only a little after eight, but exhaustion made her head feel heavy. She eyed her knitting basket in the corner. Knitting. Precise, logical, and yet somehow creative. Mrs. Lilly, one of her favorite foster mothers, had taught her when she was eleven. Before Mrs. Lilly got too sick to take care of lost kids. More recently, her old hobby had allowed Josie to make friends in a strange city and show a side of herself she often hid.

With a smile, Josie noted a striped hat perched on the dresser she'd recently knitted for her secretary. Sassy, bright, and bold, the woman would love the pattern. It was so different than Josie's first disastrous attempts on her own. Now she could picture the final result in her mind while buying yarn at the specialty store on the other side of town. The owner knew her there...and while shopping, Josie became part of something. A community of people who created.

Times were tough. People knitted to make money, to keep their families warm. While women with adorable kids searched the cozy aisles, Josie could almost pretend she had a family, too. That she had a skill to pass down and share with somebody else.

A somebody with Shane's eyes and her nose.

Even if she stayed alone for life, she could create. Something of her would remain...so long as the yarn held true.

Shane had loved her knitting. Something old-fashioned and feminine about the process. A part of her wanted to go back to the living room. To be near him. But they really didn't have anything to talk about except the need for him to sign the divorce papers. What if he wouldn't sign?

What if he would?

The phone rang, jarring her from thoughts of Shane. She grabbed the handset. "Hello?"

"Mrs. Dean, it's Detective Malloy." Rustling papers and ringing phones sounded across the line, surrounding the detective's voice in noise.

"Hi, Detective." A shadow crossed her doorway. She glared at Shane. He more than filled the entrance, his large bulk contrasting with the feminine tones of her room. Wet hair curled at his nape.

The detective cleared his throat. "We've had some developments in your husband's case, Mrs. Dean."

Unease straightened her posture. "Developments?"

"Yes. I know it's almost eight at night, but I'd like for you and your husband to meet me at the station in thirty minutes." The detective hung up.

Josie pulled the handset from her head, turning to stare at it. Developments? Malloy needed a book on proper phone etiquette. She hung up the phone and turned toward the doorway.

"Angel?" Shane leaned against the door frame in faded jeans and ripped T-shirt, the casual stance belied by the sharp gaze in his too-pale face. His head was probably killing him. His scent of heated cedar wafted her way, suffusing a maleness into her comfort zone.

"Detective Malloy would like to speak with us." Her hands clutched the thick comforter with its pattern of homey tulips. She'd purchased the cover from a catalog, waiting impatiently until it arrived before choosing the whimsical table lamps that matched. She normally counted her pennies, but she'd splurged on creating her home.

The king-sized bed had been another indulgence.

Memories of heated nights and fun mornings spent grappling in another bed with Shane filled her mind. He was a big guy and needed a king-sized bed. She fought a blush.

Shane lifted an eyebrow, leaning against the wall she'd painted a soft beige. A shadow lined his sharp jawline, giving him the look of a rebel. "Why does the detective want to speak with us?"

She shrugged. "I don't know." Blood stained Shane's ripped shirt, a testament to the violence that stalked him. "Give me a second while I change, and we can go see what this is about."

His eyes warmed. "Need help?"

Her abdomen heated. "No."

His shrug made him wince. "Suit yourself."

"Are you okay?" The unwanted concern reminded her of emotions she thought she'd destroyed.

"Fine. Just a headache." He pivoted on his bare feet and disappeared from view.

Yeah, there was the Shane she remembered. Blocking her out on the pretext of protecting her delicate nature. Dumbass.

It was time to move on and unravel the hold he had

on her. The emotions Shane evoked were raw, dangerous, and so deep. She'd never completely expel him from
inside her heart.

He was a soldier and he'd staked his claim.

The sooner he left, the sooner she could return to
pretending she'd moved on. Maybe someday she actually would. Her feet hit the cold wooden floor. She'd
been searching for a rug for the bedroom for more than a
year—someday she'd find the perfect one.

She dressed in comfortable jeans and a blue sweater
that brought out the varied hues in her eyes. Not that she
was dressing to impress Shane. She just liked that sweater.

Indecision had her biting her lip until, with a shrug, she
grabbed a faded men's T-shirt out of the bottom dresser
drawer. On cold nights, or lonely nights, she often slept in
one of Shane's old shirts. He couldn't very well go to the
police station in the ripped one.

She found him at the kitchen table, eating the rest of
the cold lasagna. "You're hungry again?"

He finished chewing. "I like your cooking."

The T-shirt landed on the table with a quick toss. "I
have one of your old shirts. It's clean."

He wiped his mouth with a napkin, his gaze on the
shirt. "Am I supposed to read something into this?" Deep
and dark, his voice lowered to a rumble that sped up her
heart.

"No." Only that she hadn't gotten over him yet. No
matter how hard she tried to lie to herself. "Some of your
clothes must've been mixed up with mine when I moved."
Nothing would make her admit she also kept a shirt of his
she refused to wash, hidden in the back of her closet. Even
after two years, his unique male scent still clung to the
worn cotton.

"All right." He whipped off the bloodied shirt and pulled on the clean one. "Thanks."

"Sure." One glimpse at his impressive chest and she wanted to lick him head-to-toe. Man, she needed to get herself under control. She grabbed a jacket from the small closet near the door. The emotional walls between them were suffocating her, and she needed to get outside. "We should get going."

Shane nodded, unfolded himself from the kitchen chair, and opened the door slowly and deliberately. "Okay."

Concern stilled her movement. "Are you all right?"

"Yep. Just a headache. I'll drive."

Josie thought about arguing. But why bother? He'd end up driving, and frankly, driving at night wasn't her favorite activity. She'd liked that about Shane during their brief marriage. Driving was a pleasure for him, and she could just sit back and relax during the ride. "Whatever."

She waited until he'd backed them out of the driveway before giving him directions. They drove in silence until he reached town. Josie picked distractedly at a fray on her jeans. "Any memories come back?" Only stubborn will kept her gaze off the capable hands on the steering wheel. She'd loved those hands.

"No." Shane glanced again at the rearview mirror.

Josie turned to look at the cars behind them. "What are you searching for?"

"The van that followed us earlier today."

Maybe his concussion was worse than they thought. "I think your imagination took over. You do have a head injury."

"Perhaps." He checked behind them again. Frustration and doubt slid across his face, to be masked by a pleasant smile. One that didn't fool her a bit. "Regardless, I don't sense any danger now."

Yep. He still kept secrets now, didn't he? Josie turned her focus to the night outside the car.

Shane exited the freeway, drove for a mile, and parked the SUV in front of the three-story brick building. Bright lights surrounded the station, banishing the night. Jumping out, he crossed to open her door before she grabbed the handle. Strong hands helped her out of the vehicle, where the autumn breeze cut into her skin.

"Ah, Josie? How about letting me do the talking with the detective?" The door shut with a soft click, and Shane gestured her forward.

"Why?" She was perfectly capable of answering questions from the police. Not only had she done nothing wrong, but she'd grown up in foster care. Dealing with authority and its agenda was nothing new for her.

Shane opened the door. "I have a feeling Malloy is after something. I don't like that he didn't tell you any details about his new developments."

She was surrounded by manipulative people keeping hidden agendas, and that included Shane. Even if the amnesia was real, he wasn't exactly forthcoming with the truth.

The waiting room of the police station held two leather couches, a myriad of live plants, and several wide orange chairs. Homey and comfortable. A slice of small town in a city that had grown unexpectedly. A forty-something woman with riotous red hair sat behind a broad counter walled off by thick glass, humming contentedly through the night shift. Behind her spread a wall of photos depicting police officers at various award ceremonies. She smiled and spoke through the speaker, her voice emerging tinny. "May I help you?"

Shane stepped forward to answer just as a buzzer rasped and a door opened next to the counter. Malloy held it open with one beefy hand. "Come on in."

Josie pivoted to walk into a wide, quiet hallway. Shane's broad hand settled at the small of her back, pressing her along. Possessive and protective—completely in charge. She'd forgotten that feeling of being his.

Several closed doors lined the hall as the three approached a large double door that blocked the hub of the police station from the public. Malloy pushed open a scratched metal door, gesturing them inside a conference room with a thick oak table and leather chairs. Josie slid into the chair Shane pulled out for her, glancing at the pleasant watercolor of a snowy mountain scene adorning the side wall. "Where's the two-way mirror?" she asked.

Malloy snorted, walking around the table to sit and drop manila folders on the polished wood. "The interrogation rooms are closer to the cells. This is just a meeting room."

Shane sat next to Josie. "Right. Exactly what are we *meeting* about, Detective?"

Josie leaned back in her chair and away from the comfort she'd find leaning into Shane.

Malloy rubbed his chin, studying them with shrewd and tired-looking eyes. He'd discarded the rumpled suit coat and old tie, rolling his shirt up to reveal dark hair along his arms. He focused on Shane. "Have any of your memories returned?"

"Not yet, but they will." Shane ignored Josie's move away and reached out to place one broad arm across her shoulders. "Have you heard from Pendleton?"

"Not yet, but I will," the detective parroted Shane's tone. He eyed Josie. "When you were married, did your husband ever talk about his skill set in the military?"

The arm around her shoulders stiffened, but Shane's body remained relaxed and his expression unconcerned. Josie stilled. "No. Shane didn't talk about his past, about his future, or about his job, Detective. I believe we've covered this." Admitting her marriage was a sham settled like a rock in her stomach. She crossed her legs. "Why do you ask?"

Malloy glanced at Shane and flipped open a file, taking out three photographs to place on the table. "I ask because we found three dead bodies down by the river a couple hours ago."

Josie sucked in air, her gaze glued to the pictures of dead men lying on metal slabs, their bodies covered by flimsy sheets. Just like on television. Shock set off a roaring in her ears. "Who are they?" she croaked out.

Malloy shrugged. "We don't know yet. But a preliminary examination shows the first two died from broken necks." His finger tapped on the third picture of a man with mottled bruises and cuts marring his face. "This guy probably died from an intense beating that crushed his skull—we'll know more after the autopsies tomorrow." The detective glanced at the damaged knuckles of Shane's hand resting on the table.

"Any forensics?" Shane's voice remained pleasant and unconcerned.

"Not yet. But I'm sure we'll find something." Malloy raised an eyebrow. "Do either of you recognize these men?"

Josie studied the pictures, a lump forming in her throat. Had Shane killed three men with his bare hands? Was he capable of such an act? Her skin pricked with awareness and a new sense of self-preservation. She didn't know the man she'd married. "I don't recognize them."

Shane's hand settled at her nape.

She jumped.

Malloy's eyes narrowed.

Shane rubbed her neck in soothing circles that failed to soothe. "I don't know them."

"We found a baseball bat near one of them." Malloy took out a picture of a metal slugger. "It was in the river, but we'll find prints on the handle."

Shane shrugged. "We both know you already printed the bat, and if you'd found any, you'd have said so."

Josie stiffened. How did he know that?

Malloy surveyed her. "Are you sure you don't recognize any of these men, Mrs. Dean?"

"Yes." She kept her voice low to prevent it from quivering. "Why do you ask?"

Malloy reached into a second file for an evidence bag holding a battered piece of paper. "Because we found your picture in the pocket of a dead man."

CHAPTER
5

JOSIE REACHED OUT with trembling fingers to touch the wrinkled paper. The picture was from her firm's website and had been printed on cheap computer paper. Her knees trembled and the air in her lungs chilled. "Why would someone have my picture?"

Shane shook his head. "So the mugging wasn't random."

"No." Malloy tapped his pen on the table. "These men were looking for Mrs. Dean."

"Why?" Josie turned toward Shane. "I don't understand. Why would these guys be looking for me? And why hurt you?" Reality began spinning away from her along with her sense of safety. Fear tasted like acid in her throat. "How did you meet up with them?" So many questions, and the answers remained locked in Shane's hard head.

His jaw tightened. He grabbed the paper, studying her smiling face. "I don't know. But this picture is off the Internet, right?" At her nod, he exhaled. "We'll discuss the safety in posting your face online later." He tossed the paper back down. "They needed the picture to identify you. My assumption is they were looking for me, considering someone bashed my head in." The chair creaked as he sat back. "Of course, we need to get you somewhere safe while we figure this out."

Had those men been looking for her? What if they'd found her? No way could she have defended herself against all three of them. "The three guys with my picture are dead." Probably by Shane's hand.

He eyed the picture. "There could be more men after us."

"After *you*." Or maybe after her. What was she going to do? "Maybe I should take a vacation. By myself."

He shifted his focus, his gaze wandering her face, a smile flirting with his lips. "You're stuck with me for now, angel. Deal with that fact." The smile did nothing to camouflage the determination setting his hard jaw.

Malloy cleared his throat. "I can put you somewhere safe, Mrs. Dean." His chest puffed out.

Josie fought to keep from choking on the testosterone that thickened the air. "I need a minute to myself, gentlemen." The word probably didn't apply to either man sitting in the room. What should she do?

Hiding out didn't seem like a smart option . . . especially without a timeline. She couldn't just abandon work, especially since she needed to correct Billy's files—and then make partner. The security from such a position would allow her finally to relax a little bit, and the only way she'd get the promotion would be to stay visible. At the firm, anyway. "Is there another alternative?"

Malloy sighed. "I can have a black-and-white check by your house during patrol. We don't have the manpower to put someone on your house twenty-four hours a day, but I'll do what I can." He slid the paper into a file, tapping the entire stack into a neat pile and eyeing Shane. "I'm assuming you'll be staying with her?"

"Yes."

Josie blinked several times. Why would those men want her? What was Shane involved in? What if they came after her? Sure, she remembered some self-defense. Not enough, though. She'd purposefully decided to take yoga instead of karate to keep in shape. The exact opposite of what Shane would've told her to do.

Malloy stood. "I don't have any other questions for you right now but would appreciate you keeping me informed of your location."

"Of course." Shane pushed back from the table and stood, assisting Josie to her feet. "Let me know if you identify the men in the morgue."

"I will. Although you'll probably remember them soon, I'd think." The detective crossed around the table. "I'll show you out."

Well past midnight, darkness filtering in the window, Josie finished knitting a scarf and laid it on the bed to admire it, her mind ablaze with thoughts. Shades of copper speckled the scarf's pattern, guaranteed to bring out the amber flecks in Tom's eyes. She'd been working on the scarf for him for about a week. Maybe she should've called him back after dinner. Should she tell Tom about Shane staying with her? She and Tom were just friends, but something more had hinted between them lately, and she liked him.

A year or two younger than her, Tom was a good guy, a construction worker with big dreams. And he believed in her dreams. Of course, right now her biggest dream was getting back to her safe life.

Was she in danger now? Were the men after her, or did they have her picture because they sought Shane? She and Shane had left the police station and run to a clothing store to buy him jeans. He'd scowled the entire time and had been quiet, lost in his own thoughts. Not sharing them with her and not providing any answers—just like old times. Once home, they'd both headed to bed.

Charming in a boyish way, Tom never hid his emotions from her.

Pressing her hand to her abdomen, she centered her thoughts and concentrated on breathing, allowing fear to slide away. For two years she'd taken meditation and yoga classes in an effort to stay calm. Maybe she should've been taking shooting lessons.

The knife she'd grabbed from the kitchen gleamed on her nightstand. The blade was big enough to cut through a twenty-pound turkey. Just in case the muggers returned—she wanted the weapon near.

The cell phone buzzed, and seeing Tom's number come up, she answered it.

"There you are," Tom said. "Sorry it's so late. I can't sleep."

"Me either." She and Tom often spoke late into the night, both too tired to sleep after a hard day's work. Now, more than ever, she needed to talk. She needed to get the words out to someone she trusted. To someone who would understand and hopefully have insight into fixing everything.

She took a deep breath. "Remember when I crashed into you in the elevator a couple of months ago?"

Tom chuckled. "When we met? Yes. You were late for a meeting and tripped—and you apologized for being a mess."

She had been a disaster, just having found out about the possible promotion. Tom, catching her attention with his shaggy hair and strong jawline, had quickly helped her right all the papers, telling her to take a deep breath. He'd also grinned and promised she wasn't a mess.

Swallowing, she settled against the headboard. "I'm a mess again. You wouldn't believe the night I've had." Tom had become her confidant, and she couldn't stop now. Taking a deep breath, she told him the entire story, starting with the phone call from the hospital. Tom had known about Shane from the beginning and had encouraged her to file the divorce papers without waiting for Shane's input. Of course, Tom's divorce had him miserable, so she hadn't wanted to follow suit right away.

Dead silence met her when she wound down her story. Unease pricked the back of her neck. "Tom?"

He exhaled loudly. "Wow." More quiet pounded between them. "I'm not sure what to say. I mean, this sounds like something from *Law and Order*—with amnesia, dead bodies, and your photo trampled in the mud at a crime scene. You know this isn't good, right?" Concern animated his deep voice. A fridge closed at his end, echoing across the line. She could almost see him prowling through his half-finished house with the phone pressed to his ear. He lived in the finished part while he waited for the money to build the rest.

"I know it sounds unreal." There was no rational way to explain why she let Shane sleep in the next room. "I wish I could explain."

Tom sighed. "You don't owe me an explanation. I understand you're married and the ties that implies, even if you are seeking a divorce. And I sure as hell understand how a divorce can cut you down at the knees." Tom had discovered his wife of three years was sleeping with their optometrist, a rich guy with a winter house in Belize. Of course, this happened just as Tom's construction business had floundered and disappeared in the tough economic times. Very tough. He'd moved from Texas to Washington for a fresh start.

Emotion clogged Josie's throat. Tom's friendship had quickly become a rare anchor in her life, and she relied on him. "I can't tell you how much I appreciate you."

"Well, on that note, how about I tell you how much I can't stand that your soon-to-be ex is sleeping in the next room?"

And *that* was why she counted on Tom. He told her the truth, sharing his feelings. Both good and bad. He trusted her to be strong enough to deal with anything. She allowed her shoulders to relax. "I know."

"It's incredibly difficult for me to make a move with a guy in your house." Humor and a hint of seriousness echoed in his low tone. Chiefly humor.

Josie smiled. So Tom had been gearing up to make a move. She'd wondered. A tiny part of her was glad for the reprieve—she obviously wasn't ready to abandon Shane if their kiss in the kitchen was any indication. "I imagine it would be."

"Well, all things in good time. For now, how about you let me get you out of here? Away from danger and dead bodies?" The sound of leather crackled across the line as she pictured Tom shifting in his favorite chair in what he called his "man cave," an empty room with new sheetrock he'd taped himself that would someday have a pool table and plasma television. When the economy bounced back. "We can both take off from work until things are safe for you. No pressure, no stress, just away from here until the police get everything figured out. Please."

The heartfelt entreaty in the last word moved her to

close her eyes. Tom couldn't afford to leave work any more than she could right now. Yet he'd offered. "I appreciate it. But for now, let's wait and see what the police find." An odd part of her, deep beneath the fear, truly couldn't imagine the bad guys wanted her. It just didn't make sense. "Did you hear about the ninth floor yet?"

"Not yet." The ninth floor of their office building was being remodeled, and Tom had made a bid for the job. "Josie, don't change the subject. You need to get out of town—you're mixed up in something dangerous."

She stiffened against the stack of pillows in her quiet bedroom. The pillows were a reminder of a happier time and what she thought happy married people had to have on their beds. The best foster parents she'd ever had were named Arthur and Claire. Their bed had had so many pillows it had taken Claire a full five minutes to make the bed. Josie had helped before school each day, telling herself that her grown-up bed would be the same someday.

But sitting there, in her wonderful bed with its multitude of colorful pillows, Josie felt a heaviness in her chest. "I can't leave." A hoarseness crackled her voice.

"I get it. If my wife showed up tomorrow and wanted another chance, I don't know if I could say no. I mean, ex-wife."

Josie's chest warmed. "The woman was crazy to leave you."

Tom sighed. "Thanks. I have to ask, are you safe with Shane? I mean, how well do you really know this guy?"

"Not very well." She considered allowing Tom to whisk her away to safety, away from the raw need she felt whenever Shane was near. The irony almost made her smile. She'd be seeking shelter from the one man whose entire focus had been to protect her during their marriage.

Before he'd left her alone and devastated. A small part of her had always thought Shane would find her again.

She had been right.

Tom took a moment, probably swallowing some beer. He liked Bud out of a bottle. "Don't take this the wrong way, but you kind of remind me of one of those women in movies that get beat up and can't leave the guy because they love him."

Her head jerked back. "Shane has never hit me."

"I know. But he left you high and dry...and now he's in your guest room."

"Yeah, and you went to couples counseling after you found your wife doing a guy who touches eyeballs."

Tom snorted. "You have a great point, my friend. We're suckers...the both of us."

"A perfect pair." She stretched her legs out under the covers. "I need answers. I need to know where Shane has been the last two years. Crap, I need to know who I married. Finally." Then maybe she'd be able to move on.

Silence came across the line for several heartbeats before Tom spoke. "I understand. But promise me, if you need help, you'll call me. Immediately."

"I promise."

"Fair enough. I'll try and swing by your office tomorrow to say hi. Night." Tom hung up.

Josie slid her cell phone onto the night table and turned off the bedside lamp. She yawned. Yet her mind swirled. Was Tom right? Was she some victim caught in domestic disaster? Shane had earned her trust and then deserted her. He'd known all about her past and what abandoning her would do—and yet he'd left anyway. Was she weak in allowing him in her house?

Memories, ideas, possibilities whipped through her

brain for an hour. Exhaustion pulled at her, though her mind took half the night to finally wind down. As she slipped into a shallow sleep, odd dreams in which she was lost in unfamiliar forests prodded her into wakefulness around dawn.

A low growl rumbled through the bedroom wall. Josie sat up, her heart pounding. Shane. He was hurt. The man had refused even over-the-counter medication before bed. She reached for the knife on her nightstand.

Her bare feet pattered across the wooden floor as she hurried into his bedroom. He lay on his stomach, tanned arm outstretched, covers pushed to his bare waist. Such a broad, masculine back, showcasing a life of battle. Scars, some quite old, testified he'd seen pain before. The dark tattoo covered his left shoulder, the graceful lines creating a tough-looking Chinese character. *Freedom*. He moaned low.

She stepped lightly, leaning over to pat his heated back. "Shane. Are you okay?"

Swifter than sound, he pinned her under his hard body, his hand at her throat. He pressed into her, his mouth near her ear. "Not this time. I told you never again—no more training like this."

Josie struggled. Training? "Shane. I can't breathe."

He stilled. His eyes flashed open. "Josie?" The hand on her throat loosened. He shook his head, eyes focusing. The darkness failed to hide the still-fresh bruises that mottled his face. "What are you doing here?"

"You cried out." She blinked back tears. Who moved that fast? "I thought your head was hurting you."

"It is now." He hardened against her, settling between her legs. The sweats failed to mask his sudden erection. Shadows danced across his angled face, making him both handsome and mysterious. His deep voice roughened to an almost guttural tone. "You want to take the hurt away, baby?"

Need flashed through her on the heels of apprehension. Instinct kicked in. "You're scaring me, Shane."

He instantly rolled over, releasing her. She hated that about him. Always had. He was so easy to manipulate with weakness, with fear or softness. But try to meet him head-to-head, and he ran right over her. Without causing a bruise. Apparently the real Shane was returning. "God, you piss me off."

"I'm sorry I scared you." He raked both hands over his face.

She wouldn't scream. Not a chance. Levering up, she leaped onto his stomach, her knee pressed precariously close to his balls, the knife at his throat. "Now who's scared?"

Soft light filtered in, making his eyes glow in the near-darkness. His entire body stiffened below hers. Ready to fight. "What do you think you're doing, angel?" Warning melded with curiosity in his tone.

"You don't know me, you moron." She tightened her grip on the handle. "Maybe I did hire those men in the morgue. I could've been the one to injure you. To put you in the hospital and take your memories." Her knee inched closer to his boys. Just once, she needed to see the real man behind the calm mask. "Yet you trust. So easily. Why?"

"Because you're half my size and look like an angel."

"That's fucking stupid." One swift move and she could sever his jugular. A move he'd taught her so long ago. "If you have a blind spot, Shane, it's for women who look soft. I don't know why."

He frowned. No concern filtered in his eyes from her threat, so she pressed her knee up. His sharp intake of breath made her smile.

"Josie, move your leg away from my balls and get off me. Now."

"Or what?"

"Or I'll forget you're soft and teach you a lesson." The Southern drawl escaped, though his tone remained calm.

Finally. His façade was cracking. "Bring it on, asswipe."

She flew into the air.

Her yelp echoed around the room. He'd levered his feet and tossed her up without moving his arms. Strong hands flipped her around on her flight down. She found her back pressed to his front, the knife at her jugular. Heat enfolded her. His broad hand in her hair tugged her head to the side, exposing her neck to the cool night air. "Asswipe?"

Both her elbows shot back into his gut. Her wrists were quickly secured by one of his hands at the small of her back.

"Did I ever tie you up, darlin'?"

Desire shot through her like a shot of hard whiskey. "No." She tried to move, to tug her wrists free.

"Too bad. Restraining you excites me." His head dropped and his mouth engulfed her collarbone. The knife clattered to the floor. "If you don't want gentle, you should've said so." He flipped her around, and his lips crushed down on hers.

She didn't want gentle. She wanted Shane—all of him. Her nails bit into his chest while a moan filtered up her throat. Finally. Oh, she'd worn bruises after a particularly passionate and athletic night during their marriage, and they were well worth it. But something new had just

sprung free. She sensed it. A wildness in Shane, something he normally trapped and kept veiled. Somehow,
finally, it roared.

His mouth locked on hers. No gentleness. No softness.
Just pure, raw lust.

She stretched up on her tiptoes, cradling his cock
between her legs. Oh God. She wanted.

He stilled.

No. She clutched him closer.

A rustle sounded outside the window, and a scrape
echoed from within the house.

He stepped back, grabbing her arms, his head turning
toward the door. "Do you have a gun, angel?"

A gun? She gulped in air. What?

He shook her. "Gun. Where is it?"

"Um, I left it in the glove box in my car." Fear slid
through the desire.

Glass shattered. Something clattered across the floor.
"Fuck." Shane threw her onto the bed and rolled to the
other side, yanking the mattress on top of them as they hit
the floor. A bang echoed.

What? Smoke filled the space. Static. Her mind fuzzed.
Her vision blurred. She reached out for Shane, for safety.
Gone. Where was he?

Male grunts echoed. Flesh hitting flesh. She pushed
the mattress away, grabbing the night table and pulling
herself to her knees. Smoke hazed her vision. A ringing
filled her ears. Smoke swirled around her.

A grunt pulled her attention from the smoke. Shane
battled with a man in all black, fists flying, hands grabbing, bodies struggling. Shane's knife flashed, wicked
and sharp.

Blood sprayed. The attacker dropped to the ground,

his eyes wide-open in death. Shane turned to fight another man.

Her hands spread out over the smooth bedside table. The phone. She grabbed it, squinting to dial the numbers. A roaring filled her head. She dialed 911, dropping the phone just as a voice echoed over the line.

Male voices bellowed behind her. Where was she?

Darkness fell across her vision. She lost her hold on the furniture, plunging toward the soft rug. Then, nothing.

CHAPTER
6

PAIN EXPLODED ACROSS Shane's cheek as the second man landed a punch. Flashes sparked behind his eyes. Memories. Noise, fighting, brutal and deadly.

He dropped to one knee, next to the man he'd just killed. The knife was kicked out of his hand to go spinning under the bed. Explosions ripped through his brain. A firefight in Asia. A training field with the dead littering the ground. Flashes of moments in time. Blurry, loud, confusing, the thoughts hit him harder than the bastard throwing punches.

Something ripped through his ear canal. Sounds...so many, so harsh, flooded his senses. Sounds beyond the normal. A car honked miles away. Cats hissed in a fight four neighborhoods over. Memories of other cars, other animals, tumbled through his mind.

Shane tried to yank his attention to the present, blocking his face from the worst of the hits. His limbs seemed weighted down with huge blocks.

A memory slammed him like a sledgehammer to the chest. Jory. Pain. Gone.

Glass crunched as a third man jumped through the window.

Shane caught a glimmer of gold from the corner of his eye. Josie's hair. Her pretty eyes fluttered closed, and she dropped to the ground, unconscious.

Time stopped. All pain receded. Focus shot through him like an electrical current. He calmed. One thing mattered, only one.

Protecting his woman.

He leaped up, both legs flying to encircle the hitter's throat. Twisting his knees, Shane cut off the guy's air supply as they fell to the ground. He didn't feel the jarring impact. An elbow to the temple knocked the intruder out cold. Rolling, Shane released him and flipped backward to his feet.

No questions, no concerns, nothing existed but the threat in front of him. The third man yanked a Sharkman Fixed-Blade out from behind his back. He stood about six foot, packed hard, with dead brown eyes.

"As combat knives go, that's a good choice," Shane said. How could he identify the kind of knife but not know his middle name? "Though I prefer the Black Frog."

The guy smiled, showing a gold tooth. "That's a good one, too."

Shane angled to the side, keeping his body between Josie and the weapon. "Leave and I won't kill you." Probably not a true statement. He could think of twenty different ways to kill the guy without moving his feet from their current position. The blood flowing through the guy's veins made a soft sound. One Shane shouldn't be able to hear. He'd worry about that knowledge later. Right now, his focus was absolute.

The guy lunged.

Shane pivoted, slamming the heel of his hand against the man's wrist and smoothly stealing the knife. Two steps forward, and he plunged the knife into the side of the guy's jugular. Following his prey to the ground, he used both hands to slice open the man's neck, fighting against cartilage and bone. Knowledge slammed into him that, although difficult, the task was easier than it should've been. His strength wasn't normal, either.

Sirens trilled in the distance.

He stilled, glancing at the phone on the floor. Josie had dialed 911.

The blood rushed through his ears as he took in the bloody scene. He'd killed two men and knocked one out. Something whispered in the back of his head that he should take care of the unconscious man. Kill him so he couldn't seek revenge.

Shane tried to take a deep breath and regretted it as the stench of death filled his lungs. God, who the hell was he? Why could he do such amazing things? None of the memories flashing back were good—none showed a decent life. His head pounded, and his gut clenched tighter than his fists. His bloody fists.

But instinct ordered him to take out the last man for good. So he stood and took a step toward the prone figure.

Josie groaned.

He stopped cold.

For the first time that night, his hands began to tremble. His angel lay on the floor surrounded by death and blood. What kind of a monster was he?

He'd left her, and now he'd brought danger to her door. Her distrust of him had ticked him off earlier, but now he had to acknowledge that her instincts were probably good. This time. Shame filled him that he'd left her alone. Why? Those memories had to come back.

Small, she lay curled on her side, delicate features so

pale. He had to get her out of there. Grabbing a pillow-case, he quickly wiped blood off his face and hands, toss-ing the material onto the floor. Leaning over, he reached down to gently pick her up.

Two cops met him in the hallway, young and earnest, guns aimed at him.

Fire zapped along his vertebrae. Absolute calm fol-lowed. Moves to disable them, to kill them, ran through his brain so fast his shoulders tensed.

Josie stirred in his arms.

The closest cop settled his stance, his gun aimed at Shane's head. "Put her down." The kid had to be about twenty.

Shane took a deep breath. "No."

The cop's Adam's apple bobbed. "I don't want to shoot you, man." His hand wavered just enough to increase Shane's heart rate.

Shane leaned against the wall in case he needed to balance and kick out. "Call Detective Malloy. He knows what's going on. Tell him someone broke into Josie Dean's place."

The other cop, just as young as the first, tilted his head and spoke into the radio strapped to his shoulder. He lis-tened and then straightened up. "Malloy already heard the call—he's on the way. And he sounds ... pissed."

"Yeah, I assume so." Shane pivoted, fighting every instinct he owned so he could turn his back on the guns. "I'm putting my wife in her room. Feel free to follow me, but if you point the gun in her direction again, I'm taking it away from you."

Not by one whit did he doubt he could do it. So many different ways to disarm the cops flashed through his head, his skull began to ache. Memories of fights, of stripping away weapons, of his killing people, ripped through his mind.

Whoever or whatever he was...there was no way he was the good guy.

Pity.

Men's voices awakened Josie. She opened her eyes, keeping her body motionless in self-protection. A trick she'd learned from the foster parent who hit.

One voice filtered through the rest. Shane. Safety.

She sat up on her bed. "What in the world?"

Shane grabbed her hand from his perch next to her. How did they get back into her room? His gaze ran over her face. So serious. So pissed.

She fought a shiver. "What—"

"Flash grenade," he muttered, wiping blood off his forehead with the back of his free hand. A cut splayed open above his left eye, and fresh bruises mingled with the yellowing ones already on his strong face and down his bare torso. He'd somehow donned jeans.

How many bruises could one body take?

Early sunshine glinted off the sparkling wooden floor. Cops in uniform strode by in the hallway, placing markers, taking pictures. Muted voices came from the guest room. A figure pushed off from the wall, his deep brown eyes bloodshot. "Mrs. Dean."

"Detective Malloy." Josie glanced down at her bare legs. Shane grabbed a blanket off the end of the bed to drape over her. "Ah, what happened?"

"Well, Mrs. Dean, as far as we can tell, three men attacked you and your husband. Two bodies are in the guest room, and one man is on his way to the ER."

Bodies? Nausea swirled in her gut. Shane had killed

two men? So what, his body count was up to five this week? "Who were they?" Her voice cracked at the end. The men had violated her home, her sanctuary. Maybe safety didn't exist.

Shane stiffened. "They haven't been identified yet, angel." He dropped his gaze to her trembling lips. "Hold on, the next ambulance should be here soon."

"I don't want an ambulance." She tightened her jaw to still her lips. "I'm not going to the hospital again." Fear made her voice tremble, and she cleared her voice.

His focus narrowed. "Why not?"

He really didn't remember anything, or he'd never ask that question. She'd already told him about her childhood, and the story had seriously pissed him off. It was all she could do to keep him from hunting down the bastard who'd hit her. She glanced away, seeking comfort in the pretty Norman Rockwell prints of peaceful homes she'd hung on the walls. "I don't like hospitals. Most people don't."

"Josie." Low, commanding, his voice held no quarter.

They hadn't seen one another in two years, and yet her body reacted instantly to that tone. Sexy and male, it tingled down her spine. Her gaze swung to his. Deep gray, his eyes demanded an answer, as if there weren't cops all around them. She struggled to derail his concentration. "Who's after you?"

He blinked twice. His hold tightened. Finally, he ran a hand over his face. "I don't know. I'm so sorry I brought them to you." He shook his head. "I didn't think—"

Malloy cleared his throat. "I heard back from Pendleton, Major Dean. You retired over two years ago, with full honors."

Confusion swirled in Josie's brain. She'd forgotten

about Malloy. "No, no, that's not right. He stayed in the marines. I always assumed he left on a mission." That he'd be back for her someday.

"He retired on June first two years ago, Mrs. Dean." Malloy studied them both, the gun at his hip outlined through his cheap jacket.

Betrayal hit her like a fist in the gut. Shane had left her in August—two months *after* retiring. Where had he gone every day when he'd said he was going to work? Who the hell was her husband?

Shane exhaled. No expression showed on his battered face. "Any idea where I've been for two years?"

"Nope. Your commanding officer said you left without a word, just took off. Though he said you were a hero first. Saved several lives." Malloy's voice remained steady and without inflection. Cop voice.

Josie shook her head. She'd believed the lies. Just like a domestic violence victim. Tom might be right. Maybe she should get out of town. Hell, maybe she should take a chance on a guy who trusted her...a guy who let her in and didn't lie. "You lied to me, Shane." Her voice came out small, weak.

Shane exhaled. "We don't know that, sweetheart. Let me find out what was going on. Possibly I went under-cover or something."

Her vision blurred. Perhaps the flash grenade had given her a concussion. She blinked to clear her head.

Malloy scribbled in his tattered notebook. "Mrs. Dean, please relate what happened here tonight."

Josie took a deep breath and recalled the grenade and seeing the fight. "But it was all hazy. I didn't understand what was going on." Her voice trembled. She would not cry.

Shane scooped her up, blanket and all, and tugged her

to his bare chest. Scars lined his angular form, knife and bullet wounds now partially camouflaged by new bruises. Heat radiated from his hard body, an oasis of warmth in the chill of the room.

She didn't trust him, and she sure as heck shouldn't be on his lap. But the warm illusion of safety was too tempting to fight—for now. For a moment, she needed to pretend. She wet her dry lips and let him shelter her—temporarily. "How long was I out?"

"Fifteen minutes."

He'd killed two men in less than half an hour. She shivered and he tucked her closer. His familiar scent of heated cedar surrounded her. He'd killed. To protect her, but still, he'd ended the lives of those two men. Yeah. That scared her.

Malloy flipped his notebook closed. "You folks stay here." He headed out of the room toward the guest room.

Shane shifted, resting her against the headboard and rising from the bed. His gaze took in the entire room, studying each corner, each nook. "What the hell is that buzzing?" He stilled and seemed to center himself in absolute concentration.

Josie frowned, the room cooling her again without his body heat near. "There's no buzzing." Had he been hit in the head again?

Finally, with a frown, he stalked over to the phone base on her nightstand.

"What's going on?" Josie pulled the blanket up higher.

Shane shook his head, lifting the base and peering at the bottom. His jaw tightened. Flaring his nostrils, he yanked a round silver disc off to throw on the floor.

"What's that?"

Shane held up a hand and grabbed her cowboy boot

from the closet. Quick motions sent the heel smashing the disc into pieces. "Fucking bug."

A bug? Someone had bugged her room? "What are you talking about?"

"They sent the grenade into the guest room. Where I was sleeping. How did they know?" Shane swept the pieces under her dresser with his bare foot. "Don't say anything to Malloy. Something happened when I was hit...my hearing is unbelievable all of a sudden." He stalked toward her, his eyes the swirling gray of a winter storm. "Has my hearing always been beyond the norm?"

She shrugged. "Not that I know about." Of course, she wouldn't know now, would she?

He gave a short nod. "Do you need a doctor?"

"No." A shrink maybe.

"Good. Pack a bag." He glanced at his bare chest. "Damn it. I'm sure they won't let me get my shirt from the crime scene."

Josie blushed, scrambling off the bed. "I, uh...may have another of your shirts in the bottom drawer of my dresser."

He didn't comment, just tugged open the drawer and yanked on a faded Marine Corps T-shirt. "Thanks."

She panicked and dressed quickly. If they were going to argue, she needed to be fully dressed. "I'm not leaving with you."

Reaching into her closet, he tossed her clothes in a bag. "You're in danger...more than I thought. You are leaving."

He meant it. He'd try and take her, regardless of the cops in the other room. Chances were, he'd succeed. What should she do? She couldn't trust him, but he knew how to fight and win. Why didn't that reassure her? "The cops will shoot you."

His shrug made him wince as he glanced down at his torso. "I've been shot before."

She edged toward the hallway.

He grabbed her arm, his hold firm. "Josie, I know things are complicated. But three killers just stormed your house. You need protection, and I'm better than the cops."

Her thoughts slugged through her mind in slow motion. Should she leave with him? What about the police? But he was right—he'd taken care of the threat. What was wrong with her? She didn't trust him, but she couldn't walk away. Her lungs compressed. If she didn't go with him, would she ever see him again? Maybe not, and she couldn't take that chance. She had to know who he was—whom she'd married. And she wanted to live. For now, he was her best bet. So many conflicting emotions ripped through her that her stomach hurt.

He led her through the hall and into the kitchen.

Malloy met them at the door. "Where do you think you're going?"

Shane's nostrils flared. "The hospital. The ambulance is too late, and I'm taking my wife for a checkup."

Malloy frowned. "I'll meet you there when we're finished with the scene."

Confusion hazed in Josie's brain, but instinct pushed her to go. Quickly. She stumbled alongside Shane as he led her to the garage and lifted her into the SUV.

"Put on your seat belt." Quick strides put him behind the vehicle, and he backed out of the garage.

"Why didn't you tell Malloy about the bug?" She clasped her frozen hands in her lap.

Streetlights played across the dangerous angles of Shane's face. "The detective isn't prepared for whatever's going on here."

"And you are?" Okay. That did scare her.

"Yep." He circled the block, scrutinizing the homes stirring to life with the dawn. "In your neighborhood, is there an empty house, one for sale or one with the owners on a long vacation?"

"Why?"

"Because that bug sucked. The device had a radius of a block, max."

"How do you know the radius just from looking at the bug?"

He stilled. "I don't know." The vehicle slowed at the end of the block.

Josie shook her head. He knew stuff he shouldn't and was beyond trained. Trained to kill anybody in his way. What if *she* was suddenly in his way? A chill slithered down her spine.

"Josie?"

She stiffened and pointed to a small bungalow. "That house was for sale. I mean, the sign is gone, so maybe they sold it." She'd known he had training as a soldier, but just what kind of skills had he developed? His hearing must be truly excellent to have detected that bug under her phone. What was he really capable of? Besides hand-to-hand combat that resulted in the other guy being dead.

Shane nodded, drove around the corner, and parked next to the community gazebo. "Why don't you like hospitals?"

For the love of Pete. She'd known he wouldn't let it go. "I don't think this is the time to talk about it."

"We're not leaving until we talk about it." A muscle jumped in his jaw.

She'd told him her entire life story before, and yet he

hadn't told her a thing. For two months they'd shared a home, shared a bed. And she'd had no idea he was a killer. Their marriage had been a lie, one she'd jumped into wholeheartedly. She'd loved somebody that didn't exist, and the loss of that dream pierced her breastbone with a blade sharper than she would've imagined.

A stranger sat next to her.

"Josie. Answer me about the hospital," he said calmly.

She jumped. The morning pressed in. A sense of urgency had her wiggling on the seat. They couldn't just sit there, and appeasing him right now seemed wise. "Fine. I grew up in foster care. One of the houses had a drunk who hit. He took me to the hospital, and I associate the smell of the place with, ah, pain."

Shane's hands tightened on the wheel, the knuckles turning white. "Have I killed him?"

"No." Josie coughed. "Though you wanted to."

"Still do." Anger and pain bracketed Shane's mouth.

Yeah. Amnesia or not, Shane was Shane. Unless it was all a trick. "It ended up being a good thing. The doctors made a report, and I went to Arthur and Claire's to live. They were foster parents, but they planned to adopt me." Her voice sounded wistful, even to her. When she'd fallen on her bike, she'd even felt safe at the hospital with Arthur carrying her in.

"Why didn't they?"

"Claire died." Josie shrugged against the wash of sadness from what could've been. "Embolism. One day she was there, the next day she wasn't." Arthur had started drinking, nearly losing his accounting business. Social services took her away again, and probably would have even if Arthur hadn't spiraled into depression. They couldn't let her stay with a grieving single man.

Her first chance for a normal life had been snatched away so quickly. Her second, with Shane, had disappeared as well. Maybe some people were meant to live alone. Man, that was a depressing thought.

Shane released the steering wheel. "I'm sorry." He opened his door. "What did Claire do?"

"She was a homemaker. Arthur was an accountant. He loved numbers." Josie squinted to see out the window. Enough with the sad memories. Life moved on. "What now?"

Shane jumped out of the vehicle. "Stay here."

No freaking way. She could either run back to the cops, or follow Shane into the bungalow. If somebody had been bugging her house, she wanted to see who and how. She leaped from the car, swaying until she regained her balance. Quick steps had her on Shane's heels.

"I told you to stay in the car," he muttered, his gaze swinging to both sides of the road.

"I'm scared." She really should feel bad about manipulating him. "I don't want to stay alone in the car." Plus, anyone who had ever seen a slasher movie knew the person waiting in the car always ended up dead. She went for the jugular. "Please let me stay with you."

He faltered and then sighed. "Okay. But stay behind me." He took her hand, hurrying around the bungalow to open the fence toward the back. The rear yard had turned brown, weeds sprouting up. The smell of decaying brush scented the air. He peered into the kitchen window. "Empty."

Glancing around, Shane grabbed a medium-sized rock and smashed the sliding glass door near the handle. Josie cringed. A dog barked in the distance. But nobody moved.

Shane reached inside and unlocked the lever, sliding

the door open and stepping inside. He looked around and motioned for her to join him. She gingerly stepped over broken glass, her heart thundering in her ears. What was she doing? This was so illegal.

The kitchen area was empty, not even a table. Quick movements sent them hustling through the unfurnished dining room. Their footsteps echoed through the dusty space until they reached the living room.

Josie's legs froze in place.

Her eyes stared back at her from a picture on the wall. The moment captured her smiling brightly into the sun, a daiquiri in her hand. She glanced at the next picture, taken of her at a baseball game. Several more pictures of her adorned the walls. Pictures of her coming home after work. Of going to the gym. Of gardening outside her home. Months' worth. All tacked up next to a sprawl of surveillance equipment.

Shane growled, hurrying toward the equipment. "What the hell?"

Josie frowned. Her wedding picture caught her eye. The official one in the stunning silver frame. The one she'd left for him at his base when she'd moved to Washington. Just in case he wanted the memories. It sat on the end table. She looked closer at some of the pictures. Her hair was shorter. Lighter. Some of the pictures were from California. From before she'd met Shane. From three, maybe four years ago.

She stumbled back a step.

An empty Guinness bottle sat on the counter.

Guinness.

The picture.

With a soft cry, she ran for the bedroom. The scent of heated cedar filled her nostrils. The bed with its navy comforter made, the corners tucked. Shaky steps brought her to the small dresser in the corner. She pulled out the first drawer. Socks. Perfectly folded, in order of color. Just the way Shane organized them. His sole concession to being a soldier, to allowing himself one quirk.

She grabbed a discarded shirt off the floor and brought the material to her nose. Shane's masculine scent filled her nostrils. Her fingers fisted in the material as she slowly turned around.

He overpowered the doorway. She took a step back, straightening her shoulders. There'd be no crying.

He frowned, glancing at the shirt. "What's wrong?"

"Nothing." She threw the shirt down, hiding the faded Marine Corps logo. Panic threatened to stop her breathing. What should she do? He'd lied to her—he'd stalked her. Even before they met, he'd watched her. Betrayal coated her throat until she wanted to choke. She'd trusted him. Anger wanted to roar, but self-preservation won. She couldn't beat him, and she had one chance to get free. So she forced herself to shrug and walk toward him "I just don't like breaking and entering." Her voice trembled. "Can we leave now?"

She brushed past him toward the door.

His hand shot out and grabbed her arm. Dark pupils narrowed and zeroed in on her. Questioning. "Not yet. I need to check more of the equipment."

She was no victim. Her smile hurt as she swung around to face him. "Okay." The urge to run shot her into full action. She bunched, and with every ounce of strength she owned, she kneed him in the nuts.

His eyes widened in shock.

He dropped to the floor with a muffled oomph, both hands clutching his groin.

Oh God, oh God, oh God. Her hands shook and she scrambled for the next move. Pivoting, she shot a side kick to his temple and knocked him over.

She yelped as she turned and ran.

Glass cut her arm as she jumped out the sliding door, and she leaped through the open gate of the fence. A rustle sounded behind her. She cut across the front lawn, yelling for Detective Malloy. The detective looked up from her porch, a frown on his face. She ran as if the devil himself chased her, her steps pounding on the asphalt.

"Damn it, Josie. Stop!" Shane yelled.

She pushed harder. Who the hell was Shane Dean? She reached Malloy in a rush, all but tumbling into his arms. He steadied her.

Turning, she held her breath at what she'd see. Nothing. A dark, quiet street.

Shane was gone.

CHAPTER
7

POLICE STATION COFFEE sucked. Josie huddled over the Styrofoam cup, her finger probing the bite marks she'd left in the spongy top. How could she have been so wrong? But really, what had she ever known about Shane? Some of those pictures had been from before she'd even met him. Had he been stalking her? If so, why leave her for two years? He'd had her.

What kind of a crazy game had he been playing?

The heat snapped on in the small room, but it failed to penetrate her chilled skin.

Detective Malloy sat across the battered table of the interview room, the dark circles beneath his eyes widening as the day wore on. "I'm sorry, Mrs. Dean." He tapped a photograph of her leaving a gym in California holding a rolled-up yoga mat under her arm. "Since you're ready to continue, let's look at a few more photographs my men brought from the cottage where your husband apparently has been staying. Do you remember this picture?"

Considering she hadn't realized the snapshot was being taken, no. "I haven't seen this picture before." She fought a shiver at the creepy fact that she'd been photographed without her knowledge. "Though I hadn't met Shane when this shot was taken."

"Are you sure?" Malloy's gaze sharpened.

"Yes. My California yoga instructor opened her own place across town, and I followed her. I stopped going to this location at least a month before I met Shane." She'd keep using his name. No way would she refer to Shane Dean as her husband. Never again.

Malloy scribbled in a notebook, sliding another photograph in front of her. "Your hair is longer in this one."

"Yes." Josie stared for a moment. The shot had captured her leaving her office building in California dressed in her favorite green silk suit. "This was taken even before the yoga one. I cut my hair shortly after this picture, I think." Fear made her breath arrive in short bursts.

"You worked for Montgomery and Associates?"

"Yes. I moved to the local branch here when I, ah, left Shane." Apparently her instincts were right for once.

"Why Snowville? I mean, your firm has branches all over the country."

"I don't know." Josie rubbed her eyes. "Snowville is a decent-sized town, not a city, with four seasons, lakes, and mountains. Seemed like a good place to make a home." And her one and only friend from childhood was buried in the local cemetery.

"Yeah. I like living here, too." Malloy shook a picture out to the side. Dark dust flew from where the police had tried to fingerprint the paper. He slid the photo in front of her. "This was taken in front of your office building here in Snowville."

"Yes." Dread flipped her stomach over. The picture showed her smiling up at Tom, his hand at her elbow as they left at the end of the day. Probably before they went out to dinner, or to one of their homes, where they could cook and save money. She should warn Tom about Shane. "The coat I'm wearing in the picture—I bought it last week."

Malloy made a notation. "What I find interesting is we couldn't find one single fingerprint on these pictures. I have men going through the cottage now, and so far... nothing."

"Shane took those." The Guinness can, the rolled-up socks, the shirt smelling like him all proved Shane had been watching her. For years. Fear sharpened the room into clear focus. Where was he now? He'd taken her SUV and disappeared.

Malloy smoothed the photographs into a nice pile. "I have another call into Pendleton to find out more about the major."

The smell of sweat, burnt coffee, and fear swirled around the freezing room. Josie fought a sneeze, glancing at the dingy wall. The idea of being stalked for so long made her feel small and vulnerable. "I still keep expecting a two-way mirror." This time Malloy had brought her farther into the station, bypassing other detectives barking into phones and pecking at computers as they worked at their desks.

The corners of Malloy's thin lips tipped up. "The two-way mirrors are usually only on television, Mrs. Dean." He tapped his pen on his notebook. "Just like heroes protecting you for your own good and happily-ever-afters."

"That's true." Even her eyes felt bruised. "This doesn't make sense. Why would Shane stalk me? Then why leave me and come back?" Why pretend to love her? Why make her love him?

"I dunno. Maybe it's all about the chase. I mean, maybe

he likes the stalking, and since he succeeded so well last time, Dean wanted to try again." Malloy shrugged. "I'm hoping we'll get lucky and see his psych evaluation. Perhaps we'll discover why he left the marines two years ago."

"I'd like to hear the answer to that question." She picked at a torn cuticle on her pinkie. "He'd never talk about his past, about his life before we met. All he'd say was that he was alone without a family." She'd believed him. God, she'd been so stupid. "I figured he had a rough childhood and wanted the past left behind us. I could understand that."

Malloy nodded. "Yet you found out he had brothers."

"Yes." She'd never forget that night. She'd met Shane at their cozy apartment after work for dinner and he'd been... different. Distant and almost cold. He wouldn't meet her eyes. Yet when they went to bed, he'd all but burned her up with passion. So hard and fast. Almost desperate. The night had given her such hope that she was getting through to him... that he was opening up to her. That he was finally going to let her know him. "I woke up in the middle of the night, and Shane was screaming the name *Jory*."

"Jory?"

"Yes." She'd shaken Shane's arm and he'd sat up, turning away from her and dropping his head into his hands with a low sob. She'd asked who Jory was, placing her hand tenderly against Shane's heated back. Trying to offer comfort when none would be accepted.

Shane's entire body had shuddered. "My brother. Jory was one of my brothers. He's dead."

Two years later, sitting in the cold conference room of the police station, Josie could still feel the vibrations of Shane's pain as he'd said those words.

He'd left her the next day.

Malloy straightened his tie. "I'll run the name *Jory Dean,* as well."

Josie bit her lip. Did Jory even exist, or was it all some sort of bizarre trick? "None of this makes sense. I mean, say Shane has been stalking me, for whatever reason. What does that have to do with the guys found dead in the river? They had my picture."

Malloy frowned. "I'd say your husband is involved in some pretty bad stuff. Somebody's after him, and it appears they're willing to go through you to get him."

So now she had Shane and unknown killers after her. Her feet actually twitched with the need to flee. A shiver shook her shoulders, and goose bumps prickled her skin. She grabbed her purse from the floor, and a ball of yarn fell out. "Are we done here?"

Malloy exhaled. "What's up with the yarn?"

"I knit." She grabbed the ball and tossed it in the purse.

"Oh." He rubbed his chin, his eyes warming. "My granny knitted."

"It relaxes me."

"You probably need to relax." Standing, he stomped around the table and opened the door.

There wouldn't be any relaxing until Shane was behind bars. She shot to her feet and into the hall, hustling through the surprisingly quiet station and into the lobby.

Tom tossed a magazine onto the center table and stretched to his feet and away from one of the hideous orange chairs lining the paneled wall. They were all empty save for him.

Relief flooded her. She'd called him earlier, hoping he'd pick her up. Thank God. She stepped into his arms. He'd come for her. She'd called, and he'd dropped everything to help her.

Tom engulfed her in a clean, masculine-scented hug. "Josie." He leaned back, light brown eyes contrasting nicely with his worn blue flannel. "Never thought I'd be picking you up at the pokey."

Josie coughed out a laugh. "Funny. Very funny."

Tom stood back to study her face, and she studied his. Deep brown eyes glowed his concern, while the slight lines that fanned out from them marked a guy who laughed often. Full lips quirked in worry, and his light brown hair was ruffled, as if he'd been running his hands through it. His torn jeans covered toned muscle, and broad shoulders filled out his flannel. Funny, she hadn't realized Tom was as tall as Shane. Nobody seemed as big and powerful as her husband. She was so screwed up. A long shiver escaped her.

"You're cold." Tom eyed the room and put an arm around her shoulder as he focused on Malloy. "Is she free to leave?"

"Has Detective Connelly finished with your statement?" Malloy asked.

"Statement?" Josie squinted her eyes up at Tom.

"Yes." Tom smoothed a hair off her face. "I came to get you, and they asked me some questions. Where I've been the last few days, how long I've known you, if I have a camera." He grinned ruefully at the final query.

Josie rounded on the cop, her breath heating. "You *questioned* my friend?"

Tom tugged her purse strap up her arm. "I assume it's normal, and I had no problem answering the questions. Let's help the police figure this out."

Malloy nodded. "We'd appreciate that."

Tom led her to the exit. "Let's get you somewhere safe."

Safe? Safety was an illusion. She eyed Tom's tousled

hair and straight features. So different from Shane's rugged ones. She shivered and Tom tightened his hold.

"I can put you somewhere safe, Mrs. Dean," Detective Malloy said.

"You should let the police help." Tom rubbed her shoulder.

"I'm not hiding." Her voice trembled and she straightened her posture. She deserved answers, and she'd get them. Besides, something deep down whispered that the police couldn't hide her from Shane. He had skills none of them had realized. So she needed to be ready when he showed up again. And she needed to warn Tom.

Malloy nodded. "I have your contact information, Mrs. Dean. We'll be in touch."

They hurried out of the station. The fall sunshine failed to warm her face as Tom hustled her toward his battered truck. A scratched toolbox stretched across the front of the bed, holding all of the tools Tom had brought from Texas.

The hair on the back of her neck rose. Her body instinctively stilled. She glanced around the parking lot. Nothing seemed out of the ordinary. No eyes on her. But she jumped into the front seat and leaned against the clean material with a sigh.

Tom loped around the front, stepped inside, and started the engine to pull away from the station. "So. What a mess, huh?" His dimples flashed.

Josie shook her head. Leave it to Tom to try and cheer her up. "You could say that."

"How about we drive somewhere safe? Anywhere you want to go." Tom aimed them at the interstate toward his home outside of town.

"I'm tempted, but can't. You know I have that audit

all next week." The books weren't adding up at work, a fact that should be consuming her. While she'd fixed one account, she had several more to check. Plus, she'd had to start at the bottom of the Washington branch when she'd moved from California. She was a good CPA. No way was she letting Shane Dean screw up her job or her life. Not again. Besides, deep down, she knew he'd find her. No matter what.

They drove in silence for a while. Tom finally took the east exit, winding around the lake toward his home.

"I don't suppose he signed the divorce papers before you found out Dean was a stalker." Work-roughened hands tightened on the steering wheel, but Tom's voice remained steady as he stopped in the driveway and pressed the garage door button.

She huffed out a breath. "That would make life too easy. I'm so sorry." None of this was fair to him. One day in Shane's world and she'd almost slept with him. He'd taken her heart years ago, and she wasn't getting it back. "I've really screwed things up this time." She had no idea what Shane was up to, why he'd been watching her. But even now part of her hoped for a good explanation. She loved him. "I'm such a fool."

Tom waited for the automatic garage door to rise. "We'll figure this out, Josie. I promise."

His tone was soft and gentle, and she'd heard him use it before while on the phone. She grinned. "You're using your 'I'm dealing with my younger sisters' voice right now."

He started, his eyes sparkling. "I have a voice with my sisters?"

Oh yeah. As the older brother to what sounded like three wild younger sisters, he had a tone he used. "I've listened to you talking to them on the phone. Last month when Sylvia wanted to drop her business major and study ceramic pottery, you *really* used the voice."

Tom snorted. "That was crazy. Thank goodness she changed her mind. For now, anyway."

What would it have been like to grow up with siblings? With people who cared what happened in her life? Josie sighed, her gaze focusing on Tom's half-finished ranch house. A tight tarp covered part of the house as Tom waited for time and money to finish it. Cedar shakes lined the sides of the finished part of the home—a place perfect for a real family. She knew Tom wanted that family. "I don't know what to do. Nothing seems real."

Tom pulled the car into the garage and shut off the ignition. He reached for her hand, his larger one warming hers. "Life gets messy, sweetheart." She glanced up at his smile. "But you're a very smart woman. I have no doubt you'll figure this out."

Relief and gratitude flowed through her until her knees wobbled. Tears pricked her eyes. Tom believed in her. She was smart and tougher than anyone knew. It was time she woke up. A great guy sat in front of her—one who was honest with her. A man who wanted what she needed in life—a stable home and a loving family. Kids. Sometimes her empty arms ached with the need for a baby, when she could keep one safe, that was. "I need to warn you. Shane is dangerous, and he might be coming after you. There were several pictures of you and me in his house." If Shane hurt Tom, she'd never forgive herself.

Tom eyed her and then nodded. "I know. The police warned me."

"So I probably shouldn't be here." But where could she go?

"This is exactly where you should be." Tom brushed

an errant hair off her cheek. "We're stronger together, and don't worry, I can fight."

Yeah, he'd told her about his boxing for fun days. Josie sighed. "You didn't see him fight—see him kill. He's gifted in a bad way."

Tom nodded and opened his door. "We'll be safe, Josie. Come on. It's Saturday night. Let's have a wild one and watch a movie." Tom tugged her from the car, enveloping her in a hug. "Life will work out. I promise."

Shane jogged around the perimeter, the gun comfortable in his hand. He'd retrieved the nine-millimeter from the bungalow before running. His bungalow, he figured. What had he been doing spying on his own wife? He dodged around a thick spruce. Nice of Marsh to live at the edge of the forest. So many places to hide. If the bastard didn't take his hands off Josie, the man would die at the edge of the forest. Shane paused. He'd killed before. And not just earlier that day. Was he a killer? Regularly or just for the military? Did it matter? His torso and ribs had already healed, which seemed off. Way too quick.

The forest spread out empty and safe around him. Uncertainty had him pausing. He should run. Just get the hell out of there and leave Josie to rebuild her life. He should go find those brothers he couldn't remember.

The idea of leaving her, even for the right reasons, tightened his chest until he couldn't breathe. Memories or not, she was his air. The fact made absolutely no sense, yet he clung to it with a desperation that scared the shit out of him. He couldn't remember her and had certainly hurt her. Yet he couldn't leave her again. Was it some weird stalker mentality? Or God, could it be something good? Something right?

Chances weren't good on that score. But he wasn't leaving until he figured it out.

He scaled a tree, perching in the top to stare down into Marsh's sparse living room. The man ate popcorn and watched two movies with Shane's wife. Shane could hear the television as clearly as if he were sitting in the room. Maybe he should get an MRI and see if there was some sort of implant or device in his head. No way was his hearing normal.

The cutest dimples flashed when Josie laughed at a scene. Her hands worked gracefully with her knitting as she watched the movie. Looked like she was making a scarf.

A warmth heated in Shane's chest. She'd kicked his ass. A groin shot was an easy one to be expected from a small woman defending herself. But the kick to the head. Well now. That was impressive. No hesitation, no fear. She'd aimed for his temple and nearly knocked him out. Before she ran toward the cop.

Shane had thought about pursuing her, taking on the cop, and retrieving his wife. Too many men had still been in the house. He didn't need to fight the entire police force. Not yet, anyway.

His gaze wandered over her pale skin and delicate features. His woman. He wondered at the possessiveness. Had he always felt it? Or was it new, flourishing since she was the only link to the life he'd led? The man he was?

As he watched her, he settled on an answer. He'd always felt it. She was his. While his motive remained unclear, he wasn't going to figure it out while they remained apart. He needed to retrieve her and soon.

The movie ended. Tom and Josie retired to separate bedrooms. Good. Relief he probably didn't deserve flowed through him. He scouted the area again. Marsh owned an acre surrounded on two sides by expansive federal land. Pine, spruce, and cottonwood trees stood like silent sentinels offering shelter. Wildlife scampered naturally. Any predators close by were solely of the four-legged variety. All was secure. Josie was safe for a while.

Shane turned to lope back through the forest toward the hidden van. He'd traded the vehicle for Josie's SUV, leaving her car where it would be found. She needed her car.

Now he needed to question the guy at the hospital and then head to Josie's place and check out the bugs. How many had he planted? Where and why? He hoped he didn't have to break into the police station to see all the evidence. But if he did, then he would. Somehow he figured he had the skills. Knew he had them, in fact.

He needed to remember. Dark and blank, the interior of his head kept him out. Maybe for his own protection. Not knowing himself was driving him crazy. Why had he been stalking Josie? His fists clenched and unclenched. Who were his brothers? Did he hurt them, too? Did they want anything to do with him, or not? He had to remember his past. Maybe, no matter how bad he'd been, just maybe he could fix everything?

Something told him he wasn't going to like who he found. Who he was. The thought weighed heavily on him, and bile rose from his stomach.

He slid into the car and drove down the road, trying to force memories into his conscience. Only a blank slate rose to his internal search. A big, black empty hole. Frustration settled like a rock in his gut. Or maybe that was fear. If he couldn't figure out who he was, how in the world was he going to protect Josie?

If he had brothers, shouldn't they be looking for him? The name *Jory* caused something to hurt in his solar plexus. A weight squeezed his lungs.

The lights of the hospital soon came into view, and he scouted the parking lot for the best space in case he needed to make a quick exit. Finding one close to the curb, he parked and jumped out, striding toward the staff door as if he had every right to do so. It was too early to search Josie's house, so he'd make good use of his time before heading to discover her secrets, and maybe some of his own.

A nurse in green scrubs slid her card through the slider, and he opened the door for her, returning her smile as she walked inside and hurried to a large lounge set to the right.

Two steps inside and the scent of bleach slammed into him. Sparks flashed behind his eyes. He staggered against the wall as memories cut deep. A dim picture of him sitting on a gurney in a dingy hospital room with a man digging something out of his leg. Crumbling concrete made up the walls. Pain had exploded along his shin. A bullet. The man had been digging out a bullet.

Almost in slow motion, the guy rose, smiling. "Got it."

The man had gray eyes. The exact color of Shane's eyes.

The strangled gasp Shane made as he returned to the present echoed around the empty room. Jesus Christ. Leaning down, he rubbed a scar along his left leg. Nausea swirled in his gut. His hands shook. Finally, more memories were flooding back. Relief and fear slammed through him. He'd been shot, and his brother had helped him. The first look at his family made his mind spin. But now wasn't the time.

Damn it. He had a job to do.

The first few steps were more like stumbles, and then he found his stride. *Focus. Forget the past images and focus.* The voice in his head wasn't his, yet he trusted it implicitly. He continued down the hallway, pausing in front of a room that housed several dictating machines along with computers.

Dodging inside, he sat and let his fingers fly across the keyboard. Interesting. He knew how to type and rather quickly. He didn't know the name of the computer program, but he knew how to use it. Several codes led him to a screen that listed all new admittances. Two pages into the database, and Shane found his man.

The world centered again. He felt nothing. Odd and creepy talent, that.

Quiet reigned along the corridor as he strode out of the computer room, peering inside supply closets until he found a light blue hospital gown and some bandages. Concentrating, he forced the millions of sounds that whirled in his head into a blur of white noise that wouldn't disturb him. Grabbing what he needed, he hurried out of the staff area and past the emergency room, riding the elevator up to the correct floor. Disembarking, he found a restroom and hustled inside to change into the gown.

The cool breeze filtered across his butt when he stepped outside. Shane fought a growl.

An empty room contained a half-filled IV of saline, and he grabbed the piping, taping the cord to his wrist. Then he walked the hall. Room 700 soon came into view. The cop dozing outside the door may have been on the lookout for a guy in scrubs. Or a doctor's uniform.

But not a patient.

Not a bruised, lurching, wounded patient in battered

slippers tugging his IV cart behind him. As Shane limped by, the cop looked up, giving him a nod. Shane grimaced and kept walking. He lapped the entire floor, and this time when he drew near, the cop's chin rested on his chest, his snores echoing across the hall.

Shane slid inside the room. The door clicked shut behind him. The patient lay in a neat hospital bed, much cleaner than the one that recently flared through Shane's memory.

He ditched the IV cart and stalked toward the bed, flipping over the guy's chart. His name was Ray. Shane's kick to the gut had broken five ribs; one rib had pierced a lung. Ouch. Shane scratched his head. He could decipher doctor's notes. But something told him he wasn't a doctor.

Ray filled out the bed at probably six foot, two-fifty. Matted black hair pressed to his head. Dark circles slashed under his eyes. Surgery had probably been a bitch. Shane pressed his hand over the patient's mouth. Ray started, his eyes flying open. He struggled, then stilled.

Shane smiled. "Sorry about the ribs."

No response.

"So. You understand I could kill you in seconds?"

A nod.

"Good." Shane removed his hand. "Why?"

Ray's forehead wrinkled. "Why what?" He whispered, a good sign.

"Why did you try to kill me?"

Ray shrugged. "The job paid good. We were supposed to knock you both out and start the house on fire. I got alimony to pay—"

"I don't care." Shane eyed the slow breathing. The guy was drugged. "Were you watching me from a blue van the other day?"

"Yeah. We were supposed to watch you—well, until the order came in to kill you."

"Who hired you?"

"Denny hired me." Ray's blue eyes hardened. "He's the guy you stabbed to death."

"I didn't stab him. I sliced his jugular." A significant difference. The fact that dumbass Ray didn't know that showed he was just hired muscle. A moron. Certainly not trained well enough to go up against a killer. Shane might have no clue as to his identity, but something told him his enemies knew exactly who he was. Shouldn't they have sent someone better? "Who hired Denny?"

"No fucking clue, man. Paid ten large for each of us."

Ten grand. Josie's life was worth less than ten grand to this asshole. Something must've shown on his face because Ray shrank back, jaw quivering. Shane pierced him with a glare. "You're going to give me more than that, Ray. Because I really want to kill you right now—with a lot of pain."

Fear widened Ray's eyes. "Okay, I mean, okay. Denny said we had to make sure everyone in the house died, and that the whole thing burned to the ground."

So they couldn't be identified? Who wanted him wiped from the earth? Shane frowned. "What's Denny's last name?"

"Clinton. Denny Clinton. He freelances for area bookies and anyone who needs, well . . ."

Needs someone dead. Not much of a lead, though the fact that Denny was local created possibilities. Somebody might've followed Shane to Snowville and then hired local muscle. Denny could've been working for anybody. "I'm not going to kill you today, Ray." Though every instinct Shane had whispered that was a mistake.

But until he could figure out his past, he wasn't going to do something so permanent as murder when there was a choice. Something told him once he remembered his life, he'd change that theory. Maybe he'd even hunt down good old Ray.

However, even now with his brain a blank slate, there was no question Shane would kill for Josie. He leaned forward, crowding the bed with his bulk. "But if you come near my wife again, if I even seen you in the same vicinity..."

Ray lifted bruised hands, palms out. "I get it, man. I get it."

CHAPTER
8

JOSIE FORCED A polite smile on her face, letting the soft jasmine smell of her office soothe her. She'd spent the night at Tom's, and he'd driven her to work in the morning after she'd once again refused his offer of fleeing town. No way was she abandoning this life she'd built the last two years.

Plus, she needed to figure out the discrepancy in her accounts. Numbers and order made sense. When Shane had left, her job had given her a reason to get out of bed— and there was nothing she liked more than solving a good puzzle. There was no doubt she'd been distracted the last few months since she'd sent the divorce papers to Shane. If she'd made a mistake with the math, she didn't know what she'd do.

She walked her client, the CEO of Trenton Industries, to the door of her office, shaking his hand again. The company built USB flash drives and was wildly successful at it.

Eighty-year-old Joe Trenton patted her on the shoulder. "Golf awaits me, my dear. Excellent job on the audit."

Yeah, she'd spent hours working on his books. Josie's

professional smile relaxed into a natural grin. "Good luck today, Mr. Trenton."

"The magic is all in the swing, Josie. All in the swing." The man nearly skipped down the hallway toward the elevator.

To have that much energy so late in life would be a true blessing. She kept her smile in place until the elevator door closed to whisk the elderly technology genius away.

Eyeing the clock, she flipped open the file for Larson Corporation, a fancy name for a local convenience store. Her fingers danced over the calculator, and she frowned. The receipts were exactly thirteen thousand dollars off. Now that was an unlucky number.

She added again.

Yep. It looked like the store made thirteen thousand more dollars than the payables showed . . . but there wasn't any leftover cash. So was the mistake with the receipts, or was there money missing?

Her calendar dinged from her computer.

Time to go. She grabbed the blue file off her desk and hustled to her boss's corner office for their regular Monday morning meeting. Eli Johnston was waiting for her behind his massive cherry wood desk, his circa 1980 tie already askew. He gestured her to the one empty seat.

She sat and her heart sank at the large man filling the other seat. It figured her main competition for the promotion would be there. Just what she needed. "Hello, Daniel."

Daniel Mission nodded, shoving his designer glasses up his nose. As always, he appeared in control and unruffled, his Armani suit tailored perfectly to his hard body. A body earned playing basketball and working out in the building's gym.

"How's Trenton?" Johnston leaned his impressive bulk back in the chair. About fifty with rapidly thinning gray hair, he reminded her of a pit bull.

"Great. The audit went fantastic, all ducks are in a row." They'd turn the notes in to the IRS and Trenton would have another smooth year. Why the hell was Daniel present for the meeting? It was supposed to be strictly routine.

"Good. Good." Johnston's beady eyes narrowed. "Rumor has it you spent the weekend at the police station after two men died in your home."

Talk about not mincing words. "Rumors are right." She'd married a soldier, a killer. One who'd apparently been spying on her for quite some time. Embarrassment at her own stupidity heated her face. Her smile faltered, and she glared at Daniel.

He shrugged, brown eyes revealing nothing. "We have enough PR problems right now. Keeping secrets is always a bad idea."

Daniel played basketball with Tom, and the two men seemed to get along well. Unfortunately, both Daniel and Josie were up for the vice president position for the branch, and Daniel apparently had no problem playing dirty. He must've gotten the news from Tom.

Johnston cleared his throat. "Just keep it out of the business, Josie. You know we can't handle any more bad press."

Yeah, about that. She tapped the file. "I'm still doing research, but I think there's a discrepancy with the Larson Corporation account in addition to a couple other accounts."

Johnston frowned. "What other accounts?"

"Davis Bakery, Agers Hardware, and Hall's Funeral Home."

Her boss's nostrils flared. "Okay. What are the discrepancies?"

Josie shrugged. "I'm not sure. The assets aren't lining up with reported income. My guess is Billy just lost track of the math. It's probably something simple. I found one place in the Hall file which reported a lump sale where it was really spread over several months. Easy to fix." She flipped open the file. "I wish Billy had left some notes on his dealing with them. I'm sure it'll all make sense." Billy had been their accountant and main contact with the specialty shop until the previous month—though she'd been assisting him.

Daniel leaned forward. "If the files are too much for you, I can take them over. You're going through a difficult time personally right now."

Josie bit back a retort. The man was just too handsome and charming. Clients loved him. She didn't. "Thanks, but I've got it."

Daniel shrugged. "I'm settled with the files I brought over from Salt Lake and can take on more if necessary."

Josie forced a calm smile. The accountant hadn't hidden the reason for his transfer three months previous— he wanted the vice president job. "My files are covered. Though you could always seek new clients in the area."

A slow smile tipped his lips. "I just signed the Snowville School District. So, yeah, good idea."

Darn it. That was a great client. She forced a chuckle. "That's awesome. Congratulations."

Johnston glanced at his watch. "Billy should be out of rehab in another month. Maybe. I've heard meth is almost impossible to beat. He may need to stay longer." His beefy hand closed into a fist on his desk. "That's why we don't need any more bad publicity, *Mrs*. Dean."

Probably true. Billy's meltdown had put them in a bad light with several large clients. He'd missed deductions. Added wrong. And even gotten one client in trouble with the IRS. Josie only knew Billy professionally, but the guy had always been full of energy.

"I hate to ask this since Billy's my friend, but considering his drug problem, do you think he was skimming?" Daniel asked.

Josie studied the smooth number cruncher. "You're friends with Billy?"

"Yes. We've worked together, mostly via Internet and Skype, for about five years." Daniel tilted his head. "Skimming?"

"Maybe, and I always look for that. But I think so far it's been a matter of simple mistakes. Mistakes we need to catch before tax season." She'd seen what drugs could do to people and figured Billy had just been working poorly. With enough time and dedication, Josie could get the files back into order without there being an IRS issue. "Don't worry—I'll figure it out."

"I could take over the files, if you want," Johnston offered.

"No." Josie shook her head. Enough with all the men in her life trying to ease her way. The attempts always backfired. "I appreciate the offer, but I'm supposed to take over Billy's clients until he gets back." If he came back. And if she'd made the mistake while she'd been learning the file, she'd fix it. If Billy had made the mistake while on drugs, she'd fix it. "Don't worry. I can handle it."

Johnston shrugged. "Fair enough. Just keep me apprised. Like I said, we don't need any more bad PR."

Josie nodded, standing and heading for the door. "Of course." Poor Billy. Growing up in foster care, she'd befriended many a lost kid who'd coped with life by taking drugs. She'd been offered pot at ten years old, meth at twelve, and cocaine at fifteen. But she'd always known there was a way out of the system, and that taking drugs would keep her in. It was a straight shot from foster care to juvey to jail. So she'd always said no to drugs. Unfortunately, her best friend had said yes to cocaine and had died from an overdose. Josie needed to visit her soon in the local cemetery.

Drugs did kill.

For now, Josie had to concentrate on the present and not the past. This current mess with Shane could cost her the promotion she wanted.

Navy blue industrial carpet cushioned her steps as she wound through the quiet hall to the main hub of the floor. Several secretaries busily typed away in rows of cubicles filling the center space as phones rang and printers whooshed. A trill of laughter threaded among the squeaking of desk chairs. The aroma of floral perfume and vanilla coffee scented the air.

She reached her office, hurrying inside and shutting the door to keep noise out. She didn't have time to mess around—now she needed to go get a bunch of new clients to compete with freakin' Daniel.

Hurrying toward her desk, she glanced at her appointment book.

"Hi, angel." The heavy oak door swished shut behind her, the lock engaging with a click.

She froze. In slow motion, she turned around. The files trembled in her hands.

"Sit down." Shane had been waiting against the wall. He tilted his head toward a leather guest chair. She'd chosen the light brown carefully to match the chairs her foster father Arthur had had in his office so many years ago. Classy and plush.

The phone. She could get to it, or she could scream. But if she screamed, who'd come running? Her secretary, Vicki? Vicki couldn't handle Shane. Crap. She'd probably take one look at the soldier and rip his clothes off.

"Now." He wore a fresh black shirt and new jeans, kick-ass boots covering his size thirteens.

"Nice boots." Josie tossed the file on the desk and slid into a chair. She was wearing three-inch heels on her feet; they'd cause serious pain if necessary.

"Turns out I had cash hidden at the bungalow. Went shopping earlier." He stalked forward and dropped into the matching chair, swiveling her to face him. Both legs stretched out on either side of hers, trapping her. "Miss me?"

"No." She straightened her back with a sharp snap. So he admitted he'd stalked her from the bungalow. Was that a good sign or a bad one? Either way, her chest hurt. "How's the head?" A new bruise covered his left temple. From her foot. Her grin even felt malicious.

"Excellent kick, angel." He leaned forward, his hands clasping her knees above her skirt, his scent of heated cedar washing over her. "I taught you well." He wore his soldier face today, no expression showing. But those eyes. Dark, gray, and swirling with emotion. He usually veiled better.

Her abdomen began to hum... in warning and something darker. A feminine desire for him to explain everything—for him to say it was real. But the only thing that was real was the lust they'd felt. Still felt. "Don't make me kick you again."

His smile slid slow and sure across his face. Dangerous. "Ah, darlin', I'd love for you to try it again." His hands dipped under the skirt, pushing the silk up, his palms heating her thighs. "Something occurred to me last night."

Desire rippled through her with memories of what those hands could do. Even lying to her, he'd exploded her world. She grabbed his hands, halting their journey. So close to where her body was beginning to ache. The man knew her body and exactly how to play her. The thought brought both unease and intrigue. "What's that?" Her voice came out hoarse.

"I've been too easy on you." He flipped one hand over, easily trapping both of hers. "Treated you with kid gloves, kept you out of my life."

She frowned, her lids dropping. "You remember."

"No." He sighed, his free hand curving to the side of her thigh and heading toward her hipbone. "I've been thinking about what you said. What you were able to do by kicking me in the face." He traced a path over her thigh toward her core, his gaze dropping to her breasts. "Let me feel you, Josie." Three fingers pressed against the outside of her panties. "Just once. Before everything goes to shit. Open for me, baby."

Electric shocks cascaded out from his fingers. Molten lava. Fire whipped through her until she tilted against his hand. She knew the pleasure he could bring. Even with the pain that would follow, that pleasure was seductive. To get lost like that again. Sometimes to feel the fire, you had to get burned. She swallowed. They were in her office, for goodness' sake. The temptation made her catch her breath. So much temptation.

So wrong.

This time the fire would consume her. She just knew it. So she tugged her wrists free, scooting back and smoothing down her skirt. "Keep your hands off me."

Shane sat back, desire flushing red across his high cheekbones. "Never."

"Stop it, Shane." She clutched her jacket shut over throbbing breasts. Needy breasts. There was something seriously *wrong* with her. "The police are looking for you. No way can you get me out of this building."

His lip quirked. "You think I'm here to take you?"

Well, yeah. Her face warmed. Of course he was there for her. The man wanted her, didn't he? Temper lifted its head. "I assume most stalkers try to take their prey at some point."

His teeth flashed in a smile. "You're my prey now?"

Oh, most killers on television had charm, too. "You've been watching me. Stalking me. Some of those pictures in your bungalow go back three and a half years." Her voice rose on the last.

"Keep your voice down." He rubbed his chin. "I can't explain the pictures right now. There's no logical reason for me to have stalked you, and you know it. I had you." His eyes warmed. "I'll have you again."

Heat filled her body while confusion filled her mind. He was playing her, damn it. And like any victim, she was letting him. "Then where did the pictures come from?"

"I'll find out, though my best guess is that I was watching you to keep you safe if somebody is after you." He leaned forward, the rough stubble on his jaw making him look more than ever like a pirate searching for loot. "Now you need to trust yourself, Josie. Believe in your instincts, in whatever made you trust me in the first place. Give me a chance to figure this out, angel." His eyes softened with the entreaty.

"Not a chance in hell." The words came out weaker than she'd intended. Was Tom correct? Was she caught in some abusive vortex where she continued to trust when she should just flee?

"We're family, angel. Have been since we said our vows." Shane glanced at her ringless hand.

"Straight for the jugular, huh?" Typical of Shane to slice right to her heart. To the heart of a kid raised in foster care who'd prayed for a family. But she'd developed excellent instincts in that system, and she'd married the man with her eyes wide open. So that could only mean he was better than most predators—much better. She'd never even seen him coming until it was too late. Now was the time to be smart. "I'm not leaving with you."

"I know."

His easy acceptance bothered her more than it should. She bit her lip. "Why are you here?"

"There were seven bugs planted in your house, angel."

What a complete jerk. "You planted *seven* bugs?"

"No. Three matched my equipment in the bungalow." His gaze stayed steady and watchful on hers.

She frowned. "I don't understand."

"Someone else planted the other four—which makes my theory that I was watching you more credible. Maybe I was trying to figure out who had bugged your house."

Panic had her mind fuzzing. "Who the hell is after you?" She hadn't seen the man in two years. Who would go to the trouble to bug her house on the off chance he showed up after so much time? Or was she in some sort of trouble? Nobody would be after her, though. She was an accountant, for goodness' sake. "Well, at least we know how those men knew where to throw the grenade." She bit her lip, squirming on the chair. "Were there any bugs in the bathroom?"

Shane barked out a laugh. "No. None in the bathroom."

He stretched his neck. "While I think these guys were after me, we need to make sure they weren't after you. Is there anyone who would want to hurt you?"

"Besides you?" she whispered.

His eyes darkened. "I'm an asshole, I know. But I'd rip off my own arm before hurting you."

He just didn't get it. She shook her head. "Nobody wants to hurt me."

"Everything's okay at work?"

"Yes." She leaned back, picking at a string on her skirt. "I do have some accounts that aren't adding up, but they were a drug addict's files, and he's in rehab right now."

Shane leaned forward. "What kind of accounts? Anything people would want to hide?"

"No." She pursed her lips in thought. "Nothing illegal or dangerous. If anything, they'd all have a good claim against the firm for money. Most people just want money." She'd figure out where Billy screwed up, and maybe when he returned from rehab, she could help him get back on his feet.

Shane nodded. "Who's the addict?"

"Bill Johnson—he's been an accountant for about twenty years. Seemed like a decent guy."

"So you didn't know him well?"

Josie rolled her eyes. "No, I only know him professionally. I didn't even know he had a drug problem until he was admitted to the hospital, and I was assigned his files."

Shane nodded slowly. "We should check him out just in case. For now, I spoke to the man who survived the raid on your house. Someone named Denny hired him, but he didn't know why. They were supposed to kill us."

Dread slammed into her stomach. Kill? She narrowed her gaze. "The police let you talk to the guy in the hospital?"

"Not exactly."

Fear. It thrummed through her head until her ears rang. "Did you kill him?"

"Nope." Shane looked her right in the eye.

Was he lying? She had no clue.

Her mind flashed back to her wedding day, and how he'd looked her right in the eye as he'd said his vows. The moment had been the happiest in her entire life. How could she be in love with a man she couldn't read? He was an accomplished liar... and yet she wanted to trust him. But she didn't, and the desire to do so ticked her off. Her head began to ache. She glanced at her watch. "Well, thanks for the update."

"I said I wouldn't force you to leave with me today, but I'd like you to come with me voluntarily. Somewhere safe until I can figure out what's going on here. Until I can remember."

"No." Curiosity had her tilting her head. Had he spoken the truth? Would he try to force her? Did she want him to?

He sighed. "Right now you're fairly safe at Marsh's. I can keep watch periodically, but I need to do some research." He stood and prowled toward the door. "Do me a favor, will you? Call Detective Malloy for an update and see if he's found out anything about me. About my past."

"I'll call him after lunch."

"Now... please, Josie."

She rolled her eyes and punched in the number.

"Malloy."

She wiped her sweaty hands on her skirt. "Detective. It's Josie Dean calling for an update."

"Ah, yes. Well, Mrs. Dean, I can tell you that the military is quite hushed about your husband. Sealed files. Four years of service. But one interesting thing..."

She raised her gaze to Shane's. "What's that, Detective?"

"His unit worked *within* the United States. When you said he was out of the country, well, he wasn't."

She frowned. "Of course he was. While we were married, he left the country all the time."

"Not according to my buddy, the one person who'd tell me anything. Apparently your husband worked exclusively within our borders. They won't even tell me what it was that he was doing. He lied to you."

"I see." The news shouldn't surprise her. Nor should it hurt. Yet her stomach ached. "Any ideas where he is?" She glared at the quiet man by the door. One word from her and Malloy would know exactly where the lying bastard stood.

"No. My guess is that he's taken off." A rustling of papers echoed across the line.

Josie sighed. "You don't believe that."

Malloy coughed. "No, I guess I don't. He went to a lot of trouble to track you down and bug your house, Mrs. Dean. He's here for you. I doubt he'll give up that easily." More papers rustled. "I can put you somewhere safe, if you'd let me."

Dread pooled in her abdomen. What should she do? "Thanks, Detective. I can take care of myself. Please call me with any updates." She clicked the phone shut, focusing on her husband. "You're a liar."

He raised an eyebrow.

"You never left the country. No overseas missions. Just here."

"Are you sure?"

Josie shrugged. "Malloy is sure." Anger increased her heart rate. What else had Shane lied about?

"I'll have to check that out—though I'm starting to

remember missions out of the country." Shane opened the door.

"Maybe you didn't only work for our military." Could he be some sort of spy? Her stomach lurched.

He stiffened. "Maybe."

God. Who was this man?

"Don't go anywhere by yourself, angel. Stay in a group and stay safe."

She was safe so long as he was out of her life. They both knew it. Now if only her body and heart would get the hint. She should've told Malloy the truth. But what if he was wrong? The military kept secrets, right? There was no doubt Shane was a soldier. But he kept secrets, too. Families could never survive secrets, that much she did know.

"Good-bye, Shane."

CHAPTER
9

JOSIE CLUTCHED THE bouquet of flowers to her chest, the sweet scent of roses churning her stomach. She leaned back in the front seat of Tom's Chevy, her gaze on the rainy dusk outside. "Thanks for driving me."

Tom nodded, his concentration on the wet road. "Not a problem. No reason to work late tonight, anyway."

Maybe she should tell Tom that Shane dropped by the office. But why worry her friend? Great. Now she was lying and hiding facts from people in order to protect her killer of a husband. Her life had become a movie. And not a good one. "No work, huh?"

Tom grimaced and shrugged his flannel-covered shoulders. "Not so much. And it's weird being on my own now. I mean, I had a company of six people back in Texas. When I went under, I thought I'd end up hiring people here as the business took off. So far, it's just me."

"The construction business is picking up, finally." She forced her problems to the back of her head. "Right?"

"Yes." Tom flashed her a goofy grin, good humor settling once again on his attractive face. His unkempt hair made him all the more boyishly handsome. "Still, I wish you could've seen our offices and my company when things were good. I was quite the catch." He snorted, turning back toward the road.

"You're still quite the catch." And he was. Good-looking, smart, hardworking, and even better, he made her laugh. At first it bothered her that he was a couple years younger, but now she usually forgot about the age difference.

"Do you think I could catch you?" He lost his smile and his voice deepened, but he kept his gaze straight ahead.

She stiffened. "I, ah, I think you're great."

His shoulders jolted, and then he threw back his head and laughed, deep and loud.

Unable to help herself, Josie joined in. "I mean, I…" She gasped for breath, trying to speak. Her shoulders shook as she laughed, tension escaping her for the first time in days.

Tom wiped the corner of his eye. "Yeah, okay. You figure out the deal with your soon-to-be ex, and then I'll make my move." He chuckled again and then sobered. "But in all seriousness, if you're in danger, I swing a mean hammer. I can keep you safe."

Was it her smaller size that had men reassuring her they'd keep her safe? She'd been alone her whole life, and yet here she was. Perfectly capable of keeping herself safe. Even scared, she could think and plan. "Thanks."

Tom nodded. "Are you and Daniel still sparring?"

Josie stiffened. "We're competing for the same promotion. Plus, the guy's a jerk." A condescending jerk. Guilt hunched her shoulders. "I'm sorry. I know you're friends."

Tom shrugged. "You two would like each other if the situation were different."

"Not likely." The car's headlights flashed on the stone

pillars that flanked the cemetery entrance. "Turn right once inside the gates." She hated to ask Tom for such a personal favor, especially since Shane probably wanted him dead. But without her car, she'd needed a ride to the cemetery to visit Mona on the anniversary of her death. Josie had failed to be there for her friend in life…she wouldn't screw up in Mona's death, too.

Tom maneuvered his truck through the entrance, winding along the manicured drive. "All right. Who are we visiting?" He eyed the overgrown foliage.

The paper around the flowers crinkled as her grip tightened. "A friend named Mona Wilson. We were in foster care together in California." Time rarely healed all wounds.

"When did she die?" Tom followed the road, as overgrown branches scraped at the truck's cab.

"When we were seventeen." Josie pointed at a fork in the road. "Go left."

Tom nodded, maneuvering the truck over several potholes. "How?"

Drugs. They killed. "When we were sixteen, she was sent up here to Northridge, which is a drug rehabilitation center that takes indigent kids as well as people who can pay. After a year, she got out and was put in the foster system here. She got back into drugs and overdosed." Mona had attended the same drug rehab center Billy was now in because it was supposed to be the best in the Northwest. Hopefully Billy would succeed and beat the drugs.

Tom stopped the truck when a stone wall ended the road. "Is Mona why you moved to Snowville?"

Josie shrugged. "Maybe part of it." Everyone should have flowers put on their grave on the anniversary of their death. "Do you think our childhoods create our adulthoods?"

"Absolutely. One hundred percent…whoever we were as kids shapes us as adults." Tom's face held a new seriousness.

Josie nodded. She was alone as a kid, and maybe that was the only way she knew to live. Her shoulders sagged at the thought. She opened the door and slid to the ground. "I'll be back in a minute." Quietly shutting the door, she stepped over a mud puddle and onto the grass.

Winding around several headstones, she arrived at Mona's. Rain pattered down, matting her hair to her neck. "Hi, Mona." Gently, Josie leaned down and placed the flowers next to the weathered headstone. "I brought red roses this time. Something to brighten the day."

Memories of the tall, curvy brunette washed through Josie's mind. She and Mona had lived together in a small apartment owned by a lady named Judy who worked two jobs. Judy was nice but was rarely around. Josie had missed Arthur and Claire, and Mona had tried to cheer her up. But Mona had already been hooked on crack at that time, and after three months had been sent to Northridge. Even so, during their brief time together, they'd bonded as wanna-be sisters. "I miss you."

The wind picked up, scattering pine needles across the roses. Josie wiped them away. "I have another friend who's having problem with drugs. Don't worry, I'll help him." Like she should've helped Mona. Somehow. She cleared her throat. "I'm really scared, Mona." Saying the words made the reality all the more stark. While she couldn't admit the truth to all the tough men wanting to protect her, here she was safe. "I'm not sure who to trust. Or who's after me. Or Shane. It's so confusing—so terrifying."

The small tombstone stared back at her silently.

Josie shivered in the rain. Making Tom wait in the truck probably wasn't nice. Plus, she needed to figure her life out. "I'm not sure where you are, or if you can hear me. But if so, take note, will you? I could use all the help I can get. Especially with which man to rely on. Tom is safe and trusts me, but I'm putting him in danger. Shane, well..."

She couldn't find the right words. "You know Shane, if you're watching me. And...say hi to Claire for me. I mean, if heaven works like that. I'll be back." Turning in the damp grass, she hustled through the rain.

Reaching the truck, she climbed into warmth and safety where Tom's clean scent of Irish soap calmed her. She sent him a grin. "I get to choose the movie tonight."

Shane settled into the sleeping bag overarched by the thick awning of pine branches. The moon filtered through a smattering of clouds. Wildlife rustled around him. Nothing in the forest was as dangerous as him. He knew the truth in his bones, even if his brain hadn't kicked in yet.

Since awakening, he'd wanted his memories back. Now, he wasn't sure. The new ones, of pretty Josie and her strong spirit...those were good and right. But what if his memories proved he'd used her? What if the old him didn't love her? Because the new Shane did. This pounding in his chest had to mean something real—even if it was new.

He'd tamped down on the extra senses for the moment. Hearing horns miles away was just annoying. He glanced at Marsh's quiet house. Josie had gone to bed a half hour before. Alone. Safe for the time being. Though he should probably get her out of town. If he thought they'd be safe, he'd move forward and start over with her. But whoever was after him would keep coming. The only way to fight back was to remember them, but doing so could lead to the loss of Josie. He wanted a slice of time with her before all hell broke loose. He needed to show her the good side of himself—even if it was new and temporary. Just the thought of her tightened his groin. Made his heart thump faster.

There hadn't been time to sleep since he'd been injured, and despite his worries, his eyes drifted shut, his hand on the butt of his gun.

His dreams floated in and out until one came into focus.

His arm hurt. He frowned at the black cast that covered his left wrist. His small, childlike wrist. He couldn't be more than nine years old. Maybe eight.

"Damn it, Shane."

From his perch on the bed, he glanced up at a boy, a large boy, towering over him. Embarrassment heated his face. "Wasn't my fault, Mattie."

Matt's gray eyes flashed even as another boy about ten years old ran up, skirting beds. "He broke his arm?"

"Nathan, Shane broke his wrist. Sparring with Emery." Matt dropped onto an adjacent bed, one of several scattered within the concrete-block-walled room. A barracks.

"Shit, Matt." Nathan sat next to Matt, his gray gaze serious on the cast. "Does the commander know?"

"Yes." Dread slid down Shane's spine. The scent of dust and pine cleanser made him bite back a sneeze. "He knows." He glanced at his brothers, steeling his shoulders. "It's okay. The fight was good and I hurt him, too. They won't take me away." Probably. He'd get to stay this time. Unless he allowed himself to get hurt again. "I'm sorry."

His brothers shared a look.

"We need a diversion just in case," Nathan muttered.

"Already on it." Matt glanced at the large clock hanging over the door. "Jory is going to crash the computer system in about two minutes."

Shane relaxed his shoulders. "Good. That'll keep the commander busy."

"This time." Matt's young face hardened. "We need to up our own training schedule."

"We've been training all the time." Shane shook his head. "Enough already."

"Do what you're told." Nathan's eyes turned the darker gray that meant he was about to hit somebody.

Shane glared at his older brother. "You always side with Matt."

Nathan nodded. "Yeah, I do. Because if you get hurt…"

"You disappear," Shane finished quietly. Panic and fear grabbed his heart and hurt worse than his arm. "You're right. I'll do better next time."

Suddenly Shane jerked awake. What the hell? A barracks? Who the hell was the commander? If those were his brothers, where were they?

A rustle sounded in the quiet woods, and he eyed the brush. Some sort of small animal. But the forest had gone wholly quiet. The hair on the back of his neck rose.

Sliding out of the bag, he yanked on his boots and tucked his gun in his waistband. He crept to the edge of the trees where the house sat quietly. Too quietly. A shadow moved toward the garage. Then another one. He circled around, his eyes on the targets. They used hand signals—military. These guys were better trained than the others.

He listened. Nobody else. A team of two. Apparently

two were enough for Marsh and Josie. That's what they thought. At the idea of someone hunting his wife, his gut rolled. He stilled, and forced all emotion into nothingness. While the ability to do so wasn't normal, he'd use the skill to save Josie and question it later.

As quiet as death, he crept forward. He leaped for the first man, aiming an elbow just below the guy's neck. The man dropped to the ground, unconscious.

The other man turned, yanking a gun from his vest.

Shane kicked the guy's hand and the gun went flying. He kicked for the face and the soldier blocked him, jumping forward and tackling him to the ground. Together they hit the concrete with a dull thud. Pebbles dug into Shane's back, giving his shoulders a fulcrum. Bad move. Shane rolled the attacker over and shot three hard punches to the face that knocked the soldier out cold.

Shane jumped up. Man, he wasn't even breathing heavily. In fact, his entire body was calm and relaxed. What the hell was wrong with him?

Now probably wasn't the time to figure that out.

Tossing the men's weapons into the forest, Shane ran to pound on the front door. Then he rang the bell. A light went on, and soon Marsh stood in the entryway, bare to the waist with an angry scowl on his face. Muscles lined his chest and abs. The guy worked out—probably practiced swinging sledgehammers.

Josie pounded down carpeted stairs dressed in a faded T-shirt, her hair in wild disarray. "Shane? What the hell?"

He turned toward Marsh. "Two men, over to the side of the garage. They're knocked out, probably for a half hour. Call the police."

Marsh twisted his head to see around Shane. "I don't

think so, Major." He pulled out a gun, leveling the barrel at Shane's chest. "Somehow I thought you'd show up. Most stalkers do."

Josie hustled across rough tiles. "Tom! Put the gun down."

Shane tensed, muscles bunching. She was getting too close to the gun. "Step back, angel."

Marsh widened his stance. "Call the police, Josie. Tell them the major is here."

Shane relaxed his shoulders. "Do call the police. Before the men outside wake up."

Pale, her lips trembling, she nodded and hurried down a Sheetrocked hallway to do his bidding.

Shane kept his gaze on the builder, taking inventory of the entryway. The walls were mostly bare, freshly painted. One watercolor of a forest scene covered the farthest wall. Its frame would make an excellent weapon, should he need one. He focused outside. The men outside remained silent, the forest was at peace. He smiled at Marsh. "You a good guy, Tom?"

"Yes." One eyebrow rose. "Much better than you."

Probably. Shane nodded, glancing behind Marsh. Swift as a whisper, he dodged forward, grabbed the gun, and hooked a leg around the man's knee. They crashed to the floor. Shane leveled his forearm against Marsh's windpipe, digging his knees into the tile while the man struggled for air.

Finally, Marsh went limp.

Shane hissed out a breath. The guy had struggled longer than Shane would've thought. He jumped to his feet, rushing through the house toward the direction of the garage. The door stood to the right of the refrigerator, leading to a large, well-organized space. He grabbed a water ski rope off the far wall and took the outside exit, quickly tying up the unconscious soldiers.

Should he tie up Tom? He wanted to. Probably unnecessary, though. He gathered an extra length of rope and returned to the entryway.

His wife waited, her bare legs apart. His gaze ran up her smooth thighs, flat stomach, and focused on the gun in her hands. His angel held the weapon with confidence, aiming the barrel square at his chest.

"Drop the rope," she said calmly.

CHAPTER
10

SHANE RELEASED THE rope, and measured strides took him inside the house. Next to Tom's prone body.

"Stay back, Shane." Josie kept a steady grip on the weapon. For a tiny thing, the woman had long, sexy-as-hell legs. Shit. She was all leg. The shirt came to mid-thigh, leaving much to be appreciated. She'd painted her cute toes a deep red. The color of passion.

"I like your toes."

Her lips tightened while her stance widened. "I don't want to shoot you, but I will." She glanced down at Tom before lifting her gaze. "Will he be all right?"

"Yes." Geez. Shane wouldn't hurt the guy trying to protect her. Well, not much anyway. "We need to go, angel. Give me the gun." He reached out and moved toward her.

"If you ever hurt him, I'll never forgive you." She stepped back, raising the barrel to Shane's face. "We're waiting here for the police. I don't know you. Or trust you."

"Can't blame you." This was a bad idea, but he couldn't think of another way to keep her safe.

Or maybe he didn't want another way.

He took another step, putting her within touching

distance. At this point, he didn't trust anyone. His head ached. Something in his gut turned. Even if he was the bad guy, he needed to keep her safe. That had to make him somewhat good, right?

He shook his head. Probably not. With that realization, he gave himself over to the inevitable. Nothing would make him desert her this time. "We're leaving, Josie. Come easy or hard, but we're going."

Her arms trembled. "Please don't make me shoot you."

"I won't." His hand snaked out, smacking the gun from her grasp. The weapon slammed against the wall. Sirens bellowed in the distance. Leaping forward, he grabbed her by the arms and ducked a shoulder, rising when she flopped over.

"Hey!" she yelped, kicking him in the stomach.

Pain echoed in his gut. He wrapped an arm around her thighs, turned, and ran into the night. She struggled, yet he maneuvered between trees and branches. He stopped at his makeshift bed and grabbed the sleeping bag with one hand, not missing a step.

Her entire body shifted as she sucked in air, letting out a high-pitched bellow that silenced the forest.

Damn it all to hell. He swung her around and pressed her against a tree, his hand covering her mouth. Blue eyes shot furious darts, so he leaned in close. "One chance, angel." Vehicles screeched to a loud stop back at the house. She bit his palm. "Josie." He pressed harder against her face. He'd kill himself if he hurt her. "We need to get out of here," he whispered as fury rose within him. "You can work with me, or I'll take you unconscious. But either way, we're going." He let every ounce of determination and threat leak into his eyes.

Her knee shot toward his testicles. Oh no, not this

time. He slid his leg between hers, immobilizing her. If she needed a contest of strength to obey him, she'd get it. His jean-clad thigh pressed against her light panties. "You sure you want to fight me?"

A frown narrowed her eyes. "I don't think you'll knock me out."

His heart stilled. Not what he'd been expecting. Did that mean she trusted him? On some level? "You're wrong." He flexed his fingers. "To get you away from danger, to get you to safety, I'll do whatever I need to do." He fought to keep his expression blank.

She smiled. "Do it, then." Air whooshed into her lungs, and she opened her mouth to scream.

His lips crushed hers. He captured her yell in his throat, driving the air back down hers. Then his tongue took hers, mastering it, taking what he wanted. Desire lit him on fire. His cock leaped to life, fighting against his zipper to get loose. To get in her. Now.

He was going to have her. Taste her, tame her, feel her shatter in his arms. Taking the kiss deeper, he explored, seeking answers and relief. Relief from this primal need for one small woman who looked like an angel and turned him into a devil. Deep down, if he took her, no matter what, good guy or bad guy, he knew he'd never let her go. Suddenly, he no longer cared.

Shouts echoed back at the house, yanking him back to reality. Danger surrounded them.

He lifted his head. "We don't have time for this." One finger slid into a tiny hole in her shirt and he tugged. Fabric ripped.

She frowned. "Hey—"

A strip of the cotton ripped free, and he flipped her around, tying her wrists together.

Her small body jumped around. She shot a kick to his knee. He grabbed another strip of shirt to shove between her teeth, tying the jagged material behind her head. Her eyes widened with surprise and then pure, raw fury.

He dipped and tossed her over his shoulder. She kicked out. A muffled "oof" escaped him. The woman had grit. She kicked again, and he turned his head, sinking his teeth into her thigh. She tasted like strawberries. "Knock it off." He secured his arm across her legs, ensuring no more kicks.

The gag softened her response, but rage echoed in the low tone.

Grabbing his sleeping bag, he jogged into the forest toward the old logging road. A truck he'd stolen earlier in the day waited.

She continued to struggle, muffled curses leaking from behind the gag. Possibly a death threat or two.

Women. Tough to deal with. A memory filtered across his conscious. A woman's voice. *When dealing with women, undercover or otherwise, seduction is a valid technique. To gain information, to gain trust.* Seduction? Shane had the uneasy feeling he'd been trained in more than hand-to-hand combat.

His arm loosened at the thought. Had he used those skills on his wife? Was she just a job to whoever he used to be? Josie aimed a hard kick to his lower belly.

Pain slammed through his abdomen. Maybe he should've knocked her out.

"You're going to wish you'd knocked me out." Josie flopped on the bed like a fish, struggling to get out of the sleeping bag. The bastard had left her hands tied and zipped her into the bag, buckling her in the seat of a large Ford for the two-hour drive. To this dive of a motel three counties over.

She kicked off the bag, not caring that her bare legs showed. "You ripped my shirt."

Shane reached into a duffel bag and tossed one at her head. "You may borrow mine." He pivoted, his gaze dropping to her legs, his nostrils flaring. The tension in the room rose. Two steps and he stood at the bed, turning her and quickly untying her hands before flipping her back around. "Here's the deal. You behave. No screaming, no running, and you'll stay untied and ungagged." He leaned into her, both hands on the gaudy comforter on either side of her legs.

Heat cascaded off him to warm her. The room was small and intimate, and the scent of male tempted her senses. The man had carried her so easily, taking control without a thought. She breathed out, and his gaze dropped to her breasts. "Not a chance, Shane." Her voice emerged huskier than she'd hoped. "You can't keep me here."

He leaned farther into her space. "Fuck with me, angel, and you'll regret it."

The warmth in his eyes had fled. Hard lines cut into his rugged face while a muscle pounded in his jaw. Maybe the last kick to his stomach had truly pissed him off. A shiver shook her shoulders. She didn't know him like this. For the very first time, she wondered if she wanted to know the real Shane. "Just let me go."

"No." He straightened and backed away. "Whatever's going on is my fault. I brought them here...right to you." His broad hand grabbed a gun from the second bed, and he checked the clip. "Tonight, at Marsh's, they were coming for you. Not me, you."

"Why?" She hated that her voice trembled.

Shane shrugged. "To get to me, I assume." He pierced her with a hard gray gaze. "I won't let anything happen to you. You may not trust me, but you can trust that. You're safe."

Safe? She was alone in a freaking motel room with a killer who'd broken her heart. How safe could that be? Even assuming he wouldn't kill her, which frankly, she believed he wouldn't, how could she survive staying with him? Not a chance in hell he wouldn't kiss her again. There wasn't a chance in hell she'd stop him. So much fire between them.

Passion was a dangerous drug.

She knew it firsthand.

She'd spent two solid years in withdrawal.

He gestured toward the bed. "Get some sleep. We move again at dawn."

"No. You had pictures of me—from years ago." Anger beat so much stronger through her than fear. "You said you'd give me an explanation."

He shook his head. "I'm still figuring this out. Think logically, Josie."

Logically? The man was going to get kicked in the head again. Even so, she needed a good explanation for the pictures. Living with fear took too much of a toll. The fear had to go. Could she be any dumber? "What do you mean?"

"I didn't take those early pictures, it just doesn't make sense." He ran a rough hand through his thick hair. "Why keep them? Why leave you if I were some crazy stalker and I got you to marry me?"

She'd wondered the same thing. Hope was so freakin' destructive. "If you didn't take them, who did?"

"I don't know. I assume whoever planted the other bugs in your house." He focused on her, his gray gaze somber. "I need your trust, angel. You're all I've got."

The vulnerability from such a strong man tempted her far too much. The Shane she thought she'd known would've gone after anyone threatening her with a vengeance matched only by furious predators. But he had never shown her a hint of vulnerability. "What do you want from me?" Her voice came out weary. Exhaustion dragged at her limbs.

"You trusted me once." He slipped his hands into his pockets. "Trust yourself and believe your instincts were on target with me. Give me the chance to figure this out."

He was the only family she'd ever known. The only person she'd ever loved. How could she not give him the chance? Plus, she couldn't escape him on her own—he was too good. Appeasing him seemed wise. "I'll think about it."

Triumph flashed in his eyes. "Good enough. We'll move again tomorrow."

She jumped to her feet, wincing as her toes dug into the rough shag carpet. Who knew what was in the ugly orange fabric? "I have to go to work. I'm in the middle of two audits." He had to believe her. As much as she hated to admit it, she probably couldn't get free on her own. "I like my life." Usually. She'd missed him. So much. But work helped.

He scrubbed both hands over his face. "You're not safe."

"I don't care." She'd knocked him on his ass, hadn't she? "I want to help you, I really do. But I'm not losing my life again because of you." No matter what happened, he'd leave again. To pursue whatever was out there he needed to pursue. Right now that was her. But that would change.

His hands dropped. "Again?"

She breathed out. "Yes. It hurt so bad when you left, I had to leave, too. I couldn't stay where we'd lived together, to see the places we shared." Her voice caught. Tears pricked the back of her eyes. She was too damn tired to hide the truth.

His eyes softened. "I'm so sorry. I wish I remembered what happened."

"What happened was that you needed more. More than me. Something else to keep you going." He was always so driven. Looking behind them for a threat and ahead for... something. "I didn't know you well enough. I never did."

As his wife, she should have the answers he now needed. But she didn't. "I can't do it again, Shane." Starting over would be too much. She'd given him everything, and he'd left...just like Arthur. And Claire. And Mona.

Everyone left.

She wouldn't set herself up again. At one time, she'd thought Shane was different from the rest. So when he'd deserted her, it had hurt more than all the other times combined. Enough was enough.

The clock on the particleboard nightstand ticked into the silence. "I have a discrepancy in a couple of my accounts, they're new, and I need to fix it." Something in her needed to make Arthur proud. Sure, she'd never see him again, but he'd been an amazing accountant. He'd never made a mistake—at least he hadn't until Claire's death destroyed him—and he'd taught her a love for numbers. Plus, she had to save Billy. She hadn't been able to help Mona, but Billy was here and now. She could help him and get that promotion she deserved.

"Please, Shane." She held his gaze, searching for a way to convince him. "You want me to trust you, and you need to earn that. You can't take me out of my life. I'll fight you every step of the way, and you need to concentrate on whoever's after you."

Doubt had him shaking his head. "I don't want to fight you at all." He sucked in air, dropping to sit on the other bed. The minutes ticked by. "I can't hide, either. Fine. I'll take you to work and pick you up. No leaving the building. For any reason. You'll need to tell Detective Malloy something. About why I released you."

"I will." She blinked to stay calm. Shane was *trusting* her. Not only to keep herself safe but to protect him. Hope flared hot through her. As well as caution. She needed to protect herself from having her heart broken yet again. Although the indecision in his eyes was new. "You've changed."

"It's been two years. I assume we both have." He stretched out on the bed, closing his eyes. "Go to sleep. Morning will arrive way too soon."

Less than a minute and his breathing evened out. She smiled as memories assailed her. He'd always fallen asleep so easily, almost as if he could control it. Almost as if he had to take rest when available.

The smile slid away.

When they'd met, they'd had a lack of family in common. She'd thought he was like her, raised in different foster homes, never quite fitting in. Then the nightmare, when he let the truth slip. He had brothers she'd never met. When she'd asked about them, Shane said they weren't close, and that had been the end of the subject.

She should've pushed harder to understand him. But being alone, relying on herself, that was all she knew. Maybe he wasn't the only one who'd held back. Perhaps trust earned trust. Throw two broken people together who don't know how to live with others, and you get pain. What a disaster.

Soft light filtered through the cheap shades, caressing

the hard planes of his face. So handsome. Straight nose, rugged cheekbones, and those sensuous lips. But his eyes. Magic and fire lived in their odd gray color. She still saw those in her dreams.

With his amnesia, more of his true self had emerged. The parts of him he'd hidden from her, she could finally see. Was there a chance he might let her into his life? In fact, he was even trusting her. But... what would happen when his memories came back? Would he draw away and break her heart again? Or would he stay?

He twitched. Then gave a low moan. Pain suffused the sound.

Her heart lurched. Her mind spun.

During their brief marriage, although he'd had no clue, she'd learned how to soothe his nightmares. To help him rest and get needed sleep. It was so easy and natural—and just took a soft whisper and touch. No matter who he was, she could only be herself. If he was in pain, she couldn't sit by and watch. She didn't want to be a person who'd sit by and watch.

An agonized growl rumbled from his chest.

Oh, this was a bad idea. She crept forward, gingerly resting one knee on his bed. Reaching his side, she snuggled down, her head on his outstretched arm. Warm cedar filled her senses. She placed her hand over his heart. "It's okay, Shane. Only good dreams tonight," she whispered. With a soft sigh, she closed her eyes and let darkness take over.

Shane kept his breathing even, his body relaxed. His heart thumped against her palm. Awakening, he'd heard her move from the bed and had wondered. Would she head for the door? No. She hadn't. The woman had cuddled up with danger to provide comfort for him. Security. Love.

His heart warmed until it hurt. Vulnerability and need filtered through him, followed by determination. He didn't know how the hell he'd lost her before. No matter what it took, no matter who he had to walk through, he wouldn't lose her again.

A truck passed by on the interstate, and he calculated the weight load and speed. A cricket chirped outside, and he identified the species. A woman breathed deep next to him, and he measured her heart rate. With his hearing.

He knew every way to kill a person, and he could do so without hesitating. In fact, hesitating didn't seem to be part of his makeup. What kind of a monster didn't feel anything when he killed? People should fear monsters. So far, nothing scared him—nobody could stop him. He closed his eyes against the reality that if his memories came back, *he'd* be the one thing he feared.

Josie sighed next to him, and he could hear her lungs fill with air.

Jesus. Who the hell was he?

CHAPTER
11

JOSIE MUMBLED TO herself, her head bent over the figures laid out on her desk. Her head ached. She needed to get dimmers on the lights in her office. The room was almost perfect with the thick desk she'd chosen to match the chairs. Prints of famous Western oil paintings lined the walls.

Although it had taken her all day and several pots of coffee, she'd found one of the problems in the Larson Corporation file—a mistake in the revenue figures. How freaking high had Billy been the last year while doing the corporation's books? This was malpractice and not some minor math mistake. She'd have to meet with the client soon.

She tugged her gray skirt smooth. Thank goodness she'd had a change of clothing and makeup bag at work.

A blond head poked in the door. "I'm heading home, boss."

Josie glanced up and forced a smile for her secretary. "Home or out for some fun?"

Vicki grinned and stepped inside. She'd removed her blue jacket to reveal a sleek black dress. "Out for some fun. Want to go?"

Not in a million years. They might be about the same age, but Josie felt decades older. "No, thanks." Until Shane picked her up. While she still didn't trust him, he could keep her safe from whoever was after him—and thus keep Tom safe. The two men who'd tried to attack Tom's house would've killed him, and she couldn't let that happen. She focused on her secretary. "I think I'll work late."

Vicki shrugged a curvy shoulder. "I figured." Her thickly mascaraed eyes widened. "Was that cop mad earlier or what?"

"That's an understatement." Detective Malloy was no dummy. The story of how she'd gone willingly with Shane had sounded ridiculous, even to her ears. But there wasn't anything the detective could do, absent taking her into custody. Which apparently he wasn't ready to do. Though she wouldn't be surprised to find herself under surveillance. The cop had even more questions about the two men Shane had left trussed up for the police. Because apparently they weren't cooperating with Malloy.

Vicki wrinkled her forehead, concern glimmering in her eyes. "So are you really staying with Tom Marsh? I mean, now that your husband is in town?"

Josie shifted in her chair. "I didn't tell anyone about my husband because I'm getting a divorce." All she needed was a guilt trip from her secretary. "A clean start seemed like a good idea, you know?"

Vicki nodded. "Yeah, I get that. Though staying at Tom's now is kind of risky, boss."

Josie rolled her eyes. "Eavesdropping on the detective?"

Vicki giggled. "He was yelling at you. It was hard not to eavesdrop."

Yeah, Josie had lied to the detective. Was that against

the law? She needed to Google "false statements to police officials." Wasn't it a crime only if they were federal agents instead of county officials? "I'm not staying with Tom any longer. Have fun tonight, Vicki." Happy hunting.

Vicki nodded and then glanced to the side. "Hi ya, Tom." She winked at Josie and headed toward the elevators.

Tom nodded absently and stalked into the room to drop into a guest chair. A rip marred the work shirt that he filled quite nicely. The guy was religious about using the building's gym. "Are you sure you're all right?"

Josie nodded. They'd had this discussion via telephone several times during the day. "Yes. I told you, Shane left town." The lie fell easily from her lips. Growing up in foster care, she'd learned to lie early and well. Just to keep people happy. "Detective Malloy is setting me up somewhere safe until we know for sure." Another lie.

Tom kicked his legs out, crossing scuffed work boots at the ankles. "Why are you at work?"

"I can't hide. Plus, I need to fix these books."

Tom's grin brightened the room. "I'm pretty sure that didn't come out right."

Josie laughed, her shoulders relaxing for the first time that day. "Good point. I didn't mean that, and you're above accountant jokes."

He shrugged. "It was an easy one. Sorry I couldn't be here earlier—rough day. I'm bidding on three different jobs right now."

"I know what you mean about having a rough day."

Tom glanced at his watch, a frown settling on his handsome face.

"Do you need to go, Tom?" He had to go. Shane would be there soon.

Tom frowned. "I have a meeting with a pain-in-the-ass client who might want to build a fast-food restaurant, but I don't want to leave you alone."

"Why is he a pain?" Josie stretched her neck.

Tom flushed. "She. She's a pain."

"Oh?" Josie bit back a grin. "Is she flirting with you?"

"Yes." Tom cleared his throat. "The woman is all hands."

"Do you like her?"

"Maybe." His eyes warmed. "Though I've been waiting for you."

Josie shrugged, unease filtering down her spine. "I'm a mess. Don't miss out on something because of me."

Regret flashed in his eyes, followed by humor. "Good enough. So, when will Malloy be here?"

"He's on his way." She hated lying. "Also, Johnston's office is just down the hall. He's always the last to leave." Which was usually the truth. But today he'd gone to meet with the board of directors of the biggest bank in town. Gaining the bank as a client would be huge for the accounting firm.

A phone buzzed. Tom grabbed his cell from his pocket, reading the screen with a frown. "Okay. I have to go. Call me tonight so I know you're safe." His smile didn't reach his eyes.

Darn it. She'd really screwed up his life. The guy had been knocked out last night. Josie sighed. Why couldn't she have fallen in love with a great guy like Tom?

"I'll call. Good luck with your client."

He nodded and hustled toward the door, running into Daniel.

"Hey. I was just going to head to your floor and see if you wanted to go for a drink," Daniel said. He'd shucked his fancy coat and had rolled his monogrammed shirt up to the elbows. Even his Burberry tie looked askew.

Tom shook his head. "I have a meeting with a client. Plus, we have a basketball game tomorrow night."

Daniel rolled his eyes. "Drinking doesn't affect my game, Sally."

Tom snorted. "See you tomorrow." He hurried down the hall.

Daniel rubbed his clean-shaven jaw, glancing at Josie. "You're working late."

She lifted a shoulder. "I'm trying to keep up with you. Rumor has it you got the school district account on the golf course." Apparently playing golf with the superintendent led to business.

"Yes. A lot of business deals are made on the golf course." He frowned.

"I don't play golf." Especially with men. Life sucked.

Daniel exhaled, exhaustion dimming his eyes for a moment. "So you don't play golf with the guys. Many women own businesses in the area—join the chamber of commerce and meet some. Join women's groups like the PTO and meet some. Use what you have, Josie."

Why was Dan giving her ideas? She lifted both eyebrows. "That's actually good advice."

He shrugged. "I like the playing field level. Simple as that." He turned on his Italian loafer and disappeared from sight.

Interesting. Maybe Dan didn't suck as much as she'd thought. Josie grabbed her calculator, adding and reading the figures on the spreadsheet before her for Agers Hardware. Why wouldn't they match up? She bit her lip, grabbing the rest of the file from the bottom drawer.

Her door closed.

She hissed out a breath, pushing back from the desk. "Shane. I didn't hear you."

He shrugged. "Good. Hopefully nobody else did, either." A click echoed. He'd locked the door. Prowling forward, he stood next to her chair, his hands dropping to knead her neck. "There's a patrol car out front, no doubt watching for me."

Josie lowered her chin to her chest. Heaven. The man had magic fingers, and she should really move away. "Yeah. The detective didn't buy my story." She fought a groan as Shane worked out the knots in her neck.

Her thighs began to soften.

Warmth lit her abdomen.

She cleared her throat and pushed away, swiveling the chair to face him. "So, what now?"

Shane slid his hands into the pockets of well-worn jeans. A dark T-shirt covered his thick chest and brought out the deep gray flecks in his eyes. "Now I borrow your computer."

With a shrug, Josie relinquished her chair, taking her notebooks to the other side of the desk. "What are you looking for?"

Shane sat, punching keys on the computer. "First I want to hack into my military records. Then I want to find my brothers." He frowned, dark gaze shifting to her. "I had a dream. I saw them. Matt and Nathan—if I had to guess, I'd think they were both older than me. We were at some type of camp—maybe a military one?"

Intrigue sped up her heart. She'd never even known their names. "How old were you?"

Shane shrugged. "I don't know. Maybe eight?"

Josie wrinkled her nose. "A military camp at the age of eight? Seems young." She cleared her throat. "When you had the nightmare about losing your brother, you yelled out the name *Jory*."

Shane's jaw hardened. "Jory. Yeah. Mattie mentioned that name in the dream." Shane rubbed his chest. "Jory." He turned his focus back to the computer.

Josie returned to her files, working through deductions for Fuller Labs. Her favorite client. Always paid on time, always kept good records. Since they had labs all over the United States, she'd been able to keep the client as she made the move to Washington. Why couldn't all clients be this good?

She ordered a pizza and met the pizza girl at the elevator, bringing the large pie into her office and shutting the door.

Shane looked up and smiled. "Do I like pizza?"

How odd not to remember. Josie returned the smile, placing the box on the desk and flipping open the lid. "Yes. You like pizza with pepperoni and pineapple."

Shane frowned, his gaze on the colorful pie. "Really?"

Surprising humor bubbled through her. "Well, kind of. You like pepperoni, and I always wanted pineapple, so we learned to compromise the first month of our marriage and order it this way." She handed him a piece.

"Thanks." He took a bite, slowly chewed, and then smiled. "All right. The combination works for me."

"I remember." She took a bite. They'd been happy as newlyweds. She'd moved into his apartment, immediately repainting the walls a homey tan with white trim. Away from the base, so they had privacy. "We got married in Las Vegas."

He squinted, a smile playing on his face. "Just the two of us?"

"Yes." She took another bite, the pineapple cooling the

pepperoni on her tongue. It'd been two years since she'd enjoyed the combination of flavors. "You were on leave, and as a new accountant at the firm, I only had one day off." The memories rushed through her, bringing both pleasure and the pang of eventual loss. "You bought me a dress." He'd already taken her heart, but with the white dress, he'd stolen her soul. The white silk had been perfect, better than she'd ever dreamed.

He inhaled. "I can't wait to remember that day. While my brain is fuzzy, my emotions are clear, Josie. I know I loved you."

A tingle started at her heart and spread through her entire chest. She pushed the feeling aside. He couldn't make such a claim without his memories. No matter how badly she wanted to believe him. Even if she did learn to trust that the love was real, he'd still left her alone. She cleared her throat. "So how's the research going?"

He gave a short nod, letting her off the hook. "Not great. But I'll find what I need."

"Good." They needed answers before another attack came. Josie pushed the pizza box aside and grabbed the file on Agers Hardware, a small hardware store whose owners weren't as good at record keeping as some of her other clients. Good thing she knew her job. She'd find the deductions the young couple needed to pay the IRS less.

Shane went back to typing. Hours passed. Finally, Shane looked up at her and frowned thoughtfully.

Did she have pizza sauce on her face? "What?"

He studied her, his eyes the color of a stormy sky. Not moving an inch, he kept his focus entirely on her, as if she were the only thing in his world. Tension thickened the air around him, his predatory stillness a warning that he'd soon lunge.

Memories assailed her. She'd forgotten the feeling of being everything. Her heart picked up its pace, and heat slid through her veins like a fine whiskey. Desire slammed into her abdomen. With just one look from him, electricity zipped through her body to pulse between her legs.

His nostrils flared. "I remember you."

CHAPTER
12

JOSIE STRUGGLED TO stay calm as she stared at Shane. "You remember me?"

He frowned deeper and rocked back in her office chair. "Yes. At a coffee shop. You were wearing a blue yoga outfit that showed off your ass."

Josie snorted out a laugh. "The day we met."

"Yeah." Shane focused on her face, his smooth Southern drawl deepening. "Some guy was bothering you. I asked if you needed help."

"I said yes." She wrinkled her nose. "I felt like such a wimp. But you helped." Her hero. Right from the first moment. He'd stepped in and dragged the jerk outside. Then he'd come back inside and bought her an iced coffee. "You said I was smart, not wimpy."

"I remember." His gaze ran over her face. "Your hair was shorter and you had a tan."

"It was California. You had a darker tan, too." And biceps that made her want to take a bite. So maybe now he could explain why he'd been stalking her before that day. She cleared her throat. "Remember anything else?"

"Not yet."

But he would. What would happen then? "Did you find anything about your past?"

Shane kicked back in her chair, overwhelming the gray leather. "Not really. My military record is good; lots of missions dealing with problems on our soil. A couple of biological problems from factories." He frowned. "There's more. I know it. But I haven't gained access yet."

"What about your brothers?"

His face turned to stone.

Josie studied him. He seemed like one cold bastard. But he wasn't. Fire burned hot through him, so hot he forced ice into himself. To keep control. God, she used to want to make him lose it. Completely. Just with her. Only with her. She licked her lips.

Sparks flashed into his eyes in response. His gaze dropped to her chest.

Her nipples hardened to sharp points. She licked her lips again and swallowed. Her nerves fired. Oh man, this was a bad idea. "Shane. Stay focused." Her voice came out breathy.

"That tone. I remember it." His voice lowered to a rumble that wrapped around her heart. "Sexy as hell. Almost as if you're whispering, your breath heating my cock."

Jesus. The way he talked. Husky. Male. He used to whisper her name in her ear as he came. As if she was the only tether he had to this life. As if she was everything he needed.

Desire slid to temper. She wasn't everything he needed. He'd left. "Knock it off. It isn't going to happen." Liar. The word echoed through her head. She was such a liar.

"Yes, it is." His eyes darkened until nearly black. "Maybe not right now. I'll wait until we figure this out." He leaned forward, forearms on her desk. "But make no mistake. It is going to happen."

Her sex clenched. "What did you discover about your brothers?"

"Nothing. Not a thing." Anger tightened his jaw. "I found a couple military academies with pictures; nothing like the place I saw in my dreams. I searched their names, my name, hospital records. Death records." His eyes swirled with emotion at the last. "Nothing." He threw a pencil on the desk. "That's not all." Rising, he extended one hand into the kneehole of the heavy oak desk and casually lifted it a foot from the floor. "I'm seriously strong."

Josie stood. Her heart slammed against her ribs. Nobody should be able to lift the desk so easily. "Apparently."

He let the desk drop with a thud. "Did you know that about me?"

She tried for a nonchalant shrug. "I knew you were strong. Not that strong." Apparently the guy had hidden more than his past from her. Who the hell was he? Anger began to slide through her veins. What was she doing even thinking about trusting him again?

"Close your eyes. What do you hear?"

She kept her eyes open. "The hum of the heating unit." Other than that, silence echoed through the night.

Shane shook his head. "A block away a couple is having a spat about the tip the man left at dinner." He stalked around the desk. Toward her. "The elevator has gone up twenty-three times in the last couple hours; gone down twenty-seven times." His hands reached out to grab her forearms. "I need thirty-three steps to walk from here to the elevator. There are three exits from this building where I wouldn't be seen." His gaze dropped to her neck. "Your pulse rate increased when I grabbed your arms. I can *hear* it." The large hands tightened around her biceps. "And you're a liar. When you say it isn't going to happen, you're lying."

He tugged her into masculine hardness, into incredible heat.

His palm slid up her neck until his fingers tangled in her hair—slowly, deliberately. He tethered her in place, his eyelids dropping to half-mast.

Goose bumps rose on her skin. Caution warred with desire. She jerked her head back—or tried to. His hold tightened, holding her where he wanted her. *She couldn't move.* Shock and then flames licked through her.

His lips took hers, firm and determined. Her thighs dampened. He groaned low, bending her back, his hunger igniting hers.

Josie's mind spun. He wasn't asking. Gone was the care with which he'd always treated her. Pure, raw passion replaced thought.

Everything inside her melted as desire lit her on fire. While he'd always been passionate, this was new. Intense and dangerous, his hold showed no mercy.

He slammed her against the desk, the hard length of his body sliding against hers. He cupped the back of her head, his mouth moving over hers. A sharp nip triggered her to open her lips in protest, and he dove in, his body pinning her in place.

Hunger ripped through her veins.

His tongue stroked hers. The desk pressed into her back and she stiffened. He lifted her and plopped her atop the desk, her knees on either side of his hard hips, the skirt pooling up. Heat filled her sex. Her core rubbed against his erection.

"See what you do to me," he rumbled against her

mouth, giving her a reprieve to breathe. "From the first second I saw you in that coffee shop, you've done this to me."

She clutched on to his hard forearms to keep herself upright. A protest caught in her throat when his head rose so he could pin her with a look. Danger glinted in those dark gray eyes. Possession. Promise. A hard flush covered his rugged face. "Say yes, Josie."

"Yes." The word came out before she could think.

He didn't wait for a qualifier, not that her mind was working fast enough to invent one. Reaching past her, he swept files and papers to the floor. Broad hands circled her wrists, and he laid her back. He flattened her knuckles on either side of her head, palms up. "Keep your hands here."

Her fingers curled until nails bit into her palms.

His gaze slid to the buttons of her shirt. He quickly flipped them open, smoothing the shirt apart to reveal her plain cotton bra. Hunger flared in his eyes.

So much she couldn't speak. She could barely think.

"Ah, Josie." He flicked open the clasp and the material sprang apart. "Finally, something I remember. You and us. This. The prettiest pink nipples in the world." His hands dropped onto hers, holding them against solid oak as he lowered his head toward her breasts.

Fire. He engulfed one nipple in the heat of his mouth. Her eyes fluttered shut, and she pressed up against him. She'd forgotten. How had she forgotten how warm he could be? The inferno in that dangerous mouth? So unreal. Enhanced like his strength? She lifted her legs to encircle him, pressing her feet into his ass. Pressing him harder against her. Her hands ached with the need to touch him, and she tried to tug loose.

He kept her in place.

His mouth wandered to the underside of her breast, where he nipped before taking the other nipple in his mouth. A low hum of appreciation echoed against her flesh.

"Shane," she moaned, moving against him.

"Let me play." He placed wet, open-mouthed kisses up her chest to her throat. "If I remember correctly...there's a place right about here..." His tongue flicked at the base of her neck. The hollow near her shoulder. She shivered. "Yeah. I remember right." Heated lips closed over her flesh and he suckled.

His idea of playing had always destroyed her. In a seriously good way. The Southern drawl he'd let loose flashed craving through every nerve she owned. "Please. Let go of my hands." The plea came unbidden. She needed to touch.

"This time," he mumbled against her neck, lifting his hands to quickly shift her and remove all clothing except her panties. His hands went to her breasts while his mouth found her earlobe.

She grabbed the bottom of his shirt and pulled it over his head, her palms spreading across the muscles in his chest. So much strength. She'd missed him. Missed this. She bit her lip. Power infused her. He wasn't the only one remembering.

She traced a long scar along his abs, loving the way the skin shifted. Trembled. She wandered around to the base of his back to caress a spot just above his tailbone. He growled against her neck. Oh yeah. She remembered that spot. Her hands dove into his jeans. Commando. No boxers or briefs for her man. Some things never changed.

His boots were kicked off, and he yanked open the clasp on his jeans to drop them to the floor. The ties on the sides of her panties snapped in two. He grabbed one buttock and lifted her off the desk, positioning himself at her entrance. "Josie." With a swift plunge, he impaled her, balls deep.

Her body clenched around him. Her back arched. Jesus. She'd forgotten how big he was.

His mouth dropped to hers, taking, plunging, over-whelming. His hands molded her breasts. He tweaked a nipple. Fire lanced through her to where they joined. She pressed her feet into his butt and started to writhe against him.

"Wait." He hissed against her lips. "Wait a minute. You're not ready."

A craving filled every pore in her body. Her sex was wet, her clit throbbing with a need so great she wanted to cry. "I'm ready. God, I'm ready. Move or I'll kill you."

His hand manacled around her hip, lifting her into him. His other slid up her back, clasping her neck. Hold-ing her in place. Taking her.

He pulled out, then pushed back in. Slowly, as if testing the waters. He plunged in hard. His name tumbled from her lips. Fire ripped along the nerves inside her. Tissue swelled. "Faster."

He moved faster.

Harder.

Plunging in and out, consuming everything in the room, even oxygen. She couldn't breathe. She didn't care. Her feet pressed into his ass, her thighs tightened around him. Her nails dug into his shoulders, biting his skin until his mouth took hers again. His tongue thrusting in time with their bodies. So much. Definitely too much.

Her heart swelled. No, no, no, not her heart. She focused on the spiraling feeling deep inside. The physical. The overwhelming heat.

He angled his body up. His cock slid over her clit.

She exploded.

Her mouth opened on a rough scream, and he swooped in, taking the sound into his own body. From her breasts to her toes, she spasmed, riding the waves. While he rode her. Somehow harder and faster, his thrusts full of fury and need. With a hoarse growl against her mouth, he came. Heat filled her.

Memories threatened to suffocate her. The thought slid away as his climax triggered another one in her, and her entire body went rigid. She threw her head back, thighs tightening around him, the thrum of her bloodstream whooshing in her ears.

Pleasure. So deep and hard, it cut.

Her body went limp. A soft sigh escaped her as she relaxed, releasing his hips. Her feet slid from his body. She panted in air, trying to fill her lungs. An ache set up around her mouth.

Taken.

She licked her lips.

Swollen.

Her entire body was swollen.

Throbbing.

But man, she felt good.

Panic followed bliss. Kind of. She didn't have the energy for full-on panic. So much for her heart. She'd loved him from the moment those unique gray eyes twinkled at her at that coffee shop. Shane had rescued her that day, just like in a romance novel. Just like members of a family did for each other. When she'd given her vows, she'd meant them. In her lonely, solitary life, she'd given her heart once and once only.

She'd never get it back.

CHAPTER
13

A CROSS THE STATE, the ding of the phone awoke Matt from a dream where he finally found safety for his brothers. They only had three months left, and it was time to strike. "What?" he growled into the phone.

"Matt. We have a problem," Nathan said, his voice falling into a Southern drawl that set Matt's teeth on edge. They'd all worked hard to eliminate the tell, and the sound broke free only when something went wrong.

"You found the woman?" It was about fucking time.

"No. Have you?"

"No, but I'm closer." He'd become a U.S. Marshal for the sole purpose of finding one little witness who couldn't be found. Matt swung out of bed, reaching for his jeans. The soft Seattle rain pattered against the window. He'd had a tickle at the base of his neck for almost a week now, warning him something was coming. "What's going on?"

"It's bad," Nathan drawled, the sounds of his hands working a keyboard clacking over the line. "My alarms lit up last night with someone conducting an Internet search on you, Shane, me, and, uh, Jory, as well as military academies for kids."

Who would be so fucking obvious? Matt yanked on his jeans, sliding open the nightstand for his gun. He ignored the pain that slammed into his gut at the mention of Jory's name.

Nathan cleared his throat. "I think it was Shane."

Matt paused. "Shane? Not a chance." Shane was a genius. No way would he piss Matt off like this. "Where is he?"

"He broke cover a month ago apparently."

"A month ago?" Why? Where the hell was his brother? Shane wouldn't break cover. No way. "Where has he been?"

"I'm working on finding out. So far I've discovered he broke cover without alerting any of us—he wasn't due to check in until next week. Instead, Shane headed to Snowville for some reason."

"He's in Snowville now?"

"According to the BOLO out on him, he's in Snowville."

Matt dropped back onto the bed. "BOLO?"

"Well, out on Shane Dean, anyway. For now, that's him." Nate cleared his throat. "Hospital records show a Shane Dean was admitted to Mercy Hospital with head injuries on Saturday, resulting in temporary amnesia."

Dread ricocheted through Matt's gut. "You're telling me someone got close enough to injure Shane?" Shane had eyes in the back of his head. "And now, without a memory, he's trying to find out who the hell he is?" This was beyond bad. "He'll lead the commander right to him."

"Without question," Nathan said. "Shane kidnapped Josie Dean, which explains the BOLO."

"Josie?" Oh, this was getting worse by the minute. "I'm going to fucking kill him."

Nathan's Southern drawl deepened. "I warned you he wasn't finished with her. No way. No how."

Matt shoved the anger down past the concern. He

needed to think. "You're flying to Snowville. Text me your flight information, and I'll meet you at the airport—I'll drive so we have transportation." Matt grabbed a shirt to yank over his shoulders. His brothers. A ticking bomb hung over their heads, and time was counting down. "Ah, bring an identity as a lawyer, in case we need one."

"Matt." Nathan's usually humorous voice turned serious. "Can you leave? We've had you in place for less than a year."

"I have time. I'll make up an emergency." Which this fucking was. "You have your orders."

He clicked off the phone. Anger and determination swirled in his gut until his breath caught. Would he get to Shane before the commander did?

He couldn't lose another brother.

A wolf bayed in the far distance. Rain and wind clattered against the single-ply glass of the window. Josie snuggled farther beneath the threadbare covers in the cheap motel room. Heat enshrouded her from Shane's body. For the love of everything holy, what had she been thinking? Sleeping with him again.

Sleeping? Make that fucking. Hard-core, balls to her ass, fucking. The man did it well. His mind may still be playing catch-up, but his body remembered her. Exactly what to do to her.

Good thing she was on the pill to deal with menstrual cramps.

They'd always used protection. Neither had wanted a baby during their brief marriage. Sure, someday she figured they'd have kids. But he'd left. No kids.

The idea of having a baby sent her into a spiral. She'd always planned on creating a large family . . . lots to love. But deep down, fear lived. What if she died? Leaving her babies alone in life scared the crap out of her. What if they ended up in foster care, too?

She wasn't ready to make that decision.

The red numbers of the bedside clock illuminated the files sitting on the cheap table. Maybe she should get up and work.

"You're thinking too hard," Shane rumbled in her ear, running a hand down her arm. Goose bumps rose in reaction.

"I'm a thinker, Shane." Yet another thing he didn't remember about her.

He nodded. "No kidding. I have to ask...I shouldn't because we've been separated, but I need to know."

"Know what?"

"Did you sleep with Marsh?"

The question should've surprised her. But she remembered Shane's possessiveness well. He'd need to know the truth.

Of course she hadn't slept with anyone else while still married to him. "No, I haven't slept with Tom." Shane had been the one and only for her.

His body relaxed behind her. "That pleases me."

She sighed. Pleasing him wasn't high on her list. "How fantastic."

He chuckled. "So. Tell me what I don't remember about you."

What? Oh man. She hated pillow talk. She sucked at verbal intimacy. Being naked with Shane made her vulnerable enough, and now he wanted her to expose herself more with admitting to her odd life? Nobody had ever taught her how to share, how to trust. Not really.

She sighed. "You already know I grew up in foster care—moved around a lot." Rain pinged the window outside. "My childhood was all right. Most people were fairly nice, but nobody was mine."

His sigh stirred her hair. "Until me."

"Until you. Then you left." Pain caught her breath in her chest. How could his disappearance possibly still hurt?

Soft lips pressed a kiss against the top of her head. "I'm sorry."

Too much emotion for her. She couldn't handle any more. "Earlier in my office. We didn't use a condom."

He stilled. "Huh." One arm slid around her waist to tug her farther into his warmth. An erection settled against her butt. "I didn't think of the possibility of, er, ah..."

"No kidding." Heat pooled in her core. She fought to control her breathing, to keep her diaphragm relaxed. "Though I'm on the pill—for menstrual cramps."

"Oh. I guess that's okay. But about kids, we are married."

"We're about to get divorced." He didn't remember himself.

"No." He licked up her ear to bite the shell.

She shivered in response. "Yes."

"Nope." His palm spread out across her bare midriff. "I may have screwed up, and we'll find out why, but I won't hurt you again. You're mine, angel. The only thing in life that matters." A tremor of desperation filtered through his tone.

His fingers brushed the underside of her breast. She shoved a groan down. "I'm the only thing you remember right now. The rest will come back." Then she wouldn't matter anymore. Something else would take him away again, and he'd leave her shattered. Rebuilding had almost killed her last time. She couldn't do it again.

"I love you, angel. It's the one thing I remember without a doubt." The Southern drawl wound around her heart. "I'm not letting you go."

"Please, Shane." She couldn't take the promise. No more. "This is just sex."

He chuckled in her ear. Then he flipped her onto her back, his body pinning hers. Tension corded his muscles. "That sounds like an offer."

Her heart caught in her chest. A humming set up in her blood. Warning flushed through her along with desire. "That wasn't an offer."

He settled his erection at the apex of her legs. "My mistake." The rough hair on his thighs tickled her skin. He dropped his head to run heated kisses along the cord of her neck, one hand sliding to clasp her ass and squeeze, his grip implacable. "Are you sure you aren't offering?"

Stubborn pride fought with basic need. A desperate need only the man above her could fulfill. "No."

"No to sex? Or no, you're not sure about the offer?" His drawl deepened. He plucked a nipple, the bite of pain sending raw need to her clit. The palm at her butt lifted her, rubbing her against him.

Her breath caught in her throat. She lifted her gaze to find him focusing on her eyes. Not her body, but her eyes. Watching her. Gauging her reactions. Learning her secrets, delving deeper inside her, allowing her to hide nothing.

At the knowledge, something uncoiled inside her. Something dark, something daring.

His fingers continued to play, tugging her nipples over and around—until she wanted to beg. So many sensations at once kept her on the edge. The hard body over hers, his pulsing erection, his demanding fingers—and that knowing gaze. As if she were completely bare to him.

Her core ached with a need too great to fight. She tangled both hands in his dark hair. She tugged his mouth to hers, licking his bottom lip with her tongue. His eyes glowed silver through the darkness, so much hunger in them she felt devoured. He tweaked the other nipple, and his hand snaked up to tangle in her hair and tug back. "Say the words, Josie."

He'd ensnared her, rendering her immobile. If she could move, she'd toss him on his back and take him. Hard and fast. She was afraid she'd give him whatever words he demanded. "This is just sex."

"That's not what I want to hear." His hand kneaded her butt, his fingers leaving marks. His marks. "You mentioned an offer. Make it."

"I hate this about you," she hissed, even as her body slid against his. So much feeling. So much of an ache.

His grin lacked kindness. "Not true. You love this. You need this." The hand in her hair gripped tighter, an erotic pain spreading along her scalp. "I'm not letting you hide. I'm not letting you go."

His eyes held too much knowledge. Did he remember, or was she so easy to read? Her heart hurt even while her body moved against his. "Shane—"

"This is your place, little one. Take it." His mouth wandered over hers, kissing the corners of her mouth, the center of her lips, angling her to dive deep. So deep. His tongue slid against the roof of her mouth while he held her still. Held her where he wanted her.

He lifted his head. "Make the offer."

Damn him. She bit her lip, knowing she was fighting the inevitable. "Fine."

"Not good enough." His mouth enclosed the soft flesh where her neck met her shoulder. She moaned deep in her throat, waiting until his head lifted for his gray gaze to pin her.

"Fine. I offer sex." Please. Let it be enough. God. Leave her something.

"Not enough."

She pushed against him. Getting nowhere. "What the hell do you want?"

His eyebrow rose. Perfect control. She wanted to make him lose that. "Everything, Josie. You already knew the answer."

She had. She'd known exactly what he would demand the second she let him take her in the office. Could she risk her heart again? Ride the wave until it ended. Her body craved. Her heart needed. What if? What if their relationship worked out this time?

"Trust me. Please." His eyes darkened to a hue not even close to gray.

Some things were inevitable. She faced her greatest hope and her possible downfall. She knew herself. For Shane and Shane only, she'd jump. Such a terrible risk to take, and the only one with a reward that would be worth it. She'd never stood a chance against him. "Okay. Take it all." He would anyway. He'd always held her heart. Why pretend otherwise?

Triumph lifted his chin. His lips met hers in a kiss so full of emotion, tears sprang to her eyes. Slowly, so slowly, he entered her, his body fusing with hers. Taking hers. Protecting hers.

She fastened her thighs against his hips, her hands digging into his arms. He started to plunge faster, thrusting with perfect control. Not a chance, buddy. She grabbed his butt, yanking toward her while rearing up and nipping his chest. Leaving *her* mark.

He paused, mid-thrust.

Her teeth released, and her head hit the pillow.

A vein pulsed in his neck. Crimson spread across his high cheekbones. Those dangerous eyes darkened to midnight as they pierced her. His biceps undulated like the muscles of a stallion wanting to run, and his cock swelled inside her.

Her breath caught. She'd never seen him so on edge. Then, knowing full well what she was doing, she allowed a challenging smile to curve her lips.

His control snapped.

Hard fingers dug into her hip as he thrust hard and to the hilt. Fire lanced inside her, sparking each nerve. She cried out, arching into him, her eyes widening on his.

His nostrils flared. His breath panted out. He slid out and slammed back in, his eyes glittering, his hand in her hair. Keeping her in place. The headboard smashed against the wall.

Hard and fast he thrust, taking them both higher and hotter than ever he'd permitted himself to go with her, taking him beyond his keen rein. An unbelievable ball of heat uncoiled fiercely within her. This was more than sex—more than man and woman. He was all male, taking a female. Her heart hammered with the knowledge, and she clasped her ankles at his back.

Close, she was so close. Her eyes shut. Electricity zapped through her. With a sharp cry, she broke, ripping through the waves.

He pounded harder, faster, finally grinding against her and murmuring her name in that deep Southern drawl as he came.

She relaxed back into the bed, her mind spinning. He'd lost control. The darkness hid her trembling lips. Maybe things could be different this time. Though, as her heartbeat slowed and reality returned, she had to wonder. Was that a good thing?

CHAPTER
14

IF HER PERSONAL life wasn't a big enough mess, her professional life was blown to bits the next morning. A tornado had ripped through her office. Josie sucked in air, her head pounding. "How did this happen?" Shredded papers covered the floor. File folders had been torn, spreadsheets ripped in two. Cabinets teetered empty and overturned. Anything breakable...broken. She bent down to finger the shards of a ceramic vase she'd made during one outing with Vicki. Of course, Vicki had gone to the art studio to flirt with the owner, but Josie had enjoyed creating the vase and then painting the dramatic colors all over the sides.

She avoided the desk. What she'd let Shane do to her on that desk—

"I don't know. The police were here for hours earlier to process everything and look for prints." Vicki bent to pick up a pile of papers. "They said we can clean up now."

Josie glanced behind Vicki. The rest of the tenth floor didn't look any better. Whoever had torn through the CPA firm's space had done so with a vengeance. "Thanks for calling me." She'd been at Trenton Industries going through their files all morning.

Johnston stalked down the hall, his normally pleasant face set in hard lines. "Anything missing?"

Josie shrugged. "No clue yet."

He shook his head, a muscle ticking in his massive jaw. "We have financial records for some of the largest corporations in the country. If any of that information went public—"

"But those are locked away, aren't they?" Josie frowned. This appeared to be vandalism.

Her boss breathed out. "They got into everything. The vault, the computers...they even took three laptops." He tilted his head at someone behind her. "Detective."

Oh, come on. It couldn't be. Josie pivoted, plastering a smile on her face. "Detective Malloy. How nice to see you."

The detective raised a bushy eyebrow. "Mrs. Dean." He gestured toward the small conference room. "You're the only one I haven't spoken with yet. Shall we?"

Josie straightened her peach-colored silk suit and followed Malloy into the room. Thank goodness her husband was a master at breaking and entering. He'd retrieved more clothes for her earlier that morning from her home. Maybe it was time to go back home.

Malloy shut the door, waiting until Josie settled into a plush leather chair before he did the same. "Do you know if anything is missing yet?" He flipped open his tattered notebook on the gleaming dark mahogany table.

"No." Josie studied the cop. He had to be, what? Mid-forties? Today he'd worn another wrinkled brown suit, his tie a striped pink. "I like your tie."

He glanced up, a faint tinge of color sliding across his pale skin. "Thanks. It was a gift." Dark circles bagged under his eyes, and Josie fought guilt. The guy was sleep-deprived from chasing Shane. He wouldn't find Shane.

"Well, the colors are very nice." She clasped her hands on the table. "So, um, you investigate every crime that comes up?"

"Nope. Just anything related to you right now." Malloy's smile lacked charm.

Well, wasn't that just terrific? "This has nothing to do with Shane."

"We'll see about that, won't we?" Malloy tapped his pen against the notebook.

Yeah, they would see about that. Josie crossed her legs. "My boss said the computers had been hacked and the vault broken open."

"Yep. Whoever did this was looking for something." Intelligent brown eyes focused on her face. "Any idea what?"

"No." Josie shrugged. "We have varied financial information for banks, corporations, nonprofits . . . you name it. I guess they might've been looking for that."

"I think this has something to do with your husband."

A chill swept through her. "I don't see what." She spoke the truth. The timing sucked, but Shane had nothing to do with her business. Never had.

"I'd like to verify that myself."

She widened her eyes, going for innocent. Probably looked like a clown. "Shane's gone, Detective. I assume he went back to his military buddies." The clock on the credenza ticked a quiet countdown until angry clients showed up demanding answers. She hoped this had nothing to do with Shane. Or with her. "If I could help you, I would. Besides, he didn't kidnap me. He hasn't broken any laws." The smile she flashed trembled on her lips.

"So Major Dean signed the divorce papers?"

Thunder rolled outside. Josie took a deep breath. "No.

He didn't sign. I'll have to go forward on my own." But would she? What if they stood a chance this time? Concern had her biting her lip. What if she was making a huge mistake? Her stomach tightened. What if the whole mess did have something to do with Shane? She swallowed several times.

"I see." The detective pushed back from the thick table and stood. "I'd appreciate it if you contact me once you discover if any files are missing." Three long strides had his bulky body at the door. "Or if you hear from your husband, of course."

"Of course." Josie stood on shaking legs, smoothing her face into a pleasant expression. The ability to do so had helped her navigate the foster care system without many problems. Her mind reeled, searching for answers. This had to be random. But it was an odd coincidence that Shane was in town and things had started to go south.

She'd taken only one step into the hall when Mr. Johnston hailed her. "Josie, Dr. Phillips from Fuller Labs and his colleague are in the large conference room waiting for you."

Josie nodded, swiveling around and hustling toward the west wall. She entered the conference room, smiling and extending a hand to the fifty-something scientist. He took her hand in a strong grip, his faded green eyes twinkling. "So. You need a new housekeeper."

Josie laughed, moving to sit at the head of the marble table, her gaze on the woman sitting quietly next to Dr. Phillips. "Hi, I'm Josie Dean."

"Dr. Madison." Low and cultured, the tone spoke of Ivy League degrees. She could be anywhere from forty to fifty with flawless porcelain skin, dark hair, and eyes the deepest of blue. Intelligent eyes took Josie's every measure. "I'm in town from our DC branch."

Dr. Phillips dropped into a chair with a groan.

Josie smoothed her hair back. "I'm afraid someone ransacked our offices looking for some type of financial information on our clients."

Dr. Madison sniffed. "That's what we understand. As you can imagine, we're quite concerned about client confidentiality."

"Yes." Josie calculated the materials in her files. The lab worked in everything from reproductive technology to cellular research for genetic diseases. "But all of my information is financial. We have no access to patient names, medical data, or anything protected by the new privacy laws. Just your grant applications, payments, and bottom line."

"So even if there were payments from patients, those payments would be listed anonymously?" Dr. Madison wrinkled her brow, her chin lifting, her tone cultured and condescending.

Josie stamped down irritation. "Yes. Your organization assigns a number to a patient, and we just get that number in our files." The doctor appeared unfamiliar with the process. "If you don't mind my asking, what field do you work in with Fuller Labs?"

A fine eyebrow arched. "I'm a clinical neuropsychologist with a specialty in psychoneuroimmunology."

Well now. That was a mouthful. "So. Brain. Psychology. The interaction of the central nervous system, psychological processes with the body's immune system." The doctor wasn't the only person in the room who'd gone to college.

Madison smiled a perfect row of small white teeth. "In a simple nutshell, yes."

Annoyance swirled in Josie's temples, so she widened

her smile. "Sounds fascinating." Arrogant, snotty know-it-all. She met the doctor's gaze head-on, allowing both confidence and humor to show on her face. Years of dealing with people who considered themselves better than a lost kid often came in handy with handling bullies. "I'm surprised you have time to delve into the accounting side of the business."

The smile slid off the doctor's face. "While my work is far more important than simply adding numbers, I do wish to protect our clients." She picked invisible lint off her designer suit. "Which is why I'm quite concerned with the obvious breach of protocol here."

Josie forced herself to remain calm. "Breach?"

"Yes." Madison clicked her tongue. "We expect our financial information to be protected and safe. Apparently your firm is not up to the task."

Dr. Phillips patted Madison's china doll hand with his large, gnarled one. "Now Dr. Madison, let's not be hasty." He cleared his throat. "I'm sure our records are safe."

Josie nodded, shifting her focus to him. "Of course. Since we didn't have any client information to begin with, there's absolutely no risk of a breach. Plus, I'm confident the police will find whoever broke into our offices." Something in her would've truly enjoyed punching the snotty woman in the face. Just once. Or maybe twice.

A whisper of sound echoed before Daniel poked his head around the thick door. "Sorry. I just need the conference room when you're finished." His trimmed brown hair appeared slightly ruffled, but his gaze was calm.

Dr. Madison leaned forward. "You're Daniel Mission."

Dan frowned, stepping inside and smoothing down his power tie. The red tie contrasted nicely with the navy suit. "Yes, er..."

"Dr. Madison of Fuller Labs." The woman flashed a smile. "You handle the accounts for Genevieve Trogart, who is a friend of mine."

Understanding smoothed out Dan's frown. "Yes. The Trogart Corporation has been my client for about two years." He smiled, all charm. "In fact, I just got off the phone with Genny—she was anxious about the break-in."

Dr. Madison's eyes widened. "Don't tell me the Trogart files were taken?"

"No." Dan shook his head. "I keep my files on a flash drive that's with me at all times. No hard copies, nothing on the laptops I leave at work. Of course."

Irritation had Josie's hands drawing into fists. "That's not firm policy."

"Yet it's a good one now, isn't it?" Dr. Madison drawled, her gaze all but shining on Dan. "I'll bet all of your clients are very happy right now."

"Yes." Dan returned the admiring glance. "It was nice to have met you." With a nod at Josie, he pivoted and disappeared from view.

Dr. Phillips pushed back his chair and stood, assisting Madison up. "We should get going. Don't worry, Josie. I'm sure they'll find the criminals. Please keep us informed."

Josie stood, dread mixing with irritation along her shoulders. "Well, I hope I've been able to reassure you a little bit. We, of course, will be in contact when we figure out if anything was taken."

Dr. Madison glided toward the door. "I would hope so. Until that time, I should inform you I'll be discussing alternative firms with our Board of Directors. Or maybe just different accountants." She headed down the hallway toward the elevator.

"Ignore her," Dr. Phillips whispered with a wink. "She

should be returning to DC any day." He shook Josie's hand in a warm grip.

Josie walked him to the elevator. If Dan had just stolen her client, she'd beat him senseless. He'd get the promotion for sure if that had just happened. Doubt swirled in her brain. There was no doubt most of them would lose clients now…everyone except Daniel. She shook her head at the bizarre thought. Now she was seeing conspiracies everywhere.

With a huff, she returned to her office, where Vicki still attempted to put everything into order.

"Josie," Tom said, striding from the reception area to grab her arms. "Are you all right?"

"Yes." She looked up to his frowning face. "I'm fine. They destroyed the entire floor, though." And she may have just lost her biggest client to his basketball buddy.

He stepped back, running a rough hand through his thick brown hair. "I just heard. The police are on my floor asking if anyone noticed anything." His sigh stirred the air with mint. "You worked late last night, and I was afraid—"

"No, no." She reached out to grab his strong arms. "I was long gone. Really. I'm fine." He was such a good guy. Why couldn't she have felt more for him? "I appreciate the concern, though."

He nodded, his eyes narrowing. "How did you get to work? Did the police bring you?"

"No." She hated lying to him. "The police found my car and returned it to me."

He stepped back. "Did you say a while ago that Dean stole your car?"

A blush crept up her face, heating her skin. "No. I said I let him borrow it."

"Josie." Tom shook his head, his lips tightening. "Dean's dangerous. You know it. Break free now, before it's too late." Concern deepened the lines that bracketed his mouth.

Josie forced a smile. "I have. He's gone." The lie nearly stuck in her throat all the more now that she knew there was no possibility of a future with Tom. Right or wrong, she'd always love Shane.

Tom sighed, reaching out to run a finger down the side of her face. "I care about you. Let me help."

Tom. So solid and strong. She stepped back this time. "I'm a big girl. Thanks for the concern, though. It really does mean the world to me."

"Hey, boss," Vicki interrupted from her perch by Josie's phone. "You have about thirty messages. Word has gotten out, and clients need reassurance."

Josie nodded. "I have to go, Tom."

His smile was tinged with sadness. "I know. Bye, Josie."

By seven that evening, Josie's head pounded, her feet ached, and she'd bitten her nails to the quick. She needed a manicure, bad. She'd met with five clients and spent the rest of the time on the phone reassuring others that their financial information was safe. Hopefully.

She tightened her grip on the handset of the telephone. "I understand that, Mr. Larson." First Billy screwed up their deductions and now this. "You need to understand, I had your file with me last night. The people who destroyed our offices didn't get any of your information."

"I have your assurance on this?" The man's tone quickened in agitation.

"Of course." She sighed. "We should probably meet

next week and go through the documents." There was a good chance Larson might sue the CPA firm once she brought Billy's mistakes to his attention. He'd probably win. "I'll call you soon to set something up." She hung up after tense good-byes.

She grabbed the manila files to drop off at The Pound, a local bar she hoped would keep her as its accountant. The owner had been quite concerned about the break-in, and she'd spent fifteen minutes reassuring him via the phone. She'd also promised to drop by the notes she'd jotted down for creating a new benefits plan for his employees.

Her cell phone buzzed and she read the screen. Shane waited outside. Time to go. He'd assured her they'd only have to stay at the motel for a couple more nights, and then she could go home. Apparently he thought he'd be able to find out who was after him by then.

Would he want to stay at her home then? Did she want him to? The question really came down to whether or not she trusted him, and whether or not he wanted to try to make it work. How could they do either until his memories returned? Her head started to ache.

Grabbing her files and handbag, she hurried toward the elevator, waving at Johnston in his office as she passed. Man, he was angry. Nobody messed with his clients.

The elevator rode smoothly to the bottom floor. She dodged outside into the chill of dusk, and she tightened her coat, taking a deep breath. The scent of decaying leaves contrasted with the vibrant orange hue of leaves still on tree branches.

Yet the air smelled dead.

She couldn't help the long shiver that shook her shoulders. The world was suddenly too quiet. Steeling her shoulders, she forced herself to move toward her parking spot, the hair on the back of her neck standing up. Shane was there somewhere, watching her. Her body responded just because he was near. Who knew that desire and warning could comingle?

A figure moved away from the building and grabbed her arm. She yelped, jerking back. "Tom. What are you doing?"

He frowned. "Sorry, Josie. I really am." The wind tousled his hair even more than usual. He tightened his grip and began to drag her back to the office building's main door.

Daniel had just opened the door and he froze, both eyebrows raised.

She struggled. "What's happening? Let go of me."

"I will in a minute," Tom hissed, jerking harder. "I swear, you're as bad as my sisters. Don't you gals ever think?"

Another figure stepped out of the shadows. "Let her go, Marsh."

Shane. Thank goodness. Tom yanked her behind his back.

She stumbled in her heels, grabbing his flannel shirt to keep from falling on the concrete.

"Freeze!" A male voice bellowed as a man wearing a black vest labeled SWAT jumped into range. Vehicles screeched, and sirens yowled as emergency vehicles skidded into the lot.

Malloy stepped out of an unmarked black car, his gun on Shane. "Major Dean. You're under arrest."

Shane eyed the detective and the myriad of weapons pointed at him. "Quite the firepower you brought, Malloy."

"Yes, well. I've seen what happens to men who cross

you." Malloy gestured. "Turn around and place your hands on the building."

Josie elbowed Tom out of the way. "Detective! I told you Shane didn't kidnap me. You can't arrest him."

Tom turned toward her. "I'm pressing charges. He broke into my house and knocked me out before taking you. That's a crime."

Shane growled. "You had a gun on me, asshole."

Tom shrugged. "It was my house and you were trespassing. I had the right to defend Josie."

Panic heightened Josie's breath to a hard pant. "Tom. Don't do this. Please." Her mind spun. What could she do?

"I'm sorry." His eyes darkened in the soft light, his jaw hard as his voice lowered to the tone he used when dealing with his younger sisters. "You don't know what you're doing. You're not thinking clearly."

Son of a bitch. Malloy flipped Shane around, frisking him and cuffing him within seconds. Because Shane allowed him to. Thank goodness her husband wasn't fighting back. Right now, anyway.

Malloy tipped his head, resignation in his eyes. "Mrs. Dean, you can probably bail him out within hours." He prodded her husband toward a squad car.

"Josie." Shane gave her a look, his hands behind his back, his eyes a seriously pissed-off hue of gray. "Watch your tail and go home. Don't leave until I call you." Malloy shoved his head down before pushing him into the car.

Seconds later they drove away. The SWAT team packed up. The parking lot emptied.

Tom grabbed her arm, pulling her to face him. "Come home with me. I can protect you."

Fury cascaded through her system. She shot her knee into his groin.

Tom bent over with a muffled oomph, dropping to one knee. "Damn it."

She turned and glared at Daniel, who'd remained motionless at the door.

He shook his head. "You're going to ruin your career."

Without another glance, she flipped around and ran for the Toyota, keying the ignition and ripping out of the lot. Shane said to watch her tail and go home. Probably the crappy motel. She knew he had cash hidden in a large duffel bag. She'd need the money to bail him out.

The files slid out of her briefcase. She'd lose the bar as a client for sure if she didn't drop those off as promised. Okay. New plan. She'd drop off the files and head back to the motel to get money to bail out Shane. The police would need time to process him, wouldn't they?

She chewed her lip. What was the bail procedure? Did she go to the police station? Man, she had no clue.

CHAPTER
15

JOSIE KEPT AN eye on the rearview mirror as she drove across town. Shane had told her to watch her tail. Would someone really follow her? Cars zipped behind her, probably people rushing home after a hard day's work. Like she should be. But no. First she had to appease a pissed-off client, and then she had to bail her husband out of jail. She'd become one of those women from television who bailed their man out. The giggle that escaped her had an edge of hysteria to the high pitch.

She parked on the street in front of The Pound, shoving the files back in the case. Thunder rolled above. The first winter storm was about to hit.

Heavy metal music pounded as she ran into the club. The stench of sweat mixed with stale perfume and smoke filled her lungs. Lights flashed. Bodies gyrated on the dance floor. A lot of bodies, considering it was only eight o'clock on a Tuesday night. Glancing around, she made a beeline for the burly bartender who stood behind a large marble bar.

He grinned, a gold tooth gleaming in the dim light. "Hi, pretty lady. What can I get you?"

"I have some papers for Paul," she yelled over the loud music.

"He's in a meeting." The bartender nodded at a sparkling bar stool. The booming voice matched his large bulk. "Have a seat, have a drink, and he'll be done in a few."

She didn't have time for this, but neither did she have a choice. She absolutely couldn't lose any more clients. With a shrug, she slid onto the stool. "Rolling Rock, please."

The guy slid the beer across the bar. "On the house." He winked.

"Thanks." She took a deep drink. The beer was light with a smooth finish, and she allowed herself to relax. The bartender loped down to the other end of the bar to serve two young women in tight tank tops and short skirts. Really short skirts.

The outside door opened and shut. A cool breeze wafted across her skin, and the hair prickled on the back of her neck. She turned, surveying the doorway.

A man, a large man, stood just inside. Smooth and graceful, he crossed to a table close to the doorway. He prowled like a panther on the hunt. A dark T-shirt covered a thick chest, while faded jeans rode low on his hips. Black hair fell to his shoulders, giving him a bad-boy look that matched the biker boots on his feet.

Two waitresses nearly collided in a rush to serve him. The buxom blonde got there first, and her ass actually twitched as she took his order.

He shouldn't be there. Adrenaline whipped through Josie's veins. The club catered to a young crowd, a partying crowd who liked to dance. The guy sitting across the room was no partier. Even more alarming, he did nothing to hide the fact that he didn't belong. Arrogance and an air of apathy filtered around him in a deadly, frightening combination.

His glance at her increased her adrenaline rush. He looked away as the waitress dumped a beer in front of him. Long neck. The woman tripped in her heels as she moved on.

Josie's breath caught in her throat. A sense of awareness pulled her gaze from the man at the table to the rear entry near the bathrooms. Another man, just as big as the first, leaned against the wall, a beer in his hand. His gaze settled on her. No expression. Just focus.

Danger. Between the two men, a sense of danger filtered through the club.

Josie shivered. Were they following her? Who the hell were they? They didn't so much as acknowledge each other, but they didn't fit in. Not in this club.

She'd left the gun in the jockey box of the car. Without a doubt, she needed a weapon. These had to be the men after Shane. Maybe. Or perhaps she'd lost her mind, and these guys were just looking for a good time.

Nope. The one standing ignored a chippy in barely there clothes to keep his gaze on Josie. They weren't looking for a good time. The girl pouted out her bottom lip and flounced back to the dance floor.

"Hey, Paul's free," the bartender bellowed, flipping up an opening in the bar. Josie jumped, almost spilling her beer.

"Thanks." She scurried past him, all but running down the narrow hall to the offices at the back. A glance toward the bar showed an empty hallway. With a deep breath to calm her jumping nerves, she knocked on the door.

"Come on in," a male voice said.

Calm. She needed to be calm. Opening the door, she walked in wearing a smile. "Hi, Paul. I have the benefits package lined out for your employees." She crossed and sat on a pleather guest chair to face her client across his massive marble desk.

Paul leaned forward. "Great." In his early twenties, Paul had inherited a bundle from his grandfather and had quickly built his dream club. He'd been smart enough to hire the accounting firm to assist him. He pushed thick blond curls away from his face. "Sorry I was so much of a pain earlier. I just don't like anyone knowing about my finances."

Josie nodded. Especially his drug-dealing brother, who had been annoyed when Paul inherited all the money. She made a mental note to let Malloy know about the brother. Could be a lead for the break-in at the offices. "I know. And I assure you, we're doing everything we can to discover what was taken and by whom."

Paul nodded. "I know. So what papers did you bring for me?"

She pushed the manila files toward him. "The first is a plan for employee benefits, the second is a list of deductions I think you can take throughout the year." Right now she had a more immediate concern. Were the men still out in the bar? She hoped not. "The deductions should save you about ten thousand dollars each quarter."

"Great." Paul glanced at his watch. "How about I look these over tonight and give you a call tomorrow? I, er, have a date."

Josie smiled and stood. "No problem." Relief filled her. Paul wasn't going to hire another firm. Excellent.

She followed him down the hallway to the bar, her senses on high alert. Her hands tightened to fists. The guy against the wall had gone. The man at the table remained in the same place, his gaze on her as she dodged through the bar. Anger and fear slammed together. She wasn't taking this. With a huff, she grabbed her beer from where she'd left it on the bar.

Lifting her chin, she stalked toward him, plunking her beer on his table. The liquid fizzed up and spilled over the top. The bartender and two bouncers were close enough to call if she needed them. "What do you want?"

The guy raised an eyebrow and took another drink of his beer. "In general or right now?"

He appeared casual but a muscle pounded in his jaw. The words might be a double entendre, but not one ounce of sexual innuendo echoed in them. "In general."

Surprise flashed in his dark eyes. The light was too dim for her to determine color. "A quiet life." He set down his beer. "What do you want?"

She shrugged. "What happened to your buddy across the room?"

A smile flirted with the corner of his mouth. Familiar. There was something so familiar about this guy. Was he a client of the firm? "What buddy?"

"Whatever." She rolled her eyes. "I've had a long day and don't want to play. Leave me alone or you'll regret it."

"You approached me, doll."

She needed to get to the motel and then bail out Shane. "My mistake." She whirled around, her gaze seeking refuge. Plastering on her flirtiest smile, she wandered over to the bartender. "Hey, would you do me a huge favor?"

His grin split his face. "Anytime, lady."

"There's a guy at a table behind me, a big guy. Would you distract him for a few minutes after I leave?"

The bartender glanced behind her. "What guy?"

Josie turned. He was gone. Only two beer bottles remained on the sparkly table. Unease caught her breath in her throat. "Well, how about escorting me to my car? Just in case."

The bartender jumped over the bar and held out an arm. "I'd be delighted."

The rain drenched down as they hurried outside, and she checked the backseat before getting in. Empty. With a wave to her temporary hero, she pulled into traffic, keeping an eye behind her.

Darkness fell as she took side roads, driving the opposite direction of where she needed to go several times. No one followed her. That she could see at least.

Finally she arrived at the motel and parked across the lot from their room, watching. Waiting. Nothing moved. She grabbed the gun out of the glove box and stuck the heavy weapon in the back of her pants. Her purse offered little comfort at her side while she scrambled across the unkempt lot and opened the door.

Silence.

Thank goodness. She stepped inside and locked the door, flipping on the light.

Empty.

What a rotten day. She dodged forward into the bathroom, taking a moment to wash her face and use the facilities. What should she do?

Bail out Shane. That's what she should do. He may have knocked Tom out, but he was just trying to protect her. Plus, the two men at the bar were there for her. She couldn't handle them, and they had to have something to do with Shane. Sure, she could tell the police about them, but they hadn't done anything yet, and she had no clue who they were.

Shane could deal with the duo from the bar. Every instinct she had yelled they'd be back. She might not trust Shane, but he was her best bet in surviving whatever was going on. Then she'd have to figure out how to survive him. One thing at a time.

Okay. Good plan. She walked out of the bathroom.

And stopped cold. Fear slammed her heart against her ribs. Her ears burned. Adrenaline ripped through her bloodstream.

The two men sat on the ragged couch, gray eyes focused on her.

CHAPTER
16

S HE DREW THE gun, steadying her feet on the ugly car-pet. Should she point at one of them or between them? Between them.

The two men on the couch didn't flinch. Or move. The brown-haired one who'd stood against the far wall at the bar raised an eyebrow. "Did you figure she had a gun?" He cocked his head to the side, twisting his lip as if in deep thought.

"Nope." The man with black hair stretched out long legs. "She tossed her purse on the bed."

Familiar. There was something so familiar about these two. She squinted her eyes. "Who the hell are you?"

The first man scratched his head, glancing at the other. "Well?"

With a short nod, the second man spoke. "I'm Matt and this is Nathan." He tilted his head. "Shane's brothers."

Shane's brothers. Shock washed through her, and she plastered on her foster care face. "Well. That explains the eye color." Gray. Pure gray, just like Shane's. "How did you find me?"

"We followed you to the bar from your work, and from

the bar to here," Matt said, his big body relaxing into the couch.

"No you didn't. I checked behind me."

He smiled. "I know. You did a good job, too. Almost lost us on Pine Street."

Almost wasn't good enough. No way could she take these two. They stretched well over six feet, packed hard, and thrummed with the same preternatural stillness as did Shane. They were as big as Shane. Probably just as dangerous. "So why follow me? Why not get your brother out of jail?"

"We will. Shane is safe right now. You're not," Nathan said, rubbing his chin.

She shifted her aim to him. "Is that a threat?"

Confusion wrinkled his nose. "Um, no. I'd never threaten someone so soft. Did it sound like a threat?" He lifted an eyebrow at his brother.

Matt shook his head. "I didn't think so. I figured it for a statement of fact."

Her shoulders straightened. "Listen, Laurel and Hardy. Knock it off. Aren't you at least a little concerned I'll shoot you?"

A grin tipped Matt's lips. "Honey, you have the safety on."

Goddamn it. Her thumb clicked the lever loose. "Not now, I don't."

His smile widened. "Shane was right. She is something."

Pleasure rose unbidden. He'd talked about her to his brothers? In a good way? Then irritation spiraled through. "He never mentioned you. Not a single word."

Nathan's gray eyes softened. "He couldn't, Josie. Trust me."

"I don't trust any of you." Sad, but true. Not even Shane. Who were these people?

"Smart girl," Matt said. "So, ah, do you mind telling us what the charges are against Shane? I know there was a BOLO out on him for kidnapping you, but the police canceled it earlier today."

She ground her teeth. "I am pointing a gun at you." How stupid were these guys? "Get out." Home. She'd back her bags and go back home. If Shane stayed the hell away, she was safe. To get on with her life. Her long, boring, lonely life.

"Actually, you're pointing the weapon at Nathan," Matt said. "He's been shot before. Go ahead."

"You're such an asshole," Nathan muttered.

Their banter bordered on humorous, but a thick tension blanketed the room. Danger prickled through the air.

"Would you please leave?" Why was she asking them? She held the gun.

Matt's eyes softened. "No. Shane apparently wants you safe. That means we keep you safe."

"For how long? Until he leaves me again?" Her voice cracked.

"Ah, Josie." Matt leaned forward, his gaze serious. "He had no choice. Jory was killed, and we had to move. Leaving you was the only way to keep you safe and do what he needed to do."

Fire whipped through her. "Baloney. Sorry, Matt. The old 'I hurt you to protect you' line doesn't work on me." She shifted her aim to him. "How did Jory die?" The question held risk and she knew it.

They both stiffened. Already hard, their faces hardened even more. Matt held her gaze while Nathan dropped his to the floor. Pain thickened the air.

Matt cleared his throat. "We need to get Shane out. Will you help us or not?"

Okay. So they shared information as freely as Shane did. Not at all. "If I help you, you'll leave? All of you?"

Matt winced. "Nate and I will leave. You're on your own with Shane."

"Shane will leave," Nathan said.

Matt cut him a glance. "Nate—"

"Shane will leave." Nathan's jaw snapped shut. "I have one brother in the grave, and everyone close to us dies. Shane will leave. He'll move on if I have to beat him senseless to do it." He exhaled loudly. "I'm sorry, Josie. But you should cut your losses and move on. There's no future with any of us."

She'd already figured that out, but hearing the words delivered so coldly slid ice down her spine. Josie lowered the gun. Her hand ached, but she kept ahold of the weapon anyway. "How many brothers are there?"

Matt took her measure. "Four."

Surprise flashed across Nathan's face. Apparently Matt wasn't usually so forthcoming. Nathan cleared his throat. "Four counting Jory."

Three brothers still lived. A real family. "Shane might not remember you."

The sofa wobbled when Matt pushed his bulk off. "I know. We have his medical records." He stretched his neck. "Why was Shane arrested?"

She didn't bother to ask how he'd gotten his hands on Shane's medical records. "I went to stay with a friend, and two men tried to break into the house. Shane stopped them and knocked out my friend to, ah, take me."

Nathan stretched to his feet. "Tom Marsh?"

These guys could obtain information now, couldn't they? "Yes. Tom had a gun pointed at Shane, so Shane defended himself. Now Tom has pressed charges."

Nathan grinned. "Listen to you defending your man."

"It's the truth." She wrinkled her nose at him. So familiar. Must be the resemblance to Shane. Her man. Temporarily at least.

"So. Do I flash my badge?" Nathan yanked a wallet out of his back pocket to flip open the top.

Was that an FBI badge?

"No." Matt reached into a case sitting next to the couch that had been hidden by his long legs. He drew out a wallet, which he tossed to his brother. "You're Nathan Jones, attorney at law. Congrats."

Josie cleared her throat. "The FBI badge would work better. He could take Shane into federal custody."

Nathan eyed her. "I like how you think...and you really do look like an angel."

She stiffened. The nickname. Shane had discussed her with his brother. What had he said? "Thanks."

Matt shook his head. "The badge is authentic. I'd rather not have the connection between Nathan and Shane on the record. Not yet, anyway."

"Why not?" Her hand cramped around the gun. She should put the weapon in her purse, but that seemed unwise. Just in case.

Matt shrugged. Standing, he seemed even taller than Shane, who stood to six foot three.

She faced Nathan. "You're really in the FBI?"

"No." Nathan grabbed a California driver's license out of the wallet and studied the plastic.

"I don't understand. Why do you have so many fake credentials?" Unease began to make her head pound. Who were these guys?

Nathan yanked a large handgun from the back of his waistband and tossed the weapon to Matt. "I shouldn't be armed."

Matt placed it on the scarred table holding the rickety television. "We can't really explain. Shane trusts you, so we're letting you know this much. But the less you know, the safer Shane is." He turned to Nathan. "Good luck."

Nathan nodded. "I brought a suit—it's in the car." With a wink at Josie, he dodged out the door.

Silence. Alone with Matt, Josie turned to take him in. "So, you're Mattie."

He crossed his arms over a broad chest. "That's me."

"Does Shane love me, or what?"

The smell of the interrogation room set neurons firing in Shane's brain. Antiseptic. Fear. Blood. He rested his elbows on the hard metal of the bolted-down table, his hands handcuffed before him. In less than a minute, he could have them off.

The dingy green walls closed in on him, and he again counted the rate of buzzing from the fluorescent light above him. Two cameras were hidden in the ceiling, also emitting a low frequency.

Memories.

A room like this. A large man, buzz cut, dead eyes. Telling him if he lost again, he'd go to the other camp. Disappear like those other kids.

A training field. Hard packed and dusty. Boys, his age, fighting hand to hand. With knives.

Barracks. Beds for growing boys. His brother Matt teaching him how to block a side attack.

The door banged open, ripping Shane back to the present. Malloy stepped inside, followed by another man wearing a navy blue suit and bold power tie.

Malloy tilted his head. "Your lawyer is here, Major Dean."

Shane lifted an eyebrow, keeping his face blank. His stomach clenched hard. Memories shot like spikes of glass through his brain. His brother wasn't a lawyer. But his brother was there.

His brother brushed past the detective, taking a seat next to Shane. "Whatever my client said without counsel is irrelevant."

Malloy snorted, chomping his gum. He reached down and unlocked the cuffs, twirling them in the air. "No worries, counselor. Your client hasn't uttered one peep since we brought him in three hours ago." The door clanged shut as he stomped out.

Shane turned toward the man. The past slammed hard into his gut. His brother. Breathing hurt suddenly. "Nathan."

Nathan nodded. "Yes. Nathan Jones, your attorney." He peered closer. "Major Dean, how's the head?"

Memories rippled through Shane's brain—so many, so fast. Triggered by his brother. He swayed. "Great." Nathan teaching him to pick a lock. Times they'd spent together growing up, the time he helped Nathan in a knife fight. Blood spraying. For one second Shane wondered if he could trust Nathan. Instinct and memories comingled into a desperate yes. His brothers were the only people he could trust. "Memories filtering in fast."

Nathan's eyes lightened. "Good. Good to know." He eyed the ceiling. "So. I checked at the desk, and you haven't been formally processed yet."

Shane nodded. That was good considering they'd have to steal his prints back if he had been. His skull pounded as the dam holding his life back released. "I assume it's a matter of time?"

"No." Nathan flipped open a small smartphone to read

the screen. "My firm is in touch with the prosecuting attorney's office. They don't have a case, and you should be let go soon."

"Think so?"

Nathan shut the phone. "Well, you did save Mr. Marsh and Mrs. Dean from two attackers. You were defending your spouse when you took the gun from Mr. Marsh and were forced to render him unconscious. Temporarily, of course."

"Of course." Flashbacks. Nathan had always been able to spin the bullshit with the best of them. Warmth settled beneath Shane's rib cage that he remembered his brother. His life was coming back. "Where's my wife?"

Nathan pushed back from the table, his hands tapping the arm of the chair. "I'm sorry. I have no knowledge of your wife."

Shane counted the taps. Morse code. Josie was safe with Matt.

Matt?

Yeah, Matt. His oldest brother, the one who'd taught him to fight. Shane's breath whooshed out, and he blinked against light-headedness. Tears tried to prick the backs of his eyes. He remembered. He wasn't alone.

So he cleared his throat, trying to clear his head. "Yeah, well, I figure she's about done with me. After this arrest and all." He relaxed his shoulders and gave a small shrug. The woman had better not even *think* of being done with him. She was his life, and no way was he letting her go again.

Nathan narrowed his eyes, stopping his tapping. "Yes, well, that probably would be best. Considering the danger you've put her in."

If Shane had a "screw you" smile, he gave it to his

brother. "Speaking of such, any clue why danger is following me?"

"No, sorry." Nathan had a pretty decent "screw you" smile as well. "Of course, I'm just your lawyer. You don't tell me everything." The door opened, and he cleared his throat, straightening when a tall woman in a sexy red cocktail dress clicked stilettos across the floor.

She sat across from them. "Gentlemen." Her black hair had been swept away from pale skin smattered with freckles. "I'm Cynthia Miller, the prosecuting attorney. The chief of police dragged me out of one hell of a party."

Nathan smoothed down his silk tie. "Nathan Jones here for Major Dean. I do apologize, Ms. Miller. Our client here, well, he should be let go. Or charged." The smile Nathan flashed was all teeth and dare.

Malloy lumbered in, dropping his bulk into a chair next to the prosecutor. "I have a victim willing to press charges."

Nathan tsked his tongue. "You have a spurned lover who was pissed off my client saved the girl while Marsh ended up on his ass." He cleared his throat. "Begging your pardon, ma'am."

Green eyes flashed. "I know what an 'ass' is, Mr. Jones." Her tone made it perfectly clear she considered him one. She cleared her throat. "I assume the woman is willing to testify?"

Nathan sat forward. "She's willing to testify Tom pulled a gun on Shane, who just defended himself. Then she went willingly with him."

Cynthia narrowed her gaze on Shane. "Major?"

He cleared his throat. "The two men I took out meant harm. I didn't kill them and merely trussed them up for the police." He pinned Malloy with a hard glare. "Marsh pulled out a gun. Josie was too close to the barrel; I thought she might get hurt. I disarmed him, he struggled, and I knocked him out for a brief time. No damage, not even a bruise."

Cynthia sighed. "There's no case here, Detective." She stood and glanced at an antique watch around a rather delicate wrist. "Let him go."

"But—" Malloy pushed back from the table, his chair scraping across the hard concrete.

"But nothing." She opened the door. "You want to take a decorated marine to trial for saving his wife from two attackers and a spurned boyfriend with a gun. If something else comes up, charge him. Right now, there's nothing here to take to trial. Let him go."

Malloy stood, his gaze hard on Shane. "Looks like you lucked out again, Dean." He tapped files against his hand. "Leave town. For once, be a decent guy and let that little girl go. She's better off without you." His jaw hardened.

Shane straightened his shoulders and stood. "I'm never letting her go, Malloy." He pivoted and followed his brother from the room.

CHAPTER
17

JOSIE FOUGHT THE urge to thump her head against her desk. Now she had to convince three larger-than-life jackasses she needed to go to work. There was suddenly way too much testosterone in her life.

The good news was that since Shane had been freed, he could openly bring her to work. No more hiding. Which was good because she disliked lying to her coworkers. But it was bad, because the man sat sprawled in her guest chair, gray eyes focused solely on her.

"Shane. You need to leave so I can get some work done." Either that, or toss his sexy ass on the desk and have her way with him. Again.

He steepled his fingers under his chin. "So. You and Mattie had quite the discussion, I take it?"

Heat filled her face. "I had some questions." She leaned forward, her elbows on the desk. "Are you remembering your life?"

"Yes." His eyes betrayed nothing. "There are many blanks, but the holes are filling in—though my brothers have some explaining to do."

The veiled expression was one she knew well. Apparently

the real Shane was returning . . . the one who couldn't trust her with reality or with the truth. She bit back a hurt sigh. "They haven't explained everything?"

"Not yet. We're all scrambling right now, but I plan to pin them down soon."

She nodded. "Don't you have a follow-up visit scheduled with the doctors?"

"No." He stretched his long legs out and crossed them at the ankles. "What did you talk about with Matt?"

"I asked him if you loved me and why you left." She had no doubt Matt had already given Shane the rundown. She had absolutely no reason to lie.

"I told you I loved you."

"You told me a lot of things."

He exhaled, giving a short nod of his head. "That I did."

"Matt also said you were a bad bet, that all of you were bad bets." He'd said the statement with sadness and a determined jaw.

"We are." Shane stretched his hand, curling the fingers over. "But that doesn't mean you're not rolling the dice, angel."

"Excuse me?"

"This time, I'm not letting you go." His voice remained steady and sure, while his jaw tightened.

Her heart thumped hard against her rib cage. "Why did you leave me, then? Why did you lie about remaining in the marines?"

He sighed. "I'm not sure. But I will find out the truth, I promise."

Hurt filtered through her skin until her heart ached. "Why couldn't you trust me? Why couldn't you just tell me?"

"I do trust you, and I will tell you as soon as the memories come back." Determination flashed in those dangerous eyes. Rough cedar and male scented the space. He sighed. "You're about to become pissed off at me, and before you do, I'd like you to understand I do love you. Have since the second you flashed those baby blues at me."

Oh, this so didn't sound good. "I already am pissed off at you." She flipped closed the file she'd been pretending to work on. "What do you have to say?"

He cleared his throat. "I want you to quit your job and move to our, ah, headquarters. Where I can keep you safe."

"Where is your headquarters?"

"I can't tell you."

Disbelief had her catching her breath. "You don't even trust me enough to explain what's going on, and you want me to pack up and move with you to someplace you won't reveal?" Anger battled with a temptation she'd never admit out loud. He wanted her with him. How easy would it be to kick reality out of the way and go? "I want to try and trust you, Shane, I really do." She gripped a pen so tight her knuckles turned white. "But I don't know you. You won't let me." No way was she giving up this life she'd worked so hard to create the last two years. Not without knowing everything.

"You know what you need to know." He dropped his elbows to his knees, leaning forward. "You're everything to me, and I'll keep you safe. I promise."

He didn't understand. "I don't want safety."

A puzzled frown settled between his eyes. "Sure you do. A woman like you, you need safety. I can provide that now." He rubbed his chin. "Or I'll be able to soon."

"A woman like me?" Who the hell did he think he married? Sure, she wanted to be safe, but she was no frightened victim.

"Yes. Soft, smart, sexy." He licked his lips. "Fragile."

Fragile? Not in this lifetime. Where did this distorted perception of women come from? "What was your mother like, Shane?"

He started. "Ah, I'm pretty sure I didn't have one."

"Like you didn't have brothers? Or you honestly didn't have one?" He could evade with the best of them.

He grimaced. "No. I kind of remember wanting a mother but not getting one."

"Father?"

"Don't think so."

So that much might be true. He was an orphan like her. "You know your brothers. Who would take in four boys?"

Shane shook his head. "That's a tale I'm not ready to tell today." He placed both palms on her desk. "I will, I promise. Once you're somewhere safe and I can remember everything." He frowned. "Some of my past is still so hazy."

His memories were returning. When they did, he might leave again. "Do you remember why you left me?" Fire rippled through her blood.

A matching fire flashed through his eyes. "I'm sorry. I know Jory died around that time. Maybe I left because I didn't want anything to happen to you. Matt said I went undercover to find out what happened to Jory."

So many questions. "How did Jory die?"

He stretched his neck, exhaling loudly. "We're still figuring that one out, angel. I went undercover for two years to find out. Unfortunately, the memories of the last two years haven't come back."

"Do you think you found out who killed him?"

"I assume so, considering someone's after me. Someone has learned enough about me to bug your house." He stood and leaned closer, his palms still on the desk. "Matt and I are meeting later to go over the files and try to make sense of the whole situation. Apparently I went so deep I couldn't make contact, and he doesn't know much more than I do." Shane leaned even closer. "But obviously they discovered you, so keeping away is no longer necessary. You're in danger from whoever is hunting me, and I have a feeling they'd use you to get to me in a heartbeat. I'll do what's necessary to keep you safe."

What about her heart? He wouldn't keep that safe. He towered over her. Even with the desk between them, he exuded deadly promise. She shivered. "I refuse to make a decision concerning the rest of my life without all the facts." She was a CPA for goodness' sake. What else could he expect?

"I understand, and I will tell you everything." He straightened, sliding his hands into the pockets of well-worn jeans. "However, you'll get to safety first. Like it or not."

Fury set up a ringing in her skull. "You try to take me again, and I will press charges for kidnapping." She jumped to her feet, slapping her hands on her desk and leaning toward him. "I wonder how well you can bother me from a jail cell."

His upper lip quirked. "You are so cute when you're threatening me."

The anger zipped through her until she feared her head would explode. "Don't you dare get condescending with me. I took one jerk to the ground with a well-aimed kick yesterday, I have no problem doing it again."

Both eyebrows angled up. "Were you in danger? Who exactly did you need to kick?" Tension tore through the air.

She cleared her throat, ignoring the ripple of unease filtering through her skin. No way should she back down. Detective Malloy had already taken Shane away when she knocked Tom's balls to the roof of his mouth. "I'm not prepared to discuss that with you." See how he liked not having the proper clearance for the truth.

He lowered his chin, his eyelids at half-mast. "You want to play games with me, angel?"

Talk about intimidating. She straightened her posture. "Bring it on, Major."

"Not wise, little one." The smile revealed both a dimple and odd light in his eyes. "I know rules for games you've never heard of. I promise."

A delicious shiver ran up her back. Only pride kept her in place. "Do you? Interesting." Something had happened in the two years they'd been separated. Or while his memory had fled. Shane was different. He was finally revealing parts of himself. She'd wanted so badly to know him. All of him. "Where in the world did you learn such games?"

"Oh, baby," he breathed out. "Some of the thoughts scattering through my head would scare you spitless." He shook his head, regret twisting his lips. "You don't want to challenge me, Josie. You won't win."

Wouldn't she? The temptation to see where he'd go flirted with her. The sense of danger softened her sex. "What thoughts scatter through your head?"

"No." He moistened his lips, and she fought a groan. Then he flipped open his phone, reading the screen. "We'll finish this discussion later, sweetheart."

Why did that sound like a threat? "Think so?"

His phone snapped shut, his gaze pinning hers. "I guarantee it." Two strides had him at the door, where he halted as he ran into Vicki. The woman stared up at him, her red-painted mouth open. Shane stepped back.

Josie fought a snort. "Shane, this is my assistant, Vicki."

Vicki stuck out her hand, her eyelashes fluttering rapidly. "You must be the husband."

"Yes." Shane briefly shook hands, sidling around Vicki toward the door, giving the woman a wide berth. Once safely out of reach, he faced Josie over Vicki's head. "Stay in your building until I get back. I'll give you the rest of the week to wrap things up here. Then we leave." He strode away before she could answer.

Josie dropped back into her chair. Her hands trembled. What that man did to her.

Vicki fanned her well-endowed chest. "That man is seriously hot."

Josie snorted. "That's an understatement." She pushed back from the desk. "What's going on?"

"Tom Marsh called." Vicki rolled her eyes. "I don't blame you for ignoring him with the sexy-as-sin husband back in the picture."

"Thanks, Vicki." Josie bit her lip. "I'll take care of Tom."

Vicki nodded and headed back down the hall, smacking her gum on the way.

Josie straightened the papers on her desk, guilt swirling in her abdomen. Tom was a good friend and had been since she arrived in town. While he was wrong to turn Shane in, he did it to protect her. To help her.

She glanced at her watch. Maybe she'd run down to the

cafeteria on the first floor and grab cappuccinos for them both as a sort of apology. Escaping her office, even for just a coffee, was so appealing. She'd stay in the building so Shane wouldn't be upset, but she needed some caffeine, as well as a chance to make things right with Tom.

She stretched her calves on the way to the elevator. It'd been way too long since she'd gone for a jog. Something she and Shane had done together during their brief marriage. She'd loved running with him.

Her punch card took care of the coffee on the first floor, and she took another elevator up. Would Tom be angry? She had really clocked him.

Tom's floor consisted of several smaller businesses, all sharing space. The tray balanced easily in her hands as she smiled at the receptionist the floor shared. The young brunette said something into a phone and looked up with a smile. "Tom said to go on back."

Well, at least he'd see her. Josie nodded, walking down the minimally decorated hallway, past closed doorways, to Tom's small office. She entered without knocking. "I brought you coffee." Careful movements and she placed one cup in front of Tom, taking the other for herself as well as a seat.

Tom sat behind his scarred desk, flannel sleeves rolled to showcase muscular forearms. Building plans perched against a far wall, and a set of ancient tools decorated the side wall. "Is this an apology?" His brown hair was mussed, as if he'd been running his hands through it. An array of papers spread across his desk, all bidding contracts.

Josie fought a blush, concentrating on her friend and not the spectacular view of the mountains outside the small window. "Yes. I'm sorry I kneed you. Though you were wrong to turn Shane in to the police."

A smile played on Tom's lips. "Even so, you didn't need to turn me into a eunuch."

She cleared her throat. "Ah, well, are you all right?" She so didn't want to have a discussion about his balls. Not that he wasn't hot, because good-looking was an understatement. But her heart lay elsewhere.

"I'm fine. It was a good move—one I hope my sisters know to use if anybody ever threatens them." He took a drink of the coffee. His throat moved when he swallowed, a masculine movement in a fit man.

Relief filled her. She didn't have many friends and certainly hadn't wanted to lose him. "I'm sorry. I really am."

Tom placed his cup on the desk. "Is there anything I can do to help you?"

"No." She took another sip. "I'll figure out my path. I will." Wouldn't she?

He shook his head. "I hope so." He sat back and she was struck again by the perfect evenness of his features. Straight nose, high cheekbones, full lips.

"You're a good-looking man, Tom."

He rolled his deep brown eyes. "Thanks." A line of numbers scrolling across his screen caught his attention. He turned back to her. "Any news on who trashed your offices?"

"No."

"That's so weird." The screen caught his eye again before he focused back on her. "They had to be looking for something. What do you think they wanted?"

"No clue. Possibly financial information on random big clients. Who knows." The numbers flashed yellow. "What's keeping your attention?"

Tom shrugged. "The county is granting bids on three projects, and all the subcontracting awards are going through."

"I hope you get a couple." The man had a job to do, and she was distracting him, so she stood. "Anyway, thanks for being so understanding about the entire situation. I appreciate your friendship."

He leaned back, dark eyes appraising and making him look older. "I want more."

She opened her mouth to speak, but nothing came out. So she cleared her throat. "I know—"

"No, I don't think you do." The numbers flashed by on the screen, but this time Tom ignored them. "I'm not going to let you ruin your life."

She stepped back. "I, uh, I'm not ruining my life."

"No. You're not." Determination lifted his jaw.

Irritation swirled through her. Enough with overbearing men. "I haven't promised you anything."

"Haven't you?" He tilted his head to the side. "That's debatable. Regardless, I will figure out what's going on with your soon-to-be ex-husband. He's not the only one with contacts in the police department."

That couldn't be good. Shane needed to keep a low profile, as did his brothers. "I'd appreciate it if you let me handle it."

Tom turned back to the screen. "Thanks for the coffee."

As dismissals went, it was a good one. Turning on her heel, she headed directly to the elevator. How could Tom think she'd promised him anything? Guilt had her flushing. She had discussed the divorce with him.

Her mind swirled as she stepped into the crowded elevator. Great. It would take forever to get back to her floor, and she had work to do. After several slow stops, most people had disembarked. She eyed her watch. Only she and one person remained, and he'd get off first.

The door opened on the ninth floor. A broad hand

between her shoulder blades shoved her out of the elevator. "Hey," she protested, flipping around.

The man crowded her away from the lift. The doors slid shut.

Silence.

Josie turned around. The entire ninth floor of the high-rise building was being renovated for a legal firm to take over at the end of the year. In fact, Tom had bid on the job. Sawdust littered the floor, while tools remained scattered about.

She pivoted and took a step back, her gaze flashing to the man who'd shoved her. Just under six feet, broad across the shoulders, he had a nose that sported several old breaks. "Um..."

"Mrs. Dean, I suggest you cooperate with me." Raspy and tough, his voice promised pain.

Panic heated the air in her lungs. The guy knew her name. Memories of Shane teaching her self-defense moves ran through her brain in rapid succession. She'd go for the balls again. "What do you want?"

The man's gaze slid down to her toes and back up.

Fear caught in her throat.

He sighed, shrugging his shoulders. "Unfortunately, not what you think. This time, anyway." His hand snaked out and manacled around her arm before he dragged her toward a room partially framed in. "Please have a seat." While the words remained polite, the shove he gave her onto the folding chair held barely controlled violence.

She hit the metal hard, struggling to stay in place. "Wha-what do you want?" She straightened her pin-striped skirt over her knees, searching for a plan.

He crouched in front of her, hands going to her knees. "Here's the deal, blue eyes. We're going to wait here until closing time, and then go up and grab a few of your firm's files."

Awareness filtered through the buzzing of fear in her brain. "You ransacked my office."

He tightened his hold on her knees. "Wasn't me. My boss ransacked the entire floor looking for the files he needed."

She yanked her legs to the side, dislodging his beefy hands and trying to focus past the fear. "What files did he need?"

The guy's grin revealed a large gap between his front teeth. "Oh, we'll find them when we go up later, don't you worry."

"I don't understand. What's going on?" Would Shane be looking for her yet? Though why would he check on the empty ninth floor?

The man stood, reaching for a power saw. "If I were you, I wouldn't ask too many questions, Mrs. Dean. People with too many answers end up dead."

A death threat. Silence echoed around the floor. It wasn't quitting time, so either the guy had enough power to send the construction crew home for the day, or he knew their schedule. Was it her files or Daniel's they wanted? Though, once the guy got the files, would he kill her? Maybe she could keep him talking. "Tell me what files, and maybe I can give you the information now."

"No." He slapped the blade against his palm, licking his lips as his gaze wandered over her legs. "Though you can call me George."

The guy was probably a killer. Her heart beat hard enough to bruise her ribs. Could she get the saw from him? If the tool was plugged in, she could inflict some serious damage. Did she stand a chance? "Is that your name?"

"Sure." He twisted his wrist to glance at a battered sports watch. "We have about two hours to spend together." He smiled again. "Then we'll get my files, and you can go on your merry way."

He had to be lying. If that was his real name, he had no intention of letting her go. She forced her foster home smile to her face, her breath heating. "Sounds good to me. Is your boss a client of mine?"

He shrugged. "I don't think so."

If she could keep him talking, maybe she could distract him somehow. Was Dan's habit of keeping all his files on a flash drive with him the problem here? "Is he a client of Daniel Mission's?"

"No. He just wants *your* records—nobody else's. So shut up and wait the time out."

The boss wanted her files—not Daniel's. Probably the files she'd taken home that night. Four accounts, four clients. Had Billy been involved in something illegal? If so, what? "Why take the laptops?"

"We pawned them in the next state. After wiping them down."

Relief echoed in the back of her mind. Behind the terror. Growing up in foster care, she was always on the outside, and rarely trusted. Now, she knew secrets, and she was actually trusted. That mattered. Her clients' sensitive information was safe, and she could be pleased.

"After we made copies of everything, of course." George snorted. "My boss has a buddy who can figure out that kind of stuff. Maybe we'll make some extra money on the side." One bushy black eyebrow wriggled. "I don't suppose you teach people how to hide stuff from the IRS?"

"No. I teach them how to take legal deductions so they

don't end up in jail." She lifted her chin. "You been to jail, George?"

Creases cut deep alongside his mouth as he frowned. "I served a dime." He leaned toward her, the smell of old tacos wafting from him. "I'll kill before I go back, Mrs. Dean. You might want to remember that fact."

Her knees wobbled. "Apparently you haven't let go of your life of crime."

He wrinkled his mouth, biting his lip. "True. Sometimes you get into a life, and there's no getting free. You are who you are." He gestured with the saw as he spoke.

Killing was a philosophy to the guy. Panic heated her lungs—she had to get out of there before he killed her. Large bolt cutters perched on a sawhorse to her left. A power drill lay on the floor ahead of her. George held the saw. She toed off her three-inch heels as he admired the power saw in his hands. Was he imagining using the jagged blade on her? She shivered. Her thigh muscles bunched as she calculated the best way to take him down. Nothing seemed good.

But it was now or never. Steeling her spine, she tried to focus her energy. Then she leaped forward and grabbed the bolt cutters, swinging toward George.

He jumped back, out of the way.

The metal weighed heavily in her hands. The end of the tool thunked against the floor as gravity took over. She panted out a breath.

George shook his head. "Now I have to teach you a lesson. I really didn't want to have to hurt you." His smile hinted he was lying. "Put down the cutters, Mrs. Dean."

"Not a chance, asshole." Panic hazed her vision. The man was going to kill her. Her mind spun, and she eyed the elevator.

"Okay." He jumped toward her, saw in hand.

She yelped and swung again with the heavy tool, missing once again. But as George took another running step, his feet tangled in the power saw's cord. He went down. The floor rumbled in protest.

Crying out, Josie swung the cutters at his head.

Crack.

Blood arced across the rough floor.

"Bitch." Blood poured down his temple. He yanked the cutters out of her hand, throwing them across the floor. "I'm going to kill you." He reached down to untangle his legs.

Run. Josie dodged to the side and ran.

Oh God.

CHAPTER
18

H ER STOCKINGS SNAGGED on the subfloor as Josie ran for the elevator. Slivers cut into her feet. Sobbing, she punched the up and down buttons.

Behind her, something crashed against the wall. George had thrown the saw.

"Hurry, hurry, hurry," Josie chanted, pushing the buttons. The blood rushed through her ears. Her knees trembled. She glanced toward the makeshift office. George teetered to his feet with a roar, stumbling toward her.

No time. She pivoted and ran toward the far wall. Toward the stairwell. Her feet slipped on new marble tiles. With a cry, she yanked open the door and ran inside.

Shit. She wasn't in the stairwell. The room was a large closet, probably a janitor's storage area. A stinky room. Rows of metal shelves stood next to the door, awaiting some sort of order.

Footsteps pounded closer. Reason fled, and she panted out fear. Survival was all that mattered. She slammed the door shut, engaging the lock. Would George have a key?

Someone had left the light on, thank goodness. She leaped forward and yanked a shelving unit down in front of the door. Then another. Stacks of marble tile rested against the far wall. Her fingers shaking, she grabbed several tiles and piled them between the downed shelves. Her nails split. The rough edges of the tiles cut into the pads of her fingers.

George pounded on the door. "You little bitch. I'm going to kill you."

She bit back a sob and kept piling tiles. Back and forth. Tiles. Until they were all between the shelves, keeping the door shut. Even if he had a key and could unlock the door, no way could he push it open.

Panting now, she backed away from the door. What now? How could she get a message to Shane?

Josie sniffed, tears burning her eyes.

George continued to pound.

She scanned the room frenziedly for a weapon. Near the tiles. A box cutter. She leaped for the large razor blade, holding the tool in front of her toward the door. Her hands shook. Blood from her tile-mangled fingers dripped to the floor.

George continued to pound.

He didn't have a key. She needed to focus.

What stank? Did new tile smell like rotten tomatoes? She eyed the small room. Stacks of wooden flooring piled up at the far wall. She edged toward them. Was there a dead rat in the corner?

Holding her nose, she skirted the edge of the wood and glanced behind the stack.

She screamed. Billy lay on his back, his eyes wide and unseeing at the ceiling, a hole in the center of his head. His hands were tied in front of him, his wrists rubbed raw.

Dead.

Coughing, Josie forced bile down. Her mind sheeted white, and she stumbled back. Why wasn't he in rehab?

She shook her head. Focus. She needed to focus. They'd killed Billy.

Silence descended outside the stifling room.

She slowly turned around, her heart pounding. She glanced up. Where was a vent? Way up, in the wall. No way could she reach so high.

Her mind scrambled.

Something hit the outside wall. Hard. She yelped, jumping back. Toward Billy.

"That's right, little girl. I'm coming," George bellowed. Something slammed into the wall again, and dust flew.

He was going to tear down the wall. Maybe he'd hit electrical wires and fry himself. Was that even possible?

She needed to think. Think, damn it.

Her fingers hurt. Breath heaved in and out of her lungs. She eyed Billy.

A large thump echoed, and Sheetrock dust flew toward her. Panic had her gasping. George would be inside soon. Why hadn't she spent two years learning karate instead of yoga?

She slid the razor closed and put the tool in her pocket. With a gulp of a swallow, Josie fell to her knees, reaching for Billy's pockets. Hopefully he had a weapon.

Nothing in his front pockets.

Closing her eyes, breathing through her nose, she yanked him to the side to check his back pockets.

A phone!

She grabbed the cell, punching in numbers to her office with slippery fingers. Hopefully Shane was there. If not, Vicki would pick up. Billy fell back with an inanimate thud.

"What?" Shane growled in answer.

"Shane!" Josie hissed, forcing herself to lower her voice.

"Josie. Where the hell are you? Whose number is this? I'm in your office—"

"Listen. I'm on the ninth floor in a maintenance room. Billy's dead. George is going to kill me—"

The head of a sledgehammer plowed through the Sheetrock near the door. Josie screamed and jumped back, stumbling over Billy's body and falling to the floor. Her butt bounced against the tiles, causing fresh bruises. The phone flew out of her bloody hand, skipping across the room.

Eww. She kicked against Billy's legs, scrambling to get away from the dead body. Hand over bloody handprint, she crawled up the wall to stand on shaking legs.

She grabbed the box cutter out of her pocket, shakily working to slide the blade out. Her bloody fingers slipped, her nerves screamed in pain. Holding the tool with both hands, she finally pushed hard enough to expose the blade.

George broke the hole in the wall wider, pounding either side of the opening and sending chunks of Sheetrock dust flying. He poked one thick boot through the bottom, kicking drywall toward her. Both beefy hands pulled at the broken wall to open a man-sized hole.

He stepped inside, blood pouring down his face, his brown eyes wide and crazed.

Chills ripped down her back. She lifted the inch-long blade toward him. "I called for help." Her voice trembled more than her hands. "You should run. Now."

He grimaced, his gaze on her meager weapon. "You didn't call nobody."

She shoved fear to the back of her mind. Think. Focus. Shane's words from so long ago came flying back. *Accept you're being attacked, breathe, and face reality.* Her stance settled.

George leaped forward, both hands grabbing her wrist and swinging her toward the wall. Her knuckles crashed into hard Sheetrock, and she cried out, the blade clattering to the floor. Her foot shot out to kick. George reared back and punched her in the jaw.

Pain ripped through her face. Josie went down.

He grabbed her by the hair, dragging her through the hole and out of the closet. Agony scorched along her scalp.

Bunching her fist, she plowed it into the back of his knee. He yelled, loosening his hold and turning toward her. Scrambling for her feet, she jabbed him in the groin on her way up.

Somebody yanked him away. He released her, bellowing in protest.

Josie dropped to the floor, her vision blurred, her ears ringing.

"Angel," Shane breathed, gathering her into a seated position. He lifted her chin. "Where are you hurt, sweetheart?" Concern and fury comingled in his eyes.

Josie shivered. "My hands." Her entire body began to shake. "My jaw." Where did George go? She glanced around in terror.

The breath caught in her stomach. Matt held George in a headlock, a wicked double-edged knife at her kidnapper's throat. George's eyes had gone wide, his body slack. Nathan stood to Matt's side, a gun in his hand. They'd come for her.

Like a real family would.

Shane eyed her jaw, and his snapped shut. Swiveling to full height, he shot a punch to George's face. A loud crack split the air. George went limp, and Matt let him fall to the ground. Shane instantly stomped on George's hand. The sickening sound of knuckles breaking destroyed the silence. He moved for the other fingers.

"Wait." Matt held up a hand.

Shane circled George like an eagle hungry to strike. "No. He hit her."

"I know." Nathan stepped between Shane and George, ignoring his brother's warning growl. "We need answers, Shane." He glanced at Josie, his gaze softening. "How badly are you hurt, sweetheart?"

She pushed to her feet. "I'm not. I'm fine." Her jaw was on fire, and speaking forced tears to her eyes. She batted them back.

Nathan's upper lip quirked. "Good on you." He raised an eyebrow. "Why did he take you? Does he know about Shane?"

Josie frowned, rubbing her smarting fingertips together. Blood smeared. "No. His boss is the one who trashed our offices because they want some of my records."

Shane frowned. "Which records?"

Josie shrugged, trying to catch her breath. "George wouldn't say. It had to be in one of the four files I took home the other night. Those are the only files they couldn't get at the office."

George groaned, rolling to the side.

Shane reached for her wrists and turned her palms over. "What the hell happened to your hands?"

"I grabbed the tiles to block the door." She bit her lip against tears. Now that the danger had passed, fear clutched her around the throat. No crying. She would not cry.

"Smart girl," Shane murmured, his hands warm under hers. "You go with Mattie, angel. We'll be along shortly." He pushed her gently toward Matt, who put a reassuring arm around her shoulder.

"Oh but—" Reality crashed back. "Billy's dead. I mean, his body is in the storage room." Poor Billy.

Nathan raised an eyebrow and hustled through the hole in the wall, plunging back out after a couple moments. "Thirty-five to the head. Point-blank."

Her knees quivered. George would definitely have killed her. "All four of the accounts I brought home with me were Billy's clients first." They were good clients. What did George hope to gain by obtaining their financial information? Or was he trying to cover up Billy's mistakes? Had he stolen from the companies? If so, for whom?

Shane's face turned to stone. "Well, then. We need to find out what this guy was looking for, don't we?" Anticipation and deadly promise whispered through his deep tone. "Matt, please take my wife out of here. We'll meet you shortly."

Josie shivered. "No, Shane. I think we should call the police."

The smile he flashed was one she'd never seen. Hard and dark. "We will. After I get the answers I need." He nodded at Matt. "The police have seen both Nathan and me—let's keep you out of this. Take her out of here."

"I can figure it out from the paperwork—we don't need this guy." She struggled against Matt.

Shane shook his head. "No—we need the answers now."

She faltered. "But, I mean, what if he won't tell you?" Shane wouldn't really kill George, would he?

Shane dropped the smile, sadness curling his lip. "He will. I promise."

Matt tugged her toward the elevator, gently, but not giving an inch.

Josie stumbled, glancing back at her husband. "Do you know how to do this, Shane? I mean, interrogation."

His eyes turned slate hard. "I know how to do this, angel."

She faltered, pushing away from Matt.

Shane shifted his gaze to the man writhing on the floor. "Now, Matt."

Without a word, Matt swung her up in muscular arms. The scent of man and spice surrounded her. She began to struggle even as he stalked to the far corner, his boots thumping on the tile. Her elbow shot tentatively into his gut, and she squirmed in his arms.

Matt tightened his hold and lowered his head. "Stop it. You'll upset Shane if he thinks I'm hurting you." He opened a door, stepping into a wide stairwell.

Frustration welled up. How could Shane just let his brother carry her off? Matt was seriously strong, and she couldn't get free. "Let me go."

"No."

"Stop, Matt. Shane's going to kill George."

Matt shrugged. "I wouldn't care if Shane killed the asshole who attacked you, sweetheart. But Shane told you he wouldn't kill George. So he won't." Matt loped down flights of stairs until he kicked open an outside door. Wind whipped hard rain into them, and Matt hunched his body over her, giving shelter. Quick strides had them at her car, where he buckled her in before jumping into the driver's seat and maneuvering out of the parking lot.

Matt drove quickly through town, taking an unfamiliar exit off the interstate. Businesses and then homes passed by until trees and fields filled the view. The rain slashed against the window of her Toyota, and Josie burrowed farther down in the passenger seat. "We shouldn't have left Shane to torture that guy."

Matt's jaw tightened. "Shane will be fine."

Then why was tension suddenly filling the cab? Josie sighed. Matt wouldn't turn back, and there was no way she could help Shane right now. But her clients were another matter. "I should've gone back to my office and gotten those files."

He kept his gaze on the narrow road, his large hands relaxed on the steering wheel. "Your face is pretty banged up. It's Friday—surely you take off early on Friday sometimes."

The Hercules hadn't given her a choice. Just hustled her out of the building. "Why don't you like me?"

His head jerked. Muscles in his large chest shifted as he exhaled. "I do like you."

"Do not."

A dimple flashed in his cheek. Just like Shane's. "Sure I do." Matt's gaze focused on her aching jaw, and he gritted his own, turning back to the road. "Enough to know you don't belong in our world. You're too—"

"Soft." She sighed it. "All three of you have used that term." It didn't make any sense. "Maybe you're all wrong. Whatever shaped you, whatever you think about women...maybe you're all wrong." Fog filled the windows, so she reached forward and flipped on the defrost. "I can be pretty tough."

"I know." He nodded. "There's no doubt you're a tough little thing."

Why did that not sound like he was agreeing? "You don't know anything about me."

Matt had a deep chuckle. "I know everything about you."

"Is that so? Like what?"

He inhaled. "I've read your records, sweetheart. Your hospital reports, your school reports, all the social worker reports. Your school transcripts, any e-mail you've ever sent. The court documents when Arthur and Claire Bomont began adoption proceedings."

What? He'd investigated her? "The adoption proceedings didn't go through."

Matt eyed the rearview mirror, his shoulders relaxing as he took another turn. "I know. Claire died, and it took Arthur almost six more months to press forward."

Surprise had Josie's hands clutching together. "Six more months? What do you mean he pressed forward?"

Matt flashed her a glance, eyebrows raised. "Ah. Well, he tried to continue adopting you. Wrote letters, even wrote the governor to help. But the officials wouldn't let a widower, a single man, keep you."

Warmth, surprise, sadness all flushed through Josie that Arthur had still wanted to keep her, that he'd made an effort to get her back. "I thought he forgot me." Maybe she should look him up—he was the closest thing she had to a father.

"No. He wanted you, sweetheart." Matt rubbed his chin, one hand casual on the steering wheel. "Arthur remarried about a decade ago. The woman had three kids, and he seems to have made a good life. I have his contact information if you want it."

"Maybe." She needed to think about it and get her life in order first. "So you know all about my childhood. Shane has memories of you as boys at some camp. A military camp."

Matt's knuckles tightened on the wheel. "Yeah. We attended military camp." He increased the speed of the windshield wipers with a flick of his wrist. "What did Shane tell you?"

"Everything." Could she get information out of Shane's big brother?

"Ah." Matt turned on the lights as the forest sped by around them. They were heading into nowhere land. "I see."

Okay. So he wasn't going to bite and reveal everything. "Where are we going?"

Matt shrugged. "We rented a cabin for the duration. It's safe and we can keep an eye on who approaches it."

"I think I'd rather go to my house." Enough hiding. "I mean, this whole thing was about me and not Shane, right?" She'd been thinking about it. Apparently Billy had done something or known something that had gotten him killed. Taking another look at those accounting records was a good idea. "My house was bugged because of a client, not Shane's past."

"It's starting to look that way." Matt turned onto a barely visible dirt road. "Any idea which client? Or why?"

"Maybe. The numbers for a few of the accounts weren't adding up, but I haven't figured out where the money has gone. I need to look again."

"You think someone was skimming? Or laundering money?"

"I don't know." The words clicked out before she could weigh the question. "I guess it's possible Billy was stealing to support his drug habit." And she should check the other twenty accounts she'd taken over from Billy. Chances were he'd done a good job of hiding the theft but had probably also goofed up on the other files. Negligence and malfeasance from the drug addict. The Toyota bounced along rough potholes. "We're in the middle of nowhere."

"That's the idea."

Should she be afraid? For some reason, Matt exuded safety and comfort. "You know, I'm still married to Shane."

"I know."

"That makes you my brother."

Matt stiffened. His eyes closed briefly, and he lifted his head to reopen them. "Yes. I guess it does."

Ah, so much like Shane. The need to protect was ingrained. "I always wanted a brother." She ignored Matt's loud exhale. "Alone in the foster homes, sometimes scared, always lonely. I prayed so hard for brothers." It was the truth. So many times she'd hoped a brother would show up to protect her. Love her. Just be hers.

"You're killing me." Matt's voice dropped to a rumble that sounded just like Shane.

"I know," she whispered. The second they'd all shown up when she needed help had cinched it for her. She wanted a family—no matter how damaged it might be. "But I'm not letting him go this time. You might as well get on board now." Realizing the truth, admitting it out loud, filled her with determination. "I've wanted a family my entire life. Now I've got one." Whoever they were, whatever they'd done, they were hers. Right or wrong, she was keeping them. "That includes you, Matt."

The sound he gave may have been a groan. A strangled groan. "You don't know what you're saying."

"Of course I do. The danger is over. We know one of my clients bugged my house. This isn't about Shane. He's safe."

"Ah, darlin'. Shane will never be safe. And if he alerted us to his presence, he alerted the—"

"The?"

Matt cleared his throat. "Jesus. You're good." He took a turn between two large blue spruce trees onto a weed-riddled path. The Toyota jerked and dipped along the uneven road. "You need to understand we have enemies, and now they probably know exactly where Shane is."

"You could get him to safety."

Matt nodded. "Yes. I will get him to safety—whether he likes it or not."

Relief had Josie's shoulders relaxing. "Thanks. Now tell me about the military camp you all went to as kids. It sounds bad."

"No." Matt squinted into the pelting rain.

"Okay. Tell me about you. What do you do?"

"Um, I'm a U.S. Marshal."

Now that made no sense. Otherwise he would've called the cops and not let Shane torture George for information. "No, you're not."

Matt flashed a grin. "Yeah, I am. For now, anyway."

"Why?" She actually felt like a pestering younger sister. Warmth filtered through her along with curiosity. "I'll bug you until you tell me."

He rolled his eyes. "I need to find somebody, and Marshals find people."

"Who are you trying to find?"

"A woman who has answers I need." His jaw hardened.

"It sounds like you don't like her much." Josie shivered. Having Matt as an enemy would be downright terrifying.

"No. Let's just say she's not a softie like you."

Frustration ripped through her nerves. "Tell me something. What the hell is up with you guys and soft women? I mean, what makes you think most of us can't face this world?"

"Ah, Josie. There are parts of this world you can't even imagine. I wouldn't want you to." He shook his head. "More importantly, I wouldn't want someone to hurt you to get to Shane. There are people out there who would be overjoyed to harm you."

So much responsibility and determination in the set of Matt's shoulders. "You're the oldest, aren't you?"

"Yes."

"Responsible for everybody?"

"Yes."

"That's quite the burden, Matt. Three brothers to be responsible for."

He pulled abreast a large log cabin, switching off the ignition and turning to face her. "Two brothers these days. And now one sister."

CHAPTER
19

SHANE SLIPPED OUT of the SUV, his gaze on the quiet cabin. Blood covered his clothing from his interrogation. Was Josie already asleep? "I just need to walk for a minute."

Nathan shut his door and tossed a flask at him. "Drink." Highlighted by the moon, he leaned against the Jeep's grill, arms crossed. Broad and dangerous, even leaning he didn't appear remotely relaxed.

Shane unscrewed the cap and took a hit of bourbon. The blend burned down to his gut.

"Now, talk." Nathan didn't move an inch from his position.

Shane shuffled his feet and threw back the flask. "You talk. I need to know about my past."

Nathan turned, pinning him with a dark gaze. "How's your gut? Your head? Your legs?"

His gut hurt, his head spun, and his legs felt wobbly. "Fine. Why?"

"I'll hit you if I have to, Shane. I'd rather not." Nathan tipped back his head and drank.

Shane jerked his head. "I feel sick." Now. But while

he'd been interrogating George, he'd been calm as a dead pond. "I knew just how to get answers from that bastard." Frankly, he'd scared the shit out of himself. Well, afterward. During, he hadn't felt a damn thing.

Nathan wiped off his bottom lip. "Our training is good."

"We're not normal." There was no way they were normal. God. The things he could do—the things he would do. He was a fucking abomination.

"Not even close."

"Tell me." Shane steeled himself for the blow.

"Take a shower, wipe off the blood, and then Matt and I will tell you everything." Nathan slid the flask into his boot. "You should spend time with your wife before you have to leave her again."

Heat roared through him. "I'm not. Not leaving her again."

"Yes, you are." Nate shook his head. "Our war is just starting, and she'll get killed. Then you won't be able to function at all."

Shane coughed. "So it was never meant to be permanent?"

Nate sighed, glanced down at his boots. "I think it was—I think you wanted to take a chance on forever."

"I still do," Shane said softly. But at what cost? Bad people were after him, and they'd probably go right through her to get to him. What about his brothers? "It's always been just the four of us, hasn't it?"

"Except for a short time, yeah." Nathan pushed away from the Jeep. "We fight for each other, we kill for each other, and we'd die for each other. Sometimes, that's all you get."

Shane lifted his head as his memories finally cleared. "If I lose her, I weaken and put you all in danger." They were each other's weak spots. Always had been.

"Yes."

"Is that why I let her go?" The thought of letting her go again made him want to punch the Jeep. Hard.

"No. You left to find out what happened to Jory." Nathan pivoted to stride toward the cabin. "We need to unlock your memories to find what you discovered."

"Nathan, I don't think I can let her go."

"You don't have a choice," his older brother said, not turning around.

Shane shut his eyes for a moment. His gut hurt worse than when he'd tortured George. Steeling his shoulders, he opened his eyes and followed his brother into the cabin.

The rain beat against the window of Josie's bedroom, and she snuggled down under the heavy comforter. She and Matt had quickly eaten sandwiches for dinner before spending several hours putting together an impressive array of computer and surveillance equipment. After Matt had carefully bandaged her wounded fingers, of course.

The sprawling cabin was luxurious rather than rustic and sported five bedrooms with attached baths as well as a large playroom. The pool table had beckoned her, but she decided to go to bed. Her jaw ached.

She heard a door somewhere in the house open and close. Male voices echoed. Shane and Nathan had arrived. They spoke for several moments with Matt before heavy footsteps sounded down the hall. Closer and closer. The door opened.

She sat up in bed. "Hi."

Shane shut the door, kicking off his boots. "Hi." He stalked into the bathroom. The shower surged on.

Unease wound through her. Why did he need a shower? She scrambled out of bed, hurrying to the bathroom. Sliding inside, she studied his clothes lying on the tightly woven bath mat. His black shirt appeared all right, but dark stains marred his faded jeans. Blood.

She pushed the door open farther, striding inside. Thick stone lined the large shower behind a glass door. Shane stood, his back to her, one hand against the tiles, his head lowered as the water beat against his neck. Steam rose. "Either get in with me, or get out."

No warmth, no kindness existed in his matter-of-fact tone. A quiver ran through her legs. She ignored her fear, stepping over his clothing. "Did you kill George?"

"No."

"Good. Did you call the police?"

"No." Shane didn't move.

They needed to call the cops. Someone had killed Billy, probably George. "I'll call them, then." She pivoted to go.

The glass door shot open, and two strong hands grabbed her biceps, pulling her against a wet chest. Shane dropped his head closer to her ear. "No cops."

She struggled, swinging around to face him. His rugged face appeared cut from granite, his eyes a hard, cold gray. "What did you do?" Her voice came out a croak. She tried to take a step back, but he kept her in place.

"What I had to do." No emotion, no expression rode his tone. No concern whatsoever for his nudity.

"Did you kill him?" She had to know. Was Shane a cold-blooded killer?

He sighed. "No. I didn't kill him." The pads of his fingers caressed her arms as he wandered down to her hands. "We let him go."

She frowned. "Bullshit." The stained clothes at her feet whispered another story. "There's blood on your clothes."

Shane's smile lacked warmth. "I didn't say he wasn't bleeding. He bled." Shane reached out and ran a gentle knuckle along her bruised jaw. "For this alone, he deserved to bleed."

A shiver shook her entire body. "I don't understand." Even through fear, desire awakened.

"I know." The shower sprayed behind Shane, sending steam to coat the mirror over the sink. "Torture isn't a distance game, sweetheart. It's close and personal—even intimate. Believe me. George told me everything he knew. So I let him go."

Nausea swirled in her stomach. Who was this man? She shook her head. "I don't believe you let George go. There's no reason you'd let him go."

Shane stepped even closer, his body almost touching hers. "I promised I wouldn't kill him, so I didn't. I let him go because he's seen Nathan. My so-called attorney. He also saw Mattie. If we called the cops, we'd have to explain. There'd be records, and right now we can't have that."

"What about Billy?"

"He'll be discovered."

"Who are you, Shane?" He stood before her. Naked, strong, and sure. She'd made the claim to Matt that she wanted to keep Shane. But could you keep someone you didn't know? Once again, she was on the outside looking in. Looking into an incredibly dark world. Shane's world.

"I'm the guy you married, angel. The guy you love." His lips took hers. Soft, seductive, so sexy. Teasing and tempting. The coldness fled, to be replaced by heat. He lifted his head, his eyes glittering with hunger.

She shook her head against temptation. Need trapped a groan in her throat. "But George killed Billy."

"No." Shane's gaze dropped to her throbbing lips. "He was as shocked as you by the dead body."

"He lied to you, Shane."

"He didn't lie. Believe me, he told me the truth." Dead certainty colored Shane's words. "Interrogation is one of my specialties, sweetheart."

Her hands went clammy. "So who killed Billy?"

"George was hired by a man named Max. My brothers are trying to find out who Max is right now. Max probably killed Billy, and I promise you, I'll find him."

"What file did George want?" Her mind had been spinning and she couldn't find an answer.

"He didn't know which file. George was supposed to call his boss once you two were in the office for more direction."

Darn it. There was no way she could figure out which file everyone wanted. Josie's head began to hurt. "I have to figure this out."

"I'll look into it."

"No. I will." Her brain began to click facts into order. "So George failed."

Shane's eyes narrowed. "George's job was to ride the elevator up and down all day, waiting for a chance to get to you. You gave him the opportunity." Shane's jaw tightened. "Next time I tell you to stay someplace, you damn well better do it."

"Or what?"

Shane jerked his head back, surprise flashing through his deep eyes. "Excuse me?"

"You're always telling me what to do, Shane. I'm tired of it." She jerked out of his hold. For better or worse, she'd made a vow to him. His world was dark, and maybe she could bring some light into it. Even a little.

"I'm tired of you thinking I'm too soft. That I can't handle myself."

"So you can handle yourself, can you?" A low warning threaded through his deep tone.

Pinpricks scattered along her skin. She sensed a trap hidden in the innocuous words. But she tilted her chin. "Yes. I can."

"Good." His smile could never be considered kind. "Let's see you handle yourself." He grabbed her arms, lifted her against him, and stepped into the shower.

"Hey—" she protested as she slid down his hard body and dampened her pajamas.

He pivoted and the pelting spray drenched her back.

Fire slammed into her abdomen. She struggled. "Damn it, Shane." He wanted to see her skills? Fine. Wounded fingers curled into a fist, which she shot toward his throat.

Shane dodged, allowing the blow to glance off the side of his neck. "Impressive." One arm wrapped around her bare waist while the other whipped off her top. Her breasts sprang free, her nipples already pebbling with need.

She struggled against both Shane and desire, punching him in the shoulder. Pain ricocheted up her arm.

Shane dropped her to her feet. "If you hurt yourself, I'm going to be seriously pissed off." He shoved her sopping pajama pants and panties down, lifting her with one arm and yanking them out of the way.

Oh, this should so not be turning her on. Her breath came faster. Her heart beat harder. Temper battled with need. Her body fought with her mind, with her stubborn will. "Who the hell do you think you are?" Maybe she should aim for his knee. The temptation to knock him on his ass, just once, narrowed her focus into sheer determination.

"Your husband." He jerked her to him, his body hard

against hers. Taking her mouth, his tongue shot past her lips, commanding a response.

A whimper lodged in her throat.

One thick hand tangled in her hair, tugging her head to the position he wanted. He went deeper. His mouth claimed, his tongue possessed. An odd sense of desperation hinted in his kiss.

Without warning, he flipped her around, placing her hands on the smooth tile. His tongue flicked the shell of her ear. "Is your jaw all right?" Rough and hoarse, his voice triggered liquid need to coat her thighs.

"Fine." She pushed back against him, her bare butt against his erection. Her eyelids fluttered shut.

He grabbed her hip, holding her still. His other hand flattened against her belly, sliding up across her breasts to her throat. Flames licked her skin. He cupped the unbruised side of her jaw, and tugged back, stretching her neck. "Keep your hands on the tile."

He held her immobile, resting her head against his shoulder and dipping his mouth to her exposed jugular. His warm palm curved around her neck, holding her where he wanted her. His teeth sank into the soft area of her shoulder. Marking her.

Her thighs quivered. A spiraling started deep inside, and she pushed back against him.

A sharp slap against her ass had her crying out. "Stay still."

She stiffened, too many emotions whipping through her to concentrate on just one. An edge had always existed in Shane, especially in the bedroom. But something had been let loose. A wildness, a darkness she'd always suspected he hid. His memories were returning, and yet he hadn't retreated behind that wall.

Maybe things could be different this time.

His mouth found her ear to nip her earlobe. Tingles sprang up on her skin as he covered her breasts, tweaking both nipples before sliding south. Parting her, he slipped two fingers into her heat. "You're so hot for me."

Her knees softened. She pushed her flattened hands harder against the tiles, trying to maintain balance. To maintain control. He angled his palm, sliding against her clit. She cried out. Too much. She needed him now.

He chuckled hot breath against her ear, the sound wicked and arrogant. "We stayed at a hotel with a small pool once. Right?"

Her sex clutched around his dangerous fingers. "Yes. You remember?"

"The water, you, the steam...a memory is coming back." His erection jerked against her ass. His fingers played, crisscrossing inside her. His other hand kneaded her breast, concentrating on rolling the nipple between two fingers. "We made good use of that pool. You screamed my name as you milked me dry."

Yes, but he'd been so gentle, even then. She hadn't wanted gentleness. She'd wanted him. Memories flashed through her mind, showing how very different he was now. Man, she wanted him like this. "Shane, please."

"Ah, angel. I love how sweetly you ask." Bending over her, he slid a rough palm down her hip and leg, lifting her knee to place her foot on the narrow bench. A quiver began around his fingers. He withdrew and she hissed in protest. "Not yet," he murmured, "We have a few things to get straight first."

Focus. Her mind spun while her body throbbed. "What are you talking about?"

"You're in danger, and you're going to let me handle

it." He pressed against her entrance, sliding forward so slowly, too slowly. She pushed back against him, crying out when he filled her. Both eyes opened wide.

Muscles vibrated in her shoulders as she straightened her arms, taking more of him. Taking all of him.

He groaned against her ear, his body protecting her back from the hot spray. "You're a dangerous woman, Mrs. Dean."

Her laugh came out strangled. "I appreciate that, Major Dean." She tilted forward and then slammed back.

His hands instantly clasped her hips, keeping her in place. "Slow down, darlin'."

"No." She struggled against his hands, causing sparks of pure pleasure to ripple along the sensitive nerves holding him captive.

His indrawn breath made her smile in triumph. She did it again.

"Damn it, Josie. I want to talk." But he slid out and then impaled her.

She closed her eyes. Fire sheeted white behind her eyelids. Using the wall for leverage, she pushed back, throwing her head against his shoulder, biting her lips.

Shane snapped. With a growl, he dug his fingers into her hips, yanking her against him. Then he started to pound. Harder and faster than ever before. Furious and forceful, he settled his mouth at the base of her neck. He was finally being himself, finally taking her like she needed. For the first time, she felt like he was hers— completely. All of him belonged to her and her only.

She cried out, the delicious friction so fierce her breath caught on the scream. Pleasure stabbed through her at his relentless strokes. Need whipped along her nerves to the point of pain. The pinnacle she needed to crest or die.

His hand slid down and found her clit.

Fire ripped through her nerves. She broke, tumbling over. Her mouth opened on a silent scream as she arched her back, letting the overwhelming pleasure ripple through her. She sobbed his name.

With a tightening of his hold, he pounded harder. Faster. His large body tightened around her as he came, his breath hot at her ear. Finally, he stopped moving, remaining inside her, his heart beating a rapid tempo against her back. "I love you, angel."

The words were soft.

The tone possessive.

The promise absolute.

Shane tossed in the big bed, wandering through the twilight between dreams and reality. His brain relaxed, and he let memories wash over him.

Two years ago, he'd whistled a country tune, walking home from the bakery to his woman. Josie. Doubt had still assailed him, but maybe he had a chance at a normal life. Sure, what had happened to his brother Nathan was a tragedy, and when Nathan was betrayed by Audrey, his life pretty much stopped. But Nate had never talked about the whole story. Something else had happened, and he wouldn't discuss it. But now, maybe Shane could find a better ending.

The hair on the back of Shane's neck had prickled. He had shifted the freshly baked baguettes to his other hand, reaching for the knife in his back pocket.

"Not necessary," a low voice muttered from the alley.

Relief relaxed his shoulders as Shane dodged into the alley to face his brothers. "Matt, Nate. Why are we in an alley?" Humor tilted Shane's lips. Matt hated drama, while Nate had once lived for it. When he lived for something.

Matt didn't return the smile, just stared at him with those dark gray eyes.

Dread whispered along Shane's skin. His ribs instantly had ached. No. "What?"

"Jory's dead."

Two years later, the words made Shane sit upright in bed, his gut revolting. Pain filled his body. Jory. The youngest kid, the smallest, the one who tried so much harder than the rest of them. Until he grew and kicked ass.

Shane breathed out, glancing at the sleeping bundle next to him. Tiny. She was so tiny, curled up like a kitten. Her lips pouted in her sleep, and he flashed back to the many times he'd lounged next to the bed. Watching her. He'd meant to talk some sense into her in the shower. Show her who was boss. She'd taken him. Wrapped her little body around him as tightly as she'd bound his heart.

Jesus. He couldn't keep his own brother safe. How could he keep Josie safe? While memories were flashing home, there were more he needed to find. He'd told Josie he was keeping her, but what if that was a death sentence? Maybe loving her really did mean releasing her. But could he?

His hand trembled when he reached out and smoothed back the wispy hair on her forehead. Her skin felt like the finest of silks. Though the bruise spreading across her jaw made him wish he had killed George.

How could he see so well in the dark?

Time for some answers.

He rolled from the bed and pulled on his jeans, stalking on bare feet down the hallway to the living room.

Nathan glared at him from the table, where he had put

together a scanner. His wet hair lay curled against his neck. "You used all the hot water, asshole."

"Sorry." He ran a hand through his hair. "Why can I see in the dark? How can I guess the speed of a vehicle thirty miles away? Shit, how can I *hear* a vehicle that far away?" Anger fought reason for dominance in his brain. "How did I know how to interrogate that bastard earlier?"

Nathan sat back, his eyes thoughtful. "What do you remember?"

Shane growled and strode to the kitchen, grabbing two beers from the refrigerator. Guinness. He handed one to Nathan and dropped into a thick leather chair. "I remember a military academy and breaking my arm. Then I remember Matt telling me Jory was dead." Even now, pain caught the air in his throat. "Small scenes, small memories scattered throughout. I'm starting to remember everything about Josie." Shane squinted his eyes, looking into the past. "I know we don't have parents. I don't know how I know that, but I remember wanting parents."

"At two years older than me, Matt's the closest thing we ever had," Nathan said softly. He rubbed his chin. "It might be easier not knowing. But you're right. We don't have parents."

"Why not?"

Nathan exhaled. "We're experiments, Shane. Genetics, psychology, and test tubes."

CHAPTER
20

S HANE EXTENDED HIS legs, stretching out. The more his mind spun, the more relaxed his body became. Interesting reaction. "Test tubes?"

"Yes." Nathan took a deep drink of the dark brew. "We're part of a military experiment. Trained to fight, trained to kill since birth."

A soft pattering sounded down the hallway. Shane tilted his head to listen. Josie had crept forward. The little eavesdropper. He could whisk her back to bed or allow her to hear everything. It was past time to have his cards on the table. He pinned his brother with a look. "So we're not brothers?"

Nathan cut his eyes to the hallway and then back at Shane. With a shrug, he shook his head. "We're brothers. Part of the experiment was to see how we related, how we trained, what motivated us." A warning light entered his eyes. "We weren't the only team. There were several." He shook his head at the hallway.

Too bad. Let her learn the truth. "That explains the eye color."

Nathan's jaw tightened, but he continued. "Yes. Same

father. Some ultra-soldier, from what Jory was able to hack. Take a genius female and her womb, some serious genetic engineering, and they created us."

"Different females?"

Nathan shrugged. "Yes. Hopefully all human DNA—but who knows. If documents exist about that, we haven't been able to find them."

"Josie thinks I have a hang-up about kind women."

"Yeah." Nathan took another deep swallow. "The women we knew were either stone-cold scientists or really rough soldiers. Mainly." His gaze slid to his boots.

The hair on the back of Shane's neck prickled. "Mainly?"

"Yeah, ah"—Nathan cleared his throat—"let's just say they sent other women to us while we were in our teens." A muscle ticked in his jaw. "There isn't much we don't understand about sexual manipulation."

Jesus. Shane dug a palm into his eye. "The barracks I remember. We lived in that place?"

"Yes. Different groups were assigned divisions, all created with similar DNA. Brothers."

"No girls?"

"Hell, no." Nathan exhaled. "Until Audrey."

The name filtered unease through Shane's brain. "Audrey. Your Audrey." Pain there, too.

"Yes. She was the head doctor's daughter. They wanted me to train her in self-defense."

"Why?" A picture of deceptively innocent blue eyes and long black hair slammed behind Shane's eyes.

Nathan growled. "I don't know. If you ask me, it was another experiment. But I fell for it. I wanted a normal life so badly."

"You were betrayed." Certainty settled a heavy weight

around Shane's heart. "I remember. She, ah, didn't turn out to be on our side?" Nathan damaged—nearly destroyed.

"Yeah. They worked me over and good—killing several of our friends in the process. People around us end up dead." Nathan spoke to the dark hallway. "That's when we decided to leave."

An explosion filled Shane's memories. He set detonations, killing on purpose. The fires had burned high and hot...the screams echoed and then died out. "We blew the place up."

"Yes. We had to get free of those people so we could seek revenge. We blew everything and scattered. Almost five years ago." Nathan glanced at his disposable cell phone. "We knew they'd need about five years to regroup and come after us."

"Regroup?"

"I'm sure we're just the first wave of experiments. So we wanted time to get away, get positioned, and then take them down." Nate's eyes hardened to slate. "Of course, we thought we'd be further ahead than we are right now—considering we have three months to live."

Shane stilled. "Excuse me?"

Nate's slow smirk lacked humor. "You didn't think geniuses smart enough to genetically engineer us would fail to have safeguards in place, did you?"

Shane's gaze dropped to his hands. A familiar but unremembered fear washed down his entire back. "I guess not. What's the safeguard?"

"Kill chip in your spine." Nathan scratched his neck. "Needs to be reprogrammed every five years, or smush."

"Smush?"

"Yep. The thing blows and you die." Nathan picked at a string on his jeans. "If we try to remove it..."

"Smush." Shane eyed the too-quiet doorway. He should've sent her back to bed. "What's the plan?"

"Jory was looking for the code or how to remove it, and so is Matt. We'll find it. For right now, we need to concentrate on the current problem."

"Matt said he's a U.S. Marshal," Shane said.

"Yes. And I'm the head of Sins Security, which is a corporation owned by the four of us. I mean three of us." Nathan frowned. "We supply support, protection, and such when necessary. We've been shoring up resources for when we strike—which has to be soon."

"What group was I with in the marines?"

"A specialty unit in the United States dealing with bioterrorism."

Bioterrorism? "What did that have to do with our childhood?"

"Some of the top scientists in our government created us in the first place. You were hunting them."

"I left when Jory died." A statement. He'd left more than the marines, and he knew it.

"Yeah. We think he got too close to the commander."

The name sent a rock of pure hatred blasting under Shane's skin. "I remember him. He needs to die."

"Yes, he does," Matt said, stalking into the room.

Shane scratched his head. "What's up with my super hearing? And sight?"

Matt shrugged. "Along with the abnormal strength and reflexes, we all have special gifts. Might be hereditary and experimental, or just flukes from all of that. We all have hyper senses, but yours are the best."

"What's your gift?" Shane asked.

Nearing the sofa, Matt pivoted, his gaze on the dark hallway. "Your woman is eavesdropping," he mouthed.

"I know." Shane stretched to his feet. "Gifts?"

"I sense movement right before it happens. Might be slightly psychic, empathic, or just notice the shift of air. They've never been able to explain it." Matt eyed the hallway.

"Must be handy in a fight." Shane jerked his head at Nathan.

"I read people. Facial expressions, movement, everything. I'm a human lie detector." Nathan grinned, all rogue. "Very handy with the women."

Matt lowered his tone. "Josie shouldn't know all of this."

Shane nodded. "I'll discuss the matter with her, and then you and I can go over Jory's death. Maybe figure out where I've been the last two years."

"Sounds good. And we need to get out of town as soon as we solve her problem." Nathan grabbed his cell phone again. "My contacts are supposed to check in with any new information."

Shane nodded, stretching his neck as he strode toward the hallway. A scurrying sounded before a door clicked. *Ah, angel. Nice try.*

Josie's heart beat a rapid pattering in her chest. She kept her gaze on the dark entrance to the room. The door opened. Faint light from down the hallway filtered inside, silhouetting Shane's strong form in the doorway.

She caught her breath in her throat. Still. Stay very still.

"Did you hear everything you needed to hear?" he rumbled, crossing inside and shutting the door. A rustling sounded and his jeans hit the floor before he tugged open the sheets and slid inside.

The scents of warm cedar and male filled her nostrils. Heat encompassed her.

He yanked her butt into his groin, curving an arm around her waist. "Well, did you?"

She shrugged, her mind spinning. "Your childhood sucked."

A barked-out laugh stirred her hair. "Yeah, sounds like it." He sighed. "Though the scientific explanation rings true. I mean, some of my senses aren't normal."

"Not even close." She wiggled to get more comfortable, her chest aching. "Do you think Nathan is right? Are you going to die in three months?" The words hurt to say.

"I think Nate is right that there's a kill chip in my spine, but no, I'm not going to die. We're going to figure it out." Calm reason filled his tone—too much calm.

That was a promise he couldn't make. He seemed so invincible—how could he die? Tears welled in her eyes, and she shoved them back. Crying wouldn't help a damn thing. "How is genetic manipulation possible? I mean, I can understand taking a soldier's sperm and making babies, but how do you explain the enhanced hearing? Sight? Strength?"

"I don't know." He ran the rough pads of his fingers along her bare arm. Goose bumps rose. "We can clone cows. Eliminate genetic diseases in crops. I guess the thought isn't too far-fetched to think we can manipulate genes that deal with strength and senses."

"Especially if funded by the government. Think of the money involved."

"Yeah. Money." His body tightened around her. "You know, it was one thing to be certain about my ability to kill. That I had training. But to discover I was created in a test tube to be a killer, well now . . ." His tone went hard and flat, but pain echoed.

Sadness filtered through her. The need to comfort him, to heal him, made her heart actually ache. He must've been such a scared little boy to turn into such a hard man. "You don't know that. Sure, you're trained. But you're freaky smart, too. Maybe you were created to do something great. Cure a disease. Fix the economy." She turned in his arms to face him. Only the deep glow of his amazing eyes filled her sight. "What you do with your skills... well, that's up to you. Not them."

He exhaled. "Right now I want to find out who killed my brother. In fact, I'd like to remember my brother." Shane's large hand spread out between her shoulder blades, and he caressed down to press her lower back into him. His erection jumped against her clit. "After making sure you're safe."

He kissed her temple. So much emotion rose in her, she curled her fingers over his shoulders. His heated mouth wandered down the side of her face to take her mouth.

Safety was an illusion she didn't want—and one she didn't believe in. This, this she wanted. *He* was what she believed in. With a sigh, Josie sank into the kiss

Several hours later, Nathan cast Matt a look. "Think he's coming back?"

"Would you?" Matt flipped open a file folder, irritation swirling through his thoughts.

"Probably not." Nathan punched in keys on the laptop. "He's lost, Matt. He doesn't understand he needs to let her go."

"It's more likely she isn't letting him go this time," Matt returned. For which, well, he couldn't blame her. As he perused her file again, he understood her need for family. While death had hung over his childhood, at least he'd shared his days with his brothers. Family. They fought with each other. Shit, they fought *for* each other. Little Josie had been all alone.

"Perhaps. If she discovers the full truth, she may kick him to the curb." Nathan grabbed a bag of chips half smashed underneath yet another monitor.

"Yep." Matt leaned back in the sofa. He was so fucking tired. But sleep had become a luxury. "Have you been able to hack into her files at work yet? We need to find out who bugged her house."

"You think the situation has to do with the commander?"

"No. I think this has something to do with her job. Not us. But she's family, and we need to figure out who's gunning for her."

Nathan started, swinging a startled gaze at his older brother. "Wow. She got to you."

Yeah. The little blue-eyed minx had wormed right into the small circle of people he gave a crap about. Matt fought a growl. "She's Shane's wife. Like it or not, we put her in danger two years ago, and it's even worse now. Shane might have alerted the commander when he tried to Google his past."

"Yeah. Every instinct I have says they're coming for us now." Nathan rubbed his neck. "The commander is close. I can feel his presence." He cleared his throat. "Do you think Shane found out who killed Jory?"

Matt exhaled, forcing the heavy weight of guilt out of his body. For now. "I hope so." The need to draw blood roared like a tempest between his ears. "I shouldn't have let Jory go."

"You didn't have a choice. Jory was good at his job and did what needed to be done. If he had a lead, nothing could've stopped him in pursuing it." Nathan glanced at his phone with a frown. "Not even you, Mattie."

The thick taste of the foreign beer failed to wash away the bile in Matt's throat. "I failed him."

"No. It was my job was to keep track of the three of you in the field—I failed him." Nathan reached for a plain manila file holding a list of Josie's current clients.

The blame game was useless, and they didn't have time for it. Matt threw his file down on the coffee table. No need to read any more—he knew Josie's life by heart, had since Shane married the woman. "Shane took the news of his imminent death well."

"What choice did he have?" Nate sighed. "We'll find the doctor. I promise."

"It had better be soon." Matt shook his head. How the woman had managed to hide from him for so long was a mystery.

A monitor beeped. Nathan punched in keys. "My results are in. I hacked the ME's office for the autopsy results on the three men found down by the river. No evidence left on the bodies."

"How did they die?" Matt asked.

"They all had lacerations from a good fight but died from broken bones in the neck." Nathan raised an eyebrow. "Military style. The cops found a metal bat by the bodies, but the river washed away any and all DNA."

Jesus. Matt huffed out a breath. Three guys had gotten to Shane with a bat. "How did they get so close?"

"My best guess is that our brother was distracted." Nate's face remained impassive, as usual. No emotion for so damn long. At least, none Matt could see. God help them all when he finally exploded. "I've traced Shane's movements and hacked into the files of some of his old contacts. I've confirmed his theory that he bugged Josie's house."

"Why?" No way would Shane bug his wife's house just because she was dating some construction worker. He'd be more likely to break down the front door and beat the guy to a pulp.

"My guess is that he discovered the other bugs and figured the commander was watching Josie. Knowing Shane, he wanted to trace the bugs back to the bastard." Nate crunched a chip. "So, what's our plan here?"

"First we figure out who's after Josie while Shane gets his memory back. Quickly, considering we're sitting ducks here. Then I assume he'll try to send Josie to the compound with you while we deal with Jory's killer."

Nate visibly jumped. "He's not keeping her, Mattie. He can't."

"I know. He'll figure that out soon enough." Matt kept his face expressionless. He steeled his shoulders. "You're flying home to Montana tomorrow."

Nathan tossed his file down. "I'm not leaving."

Exactly what Matt expected. He hardened his face into true big brother mode. "Yes, you are. We don't know how long it'll take for Shane to get his memory back, and I sure as hell don't need help with whoever's after Josie. Go home and do your job."

Shane loped barefoot into the room, yanking a T-shirt over his head, wearing ripped jeans. And a relaxed jaw. Bastard.

He glanced at Matt. "I need to fill in the blanks. Now."

Matt nodded. "Let's get down to business."

CHAPTER
21

EARLY MORNING, JOSIE pinned her wet hair up, smoothing lip gloss on her face. Shane had retrieved clothes and toiletries from her house. Thank goodness. Though the isolation was beginning to bother her. She needed to get back to work. Now that might be a battle.

The thick socks masked her steps as she meandered down the hallway toward the smell of coffee.

At the living room, she stopped short.

Matt and Shane lounged on the couch reading files while Nathan stood near the door, a ball cap on his face and thick sunglasses over his eyes.

Josie's heart began to pound. "Nice glasses."

Nathan shrugged. "Yeah. Helps with the security cameras everywhere. Standard when I travel."

Her breath caught in her throat.

Shane glanced up, a frown settling between his eyes. "Angel?"

Memories shot through her head in rapid succession. She took a step back, her wide-eyed gaze on Nathan. "It's you."

He cocked his head to the side. "What's me?"

She breathed out. Hard. "In the coffee shop. Ball cap. Eyeglasses." Her gaze slashed to Shane and then back again. "It's you." She knew he looked familiar. Rage and fear boiled into a lump in the pit of her stomach.

Shane unfolded to his feet, his gaze moving from Josie to Nathan and back again. "Honey, a lot of people have aviator glasses."

Pure raw fury ripped through her so fast her breath heated. "Don't lie to me. He was as big as you. Built like you." She turned on Nathan. "It was you. The asshole in the coffee shop."

Pain splashed ice over the fury. She rounded on Shane. "You didn't save me. You set me up." Two years ago. The scene where Shane had been her hero. When everything started. They'd planned the confrontation. No wonder the bully had left so easily without argument. The bully was Nathan.

He cut his eyes to Shane.

Josie leaped for the black gun on the table, flipping off the safety and backing away. She kept all three men in her sight. "The safety's off this time, Matt." Her voice trembled low with fury. Her hands shook.

He remained relaxed from his perch on the sofa. "You know, this is the second time you've held a gun on me this week, little sister." He cleared his throat. "If one of these two tried that, I'd break their hands."

"You'd try," Shane and Nathan said in unison, gazes locked on her.

Matt tilted his head in acknowledgment. "Put the gun down, Josie. Let's talk."

The keys to her Toyota sat on the coffee table. "Throw me my keys, Matt."

Shane stepped between the table and Josie. "Not going

to happen. Now put down the gun before you really piss me off."

She widened her stance, swinging her aim to the center of his chest. "So, genetically enhanced boy. Can you stop a bullet?"

"No." Anger began to burn slate through his eyes. "Now, Josie."

"It's true, isn't it? You set me up."

"Yes." His gaze remained on her eyes, not on the gun.

"The whole thing…meeting me, marrying me…you fucking set me up." Her grip tightened on the weapon.

"No." He took a step toward her. "The meeting was a setup. The rest was real."

"Bullshit." She dropped her aim to his knee. Her own stupidity slapped her in the face. "Take another step, and you'll limp for life, Shane. If that's even your name."

"It is," Nathan chimed in. "Always has been."

Her breath began to come out in short pants. "Give me my keys." She needed to get out of the cabin. Confusion rioted through her mind.

"No," Shane said.

Did he just get closer somehow?

Josie backed up until she met the wall. "Why? Why me?" Did he need a cover for a couple months? If so, why had he come back?

"You had something I wanted." His gaze swept her body, a slight smile tipping his lips.

Even when she was scared and pissed off, her body responded to him. Warmed and tingled. She lifted her chin. "What did you want?"

He raised an eyebrow. "Give me the gun, and we'll discuss the matter."

Nathan eased toward the door. "I'll give you some

space. Good luck with this, Shane." He dodged outside, whistling the Dixie Chicks' "Ready to Run."

Josie gasped, starting to swing the gun toward the door and then refocusing the weapon back on Shane.

He smiled. Studying her. Knowing her. "Matt? Take off, would you? I need a moment with my wife." He emphasized the word *wife* just enough to snap her spine to attention.

She kept her gaze on her husband. Betrayal burned like cigarette ashes down her esophagus. "You move, Matt, I'm shooting him. Watch me."

Matt stretched to his feet. "That's okay. He probably deserves it." Then Matt opened the door. "I'm going for a jog. See you folks later." The door shut behind him.

A strangled scream filled Josie's throat. The gun did not even remotely scare these guys.

Shane blew out a breath. "Josie—" Quick as a whip, he struck, pinning her arm against the wall. His body boxed her in, while the grip on her wrist tightened. "Let go of the gun."

She bit her lip, holding on with every ounce of stubbornness she owned.

With a growl, Shane yanked the gun from her grasp. He stepped back, flipping on the safety. "I've about had it with your defiance, angel."

Fury. Pure, raw, and deadly rage raced through her to light her veins on fire. She saw red. Jumping forward, she pivoted and shot a hard kick into his gut. He blocked her with a casual swipe of his hand on her foot.

One eyebrow rose. "Sit down, or I'll sit you down."

The tone. Low, dangerous, and commanding. He'd never used it with her before. Never. She faltered, her gaze on the sofa.

Well, it wouldn't hurt to hear the truth. Finally. "I'll listen. Then I'm leaving." With a huff, she flounced to the sofa and sat.

"You're not going anywhere." He stalked to the deep cherry wood cabinets in the kitchen and placed the gun on top of one. Where she couldn't reach it. Then he returned. "You want me to stop treating you like something fragile? Make sure you understand what you're asking for." Cushions dipped as he sat next to her on the couch. Broad hands wrapped around her arms and lifted her from the sofa.

She yelped, pushing her hands against his chest, struggling.

"Stop." He sat her on his lap facing him, her legs straddling him. His hands manacled around her arms, holding her in place. "You want the truth. Sit here and take it."

His eyes glittered an angry gray. The hard thighs beneath her heated her butt.

Desire, unwilling and unwanted, caused a swirling in her lower stomach. "Fine. Give it to me, then." He wasn't the only one who could play word games.

"We targeted you because of Fuller Labs."

She stilled. In a million years she hadn't expected his answer. "Why?"

"Scientists at Fuller used to work with the commander. We think. Some of Fuller's research includes genetic engineering."

Her mind spun. "Who's the commander?"

"The monster who trained us from birth. The man in charge of our program."

"You remember?"

"Yes. Everything but the last two years."

His childhood was sad and had damaged him. But he'd

made the choice as an adult to use her—to hurt her. Right now she needed to let go of her dream of a happy ending. "So you used me to get their financial records?"

"Yes." Shane's voice remained steady. "I monitored their finances before and then during our marriage."

Sharp knives slashed through her insides. Only true force of will kept her from doubling over. Even so, tears pricked the back of her eyes. "Wait a minute. All of my computer problems—the ones you helped me to fix…"

He shifted. "Yes. I messed with your computer to gain access to the files."

No wonder her laptop was always having issues. She'd been so grateful to Shane for fixing the problems. The bastard had created the problems.

Heat blazed between her ears. Memories followed suit. All those late nights when he was supposed to be working, where was he? All those little coincidences of her files being slightly rearranged in her office gave her a clue. "Did you break into my office, too?"

"Yes."

She shook her head. "How? I mean, they had cameras."

"I took care of the cameras. Apparently nobody really checked them, because there was never an outcry."

There was never an outcry because nothing had ever been taken. There was no warning.

Another memory almost had her scratching at his face. "What about when I fainted the night we went to pick up the file folders I thought I'd forgotten?" She'd never fainted before—and she'd been sure she'd taken the right folders home.

He flushed a dark red. "I hid the files so we had to go back to your office, and ah, you didn't faint."

She'd come to lying on the sofa in her office, and Shane had been so concerned, so gentle. "You knocked me out?"

"Yes." His eyes darkened. "I'm sorry."

He was fucking sorry? Rage had her almost seeing double, while hurt pounded through her entire body. "You asshole. Why did you marry me?" She struggled to keep her lips from trembling. "Why not just continue to screw me?"

Shane gave a short nod of his head. "Marrying you was not part of the plan. Believe me, my marriage pissed off my brothers to no end." Emotion deepened his voice. "I wanted you, Josie. Still do. With everything I am." He tugged her closer. Pain twisted his lips, and his eyes glimmered. "I knew I shouldn't marry you. I knew what the danger would mean. But I convinced myself I could keep you safe."

Such pretty words. "You lied to me. The entire time we were married."

"Yes. I abandoned you, thinking it would keep you safe." He looked up and shook his head, his nostrils flaring. "I didn't know how badly it would hurt you, and I'm so sorry." His voice lowered to guttural, his pain palpable.

The room hazed. She looked away, trying to dispel the hurt in her chest. Soothing him wasn't her job. "I don't believe you really wanted me. When you'd finished the job, you discarded me. Like an old coat, one that didn't matter."

"Not true. Jory died, and we knew there was only a short time to get information. I had to go and fast." His grip tightened. "I didn't think the investigation would take two years. I planned to return for you. No way could I stay away forever."

Incredulity had her breath catching. Anger slapped

pain to the floor. "Wait a minute. You get the divorce papers, head up to see me, and instead of knocking on my door with a 'Hi honey, good to see ya,' you bug my house?"

"Well...I don't remember that yet, but I assume I checked out your house, found the bugs, and decided to find out what was going on." Doubt wrinkled his forehead but was quickly smoothed out.

"So you used me as bait. In case the commander had found me." Hurt flashed hard and bright. She couldn't believe it.

"No. I may not remember, but no way would I ever use you as bait." His hands tightened on her hips. "From the pictures we found in the little house, I was keeping you in my sight at all times—and I had a go-bag packed for you."

"Is that so?" If she grew any madder, her head might blow off. "So kidnapping was a possibility."

"Sure."

Reality settled in her stomach like a flare of light. "No. We started on a lie, and we ended on a lie." She met his gaze head-on. Not flinching. "We're done."

His eyes softened. "I know I hurt you, baby. I'm sorry."

"You can't keep me here."

He huffed out a low chuckle, weariness tightening his face. "You have no idea what I can do, angel. What I will do to keep you here. Keep you safe."

"I have a pretty good idea how far you'll stoop." She aimed her words to cut. "Nothing would surprise me now." Her thigh muscles bunched to leap off him. His hands pressed her immobile, and her anger flared back to the surface. "Let me go."

Self-disgust curled his lip. "I can't." Heat coursed off his palms to her thighs. "Right now we need to figure out who is after your files, and I need to keep you safe." His long fingers curled around to grip her legs.

Even now, with hurt and anger riding her hard, she longed for what might've been. But she'd listened to her heart long enough with Shane. She was a smart woman, and it was time to let her brain take over. "No. We're done."

Genuine surprise flashed in his eyes.

Her focus cleared. "You truly think I'll let you treat me like this? That you're so irresistible I won't walk away?" She lowered her chin. "Watch me." Determination straightened her shoulders. The arrogance of the man. Yes, she'd been stupid to even think about trusting him again, and she was now paying the price. But enough was enough.

"I left because I knew you were safe. Or at least I thought you were."

"I don't care." Anger filtered through his eyes, but she really didn't care. "It doesn't matter *why* you lied, *why* you left. What matters is the fact that you lied and you left. How can you not understand?"

"You love me." His lips tightened into a straight line. "To a good woman, to a soft woman, that means everything."

She snapped her teeth shut, almost relieved when her brain took over. When focus became easier than hurt. "I do love you, Shane." Her frown actually made her forehead ache. "But do you really think you're the only one able to walk away from us? You were right to leave. It's better that way." She blew out a breath. "I can walk away, too."

Sympathy for him almost stopped her words. Almost. He really didn't understand. Poor guy raised without a mother, with some idealized view of what women should be. She'd been alone her entire life. Even during her marriage. Seeing the real Shane this last week only made that truth clearer. She leaned closer, her eyes an inch from his. "I. Can. Leave. You. And I will."

This time, hc let her go.

Matt stomped his feet on the porch, just in case his brother was getting busy. He hoped Shane figured out the right path—away from Josie. Though Matt understood. From a young age, they'd all had a fantasy about what real families were like. They'd wondered what they'd done wrong to be so alone. Maybe being created by men instead of God marked them for life. Deep down, he was pretty sure of it.

He nudged open the door, slipping inside.

Shane sat on the sofa, a notebook in his hand, his gaze unblinking on the far wall.

"Ah, where's Josie?" Matt ripped off his shirt and wiped his brow. It had felt good to run through the woods in the cold of fall again. To hear the wildlife and be kissed by the sun.

"In the bedroom." Shane looked up with blank eyes. "I think she just dumped me." Incredulousness whipped a flush over his cheekbones.

Matt raised an cyebrow. "Dumped you?" The innocuous words tasted weird on his tongue. "As in a regular relationship type of *dumped* you?"

"Yeah." Shane frowned at the empty hallway.

"Huh." Matt kicked off his combat boots. "I don't think any of us has ever been dumped." Sure, they'd had lovers try to kill them. But never just . . . dump them. "So, ah, what are you going to do?"

Shane shrugged. "I have no idea."

Maybe it was better this way. Though the frown on Shane's face revoked that thought. "Shane, we've been trained by the best psychologists in the world to manipulate people. You can win her back."

"No." His brother threw the notebook down on the sofa. "This is real. Not the same."

Well, now. That was true. Matt rubbed his chin. "I'll talk to her."

Shane snorted. "You can't fix everything." He stood, stretching his neck. "I may not remember all of my childhood, but you, I remember. Always present, always trying to protect us." His eyes darkened. "Thank you."

Matt shook his head. He didn't deserve the gratitude. Nathan had spent a lot more time raising Shane and Jory than he had. Besides, if he'd done his job, Jory would be alive. "I'm taking a shower."

Shane stood and headed for the door. "I need some fresh air."

Matt sighed. "We should get out of here. Your wife needs to get those files from her work tomorrow."

Shane nodded, his back to Matt. "She will."

CHAPTER
22

SHANE SAT ON the rough porch step and threw rocks across the field, his mind spinning. Thunder rolled across the sky, a perfect match for his mood. Josie had meant the words—she really was finished with him. Maybe it was for the best.

The idea of losing her ripped him apart, and the thought of betraying his brothers sliced deep. Why would staying married betray his brothers? Because it added that much danger to all of them—especially to him. As brothers, they'd always been each other's weak spots. He shook his head. This was all so fucked up.

The sky opened up, and rain slashed down.

Nathan stalked up from the forest, casting a large shadow. He'd been walking all day.

Shane stretched out his legs. Irritation heated through him. "Where the hell have you been?"

"Out." Nathan glanced up at the clouds covering the moon. "My red-eye leaves in an hour, and I thought I'd grab my laptop."

"Good idea," Shane snapped.

Nathan lifted an eyebrow. "Is there something you'd like to say?"

"No." Shane's hands curled into fists.

Nathan stomped dirt off his boots, squishing wet leaves. "Out with it, Shane."

Shane bounded to his feet and into the deluge. "My memories aren't all the way back, but you've always been a bossy bastard, haven't you?"

Nathan's eyelids slowly rose, while his chin lowered. "Watch yourself, little brother. That head injury gives you some leeway, but not much."

"Screw you." Frustration needed an outlet, and Shane was looking at a good one.

Nathan slowly removed his coat, folded it, and set it inside the SUV, his gaze never leaving Shane. Rain matted his hair to his head. "What's your fucking problem?" Curiosity, not heat, rode his deep voice.

Shane eyed his brother. "Oh, you're so damn calm, so uncaring, aren't you?" The instant flare in Nate's eyes pleased him. Instinct told Shane just where to strike. "You can't keep a woman, so nobody gets one? Really?"

Nathan smiled, and his fist shot out.

The right cross threw Shane against the porch railing. Satisfaction welled through him along with the pain. "That's what I thought." He ducked his head and charged his brother, hitting him in the midsection. Metal crunched when they crashed into the wet Jeep.

He shot a hard punch into Nate's jaw.

Nate's head snapped back, and he rolled them over, straddling Shane. Wet pine needles coated his neck. Two hard punches to the face, and Shane saw stars.

Damn it.

He shoved Nathan off and pushed to his feet, kicking

Nate in the chest. His brother rolled backward and flipped to his feet.

Shane stepped back and then settled his stance.

Nate wiped blood off his mouth. "No matter how hard you hit, or how hard I hit you, the pain won't go away. Deal with it."

The ring of truth made Shane see red. He rushed forward in a tackle, and Nathan fell back, tossing him over his head. Shane twisted, turned, and moved to tackle again, only to run smack into Matt.

No expression sat on Matt's hard face. Nathan spat blood on the leaves behind him.

Shane backed up. Rain drenched his clothes. "Get out of my way."

Matt's eyebrow rose. "Why? You're mad at yourself, not at Nate."

Nate stepped to the side. "That's all right, Mattie. I don't mind beating some sense into this jackass."

Matt cut a hard look at Nate. "Knock it off."

Nate faltered and then sighed. "Fine."

Shane snarled. "Always the obedient soldier, aren't you?"

The punch to the jaw from Matt caught him by surprise and hurt like hell. "I said, knock it off." Matt nodded toward Nate. "Get your stuff, and get to the airport."

Nate eyed Shane. "We can't leave it like this."

"We'll deal with this later. For now, we're under a deadline." Matt turned back toward Shane. "Now, Nate."

Grumbling, Nate turned and hustled toward the cabin.

Shane stepped to the side. He had to make his brother see reason. "Nate? This will all work out, you know."

Nate slowly turned, a massive man standing in the rain, pure regret in his dark eyes. "We'll go down fighting,

Shane. That's always been the plan." He rubbed a hand through his hair, sending droplets flying.

"I know. We'll win the fight," Shane said.

Nate shook his head. "The fight ends bloody, and the fight ends sad. I'm sorry." He moved into the cabin.

Shane frowned. "Is he right?"

Matt kicked a rock out of the way. "Probably."

"He always does just what you say." Was Nate a soldier or a brother?

Matt sighed. Emotion darkened his eyes. "Our childhood shapes us. Nate learned the hard way that orders matter—and that most things end bloody and sad."

"Someday you're going to have to explain that to me."

Matt pinned Shane with a hard glare. "Fighting each other doesn't help."

Shane shuffled his feet. "He hit me first."

Matt barked out a laugh. "We're not teenagers. You're fighting because you can't figure out your life. And if you're still standing, Nate seriously pulled his punches."

So had Shane. "I know." His chest hurt. He glanced down at his bloody knuckles. "Do you think he's right? Does Josie make me weak?"

"Yes." Matt shoved his hands in his pockets, allowing the rain to beat down on him. "And no."

"What the hell does that mean?"

"Anybody you love is a weakness the commander will use. That's how they kept us in line for so long—they used the threat of death over a brother." Matt wiped rain off his face. "They'll use Josie."

Desperation felt like knives slicing his gut. "I can keep her safe."

"Maybe. What about in three months when the chips

activate?" Matt stepped wearily up the stairs. "Or when we finally find them and die taking them out?"

Shane stilled. "You don't think we'll find the code in time?"

Matt turned. "No. Where does that leave Josie then?" He shook his head. "Let her go, make her believe you're letting her go so everyone else believes it, too. If you love her, you'll let her find a life." He opened the door. "We need to get to work now." Slipping inside, he shut the door.

Shane stood in the rain, his thoughts swirling. What the hell was he going to do?

He'd left her alone. Given her space. While she'd slept in the big bed last night, Shane had worked with Matt on the computer. Trying to figure out where he'd been the last two years. Didn't those men ever need sleep? Josie tapped her heel on the floorboard of her Toyota, refusing to look at her husband in the driver's seat. God forbid he let her drive her own car.

A new hardness cut lines into the sides of his mouth. "We'll go in and get the files, angel. Then we leave."

She continued her study of the trees outside. She felt numb inside. "No. I have thirty clients, Shane. I need to work." Especially since it now appeared her new life was permanent. Without him.

The SUV bounced along deep potholes. "I'm not completely unreasonable." He ignored her snort of disbelief and continued, "I understand your job. If you need to finish up with your current clients, we can work something out." Deep, sincere, and so full of compromise, his voice pissed her off beyond belief.

"We have nothing to work out." Once he left, she'd be fine. And alone. So alone. She rubbed chilled arms.

"Listen, I'm trying to compromise here. If I had my way, you'd be secured at the cabin right this second. You said you needed to wrap things up at work, and I'm going against my instincts in agreeing." Shane reached forward and flicked on the heater. He cleared his throat. "I actually remember my childhood. All of it."

She stilled. "How?"

A masculine exhale filled the vehicle. "Matt. Once he started talking, memories came flooding back. So many." His hands tightened on the steering wheel. "My first mission was to assassinate a drug dealer in New York."

Her breath caught. Did she really want to know this? "How old were you?"

"Twelve." His inflection didn't change.

So young. Josie straightened her shoulders. She wouldn't feel sorry for him. "Did you?"

"Yes."

She didn't want the details. "Oh. Do you want to talk about it?"

"Shit, no." His voice softened. "There are things you shouldn't know. Things I can protect you from. Please let me."

The entreaty from such a strong man tempted her far too much. Though the pedestal he wanted to trap her on wasn't a good fit. "I can't be the helpless girl you want hiding behind you." The scenario wasn't what he needed, either. "I'm sorry."

He sighed. "I trained you to fight, darlin'. Of course I don't want you helpless." His grip tightened. "Speaking of which . . . why haven't you kept up the training?"

"I didn't want to." She wanted to live peacefully, and there was only so much time in the day. It was either yoga or karate . . . and she'd chosen peace.

"Your training will continue starting tomorrow."

"No, it won't." He had lost his place in her life and didn't get to dictate any of it. She folded her hands in her lap. "Do you remember where you've been the last two years?"

His arms stretched out, showcasing solid biceps and granite hard muscles. "No. Matt's going to try some deep relaxation methods with me tonight."

Deep relaxation? "You mean, like hypnotism?" Was Matt a psychologist?

"Yeah, something like that. Our training in interrogation includes more than dishing out pain." Shane turned from the dirt road onto asphalted county road. "Methods exist to get information from friends as well as enemies."

She cleared her throat. "So, ah, interrogation. A specialty of yours, right?" Darn her curiosity. The thought was so far out of her realm of experience, and somehow, even though she wasn't proud about it, the thought of Shane being so tough intrigued her.

He shook his head. "Don't romanticize the idea." Thunder rolled high above them. " 'Interrogation' is a military euphemism for torture." He sighed. "And yeah, I'm good at it."

"Why did you marry me?" Her lungs seized. She hadn't meant to ask that question.

The empty road before them kept his gaze. "You made me believe I could have a life. A good one. Someday." He turned his head, his eyes a stormy gray. "The idea of not marrying you hurt more than any pain I'd ever felt." He glanced back at the road, the profile of his rugged face so strong. So enduring. "I don't think you're weak, sweetheart. I think you're kind...and good." He shifted in his seat.

So much longing. Something in her broke free. With her words the day before, she'd wanted to hurt him. Not only that, she'd needed to know that she could hurt him—that she mattered that much to him. How screwed up was that? "I don't think I can try again."

His lip twisted. "I know. But always remember that you're strong, baby. So strong." He pulled onto the interstate toward the city. "Steel wrapped in flower petals."

His acceptance hurt, even with such sweet words. Too bad they were way too late. Plus, the man didn't make sense. "Then why do you try so hard to stand in front of me?"

He whirled toward her, his hands sure on the wheel, his speed steady. "Because you're mine." His dark hair flew when he shook his head. "I've never had much, but what I do have, I protect. With everything I am." He focused back on the road. "Even if we're not together."

Holy crap. He was agreeing to leave her. The hurt almost doubled her over—even though that's what she wanted. She shook her head. Too much to deal with right now.

Shane exited the highway, driving toward her building downtown. He pulled into the lot and cut the engine. "What are the rules today?"

How irritating. "Don't speak to me like I work for you. I don't."

He licked his lips, wiping the bottom one off with his thumb and forefinger.

Heat swirled in her abdomen. She fought a groan.

He pinned her with a hard gaze. "This isn't a job. If you can't do this right, if you can't follow my lead, we'll go back to the cabin."

"Don't threaten me." She turned to grab the door

handle, stopping only when he wrapped one hand around her upper arm.

He yanked her across the seat to settle on his legs. "My way. No other choice." His hand tightened, and his voice roughened. "Agree or we go." He cupped her cheek with his free hand, holding her in place on his lap, his Southern drawl breaking free.

A soldier's intensity filled the cab. She met his gaze, biting her lip to keep from speaking. As patient as any stalking predator, he waited. She knew him. He could and would wait all day. Struggling would be a useless endeavor. "Fine."

His cheek creased as if he might smile. "What are the rules today?"

He drove her crazy. She rolled her eyes. "We go to my office. I meet with clients in my office. I don't leave my office unless you're with me."

"Where will I be?"

"Either in my office or in the waiting area if I'm meeting with a client."

"Good." His drawl deepened. "What happens if you disregard any of these rules?"

Enough of this crap. "Well, last time I followed my own path, I ended up stumbling over a dead body with a rabid jerk breaking down Sheetrock to get to me. So I'd rather not think about it."

Shane's long fingers caressed the side of her face. "Ah, Josie. That's nothing compared to what you'll face from me if you put yourself in danger again."

She shivered with desire. From any other man the threat would be silly, but from Shane. Well now. Sexual. Damn if her panties didn't moisten in response. "I'll keep that in mind."

He tugged her out of the driver's side, keeping her tucked against his body through the lot and to the elevator. Once at her floor, he followed her to her office, dropping onto a guest chair. "Why don't you hand me the Fuller Lab files?"

She couldn't help but blanch as she slid into her seat. "I can't give you those files right here in my office." Did he want her to get fired or what? She'd agreed to help him find out what happened to his brother, and then he needed to leave her for good this time. "I mean, I shouldn't even remove them from the office tonight and let you see them. The lab is a client and has a right to confidentiality."

"I don't give a shit."

Exasperation had her grabbing a pencil too tightly. "I know. What if you're wrong?" Her jaw firmed. "In the time you spent betraying me and spying on the lab, did you find anything off?"

His jaw snapped shut. "No, and I wasn't betraying you."

"Right." She punched up her computer. "I'll bring the files with me tonight, and you can take a look. But that's as good as you're going to get."

Vicki poked her head in the office. "You have a full calendar today, boss." She grinned. "Can you say 'quarterly tax time'?" Her gaze wandered across Shane's impressive form before she looked back at Josie. "The officers of Hanson Industries are first, and they brought three boxes of receipts." She wrinkled her nose. "They even want to write off a trip to a strip club."

Josie sighed. "Oh, no. Not again."

Shane nodded, stretching to his feet. "That's my cue. I'll be in the lobby. Keep in mind our discussion."

Which one? Once again, her mind was filled with Shane Dean.

• • •

The potato soup Josie had eaten for lunch lumped in her stomach. She stretched her neck, awaiting yet another client. Talk about stressed out. Plus, the warning glare from her husband hadn't eased any of her clients' minds as he had dropped by her office several times, poking his scowling face in the doorway. She was going to kill him when this day was finished.

Daniel stalked by her doorway, halting suddenly to lean against her door frame. "Rough day?"

She was too tired to spar. "Yes."

He nodded, his dark eyes serious. "I meant it about helping if you need help. Believe it or not, I do understand the concept of teamwork." Amusement lifted his upper lip.

Josie grinned. "That's good to know. Though I still want the promotion."

He nodded, the grin widening. "Ditto. But either way, I'm here if you need help."

"Thanks." Maybe he wasn't such a bad guy.

"Anytime." He turned, whistling as he maneuvered back to his office.

Josie flipped back open the file folder for Hall's Funeral Home. Something was just plain and simple bothering her about these accounts, and she couldn't figure out what. The client had purchased several different types of coffins from different vendors, and the information was all misfiled.

She carefully cataloged them in the right place and then subtracted the costs from the operating budget. Days ago she'd meant to do so, but since she'd already thought she'd found the problem, she'd concentrated elsewhere. And of course, between finding bodies, being kidnapped, and trying to figure out her life . . . she'd been busy.

The number flashed on her calculator. There was a surplus of thirteen thousand dollars.

Exactly.

The exact amount that had been missing from Larson Corporation. Son of a bitch. She double-checked the figure, her mind spinning. Yep. Unlucky thirteen. Billy had been laundering money throughout several businesses. She hadn't thought to compare the different accounts to each other. Excitement sped up her breath. She could solve this.

Vicki escorted a young woman inside. "Mrs. Ager from Agers Hardware is here."

Josie took a deep breath, closing the file. She'd figure it out after the meeting.

She stood, a genuine smile sliding across her face. Hopefully Billy hadn't stolen from Agers. But chances were looking good that he had. Should she tell her client or wait until she had it all figured out? She definitely had a duty to inform the client. Man, she was going to get the firm sued. "Madge. It's good to see you."

Madge grinned back, wiping her hands down dark jeans and taking a seat. "Thanks for seeing me. I'm not sure about taxes and whether or not we can write off the trip we took back East." She'd pulled her dark hair back into a ponytail, and her face was free of makeup. Her husband, Sam, had inherited the family business along with his brother about two years ago. "You know we have to do everything just right since Sam's brother is a prosecutor who owns half of the business." Bloodshot brown eyes glanced at the walls. "Oh, I like your horse painting."

"Thanks." Western art had always been one of her interests. "So did you bring receipts?"

"Yes." Madge dug into a large backpack, yanking out a stack of tattered receipts. "Uh, they're not in order."

"That's okay." Compared to the tattered papers from the strip club earlier, these were pristine. Josie tapped them into a neat pile. She needed to find the right words to tell Madge about the discrepancies in the files.

"So"—Madge leaned forward—"I, uh, have a weird question for you."

So long as it didn't deal with strippers or writing off golf clubs, it wouldn't be the weirdest question of the day. "Fire away."

Madge cleared her throat. "Hypothetically, if Sam and I split, do I get half the business?"

Josie sat back, mind whirling. The tick-tock of the antique clock on her desk sharpened. "Oh, Madge. Is everything okay?"

"Yes." Madge crossed her legs and settled into the seat. "But a girl should always plan."

Wasn't that the truth? Josie smoothed hair away from her face. "Well, the short answer is no. Washington is a community property state. An inheritance is separate— not community—property, and since Sam inherited his half of the business, it's technically not yours."

Madge grimaced. "Yeah, that figures." She rolled her neck. "So did they find out who broke into your offices?"

"No, not yet." Josie kept waiting for the phone to ring or the police to show up. Somebody had to have discovered Billy by now. Didn't a body start to smell really bad at some point? Not that he hadn't already smelled.

Josie focused on Madge, trying to forget that terrible day. "But I want to reassure you that your file was with me that night, as was my laptop, so nobody obtained your financial records."

"Thank goodness." Madge leaned back with a sigh. "Things are so stressful between Sam and his brother, you know? I mean, if any of the financial stuff got out, we'd be screwed."

Josie frowned. "So you're aware that there are financial issues with your account."

Madge nodded, reaching into her bag. "Well, yeah. That's kind of why I'm here." She lifted out a small silver handgun. Her nose wrinkled. "I'm really sorry about this." Her elbow tucked into her stomach and kept the weapon hidden from anyone in the hallway.

Fear slammed into Josie's stomach. She leaned back and away from the weapon. "What the hell?"

Madge's eyes glittered. "Well, we were working with Billy, and everything was fine, until he went to rehab." Her lips tightened white. "I guess he found religion. Or a conscience or something." She stomped her foot and cackled out a laugh. "Moron."

Josie shook her head. "I don't understand."

"Yeah, well...before Sam and me inherited the hardware store, we, uh, kind of were helping this guy named Max Penton with his business." Madge's eyes flashed a wild blue.

"Which was?" Josie could scream and duck under the desk, but would Madge shoot Vicki if she came running? Or Shane?

"He sells meth. A lot of it." Madge picked at a scab on the hand holding the gun. "But not to kids. Never to kids."

Was the woman on something? Josie forced anger away. She needed to focus. Shane wouldn't have been worried by the sweet-looking Madge; he wouldn't come check on her. Pudgy Madge looked softer than Josie. "So Billy helped you break the law?"

The gun wavered. "Yeah. The guy would do anything for meth. Actually, he showed us how we could take the money from helping Max and make it look like it came through the business. A way to keep the money from Sam's brother." She snarled. "You have no idea what it's like working your ass off every day. Everything goes to his brother. The favorite one—the prosecutor. Asshole."

Crazy. The woman was bat shit crazy. "So Billy taught you how to launder money." How deep did Madge's resentment go toward her brother-in-law?

"Yeah. Billy had the extra ledger so we could keep track and give the good receipts to his brother. We hid the extra money in off-shore accounts—and Billy used the accounts of his other clients without their knowledge." Madge hissed and spittle bubbled at the corners of her mouth. "But then Billy went to rehab, and you got the ledgers." Light glinted off the steel barrel of the gun as she gestured. "I'm due this money. I deserve it."

Josie's shoulders bunched with the need to duck to the floor. The knitting needles in her bottom drawer wouldn't be enough protection from a gun. There had to be some way to reason with the lunatic. "You know Billy's dead, right?"

"Yeah. Max shot him. Then George was supposed to get the files from you, but he didn't." She tilted her head, the gun settling to point at Josie's chest. Dark circles of sweat stained her flowered shirt. "What happened to George, anyway?"

Josie's chest pounded. "I'm still not sure about George." She surveyed the empty hallway. "What's your plan here?"

Madge sighed, regret flashing across her face. False regret. "I'm a good person, you know."

"In my experience, people who spend time trying to convince people they're a good person are actually trying to convince themselves." Where was Shane? "You know you're not a good person."

Madge's head jerked up, her eyes a crazy, wide blue. "We'll see about that now, won't we? Give me the files."

Josie pushed them toward Madge along with the ledger.

"Thanks." She shoved them all in the big bag. "Now here's the deal. I'll shoot you." Her gaze hardened. "I really will."

Josie believed her. "This won't work."

"Sure it will. We get up, go toward the conference room in the back, and head down the east stairwell." Madge sneered as she stood.

Josie swallowed. "What then?"

"Then we meet Max and give him the ledger. He'll figure out what to do." Madge gestured for Josie to get up.

"He'll kill me. You know that, right?" Josie edged around the desk, her gaze on the gun. Madge had about six inches and forty or so pounds on Josie.

"Maybe not. I mean, maybe we can convince him you won't tell."

If Madge got her out of the building, she was dead. "Okay." Josie eased toward the door.

Madge grabbed her bag. "I have the gun right behind my bag. I'll shoot you if I need to."

"I know." Josie stepped into the hallway, glancing toward the far lobby. *God, please let Shane be on guard.*

Shane sat, his legs out before him, a legal pad in his hand. He glanced up.

She tipped her head toward Madge and turned the opposite way.

Vicki glanced up from her computer screen. "How are things?"

"Great." Josie kept moving. She couldn't get Vicki

hurt. "Madge and I are heading to the conference room to spread out."

"Josie," Shane said, suddenly right behind her.

She jumped, partially turning. "Hi, Shane." She gestured toward Madge. Her breath caught. "This is Madge, my client. We're heading to the conference room."

Shane smiled, all teeth. He extended a hand. "Nice to meet you, Madge."

Madge eyed Josie and then Shane. With a hiss, she dropped the bag and pointed the gun at Shane. "Damn it." She straightened her shoulder, gaze surveying Shane. "You look like danger."

"Thank you." Shane shifted his stance like a cougar about to strike.

Madge steeled her shoulders. "Yeah. There's only one way to deal with a guy like you."

Oh God. She was going to shoot! Without a thought, Josie shot a roundhouse kick at Madge's hand.

The gun went off.

Shane bent at the waist, his hands going to his stomach. Blood oozed.

"Shane!" Josie gasped.

His eyes widened.

Madge grabbed Josie and pressed the gun to her neck. "You're next." She tugged Josie toward the elevator, backing away from Shane and a wide-eyed Vicki. Accountants and secretaries peered out of their offices, several with cell phones held at their ears. Calling the police, hopefully.

"Let her go and I won't kill you," Shane hissed through clenched teeth. His skin paled, yet he stood upright, one hand still covering the wound.

He'd been shot. How bad? Josie tried to halt their movements. Madge dug the gun in harder, and Josie winced.

Madge punched the elevator button. "If anyone comes near us, I'll kill her. You know I will." The door slid open and she yanked Josie inside.

Josie bit her lip. Shane stood near the door; his jaw set hard, a murderous glint in his eyes. Blood continued to soak through his T-shirt. How bad was the wound? Josie struggled to focus but couldn't tell.

The door slid shut.

CHAPTER
23

Y OU DIDN'T HAVE to shoot him." Josie tried to tilt her head away from the cold gun stabbing into her jugular as the elevator descended. Anger made stars dance in front of her eyes.

Madge shrugged from behind her. "Yes, I did. I could tell from one look at that guy—he's a hunter. He'll keep coming. Nice kick, by the way. Who do you think you are? Rambo?" She dug sharp nails into Josie's arm, her extra six inches of height coming in handy.

Josie blinked rapidly. Her kick had been useless. Maybe Shane was right. Maybe she was a ball of fluff. Fear filtered through the anger. What if the bullet had hit something important? What if Shane was really hurt? Without a doubt he wouldn't seek medical help while some crazy woman held Josie hostage. He'd come after her.

That's what family did.

The doors slid open. Two security guards, their stances low, pointed weapons at them.

Madge yanked her toward the door. "Make a move, boys, and I'll shoot her in the neck."

They didn't move, but a drip of sweat slid down the pudgy face of the man closest to them.

Josie hustled to keep up with Madge's longer legs across the entryway and outside into the pelting rain, her neck afire from the scrape of the barrel. She wouldn't think about it. If Madge tripped...

Sirens sounded in the distance.

"Hurry." Madge bit her lip, stopping behind a faded white van. She opened the back doors and shoved Josie in, following to slam the doors behind them. Pushing Josie against the far wall, Madge sat, gun pointed at Josie's chest. "Go."

Her husband turned around, bloodshot eyes wide. "Jesus, Madge. What did you do?"

Josie sank into bristly carpet. "Kidnapping, attempted murder, battery for a start." She glared at the balding twenty-five-year-old man she'd tried to help. Maybe she could talk some sense into him. "This is bad, Sam. Really bad."

Sam whipped the van out of the lot and into traffic. "Madge?" He glared in the rearview mirror.

Madge shrugged. "I had to get out of there and thought I could. But now, everyone saw me with a gun, and I just panicked."

Josie eyed the weapon. The stench of sweat and desperation assaulted her senses. Would they kill her? "The police are coming."

Sam yanked the wheel and flew into an alley, driving until he screeched to a stop in a narrow garage. Quickly he jumped out of the van and opened the back door.

Josie prepared to strike, then froze at the Glock Sam pointed at her. At least it looked like a Glock, similar in size and shape to the weapon Shane had taught her to shoot years ago.

"Get out." Sam grabbed Josie by the hair and tugged her out next to a dented old Cadillac. Pain lanced her scalp. "Get rope, Madge."

Josie struggled, trying to reason with him. "Max is going to kill you. You know that, right?"

Sam backhanded her, sending her head spinning. Pain rocked through her cheek. God. She didn't know him at all. He would actually kill her. He handed his gun to Madge and spun Josie around. A rough rope abraded her wrists as Sam wound it around and then knotted it tight.

Josie winced. What if she couldn't get away? "Everyone knows it was you. They saw Madge with the gun; in fact, she shot my husband."

Sam jerked her around, leaning his face toward her. His young, handsome face with the whimsical goatee that had always charmed her. "So, we get out of town for a while. Max needs us. No way will he kill us." Sam grabbed Josie's upper arms, his long fingers sure to leave bruises. "You, on the other hand..."

Quick movements had her trussed up, and Sam shoved her into the trunk of the Caddy. Seconds later the engine revved, and they were on the road again. They'd changed vehicles. Someone was directing Madge and Sam.

The trunk's rough carpet scratched her cheek. Moldy, smelly carpet. She sneezed.

She had to get free before they took her to Max. Wasn't there a television show she'd watched last year about getting out of a trunk? She hadn't really been paying attention. The car hit a bump, and nausea swirled through her stomach.

She rolled onto her back, scooting her butt under her to kick off her heels. Darkness. No light filtered inside. How much air did she have? Her arms ached, tied at the center of her back. Flipping to her side, she shimmied, pulling her knees up until her hands caught the bottom of her feet. Her shoulder muscles stretched in protest.

She needed help. She needed Shane.

She flexed her toes, and her hands slid up in front of her calves toward her thighs. Thank goodness. She breathed out in relief, her shoulders relaxing. Tugging against the ropes, she frowned. Then she brought her bound hands to her mouth, ignoring whatever germs were probably on the old rope. Her teeth dug in, trying to loosen the hold.

Nothing.

She couldn't free her hands with her teeth. The car bounced again and she yelped, flying up toward the metal to land with a thunk back on the sharp carpet. Bruises began to form in deep muscle and tissue.

Somehow she didn't think many women were taken captive so frequently. Was she born under a bad sign, or what?

Scooting her shoulders toward the backseat, she bent at the knees and kicked toward where the taillight probably was. Her toes hit hard metal. Pain ricocheted up her leg.

Her head dug into the carpet, hair getting caught. She kicked again, only to bruise her feet further. Think. She needed to think. Fear slowed her thoughts to haziness. If she kicked out the backseat, assuming she could, Madge and Sam would be there with guns. If she waited until they opened the trunk, same problem.

The car turned a corner and she rolled toward the backseat. The sound of her panting filled the small space. Was there enough air in the trunk? How long would she be able to breathe? Maybe they'd just leave her there to die. A sob rose. She sniffed. Why hadn't she listened to Shane and stayed home?

She sobbed again. How badly was Shane hurt? Why had she told him they didn't have a chance? The idea of living without him hurt a hell of a lot worse than the idea of trying to make it work. But could they? God. She was so screwed up.

The car stopped with a squeal of brakes. Josie rolled forward and then back, the stiff carpet scratching her bare arms. She dug her shoulder into the floor, shifting until her feet angled toward the back.

Doors slammed.

The trunk lid flipped open, and she shot her feet toward the opening, wincing as light cut into her eyes.

Sam batted her feet out of the way, reaching in with one slender hand to grab her bound wrists and drag her out of the trunk.

The rusty metal scratched her midriff.

He lifted her out, dropping her to her feet.

The smell of spoiled milk and rotten food filled her nostrils. An alley. Dark and wet between faded brick buildings. Josie frowned. Where in the world was she?

Madge yanked open a scratched purple door. The thump of music wafted out.

"Come on." Sam yanked Josie inside the narrow hallway.

No way. "The Pound?" Another client she'd inherited from Billy. She'd been right to be suspicious of the drug dealer's brother. "Paul's in on this, too?"

"Yep." Sam opened Paul's office door and shoved her inside.

Paul stood on the other side of his large desk, his curly hair wild and his eyes wide. "What is she doing here?"

Sam pushed her into a chair. "She found out about Billy."

"I thought he fixed all the accounts."

"Nope. Not in time."

"Well, he fixed mine before he went to rehab." Paul dropped into his chair. "You should've made sure he altered yours, too."

Sam shrugged. "I didn't get the chance. And Max is pissed."

Paul turned white. "Where's Billy?"

Josie straightened in the chair. "Billy's dead. Shot through the head. Making deals with a guy like Max will get you all killed." She assumed. It's not like she'd met Max, but the evidence was pretty clear. "Let me go, Paul. I'll help you get protection from the police."

Sam snorted. "Yeah, right."

Anger simmered beneath Josie's skin. "Okay. Then let me go, or my husband will rip the skin from your body with his bare hands." She leaned forward, her words spilling out. "You don't know him. You have no idea the training he's had. If anything happens to me, he'll kill you so slowly." The words made her shiver because they were the absolute truth.

Paul somehow paled even further, light freckles standing bold against stark white skin.

Madge dropped into the adjacent chair. "No he won't. I shot him."

Josie shook her head wildly. "One bullet won't stop Shane. Trust me on that."

Movement sounded behind her before the door snapped shut. "I'm not concerned about a wounded man, Mrs. Dean." Low and accented, the deep voice filled the room.

Josie pivoted, her gaze on the tall man. Black hair swept away from an olive complexion that highlighted odd, light blue eyes. He wore a black silk suit with a red-striped tie. Josie sucked in a breath. "You must be the drug dealer."

He smiled a perfect row of sparkling white teeth. "No. Paul's brother is a simple drug dealer—for me. I'm a businessman."

"Did you kill Billy?"

"Yes." Max glanced at Sam, who swallowed audibly. "Billy needed to learn how foolish it is to cross me." He brushed invisible lint off his lapel. "Of course, I hadn't realized the construction crew in your building would be called to the north side of Snowville for the beginning of this week." His full lips quirked. "I assume Billy is stinking up the place by now. I hope they find him soon."

A ball of dread uncoiled in her gut. Full confession from the rabid criminal. Obviously he wasn't planning on letting her go. Fear set up a ringing between her ears, and her hands shook. How could she get away? She turned toward a trembling Paul. "Are you really going to let him kill me?"

Paul sucked in air, his gaze lifting to Max. "You're not going to kill her, are you? I mean, she's a nice lady."

Max gave her a nod of approval. "Smart, too." He turned toward Paul. "She knows about your business, about how we've been not only selling meth here to customers but filtering the proceeds through several other businesses to end up clean. Laundering money is a federal offense. She'll put you away for life."

Josie straightened her shoulders. "That's nothing compared to what Shane will do to you. Trust me."

Paul's hands trembled on his desk.

Max sighed. "Sam, Madge, take the Cadillac to the cabin and wait for me there. We'll need to get you out of town for a while." He tugged a cell phone out of his jacket pocket. "I'll bring cash."

Madge's eyes gleamed, and she gave Josie a supercilious glare before flouncing out the door. Sam followed without looking back.

Several seconds later the outside door slammed shut.

Max pushed a button and pressed his phone to his ear. "Hi. There will be two problems arriving at the cabin in thirty minutes. Take care of them." He clicked the phone shut.

Paul half lifted himself from his chair. "You're going to kill them?" His voice rose an octave.

Max twisted his lips. "Of course. Witnesses saw them shoot a man and then kidnap this lovely lady." He ran a hand down Josie's hair.

Fear nearly made her gag, and she shrugged him off. "Touch me again, and you lose your hand."

He shifted, placing both hands on the arms of the chair to trap her. He leaned in, his minty breath brushing her lips. "You might want to change your tone with me, Mrs. Dean." His gaze dropped to her chest. "Or I'll change it for you." He leaned back. "How much fun we could have together."

Dread pooled in her stomach. Panic had her changing his focus. "Did you bug my house?"

"Yes." Max took a handkerchief from his pocket, wiping his hands. "When Billy checked into rehab, we realized he hadn't quite finished doctoring all the books. You took over for him, so we bugged your home to make sure you hadn't caught on before we fixed the files."

The idea of people listening in on her life made her nauseous. She struggled to concentrate and not puke. "All of the men Shane has taken care of lately? Were they yours?"

Max huffed out an irritated breath. "Yes. I don't know the full story there, either. I sent them to wait for you at your house so we could have a little talk. Next thing I heard, they were in the morgue."

"I told you crossing Shane was an extremely bad idea." So all the problems had been because of her, and not Shane's past. How badly had her husband been shot, anyway? He had to be all right.

"We'll see about that." Max whipped a gun out of a shoulder holster.

Paul shoved away from his desk, the chair scraping across the floor. "You can't kill her here."

Oh God. He was really going to shoot her. Josie eyed the gun. If she kneed Max in the nuts, would he drop the weapon?

Max smiled. "I'm not going to kill her."

Josie's sigh of relief matched Paul's.

Max took another step away. "You are, Paul."

CHAPTER
24

PAUL LEAPED TO his feet. "What? No way. Why would I kill her?" His gaze slid to Josie and then back to Max. "I'm no killer."

Max cocked the gun. "It occurred to me earlier that I'm taking all the risks here. Should you decide to turn me in, you could certainly strike a deal, considering I killed Billy." One perfectly creased shoulder shrugged. "So you kill her." He eyed the young bar owner. "Or I kill you. Either way, I won't worry about it anymore."

Paul gulped loudly. "Can't we just let her go and all leave town?"

Josie slid to the edge of her chair. The pounding of music through the walls turned ominous, the beat thumping her shoes. "Let me go." Paul's desk held a stapler, computer, and pens. No good weapons.

Max laughed, a low dangerous sound that rose goose bumps on her skin. He reached into his pocket for a silver cylinder that he twisted on to the end of the gun. "I like you, Mrs. Dean."

A silencer. She fixated on the small hole at the end, unable to look away. "How exactly do you plan to get my body out of here?" She aimed the question at Paul, feeling some satisfaction as he gasped.

A deep male sigh hissed through Max's lips. "Through the back door. Of course." Quick movements had him grabbing Paul and yanking the young man out from behind the desk.

Max thrust the gun into Paul's shaking hand and pointed the barrel at Josie. "This might make a mess, but I'm okay with that."

Paul retreated until his desk stopped him, his eyes filling with tears, his hand shaking so wildly he might accidentally pull the trigger.

Her breath caught in her throat, and the room narrowed to razor-sharp focus.

Max stepped away from Paul. "Shoot her, Paul."

"I'm sorry." Paul shut his eyes and pulled the trigger.

Josie dropped low before springing forward to smash her head into Paul's midsection. His back hit the desk. The bullet pinged off a painting. Paul's air whooshed out of his lungs. He doubled over, and Josie reached for the gun, her sweating hands slipping on the cold metal.

Max shot forward, grabbing her shoulder. She yelled. Pivoting, she rammed her elbow up into his groin. He made a sound crossed between a squealing pig and nails on a blackboard. He bent at the waist, still grabbing for the gun.

Oh God. This wasn't happening. Josie tucked her hand around the grip panel of the gun, rolling to the far side and standing up. The scent of splintered wood and gunpowder filled the room. She pointed the gun at Max. Paul dropped to his knees, tears and snot running down his face.

Max straightened, his face a mottled purple, his hand pressed against his lower abdomen. "You bitch. Fine, *I'll* kill you."

Josie settled her stance. She'd actually taken the gun from him. Unlike Paul's, her hand remained steady. Her mind clouded, the aftermath of the adrenaline rush. The room took on a surreal haze, but she kept her gaze on the threat. "I have the gun, asshole."

His smile belonged on a Halloween monster. "You won't shoot me. We both know it." He took two quick steps forward.

Josie pulled the trigger.

A small boom echoed. Louder than the first shot. Max fell back against the wall. Blood sprayed from his shoulder, and his hand covered the wound, seeping red through his fingers. "You shot me." His eyes flashed wide and incredulous.

"Of course." Josie fought to keep her hand steady. "You're lucky I'm a crappy shot. I was aiming for the center of your chest." Holy crap. She'd actually just shot him. "Did you think I'd let you kill me? That I wouldn't shoot you?" How unbelievable. She'd been a survivor since day one in this life. Apparently looks truly were deceiving.

The door crashed open.

Shane rushed inside with Matt on his heels, both holding square, dangerous-looking guns. He took in the scene, gray eyes expressionless. "Angel." He looked back and forth between the two damaged men and her. "Are you all right?"

"Fine." Though now that the danger had ebbed, her knees felt like rubber. A pounding set up at the base of her skull. Crazy adrenaline. "Are you?" She glanced down at the red that stained his shirt.

He nodded, his pale face tightening. "Yes. Bullet skimmed my abs. Bloody but not dangerous."

Sirens cut through the late afternoon.

Matt tucked his gun in the back of his pants. "Looks like you have things taken care of here." His grin reached his eyes. "You're something, honey."

Josie tried to smile in response, but her lips refused to cooperate. She'd shot a man.

Shane stepped between Josie and Max, his gun trained on Max's heart. "Thanks for the help. I'll see you later."

Matt took one last glance around the room. With a nod, he hurried out the door.

Max sucked in air. "I have money. A lot of it."

Shane's stance didn't change. "I don't give a shit. In fact, I'm having a mental debate about whether or not I should kill you."

Paul sobbed louder from where he lay curled on the floor.

Shane glanced down, his shoulders straightening. "Get off the floor, asshole."

Without warning, Max grabbed a gun from behind his waist and pointed it at Shane, pulling the trigger. The explosion rocked around the room.

Shane fell back. Josie grabbed him, holding him and easing him to the floor. Her eyes widened at the amount of blood, and she gasped. "Shane."

The pounding of running boots echoed. Three uniformed police officers rushed into the room, weapons drawn. "Drop your weapons," the first bellowed.

Max dropped his gun, raising his hands.

Shane perched on his knees, partially doubled over, yet still shifting his weight to shield Josie from the cops' aim.

Josie grabbed his arm. "How bad?" Blood gushed from his stomach.

"Bad." Shane paled. "Surgery bad."

Fear caught a sob in her throat. She glanced up. "Get an ambulance."

"It's on the way," the first cop said. "What happened?"

"I'm Josie Dean and those guys kidnapped me." She pointed to Max. "He was going to kill me, but I got his gun." Her hand wavered as she held the gun out to the police officer. "I shot him."

The cop nodded, taking the gun. "Yes. The whole force is out looking for you." He nodded to the other two cops. "Cuff them." The other two hurried over to Max and Paul to place them in handcuffs. "We'll take the wounded to the hospital first."

Josie gripped Shane's arm like a lifeline. More sirens grew louder.

Shane cleared his throat. "Did you get the two tied up in their car?"

"Yes." The officer glanced at Max and then back. "They couldn't wait to start talking about Max the famous drug dealer here."

"Good." Shane huffed out a breath. "There was another man in the alley, one who helped me tie them up, but he wouldn't say who he was."

Josie kept her face blank. So no one was supposed to know about Matt. She'd play along. But her ears rang, and her hands shook.

"We'll get descriptions from you both." The cop's thick mustache wriggled when he spoke. "You can answer questions at the hospital, Mrs. Dean."

Josie rested her head against the pale pink wall. Who made hospital walls pink, anyway? She shifted her weight onto the hard leather of the seat. Waiting. She hated waiting. Shane had been in surgery for an hour. Maybe more.

Matt dropped by every once in a while for an update, otherwise staying in the background. Just his presence somewhere in the hospital brought her some relief. She took a deep breath. Enough of the on-again, off-again plans for her future. She'd seen the worst of Shane, and she'd seen the best. It was time to make a decision and stick to it—no matter what. A near-death experience tended to put things in perspective now, didn't it?

She could go on her own way and build a pretty good life for herself. Maybe even find a nice man and have a couple of cute kids.

But something would always be missing. She'd always dream of Shane, and of what they might've had. His life expectancy wasn't great, but he had some time. And she wanted to be a part of that time—to take what they could. Maybe they'd even win and find a happy life. But she never wanted to look back and wonder—and she couldn't waffle anymore. The decision she made, sitting in the scary hospital, would be the one she stuck with absolutely.

For the first time, she had people who were hers. The sense of possession surpassed the sense of belonging she'd always craved. No wonder people died or killed for family. There was no other feeling in the world as being bound and not alone. Right or wrong, she felt safe.

She chose Shane. The risk was worth it. Peace settled through her body.

The doctor, still in surgery scrubs, sidled his impressive bulk down the hallway toward her. Bushy eyebrows rose over thick spectacles. "Mrs. Dean?"

"Yes." She straightened in her chair, wincing as bruises from her journey in the trunk flared to life.

"Your husband came through the surgery just fine."

Her breath exhaled in a whoosh of relief. She hadn't realized she'd been holding it. Her lungs cried for more oxygen, and she breathed in deep. "He's all right?"

"Yes, quite." The doctor pursed full lips. "He's in excellent shape. The bullet did minimal damage, though I'd like to keep an eye on him tonight to ensure there's no internal bleeding." He nodded at a passing doctor wearing a long white coat. "Your husband should be up from surgery in about thirty minutes, and then you can see him."

Tears pricked the backs of her eyes. Shane was okay. "Thank you, Doctor."

With an absent nod, the doctor turned and followed his colleague.

Detective Malloy sidled up from around the corner.

Josie sighed. "Is there a case in town you're not assigned to?"

Malloy grinned, twirling a toothpick in his mouth. "Lots of them. But you and your husband, Mrs. Dean, well... you're mine. Whenever your name comes up, I get the call."

"Lucky you," Josie breathed, pushing matted hair off her forehead. "I suppose you just heard?"

"Yep." Malloy dropped into the seat next to her. The cushions protested with a wheeze of air. "The major is in excellent shape and will be fine. Good to know." He flipped out his battered notebook. "So. Run me through what happened."

Josie told the tale, leaving out the parts about finding Billy's body as well as Matt's name. She explained in detail who Billy was and what he'd done for his clients. She sighed. "Max the drug dealer said he killed Billy on the ninth floor of my building. You should check it out."

Malloy raised an eyebrow, grabbing his cell phone and barking orders. "I sent two uniforms to investigate." He sat back. "So. Tell me about this mysterious man who helped your husband."

Josie rubbed her eyes. "I can't. Shane said he met him in the alley, and the guy helped out. Maybe he was ex-military or something. Those guys stick together, you know."

Malloy nodded, a slow smile spreading across his weathered face. "Just out of curiosity, how stupid do you think I am?"

"I don't think you're stupid at all." And she didn't. She'd known the detective wouldn't buy Shane's lame story about Matt. But she also knew Malloy couldn't prove it was a lie, either. If she and Shane stuck to the story, even though they all knew it was a lie, there was nothing Malloy could do about it. "What did the Agers say?"

"That's irrelevant." For the first time, Malloy allowed irritation to flash across his thick features. "Describe the man."

She shrugged. "I didn't get a good look at him. I shot Max, Shane showed up, Max shot Shane . . . it's all a blur."

"Try."

"Well, I guess he was about average size? Maybe with light brown hair and, I don't know, maybe brown eyes?" She leaned forward, her gaze running the length of the sparkling clean hallway. "I only saw him from the corner of my eye. My focus stayed on all the guns."

"Did mystery man have a gun?"

"I don't think so, but I'm not sure." She plastered her best innocent expression on her face before turning toward him. She'd learned it early in childhood. "I really wish I could help you. But the entire kidnapping was quite the ordeal, and my brain is just fuzzy."

Bloodshot brown eyes narrowed. "Do you require medical attention, Mrs. Dean?"

"No." She sighed, leaning her head back again. "I'm

just bruised and tired, Detective." The idea that Shane might not make it through surgery had made her heart hurt. Yet even then, she had faith he'd survive. Shane was a true warrior, enhanced. A simple bullet couldn't take him down. Of course, that damn chip in his spine had a countdown clock in it.

She shook her head at her own naïveté. Of course he could die. But if anyone was larger than life, Shane fit the bill. "Are we finished?"

"Not even close." The detective slapped his notebook shut. "I'm assuming there's more to your story?"

"Nope." Oops. She'd also left out the fact that Max believed Shane killed the thugs who'd been waiting at the house for her. "You'll have to ask Shane after he's rested up from surgery if he has anything to add."

"I'll be sure to do that." Malloy stood, stretching his neck.

A nurse in bright purple scrubs bustled around the corner. "Mrs. Dean? You can see your husband now."

Malloy dropped back into the chair. "I'll wait so we can finish our discussion."

Josie stood. "I thought we had finished."

"Not even close." The detective smiled.

CHAPTER
25

SHANE LET SILENCE waft over his skin, filter through his pores to his muddled brain. Drugs. He hated being numb. Pain beat feeling nothing any day of the week. A ticking clock punctuated the silence. Then footsteps, soft soles, outside the room. On hard tile. The beeping of a machine filtered through, and finally breathing. Soft, sexy, he knew that breath. He opened his eyes.

Josie.

Warmth exploded in his chest. Determination straightened his spine. Angel. His one and only. "Hey, sweetheart." His voice came out hoarse.

She scooted closer to the bed, sliding her small hand under his. "Hi." Dark circles marred the soft skin under her stunning eyes. A bruise still spread over her cheek. Her hair wisped all over the place. Even her lips had gone pale.

Damn, she was beautiful.

He forced his voice to work. "You impressed the hell out of me today."

Her smile lifted the corners of her eyes. "I just used moves you taught me." A chuckle escaped. "You should've seen Max nearly hit the floor, though."

Danger. Shane had failed to protect her from it. This time she'd protected herself. Pride filled him, chased by determination. No way would she be in danger alone again. He wouldn't allow it. The world was Josie. Period. No more wondering, and no more changing his mind. His path was clear. "I'm proud of you."

A pretty flush filled her face. "Thanks. I was glad you arrived when you did." She frowned. "Sorry I got you shot twice...today." A white tooth sank into her bottom lip.

"Not your fault." He glanced at the end of the bed. "Hand me the chart, would you?"

She nodded, handing it to him. He flipped open the lid, quickly scanning the doctor's notes. "I'm fine." He grabbed the blankets to push away.

Josie's hands on his stopped his movements. "Oh no, you don't. You're staying the night here. Period." She squared her chin.

He lifted an eyebrow. "Says who?"

"Me and the doctor."

Shane shook his head, and nausea welled inside his belly. What had they given him, anyway? "If I'm staying, so are you." He tugged her onto the bed, scooting to the far side.

Those pretty blue eyes widened with temptation and need. Vulnerability shone through and pretty much broke his heart in two.

He sighed. The boy inside him who had once cried out in loneliness and confusion, wondering why he had to fight and die, now howled out with hope. Because of Josie Dean. For the two months of their marriage, he'd been whole for the first time in his life.

He loved his brothers completely and absolutely. Without question, he'd die for them. He'd killed for them, and he would again. But he was taking the chance on forever with Josie, even if he had to live apart from them. They loved him, and they'd understand.

He tightened his hold on hope. "This is your place, sweetheart. Take it."

With a swallow, she nodded and slid into the bed. She snuggled into his good side, her breath on his shoulder. "I could sleep."

He settled back down. "Did you talk to the police?"

Her yawn shook her entire body. "Yes. Malloy couldn't wait to talk to me."

"Malloy? What are we—his pet projects?" The cop seemed like a good guy. Shane didn't want to have to hurt him.

"I guess." Josie's voice slurred with fatigue. "He really wants to know about the mystery man with you at the bar. I played dumb."

"So long as we stick to the same story, we're fine." No way would he let Matt get caught up in the clusterfuck Shane had made of his own life. They'd finally positioned Matt in Seattle, a safe place for his older brother. For now. The commander wanted Matt bad, and they all knew it. A memory shifted behind the drug haze in Shane's brain. Jory. Something there. He tensed.

"What's wrong?" Josie murmured.

"Nothing." He couldn't catch the thought. But it was there. Maybe when the drugs cleared, the last two years would finally come clear. He'd need to get Josie to safety before he went after the people who'd killed his brother. But he'd hunt them, without question.

He shifted his thoughts to allow his subconscious to take over. "Remember that hat you knitted me for Christmas?" His first homemade Christmas present, just like the families gave on television. Black and gray, she'd interwoven the strands into something guaranteed to keep him warm when they vacationed on the ski slopes.

She giggled. "Yes. I had to sneak and knit at night when you slept."

He'd felt her leave the bed each night and had known why. "I still have it."

Her shoulders stilled. "You do?"

"Yes. My hat, your picture, they're in a safety-deposit box in California. The most important items I own." He wanted that hat. Now. Wanted to feel the love and care she'd put into making it for him.

"That's sweet." Her voice thickened. "The necklace you gave me of the silver angel—I need to get it from my house."

"We will." He shouldn't ask. He really shouldn't. "Where's your wedding ring?" His was safely with the hat.

"Same jewelry box."

Well, at least she'd kept the ring. He had time later to talk her into sliding the stunning solitaire back on her finger. "Have you kept up the knitting?"

"Yes." She smiled against his skin. "I opened a store on eBay and sell stuff sometimes."

Pride. She was something. "I remember that was your dream. To drop the numbers and sell your creations."

"It's just a dream. Numbers pay the bills."

"I have money, Josie." A lot more than he ever expected to have. Nate was a financial genius at investing the profits from Sins Security—probably because he didn't give a shit and was happy taking risks. "You can do anything you want in life. Live your dream." With him. God, please let her stay with him.

"What about you, Shane? What's your dream to live?"

He sighed. "You're my dream, angel. Just you." Her scent of wild berries filled his nostrils while she filled his heart. His soul. If he had one, it was hers. Made in test tubes, taught to kill, he'd often doubted the possibility. But with Josie cuddled into his side, he felt like he had a soul. Even if it bore stains, his soul existed.

Her breathing evened out as she slipped into sleep.

He closed his eyes and listened to her steady breathing. In the dim recesses of his brain, he cataloged the noises outside the room, down the hall, and outside the building. But for this one moment in time, peace settled his heart rate.

Familiar footsteps echoed down the hallway into his room. He opened his eyes, smirking at his brother. Matt had dressed in faded surgical scrubs and somehow had found a mustache and thick copper-rimmed glasses. "Doctor."

Matt's eyes softened as he glanced at Josie before grabbing Shane's chart for a quick read. "The bullet didn't impact anything important. You're fine."

"I know that."

The chart clanked against the end of the bed. "She's something, Shane. Taking down those two men." Matt rubbed his chin.

Yeah, she was. He understood the risk he was taking, and leaving his brothers would cut him in two. But the risk was his, and he had to keep them safe. But he had to choose Josie—she needed him more than they did. Any life he had wasn't worth it without her. "I want to stay with her, Mattie."

"I was afraid of that, little brother." Matt sidled around the bed, dropping into a guest chair. "The whole happily ever after with a family…it's impossible. Does she know, I mean, ah…"

"We can have kids, Matt." If he couldn't, and Josie wanted kids, they'd adopt. Maybe. Someday when he'd taken care of the danger.

Matt frowned. "They tried, Shane. The scientists tried to create little test-tube babies with our genetic material. You know that. They never once succeeded."

"Maybe test tubes won't work for our kids."

"Maybe." Matt leaned back, stretching his neck. "It's more likely they fucked up our DNA so that we can't reproduce." Anger filtered through his quiet words. "Something to think about."

He would. "Besides, we're not exactly safe right now, Matt. Won't be until the commander and his top scientists are in the ground." That was if they figured out a way to deactivate the kill chips. If Shane were a better person, he'd think about sending those people to jail. But he wasn't. The only way his family would be safe was if the people who'd created him died. Period.

"True." Matt eyed Josie. "I spent the day hacking into the local police database. Apparently, the bugs in Josie's house were planted by Max's men."

"Yeah, I know." Shane took a deep breath. "I found the bugs, figured the commander had found Josie, and bugged her place myself. Then when I figured out it had nothing to do with me, I went after the morons lying in wait for her." Of course, he hadn't planned on getting hit in the head with a bat.

"Then you conducted Internet searches that could've brought us down. Thank goodness they didn't. We got lucky this time. From now on, we check in with Nathan once a week so nothing like this happens again." Footsteps sounded and Matt stiffened, his shoulders relaxing when a nurse passed by the doorway. "Though to be safe, we need to get out of town."

"Yeah. I need to get Josie to the ranch—just for the next three months. If we figure out the code for the kill chip, I'll take her somewhere else to keep everyone safe." The ranch was one hundred acres in the Montana mountains where Nate had set up a protected space for them all to live if necessary.

"We need to stick together, Shane."

"Not if it puts us all in more danger." Shane shook his head.

"We're not separating."

"Leaving her again is impossible, and I won't let my choices put you in the ground." Shane winced as his abs protested. "I'm so sorry, Matt."

"Don't be." His older brother leaned back, his gaze serious. "All I ever wanted was a good life for you. If you think it's possible, I'll do whatever I have to do in order to help."

Gratitude and love choked Shane. "I can't let you take the risk."

"That's a fight you're not going to win—a fight for another day." Matt steepled his fingers under his chin. "So your memory is coming back?"

"Yeah." Shane searched deep in his head where something echoed. "I'm almost there. I can feel it." Maybe he didn't want to know what happened to his brother. "Tell me what you know."

Matt's jaw tightened. "We put Jory deep into a company called Millennia Investments."

"I remember. The company has its fingers in everything from military contracts to genetic laboratories and drug manufacturing." Shane had posed as a researcher to get in quickly. "Jory was beyond a genius with computers, wasn't he?"

"Yes." Matt sighed, dropping his hands to his lap and stretching his legs out. "Jory's IQ kept him alive when he was a kid."

Memories of a scrawny kid with huge feet filtered through Shane's mind. "I remember. *You* kept him alive as a kid. It was you."

"No." Matt shook his head. "Jory's IQ was incredibly high. Too high to measure, in fact. That kept him alive until he grew into those feet." He chuckled. "Then he became downright deadly, remember?"

"Yes." Shane nodded. Jory fought with cold, hard logic. No emotion, no anger. His well-trained limbs did what that powerful brain dictated. He usually won. "What if he hadn't? I mean, did you ever wonder what really happened to the kids who left the camp?"

Matt stilled. "You've never asked me that before."

Maybe Shane hadn't wanted to know. "Do you know?"

"No. I assume they went to a different camp." Raw pain flashed through Matt's eyes to be quickly veiled. He was lying. There was no question he was hiding something. "Either way, right now we need to figure out what happened to Jory."

Shane could let it go. For now. "So Jory went undercover to filter out whether the commander and his scientists had fingers in Millennia."

"No. We already knew they did. Jory went in to find the commander and the names of the other investors. The people playing God." Matt snapped his jaw shut.

Shane breathed out. "That's right. What did he find?"

Matt lowered his tone, his gaze on Josie. "Don't know.

Six months later we received an urgent message from him that he'd been discovered and was heading out."

Something hurt in Shane's gut. Bad. And it wasn't the bullet holes. "What then, Mattie?"

Matt dropped his gaze. Lines dug into his face. "Nate hacked into the computer system, and we found a video file showing Jory being tortured."

"The commander?"

"I don't know. Just saw Jory."

Shane didn't remember the tape. "I saw the video?"

"No. Nate and I saw it before a virus uploaded and pretty much exploded his system. What a mess." He sucked in air, pain filling the oxygen around them. "I saw Jory die. Or rather, a video of his death."

"Are you sure?" Shane whispered. Videos could be doctored.

"Yes. A woman shot him point-blank in the chest."

"A woman?" Pain filled Shane's body along with air as he breathed. "Just one shot?"

"No. Several." Matt scrubbed his face. "I saw him fall. Saw his eyes go blank." He coughed, closing his eyes. "I lost him."

"Not your fault." Shane shifted, hiding a wince at the pain. "So I went undercover to find out who killed him—and what he'd found before he died. Did I check in?"

"Yes. Not with information, but you let Nate know you were alive every other month. Until a month ago. Then you took off—without a word. We didn't even know you'd broken cover until you triggered the Internet alerts looking for us."

Shane sighed, his head aching. Something there...a memory. Reality flashed through, hard and bright. "I was heading to Seattle, to you, Matt." He remembered going by his old base for mail and getting the divorce papers. "I stopped here on the way to deal with the divorce." He'd waited for Josie at her house, the buzzing of the planted bugs instantly alerting him she was in danger. "Figuring the commander had found her, I set up my own bugs to find him, and the next day I had the run-in with Max's men." Ending up with him getting amnesia. "But I was coming to you. Something happened, I knew something." He grabbed his head. What the hell was it?

"We need to figure out what you found." Matt lowered his voice. "Shut your eyes and relax."

Shane shut his eyes, forcing his heartbeat to slow. His breathing to even out. Such physical control the scientists had given him. An explosion ripped behind his eyelids. "Jesus."

"What?"

"I remember blowing the facility up five years ago." He opened his eyes. "We escaped. The barracks, the base...we blew it up and ran." The horrible place they were raised, the horrible place where they were trained to kill. Destroyed. It was easy to blow the place to hell. But they'd remained safe for the time being because of Jory. He figured out how to corrupt the computer system—with most of their records—which made them harder to track and even harder to find. Jory was by far the smartest one of them.

"Maybe you should sleep. See if anything comes back in your dreams." Matt's voice lowered to a hoarse rumble.

Sounded like a good idea. "What's your plan?" Shane asked.

"I'll keep watch until you get your memories back, and we find out what you discovered."

Doubt made Shane clear his throat. "Can you be away

from your job any longer?" Another memory...of Matt searching for a witness. "You're hunting somebody?"

"Yes." Matt stood. In profile, Matt's face appeared even harder than usual. Two strides had him at the door. "Get some sleep, Shane. I'll be back tomorrow."

His brother. The one who'd driven Shane so hard to train, so hard to fight. So he'd survive their childhood.

But they weren't kids anymore. It was time someone protected Matt. Shane ran his hand through Josie's silky hair. He'd been trained by the best, and he knew how to survive. Survival meant both Josie and his brothers lived. So he'd make sure they won. No matter the cost.

CHAPTER
26

JOSIE STRETCHED AWAKE in the hospital bed, her face tucked into Shane's shoulder. His steady breathing lifted his chest, and she wriggled out of bed to stand alongside his quiet form. She stepped into her tennis shoes, running her gaze over him. Even in sleep, an intensity lived on his face.

No softness, even now.

This was the first time she'd ever had the chance to watch him sleep. He had always been alert, ready to jump into action before she even left the bed. The doctor must've prescribed something incredibly strong in his IV.

Early light filtered through the blinds, scattering dust mites through the air. Bleach and the scent of freshly laundered linens filled her nostrils. The low murmur of voices wound through the hallway outside.

Her heart ached. Love wasn't supposed to hurt, and she guessed it didn't. The pain came from the uncertainty of where she stood with the sleeping soldier, and the damn kill chip. Would it actually take him out?

The smell of coffee out in the hall made her stomach rumble.

She reached for her cell phone on the counter and tucked it into her back pocket. Brushing her hands through her tangled hair, she tiptoed into the hallway and headed for the vending machine at the end.

"Mrs. Dean." Detective Malloy glanced up from his perch on a worn chair, where he was scribbling in his notebook. "Sleep well?"

Josie faltered. "Yes, thank you." What the heck was he doing there?

"Good." Malloy stood, sliding the notebook into his wrinkled jacket pocket. "We need to go down to the station and finish up with the paperwork."

A nurse plunked coins into the vending machine, and a candy bar dropped to the open slot. She grabbed it and walked down to a large counter. Josie watched her leave, then turned toward Malloy. "Why? I already gave my statement."

"I know." Malloy gestured toward the elevator. "But not only did you shoot a man, there are enough holes in your story to have my superiors wanting to send me back to detective school. I just need one more interview to put this entire matter behind us."

"But my husband..." Josie stumbled toward the elevator.

"Will be fine." Malloy pushed the down button, his face softening. "I checked with his doctors. We should have you back by the time he awakens later today."

The door slid open, and Josie sighed before walking inside. "My story isn't going to change."

Malloy raised a bushy eyebrow, poking the button for the parking garage. His gray suit sat frumpy and wrinkled on his large frame, but a shiny green tie brightened the entire look. Nothing brightened his hangdog face.

"Don't you ever sleep?" Josie frowned.

"As soon as we file the paperwork on the shooting, I'm taking some time off. Thanks to you, we've solved a huge case, and I deserve a break." The door slid open and he gestured her toward a brown nondescript car double-parked in a loading zone.

Josie hesitated at the car.

Malloy opened the front passenger door. "It's cleaner up here."

She slipped past him and sat, waiting until he had stomped around the car and settled his bulk in the driver's seat. "Are you going on vacation alone?"

He grinned, the smile making him seem years younger. "No." Starting the ignition, he backed out of the space, his gaze on the windshield. "But there's nothing wrong with being alone."

His scent of peppermint and tobacco wafted through the car in an odd ambiance of comfort. "Are you trying to tell me something?" She clicked the seat belt into place.

"Kind of. I like you." He maneuvered the large car out of the garage into the main road. "You're smart and spunky in a really cute way." He turned left toward the police station.

Why were hospitals always near police stations? Josie shifted in her seat. "Um, thanks?"

"You're welcome." He turned his attention back to the busy road, barely skirting a red sports car switching lanes. "Women rarely listen to my advice, but I feel the need to give it anyway. I think you should leave the past in the past . . . and move on. Away from danger."

The big bear was trying to protect her. "You're very sweet."

"I am not." The detective snorted.

"Are, too." But the man couldn't see that Shane and his brothers were her safe place to land. She loved and trusted Shane more than she would've thought possible. The realization set her firmly on her course. No matter what they'd done, or who they were, she wanted to keep them. She needed them. Family mattered, and she finally had one. "Please don't worry about me, Malloy. I promise I know what I'm doing."

He nodded. "Fair enough. You do seem like a smart gal. We'll get the final paperwork done, and I'll make sure you have a ride back to the hospital. But if you ever need anything, promise you'll call."

"I promise." She eyed him from the corner of her eye. "Nice tie. Another gift?"

A light flush filtered across the detective's worn face. "Yes."

"Really? Who from?"

Malloy was actually blushing.

He pulled into a parking spot in front of the two-story brick building. "Let's go inside, Mrs. Dean."

She jumped out of the car and followed Malloy through the bustling entrance, past several uniformed young men to the same conference room as her earlier interview. The cold metal of the chair instantly chilled her butt. "You gave me coffee last time."

Malloy smiled. "The receptionist will bring some in after she's off the phone." He slapped his notebook onto the scarred table. His chair scraped across the floor as he pulled the heavy frame away from the table before dropping his bulk down. His deep brown gaze settled on her face. "So. Please explain to me how your fingerprints ended up on the dead body of Billy Jones."

• • •

Shane struggled to rise to consciousness. Bleach and medicinal plastic scented the air. Drugs. His blood pumped slower, his brain fuzzed. The doctors had drugged him. Probably class A narcotics—good painkillers. But something in the back of his head insisted he awaken. He needed to wake up.

But the drugs pulled him under. The dream caught him unaware, and he slid into it, accepting the return of memories.

In this dream he was an adult.

He sat against the trunk of an old pine tree, his legs extended before him, his gaze on the training field. The dusty field of hell where he'd learned to fight, where he'd learned to kill.

Matt and Jory sat with him, their gazes hard on Nathan as he beat the hell out of another soldier. Fist to flesh, blood spraying to stain the dust red.

"We're sure Audrey was working with the commander?" Jory had asked, wiping blood off his chin from his training session.

Matt nodded. "Yes. Nate found proof—and she confirmed it just before several of the blue team were terminated."

Some of those men had become good friends—especially to Nate.

Jory plucked a lone blade of grass from the beaten earth. "We need to go. Now." His face tightened as Nathan threw the other soldier a good six feet across the field. Raw rage and pain cut deep into the hard lines of Nate's face. "Something bad is coming, and we all can feel it."

"This is the first time we've all been here at the same

time in years." *The first time the damn commander and his scientists couldn't extort them into killing in order to keep the other brothers alive. Usually at least two of them were out on missions at any given time.*

Shane studied his brothers. Of them all, Jory and Matt looked the most alike. While they all had the odd gray eyes, only Jory and Matt had pitch-black hair. He wondered once again if the two shared the same mother. Or if any of them did. He focused on Jory. "Can you do it?"

"Yes." *Jory hopped to his size fourteen feet. His shoulders blocked out the sun. So much bigger than the scrawny brainiac Shane had protected many years ago.* "I can take care of the entire computer system, if you can blow this place to hell."

"The commander will come after us." *Matt stretched to his feet, his focus on the tight form of the man standing to attention at the edge of the field watching Nathan.* "I've got the commander, but what about Emery?"

Dread slid through Shane. "You going to kill the commander?" *Could Matt kill the man who'd trained them? Even now, even as an adult with so many kills behind him, Shane still sometimes thought the commander invincible. Pure evil.*

"Yes."

Jory shook his head. "Emery deserves a chance. He was raised in this hellhole, too."

Shane rubbed the scar on his forearm that Emery had gouged with a bent paperclip when Shane was six. Two years older and just plain mean, the brown-eyed Emery was a favorite of the commander. "Emery is crazy and evil. I say we take him out, too."

"No." *As always, Jory looked to the side of fairness.* "None of us were given a choice. We fight or our brothers die." He glanced toward the computer center near the barracks. "Emery deserves a chance at freedom. To get his brothers to freedom."

Matt rolled his shoulders. "It's probably a mistake, but I agree. We let Emery live."

"For now," Shane agreed. "You know they'll come after us, right?"

Matt turned toward him, pure hardness on an already hard face. "Then it was stupid of them to train us so well now, wasn't it?" Anticipation lit his eyes on fire.

"Jesus." Shane stood. "Do you really think one of us can kill the commander?"

Mattie lifted his chin. "I started planning his death the day I turned twelve." Without another word, he turned toward the field to stop Nate from killing the other soldier. This time.

Shane jolted awake in the hospital bed. His head pounded. Jory. So damn smart, how the hell had he died?

The scent of wild berries filled Shane's nostrils. Josie. He glanced around the room. Thick sun poured through the blinds, showing the hour to be about noon. The rattle of carts sounded outside in the hall. Where had Josie gone?

Josie cleared her throat, stretching her neck. "How did you get my fingerprints, Detective?" Her mind spun. What now? Should she ask for a lawyer? Nathan had already flown out of town to wherever. Not that he was a real lawyer.

Detective Malloy sat back in his chair. "I took them off the coffee cup from the last time you sat in that seat."

"Humph. That's not legal."

"Sure it is." He leaned forward, tapping a gold pen on

his notepad. "Mrs. Dean, I know you didn't kill Billy. I've been a cop long enough to know you're one of the good ones. Just level with me, would you? Let me help you out of this mess."

Josie studied his earnest eyes. She took a deep breath. Where the hell had she left her fingerprints? On the phone, but Shane had grabbed that. On Billy's belt when she turned him over? Maybe. "Where were the prints?"

Malloy sighed. "It doesn't matter. Just tell me what happened so I can get you out of here and somehow keep my job."

"Fine. A man named George pushed me off the elevator to the ninth floor of my office building. He was working for Max Penton and wanted my files. I ran from him to hide in the room with Billy's body." Josie sucked in air. "Then he came after me, so I hit him and ran." No way would she bring Shane and his brothers into this.

Intelligence lit the detective's dark eyes. "Are you all right?"

His concern warmed her. "Yes."

"Why didn't you report the kidnapping or the dead body?"

"I was scared." Maybe Malloy had the same ingrained instinct to help that Shane did. Why not give it a shot? "I got away, but I knew George would come back after me. I thought Shane had already left town. I'm alone, Detective." She lifted her chin to meet his gaze as she lied. "You've been after my husband since day one. I figured Billy would be found by the construction crew, and I could just stay out of it."

Malloy blew out a frustrated breath. "Was your husband with you on the ninth floor that day?"

"No. Shane wasn't involved at all, Detective."

"Man, I wish you would let me help you." Malloy's upper lip quirked. "Yes, well. Billy was clearly laundering money for a drug dealer, and as you've said, Max admitted he killed the guy." A knock sounded on the door, and Malloy called, "Come in."

The receptionist, a forty-something redhead with curved hips under a tight pencil skirt, hurried into the room to set down two steaming coffee mugs. She yanked a file out from underneath her arm. "Detective Malloy. Here's the file you requested."

The scent of gardenia perfume competed with the warm coffee smell.

Malloy sat forward, accepting the file. He tugged on his tie, while a fine blush wandered across his beefy face. "Thank you, Ms. Smyth."

"Anytime." She patted his shoulder, turned on three-inch heels, clipped toward the door, shutting it with a sharp snap.

Malloy flipped open the file.

Interesting. Josie sat back, letting a smile play on her face. "Ms. Smyth is pretty."

Malloy jolted, lifting his head. "Hmm. I hadn't noticed." He glanced at the papers spread out before him.

Oh, he was just too cute. "Liar. She has nice tastes in ties."

Malloy lifted an eyebrow, and then a wide grin slid across his face. "She has even better taste in men."

"Yes, she does." Josie smiled back.

"Do you think perhaps you're clinging on to a life that doesn't exist? I mean, you're throwing your life away for a man who will destroy you?" Malloy's eyes softened.

The kernel of truth in the possibility cut deep. "Are you about to turn into a bully, Detective Malloy?"

His expression didn't change. But his jaw tightened. Ah. He didn't like that thought. Yet the cop wasn't the only one in the room who could dig under the surface. She'd navigated a scary world all by herself her entire childhood.

"Definitely not. I won't bully you, Mrs. Dean." Malloy rested his elbows on the table and exhaled loudly. "I really do want to protect you. I can. Let me help."

"How?"

"Tell me the truth about your husband—was he there that day?"

She shrugged. "No. George came after me for Max's files, told me that Max had killed Billy. I believed him."

"How did you get away from a killer?"

She smiled sadly. "I'm a survivor, Detective, and I got away from him the same way I kept Max from killing me."

Malloy gave a short nod of acknowledgment. "Tell me about your husband."

"You know as much as I do." Josie glanced at her watch. "Shane was a marine, and he disappeared for the last two years." No way would she tell the detective about Shane's life or the danger that stalked him. "I don't know where." Ironically, neither did Shane. Yet. She'd also meant it when she'd told Matt they were family. Her concept of the word might be colored by need, but she'd protect both him and Nathan from discovery. "I have nothing new to add."

Malloy studied her and then shook his head. His chair scraped the concrete as he stood. "Good enough. Are you sure you want to go back to the hospital? I can have a black-and-white take you anywhere you want to go."

"I'm sure." She brightened her smile to reassure him.

"Trust me. I've got this covered." And she did. Almost losing Shane to a bullet had made her realize she'd fight for him and for their future. They'd figure out the kill chip, and they'd move on together. It was time to get hold of her husband and explain their future. He was going to trust her, and she was going to love him. Forever.

It was as simple as that.

CHAPTER
27

D ETERMINATION ANIMATED JOSIE as she hustled through the station and into the waiting room, where she stopped short.

Tom jumped out of an orange chair. Daniel slid to his feet slowly.

Josie shook her head. "Tom? Dan? What are you doing here?"

Tom glared at the detective. "We stopped by the hospital to see you, and the on-duty nurse told us you'd left with a detective." The outside door opened and a curvaceous woman in tweed clicked Jimmy Choos toward them. "Ah. Here's my lawyer," he said with satisfaction.

The lawyer stood eye to eye with Malloy. "Jennifer Daly from Thymes, Witherspoon, and Craft." She shuffled muscular calves, handing him a cream-colored business card. "Did you read my client her rights?"

"Nope." Malloy slid the card into his jacket pocket. "She's not under arrest and was free to go at any time."

Josie stiffened. "I don't need a lawyer. We were just finishing the paperwork."

Malloy smiled at the lawyer. "Yep. Sorry to waste your time, ma'am."

Tom slid his arm around Josie's shoulders. "I'll be taking you home, Josie." He tugged her gently toward the door.

"Call me if you need anything, Mrs. Dean," Malloy said behind her.

Warmth filtered through Josie's stomach as they hurried outside into pure late-fall sunshine. Crisp and chilly. Her mind spun. Why were Tom and Daniel at the hospital? Were they going to try and save her from herself, too? She was a grown woman who knew what she wanted. Besides, she could always save herself if necessary. "How in the world did you afford a lawyer?"

Tom grinned. "That's my client—the one who wants to invest in fast-food restaurants. She's a lawyer."

"Ah. The woman with the hands. I take it you flirted?"

Tom shrugged. "I'm still waiting for you."

Sadness at what could've been caught Josie up short. Tom was a good guy who worked hard—who would've given his all to any relationship. He'd be a fantastic husband and an even better father to kids—and he'd be safe. No danger courted him. But her heart had gone another way. She smiled. "Thank you for coming."

Tom led her to his truck, opening the door for her. "Of course. I'm sorry we didn't get here sooner."

Josie hesitated and then pulled herself up into the seat.

Daniel jumped in beside her, and she scooted to the center.

Tom hustled around to climb into the driver's seat. "Have you eaten?"

"No. I just want to go back to the hospital. Will you take me?" She knew what she was asking.

He started the ignition and pulled out of the lot. "No."

"Our game is in an hour." Daniel stretched his neck. "If she wants to go to the hospital, we should take her."

Josie turned to him in surprise.

He shrugged. "I've been in love before. Yeah, it ended badly. But for a while there, I had fun." A grin lifted his upper lift. "For a brief time, I even loosened up."

"Yeah, right," Tom muttered.

Josie sighed. "Tom, you can't save me from myself, no matter how badly you want to." The words sounded as stupid as they felt. But the truth was the truth.

Tom frowned, squinting at the rearview mirror. "Sure I can."

Josie swiveled her head. "What are you looking at?"

"A van. A black van pulled out right after we did." Tom shrugged. "Now I'm imagining cloak-and-dagger stuff."

Daniel frowned, glancing in the rearview mirror. "It is keeping pace with us."

The van followed, and dread heated the air in Josie's lungs.

Shane forced the pain down, striding toward Matt's Jeep in the hospital parking lot. "Did you get my blood samples?"

Matt nodded, jumping inside. "Yes. All of your records, as well. There's no trace left of you here."

"Good." Shane edged inside, folding his arm over his aching midsection. The bullet hadn't done any real damage, though he was still sore. In fact, his entire body hurt like a raw wound. "I need a vacation."

Matt snorted. "You just spent a day in a bed. That's all

you get." He started the ignition and pulled out of the lot. "Your memory is back?"

"Yes. Everything except for the last two years. The recent stuff should be coming back next." Shane eyed the traffic. "The nurse said Josie left with Detective Malloy?" He'd called her cell phone several times, but she hadn't answered. Hopefully she'd just forgotten to turn it on. Unease and anger ripped through his skin.

"Yep. You can't blame the guy. Nothing is adding up for him."

"All of it adds up except my part." Shane grinned. "Poor detective."

Matt frowned. "You don't think Josie will tell him about us, do you?"

"No." Loyalty coursed through his little wife. But she shouldn't be facing the cop alone. Hell, she shouldn't face anything alone.

"Neither do I." Matt signaled and changed lanes. "Though I don't like Malloy dragging her down to the station for questioning."

"No. Though he seems like a pretty decent guy. My guess is he wanted to give her a chance to get the heck away from me." Shane tensed, wincing at the sudden pain. "I'm taking her out of here tonight. We're heading to the ranch in Montana."

"You could come to Seattle, if you want."

His brother would break every rule he'd created. "No. There's a reason we're all in different cities right now, Matt. You know it." Time was drawing near. They'd make their move and take out the commander as well as his scientists. "Frankly, I'm surprised you've managed to keep Nate on the ranch these past four years."

Matt shrugged. "I didn't give him a choice. Of course,

I've no doubt he's been looking for Audrey and her deranged mother on his own."

Yes. His love and the scientist who'd created them. "How are you sure he hasn't found them?"

Matt cut his eyes to Shane. "Because they'd be dead."

"So you want him still on the ranch?"

"No. He's chomping to get back in the field. If you take Josie to Montana, then you can take over the intel during the final three months." Matt signaled and changed lanes.

Nate deserved a time in the field since he'd been cooped up so long. Shane cleared his throat as his brother focused back on the road. "There's something I've never asked."

"Then don't."

His brother certainly knew how to cut to the chase. Yet it was time for answers. "Do you really think Audrey set Nathan and the blue team up? She seemed so kind to have engineered so many deaths."

"I think so." Matt's hands tightened on the steering wheel.

"Why? Why would they do that?"

Matt shrugged. "Because they could? To get Nate back in line? To get us all back in line? Maybe to show us that there would never be a normal life, we'd never be truly free."

"They had to know it would backfire."

Buildings flew by as Matt accelerated. "I assume they thought Nate would attack the commander or try to escape—anything that would give them the excuse to kill him."

Which was why they all were located at the base camp at the same time. "To motivate the rest of us. To show us the consequences." As twisted as it sounded, the interpretation made sense. "They miscalculated."

"Damn straight."

Shane shifted his bruised body on the seat. "Nate is living to find Audrey. What happens when we finally catch up to her and the commander?"

"I don't want to think about that." Matt pulled around the corner and parked next to a deli. "Something to worry about on another day. Go get your wife. I'll wait here."

Shane nodded and jumped out of the Jeep.

Josie clutched her hands together, her gaze on the side mirror of Tom's truck. "They're still behind us."

Tom tightened his jaw. "Okay. Let's slow down and get a look at them."

Panic caught Josie's breath in her throat. The two men in the truck weren't trained. An accountant and a construction worker...they couldn't deal with the people Shane dealt with. She was about to get her friends killed. "No. Just get off the highway—hurry." Had the commander found her?

Daniel shook his head. "We need to see who it is."

Tom nodded. "Trust me." He pulled into the right lane and slowed down.

The van wavered, and then sped up, coming abreast of their vehicle.

Josie cringed back into the seat, her eyes wide. A teenager drove the van, his cell phone to his ear. He sped up, and the logo for a local bread company shone on the side.

"You have got to be kidding me." Josie huffed out a laugh, settling back into the seat. "I feel foolish."

"See what Dean is doing to you?" Tom shook his head.

"Yes." Though there was nothing wrong with being a little bit paranoid. That way nobody could sneak up on her. She doubted either man in the truck would appreciate that logic. "Please take me to the hospital."

"You have to rethink your dependence on Shane." Tom sighed. "Is there any chance you'd let me buy you lunch before you spend the entire day at the hospital?"

"No." She turned a rueful smile on him. He was such a great guy . . . she needed to find someone for him. "I know you don't understand, but I really need to be with Shane right now."

"I do understand, Josie." Tom reached beneath his seat. Silver flashed.

Pain lanced across her skin as he slapped a cuff around her wrist, hooking it to a bar set between their seats.

"What the hell?" Fire ripped through Josie as she tried to yank free. "Are you kidding me?" First he had Shane arrested, now the man cuffed her? "Listen, moron. I am staying with my husband." She yanked back, slamming her feet against the floor. Pain ripped through her shoulder. "Let me go."

"I can't." Tom's jaw hardened.

"Whoa. What the hell, man?" Daniel reached over her lap and tugged on the cuff, his eyes wide. "Let her the fuck go."

Josie started. Hearing the mild accountant swear was almost as surprising as the handcuffs. Almost. She took a deep breath. Okay. "I appreciate you're trying to save me from myself here." Searching for reason, she calmed her voice. "But I'm not in danger, and I know what I'm doing."

Tom's teeth flashed in a parody of a smile. "You stupid bitch."

Josie's heartbeat sped up. Adrenaline ripped through her veins. "Excuse me?"

"Hey, wait a minute now. Knock it off," Daniel hissed. "Let her go."

"No." Tom reached down alongside his door, grabbed a gun, and pointed it at Daniel. "Shut the hell up, Danny Boy. I don't need your crap right now."

Daniel exhaled. "Come on. We agreed we wouldn't hurt her. Now let her go."

They'd agreed? She swung her gaze to Daniel. "What's going on?"

He shrugged, turning to look out the window.

She shifted her attention to Tom. Maybe she'd misread him. Could Tom be crazy? "Get out of here and run before the police catch you. And let me go."

He chuckled. "No."

Okay. She could reason with him. "I thought we were friends."

The look he gave her chilled the blood in her veins. "No. We've never been friends. Don't get me wrong." He switched lanes, glancing in the rearview mirror before focusing on the road ahead. "I wouldn't have minded fucking you." He shrugged. "Though I guess I still might."

Daniel gave a low groan. "Not this again. Leave her the hell alone."

Yeah. She'd have to take him out. Josie levered back and kicked her feet toward his face.

"Stop it." Tom slapped her feet back down without missing a beat. "I'll knock you out. Don't think for a second I won't."

She bit her lip. Confusion swirled through her brain. "I don't understand. What do you think is going to happen between us?"

He blew out a breath. "You know, when I first saw you, I figured you for a dumb blonde. Turns out I was right." The truck accelerated up the ramp to the interstate. "Do you really think I've been lusting after you this entire time? That I'm a guy who'd take 'no' from you and keep coming back for more?"

Muscles bunched in his forearms as he clutched the wheel. Why hadn't she noticed how strong he was? How big? "No. I figured we were friends. That you were a nice guy in my building who enjoyed my company." What the hell was he getting at?

"Damn, Josie." He glanced at the side mirror and switched into the fast lane. "I'm not a nice guy—nor am I your friend."

Her entire body stilled. As if frozen into an alert state. "What are you?"

Tom turned toward her, his brown eyes narrowing, and a smirk twisting his lips. "I'm a soldier, sweetheart. One who's been looking for your husband for a very long time."

She gasped, leaning closer to Daniel.

Tom laughed, the sound grating in the cab. "So is he. Good old Danny Boy is one of my brothers, sweetheart. You think the Gray brothers are the only ones who can go undercover?"

Slowly, she turned her gaze toward Dan.

He grimaced and gave a short nod. "Sorry."

She shook her head. They'd trapped her between them in the truck. "You've both been watching me? I mean, waiting for Shane to show up?"

Daniel slowly nodded. "We found you about five months ago. Our people put Tom and me in place as soon as possible. At some point, we figured Shane would come for you. At least we hoped he would."

"Why?" she whispered.

"So he can come back home," Daniel said quietly. "We have work to do."

"Or so he can die." Tom snarled. His hand shot out, his fist connecting with her jaw.

Stars exploded behind her eyes. Then darkness.

CHAPTER
28

AN ACHE FILLED Josie's entire head. She groaned, blinking her eyes open. Light lanced her pupils, and she winced, turning her head to the side and closing her eyes. Deep breaths. The sharp scent of bleach stabbed her nostrils. She opened her eyes again.

She reclined in a leather chaise in some sort of examination room. A long peach-colored counter held a stainless steel sink along with cotton balls, tongue depressors, and a blood pressure cuff.

Her arm ached. Glancing down, she gasped at the cotton ball taped to the inside of her elbow. Had they injected her with something?

The door opened. A woman stepped inside, her three-inch heels clicking on the sparkling white tiles. She tapped a manila file in her hands. "You're awake."

Josie struggled for reason. It was the bitch who'd insulted her intelligence in the conference room after the break-in at her office. What was her name—"Dr. Madison?"

Sharp blue eyes appraised her. Today the doctor wore a white lab coat and had pulled her hair back in a fierce bun. "Yes."

"What did you inject me with?" Josie asked, her voice coming out hoarse.

Madison frowned perfectly arched brows. "Nothing. I took blood to see if my young Shane had finally procreated."

The possessive tone set Josie's stomach rolling. "I'm not pregnant."

Madison shut the door. "No, unfortunately, you are not." She shrugged. "We have had absolutely no luck continuing their line."

"How unfortunate." Josie's vision wavered, and her jaw pounded. "So let me go."

"No. You're one of many sacrifices for science."

"Like you've ever sacrificed." Josie swallowed, tasting blood.

"Not true." Madison sniffed. "I gave over my only child to them—for Nathan to use temporarily. My poor Audrey."

"Audrey?" Facts ticked through Josie's mind. The woman who Nathan had loved? "Wait a minute—the head researcher was Audrey's mother—is that you?"

"Yes."

"You're psychotic. What about the kill chip?" Maybe it wasn't real.

Madison giggled. "I wondered if they were getting worried. The chip will slice their spines in three months or so, right?" She shook her head. "They really had better make up with us, don't you think?"

Rage, fear, shock all cascaded through Josie. "You're a monster."

The doctor shook her head. "Don't be silly. You might as well know that since you're not pregnant, keeping you alive isn't high on my priority list." She crossed the room toward the counter.

Josie sat up, settling her tennis shoes on the tile. She

hadn't had the chance to search the drawers for a weapon. "You're evil." If she could distract the doctor, maybe she could make a break for it.

Madison's blue eyes sparkled. "Don't be so dramatic." Her smile revealed perfectly straight teeth.

Josie eyed the door. "Rumor has it Audrey set Nathan up, Doc."

Madison pursed her lips. "Is that what they think? Hmm. Interesting." Her gaze narrowed. "Apparently my Shane confided in you. I taught him better than that."

"You know Shane?" Sadness for her husband filtered through Josie. To be raised by a crazy scientist who didn't even care about her own daughter must've been terrible. No wonder Shane had trouble dealing with women.

"Don't be coy, dear. It doesn't suit you." Madison's gaze lashed over Josie. "I have to say, you're not what I expected."

"Why's that?" She needed to find some sort of weapon. While she figured she could take the doctor in a heartbeat, stupid Tom had to be around somewhere. Or Daniel. Maybe Josie could get Daniel to help her.

The smile turned malicious. "Shane's training. The darkness in my Shane surprised even me." Her voice lowered to a throaty purr. "I really wonder what in the world my boy sees in somebody as weak as you."

"You jealous?" Josie allowed her voice to lower. "From what I've heard, you were a desperate dog in heat. Always watching, always wanting." It was a calculation and a stab in the dark. But something in the doctor's tone hinted. Josie lifted her gaze to meet the doctor's. "But they never returned your desire now, did they?"

Fire raced through the doctor's eyes before she cleared them. "That's what you think."

"No." Satisfaction lifted Josie's chin at the direct hit.

"They wanted your pretty daughter. Your innocent, sweet, and *young* daughter."

The smirk on Madison's face twisted. "Yes, well. Young Nathan wanted Audrey. And he got her for a short time—though she wasn't quite as innocent as he'd hoped." Madison crossed the room and placed the file on the counter. "But that didn't end well now, did it?"

"They're going to kill you."

"I doubt it. Believe me, I've meant way too much to a couple of them." Satisfaction lifted Madison's red lips.

Josie fought down nausea. There was no way Shane had slept with this evil bitch of a doctor. She hoped none of the brothers had been caught in her trap, either.

"Besides"—Madison's nostrils flared as she sucked in air—"I'm the closest thing to a mother those boys have ever known. They might want to kill me, but it would destroy them to do so."

But they'd do it. For each other, if one of them got the chance, they'd kill the doctor. Whoever did it would never recover. Josie settled her shoulders. "You're right. So I guess I'll be the one to kill you." She kept her gaze on the closest thing to a real monster she'd ever seen. To protect Shane, to protect his brothers, she'd kill. She'd already shot a drug dealer, in fact.

Madison smiled again. "You know, I'm starting to like you." Heavy footsteps echoed outside the door. "I think I will give Tom a chance to knock you up—or maybe Danny would like a shot at you. He seems rather irritated that Tom hit you. I wonder if I could get some ultra-soldiers out of the deal."

Nausea and fear ripped through Josie's stomach, but she kept her face bland. "You're an idiot."

The doctor shook her head, clicking her tongue.

"Name-calling, are we?" She glanced at Josie's unblemished arm. "While I haven't injected you with anything, I certainly may do so if you don't cooperate with me. Which of the brothers have you met?"

Josie rolled her eyes. "There are no brothers. Shane told me about you, about your daughter, but that's it."

The doctor clicked her tongue. "For a civilian, you're not a bad liar."

"Thanks. For a doctor with degrees in clinical neuropsychology and psychoneuroimmunology, you're stupid if you think you'll live through hurting me."

Madison's girlish laughter wound around the room. "I see what Shane likes about you."

"You must be really smart to have the degrees you do." Josie tilted her head, studying the other woman.

"I am." A satisfied smile lit the woman's flawless face.

"Why use such knowledge to harm young boys?" Something in her needed to understand. How could monsters truly live among them?

"Harm?" Madison frowned. "No, we didn't harm them. We *enhanced* them. We made them the ultimate males, the ultimate fighters." Her eyes sparked. "*I* made them incredible."

Anger tightened Josie's jaw. "You experimented on them. Like lab rats."

Madison shrugged. "Of course I experimented. We gave them the best genetics possible and then enhanced those. Before using behavioral techniques to train them as they grew."

"Aren't you concerned?" Josie frowned, truly trying to get into the crazy doctor's head.

"Concerned? That they'll come after me, not understanding?" Madison shook her head.

"No. Concerned that God will be pissed you're trying to be Him." Growing up in foster care had given her a fundamental view of God and death, but it was one she believed in. "As a scientist, you have to be open to possibilities, to what-ifs. What if God exists and is seriously pissed at you, Dr. Madison?"

Madison lifted her chin. "If God exists, He can share space with me."

Okay, the chick was crazy. No chance of reasoning with her. Time for action. Josie lunged forward, tackling the doctor around her midsection.

Madison pivoted, almost casually slamming her elbow down on Josie's spine. Pain racked Josie, and she dropped to one knee. Her mind buzzed. Her central nervous system fired.

The door opened. "What the hell?" A hulking soldier stalked inside and grabbed Josie's arms to toss her back into the recliner. She bounced against the hard leather before settling into place, her ears ringing.

Madison giggled like a little girl. "I've lived with soldiers for the last thirty years, dear. I can fight."

The man stepped back, his gaze calculating. "This is Shane's woman?"

"Yes."

His gaze ran down her form, and Josie fought a shiver. Silver hair blended with brown in his razor-sharp crew cut. He stood at about six foot two and was packed hard, his muscles clearly visible through the soldier uniform.

Josie took a deep breath. "I assume you're the commander?"

He lifted a graying eyebrow over nearly black eyes. "You've heard of me."

"My husband plans to kill you." Nothing existed

behind those too dark eyes. No emotion, no spark. Pure evil.

"I would certainly like to see him try." The commander stood at attention, his gaze dropping to her breasts and back up. "Do you think Shane mellowed out, or do you think that pretty face hides a wildcat in bed?"

Madison giggled. "I think Shane decided to slum it for a while. Though she might be worth some fun for you." She cut him a sly grin. "So long as I get to watch."

Bile swirled in Josie's stomach. "You make me sick."

Madison slid her hand down the commander's arm and ignored Josie's statement. "We should videotape her time here to give to Shane. I always figured there'd be a way to break him."

The commander nodded. "That's a good idea." He glanced at his watch. "We need to capture him first." Stepping forward, the commander grabbed Josie's jaw and tilted her head up with calloused fingers. "Who's with Shane?"

She yanked her head back, pain cascading through her jaw as he held tight. "Fuck you."

His grip tightened. Agony exploded behind her eyeballs. But she held his gaze.

He smiled, a slow anticipation of a grin. "Breaking you might be as fun as breaking Shane." With one final squeeze that had her seeing stars, he released her. A knock sounded on the door.

The commander opened the heavy metal door and allowed Tom entry. "Put her somewhere safe and meet me in the control room to call Shane." He left without a backward glance.

Tom settled his stance. He'd changed into tan silk pants, Italian loafers, and a dark Armani shirt—and he'd slicked his hair back. He glanced at Dr. Madison, his eyes warming. "Do I get her or not?"

Madison shrugged. "Sure. I haven't had any more luck using your genetic material than I have with the Gray brothers, but what the hell. Let's give it a shot." She grabbed her file and flounced to open the door. "Get her settled in and meet me in the commander's office in fifteen minutes." She smiled at Josie. "We need to call your husband." The door swished shut.

Josie glared up at Tom. "Who the hell are you?"

He shrugged. "Part of the Brown family. Brown-eyed brothers."

So they used the eye color as genetic markers. "Why didn't Shane know you?"

"A few of us were selected to train elsewhere. But Shane knows my brother, Emery." Tom grinned. "In fact, I believe Emery would like a chance with you after I'm finished."

How could she have missed the evil living in Tom? He'd fooled her so well. "And Daniel?"

"My little brother. Well, half brother."

"Where is he?" Daniel was her best ally in this crazy place.

Tom smiled, his eyes lighting. "The commander sent him on a mission, since he was so smitten with you. Good old Danny Boy is on his way to Uganda. Good riddance."

Disappointment weakened her knees. "You set me up."

"Sure." Tom's gaze dropped to her breasts. "We've had you on the radar for the last five months—constantly mining the military database finally paid off. We found several soldiers with Shane's unique skill set...and we monitored them all until narrowing our search to him. When that didn't turn up anything, the commander figured

Shane would be in touch with you ag~~~~ someday, so we've been watching you."

"The recent divorce and losing your company?"

"No bitch would ever divorce me. She'd be buried twelve feet under instead. I made it up. To get closer to you." Tom's grin lacked humor. "And no little sisters. Man, that was a tactic that got your attention now, didn't it? Poor little orphan."

Yeah. It had worked. "They raised you in a military environment—under the threat of death? Just like Shane?"

Tom's eyes swirled as he lifted his gaze. "Yes. I'm the ultimate soldier." He licked his lips. "Though I've had training you're certainly going to enjoy later."

She raised an eyebrow. "I've always considered you kind of boring. Guess I was right."

He manacled a large hand around her arm, jerking her from the chair. "Somehow I don't think you'll consider me boring for long."

Her feet slipped on the tiles as she tried to dig in and stop Tom. He continued to pull her across the room and into the hallway, passing closed industrial-sized doors.

She fought, fear heating her gut. "I have to say, I liked you better in the flannels and jeans."

He grinned. "Man, I hated dressing down the last two months. Good thing that's over."

"The laugh lines around your eyes—I don't get it." Bad guys didn't have laugh lines.

"Let's just say I love my job." His voice lowered to something dark.

Fear rippled down her spine. The guy was crazy. "Let me go."

"No." His long strides ate up the concrete floor, and Josie stumbled along.

Their footsteps echoed in the empty hallway. Dead silence came from behind the closed doors. "Why is it so quiet here?" she asked. "I mean, where is everybody?"

"This is the new building for Fuller Labs. You know that."

Oh yeah. She'd found some excellent write-offs for the lab from creating the state-of-the-art, energy-efficient new space. "The place won't be staffed until next month, when they move buildings." So she was on the north side of town. Good to know.

"Right. We have soldiers here now. I'll bet that wasn't in your documents."

"No. The fact that Fuller Labs worked outside the law to genetically engineer a soldier slave class didn't make it into the files."

"Outside the law?" He stopped in front of a bank of elevators, tugging her inside when the door opened. "You know better than that. Perhaps our entire government isn't in on it, but I can promise you many high-ranking officials fund us."

They moved up a floor. There had to be some way she could reach his conscience. "Tom. You're not this person. You don't have to be what they made you—you can be whoever you want." She tried to tug away as the doors opened.

He laughed, pulling her into a long concrete hallway that matched the one they'd just left. "I like who I am. I know how to fight, and I know how to kill. My IQ is off the charts. Normal rules don't apply to me." He stopped in front of a keypad next to a large maroon door.

She cleared her throat. "Oh. What, ah, special abilities do you have?"

"I just told you." He punched in numbers and shoved

her inside a studio apartment with sitting area, sleeping area, and small kitchenette.

So Tom didn't have any super abilities like Shane and his brothers. Was he an anomaly? Or maybe just the genetic engineering for the Gray family had produced hyper-abilities. No wonder the commander wanted them so badly.

Tom pointed toward an oak door next to the bed. "The bathroom's through there."

She yanked her arm free and backed away.

He stared down at her from his additional foot of height. "I have to go meet with the commander but will be back soon." His eyes darkened even further. "I suggest you figure out a way to make me happy."

She forced her trembling body to relax. Did Tom have any feelings for her? Surely a guy like him wouldn't like an older soldier stepping in his way. Maybe she could somehow get Tom to help her. "You don't understand. The commander said he wants to take me."

Tom smiled. "It wouldn't be the first time the commander and I shared a woman. Who knows, maybe Emery will join in this time." Stepping back into the hallway, he shut the door. The sound of the lock engaging echoed around the quiet apartment.

Fear weakened Josie's knees. Only stubborn will kept her on her feet.

What now?

CHAPTER
29

S HANE PUNCHED IN Josie's phone number again from the passenger seat of Matt's SUV as his brother broke the speed limit to get back to the cabin. "Malloy said she left with Marsh. She should be picking up her cell phone." The spinning in his gut had to be from the surgery. No way was Josie in danger. Hell. She was probably already back at the hospital looking for him.

Matt gripped the steering wheel, stretching his neck. "Then why is the hair standing up on the back of my neck?"

Good question. The phone stopped ringing and silence came over the line. A silence heavy with expectation. Someone listened, breathing softly. Lifting his eyebrow, Shane pressed the speaker button and put the phone on the dash. "Josie?"

A loud exhale sounded. "Shane, my boy. So good to hear from you." Soft and sexy, the voice dripped with false sweetness.

Rage ripped through every muscle in his body. "Dr. Madison. I'd hoped you were dead."

Next to him, Matt went rigid.

"Oh, Shane. You were always such a naughty boy." The girlish tone from the psychopath nearly made Shane puke.

Matt opened his mouth to speak. Shane shook his head, his gaze narrowing on his brother. There was a good chance they didn't know Matt was with him, and they needed all the advantage they could get. "Where's my wife?"

"Well now, she's safe right at the moment. Though I have to tell you, my Tom seems to have a nice little crush on her. Thinks he can get her pregnant and give me little soldiers." A high-pitched giggle escaped the doctor.

What the hell? Tom? How had Shane missed it? He'd been played.

Shane focused his fury until his skin prickled. Calmness settled his limbs into a state of readiness. Emotion had to go. He tuned in with his hearing, trying to get a location. No sounds echoed in the background. "Tell Tom he'll die slowly if he touches her."

"Oh. Looking forward to it, jackass." Tom's voice came clearly over the line. "Taking a dive the other night in my own hallway really pissed me off. Can't wait to give you an honest fight." He chuckled. "After I screw your wife, of course. Again, that is."

"You haven't been near my wife, dumbass." Shane lowered his voice. "You tried, though, didn't you? For two months, when she thought it was over with me, she still didn't turn toward you. Who the hell trained you, anyway?"

"You sure about that?" Tom asked. "With her background, she's quite the little liar. Are you sure she told you the truth about us?"

"Yes." Shane snorted. "You're junior league. Don't think for a second the psychotic bitch standing next to you right now won't cut your throat to get to me. To get to one of my brothers."

"You know," Tom breathed, "I think I'll have your wife call me 'Jory' as I fuck her tonight."

Raw fury threatened to blow Shane's calm façade. "I can kill you in ways you can't even imagine." Shane tightened his hands into fists, vaguely seeing Matt type something on his phone. Probably telling Nathan to trace the call.

Tom laughed again. "Think so? Well, I doubt it. We have the same training."

No, they didn't. Not even close. Matt had made sure his training beat anything the commander could come up with. At times Shane had truly hated his older brother. Now he thanked God Matt had been so ruthless in teaching them to survive. "You're going to find out how wrong you are." He needed to keep the line open for Nate.

"What's the problem, Shane?" Madison piped up. "If I recall, you've shared a woman with more than one of your brothers."

"The psychopathic whores you sicced on us don't count." He nodded as Matt gestured to keep them talking. "Of course, we wanted them far more than we ever wanted you. Not that we didn't see how bad you needed it. Or wanted it. But you never got it now, did you? Bitch." Though he had no doubt the crazy woman had screwed her way through several of the trainees through the years.

"Are you sure about that?" Her voice lowered to a breathiness that made his skin crawl. "You might want to double-check that fact with your brothers."

Shane shook his head. If one of his brothers had fallen prey to the nut job, he sure as hell didn't want to know about it. "What's your plan here, bitch?"

"Calling names? That's more Nathan's style, not yours." A rustling of paper came over the line. "How is good old Nathan, anyway? Killed himself with grief yet?"

Shane inhaled quietly, ignoring the pull at his fresh stitches. Forcing pain into a distant box, he slid calmness into his voice. "Nathan is married to a nice nurse with two kids. He moved on, Madison. Sorry to disappoint you."

"You were always such a good liar," Madison murmured. "You've lost the touch, I think. So who's with you right now? Is it my Matt?"

"Why don't you come and get me to find out?"

"Okay." A rough voice suddenly commanded the line. "You've had long enough to trace this call."

Matt whipped his gaze toward the phone in unison with Shane. The fucking commander. He was there.

"Commander. Man. I figured the devil would've taken you by now." Shane forced a deep chuckle into his voice, even as his hands closed into trembling fists. "Don't tell me you're still banging this used-up excuse for a doctor." He'd caught them once in the armory—Madison bent over a table that bore AK-47s, shrieking as she came. Nightmares had plagued him for months afterward.

"Actually"—the commander's voice matched Shane's— "I'm thinking about banging your young wife. Well, after both Tom and Emery get through with her, of course. Assuming there's anything left."

Shane leaned forward, his entire body going cold. Matt clapped him on the back, shaking his head and pointing to Shane's temple. Yeah, right. The commander was screwing with his head. Effectively. He nodded. "You know, old man, I think it's time I killed you."

"Bring Matthew with you," the commander said. "He and I have unfinished business. Oh and"—he paused—"you have thirty minutes. Or I go get closely acquainted with the babbling blonde you married. I have to say, I'm quite surprised you married a woman who cries so easily."

The line went dead.

Oh God. Shane had known the monster his entire life—there wasn't a thing he wouldn't do to get results. Pure evil. The devil as a father figure.

Matt sucked in air. "Ignore him. They haven't hurt her."

"I know." Shane turned slowly to eye his brother, and emotion ripped through him. Matt had become his father figure, giving him the strength to fight the commander's pull. "Thank you," he whispered.

"Sure."

"No." Shane grabbed Matt's arm. "Thank you for everything. Always. I never realized—"

Matt lifted an eyebrow. "Now isn't a time for girly sharing, Shane."

Shane swallowed. "Nate is right. I can't put you and Josie in danger together. We'll rescue her, and then I'll take her somewhere safe."

Matt frowned, his eyes darkening as he turned toward Shane. "We stick together. No matter what. If you say Josie is with us, then she's with us. Period."

Emotion heated tears behind Shane's eyes. They'd hash it out later. He grabbed his cell phone. The commander would hurt Josie with great pleasure. "Let's go get my wife."

Matt pulled to a stop in front of the broad cabin. "Good plan. We need to suit up."

Shane jumped out of the car, his gaze on the front door as it opened. Nathan stalked outside, dressed for combat in black fatigues, a bulletproof vest, and heavy boots.

Emotion swamped Shane until he could barely breathe. Nathan. Family. "What are y'all doing back here?" The Southern twang broke completely free with his question. Nate had made his opinion clear—and he'd been right.

Nathan gave a smart-assed grin. "You didn't think I'd let you rescue the girl all by yourself now, did you?"

"But I thought you went home."

"I did."

Shane swiveled his head to stare open-mouthed at Matt. "You called him? When?"

"Last night when you were in surgery." Matt strode forward, catching the bulletproof vest Nathan tossed at him. "I had a feeling we'd need backup."

Shane shook his head. "But the plan—"

"Plans change, little brother," Nate said. He tucked a handgun into a calf holster. "I, ah, was wrong. Josie is family, and if she's in trouble, we go in."

Shane searched for the right words but couldn't find any. "But you were right—"

"I was wrong. We'll keep her safe and with us, Shane." Nathan lifted his chin. "My anger shouldn't change your life. If she's family, she's with us. Always." As a vow, it was absolute.

Shane blinked. "Thanks."

Nathan nodded, hard lines cut into his rugged face. Gray eyes darkened to nearly black. Anger and pain all but danced on his skin. "Dr. Madison is mine. I'll take care of Audrey's mother—after she tells me where her daughter is."

Shane studied his brother. Something in his conscience whispered it'd be a bad idea to let Nate kill the mother of the woman he once loved. Memories of Nate being happy for a brief time flashed through his mind. So many moments—yet not enough. Not nearly enough.

He nodded. "Of course." No way would he let his brother live with killing Madison. Shane would take care of the scientist.

Matt cut him a hard glare. Ah. Mattie planned to protect both Nate and Shane from killing the woman who'd helped raise them. Shane straightened his shoulders, meeting his brother's stare head-on.

Matt blinked once, a dark flush crossing his high cheekbones. "Seeing us all—does it bring any memories back about Jory?"

"No." But something lingered at the base of Shane's consciousness. "The memories are so close—right there waiting for me." He examined each of his brothers in turn. They were risking their lives to save the woman he loved, and he lacked the words of gratitude. Emotion clogged his throat. The right words probably didn't exist.

"You're welcome," Nate said, his gray eyes swirling with emotion. "Come in and suit up—let's go get your wife."

CHAPTER
30

I DON'T UNDERSTAND." JOSIE wrenched her wrists against the handcuffs that held her attached to the grab bar above the door of the large SUV. Pain cascaded up her arm. From the backseat, she glared at Tom's head as he drove through after-work traffic. "I thought you wanted Shane to trace the call."

Dr. Madison sighed from the front passenger seat. "How in the world did my Shane fall for such a ditz?" Reaching out red-manicured nails, she ran her hand down Tom's arm. "You always had better taste now, didn't you, Tommy?"

He nodded. "Sure. Though I wanted to stay and wait for good old Shane."

"No." Madison settled back into her seat and crossed her legs. "We need you to protect us for now. The commander will capture Shane and whatever brother is with him. Then don't worry. We'll let you in the training ring with him."

"I can't wait." Satisfaction oozed in Tom's deep voice.

Fury swirled through Josie. "He'll kick your ass."

Tom's brown eyes flashed to the rearview mirror. "Not

a chance. Believe me, once he understands what I've done to you, anger will make him easy to beat." Tom shook his head. "You're a weakness, Josie. A big one."

Damn it, she was his weakness. Nathan had been correct. Josie was going to get Shane killed. She tugged again on her wrists. The metal cut deeper into her skin, and she fought a whimper at the pain. Anger brought sharp focus to her eyesight. A blaring of a horn made her jump. Fear shoved the anger away. Her lungs wanted to seize up. "Where are we going?"

Madison smoothed her pencil skirt down. "To a safe place until Shane is contained. Then we're going home. Thank God."

"God?" Josie gasped. No way did the psychotic bitch believe in God. "Where might home be?"

Madison twisted in her seat to flash a tight smile. "Back East. Not the facility where dear Shane grew up, but similar. State-of-the-art, in fact."

The woman had more than one screw loose. "You honestly think you'll be able to capture Shane, and he'll go back to work for you? That he'll be an ultimate soldier doing your dirty work?" Dr. Madison really didn't know Shane.

The smile widened. "Of course. Now that we have you, Shane will do anything I want. And those brothers of his will follow suit." She sniffed. "They've had an almost unnatural loyalty to each other since birth." Her exhale scented the car with mint. "I wonder if it's something we did with the genetic engineering."

Josie shook her head, trying to ignore the pounding ache in her shoulder blades from her odd position. "More likely a survival instinct. To survive their childhood and being raised by a complete nut job like you."

"Interesting theory." Madison pursed her lips, lines in her forehead creasing as she frowned. "Though the commander held death over their heads. I just studied them. Put them through their tests and so on." She turned around, her gaze wandering over Josie's face. "So who's with Shane? There must be one of the brothers close by. Close enough to call for help."

Just Matt. Nathan had headed out to a new assignment. Could Matt and Shane take the commander and his soldiers? Josie raised an eyebrow. "Shane doesn't need backup, and you know it. What kind of trap do you think will work, anyway?" There had to be some way to get a message to her husband. To warn him.

Tom switched lanes, allowing a hot yellow Ferrari to pass him on the left. "Let's just say the trap involves nerve gas that would knock out a stegosaurus. Before your boy knows it, he'll be at the new facility working to draw his brothers back in."

What kind of gas? Shane had just recovered from a concussion and surgery—and he didn't even have his entire memory back. Josie had to get out of there and warn him. How did people get out of handcuffs, anyway? The more she tugged, the harder the cold metal dug into her wrists. They were already raw. Blood oozed to coat the metal. Bile swirled up her throat, and she swallowed the horrid taste back down.

Tom signaled and took the off-ramp toward Miller's Strip.

Josie stiffened. "We're going to the airport?" Miller's was a small, private airport for the superrich. She'd picked up wealthy clients there before. If she left Snowville, Shane might never find her. Panic threatened to cut off her breathing.

"Yes. The airport it is." Tom maneuvered the vehicle around a horse trailer and followed the quiet road several miles until stopping next to a large metal-walled hangar.

Josie peered out the window. The area around the building remained quiet and empty in the gathering dusk. Clouds rolled across the sky, the wind scattering loose leaves over the deserted tarmac. She shivered at how alone she felt.

Tom jumped out of the SUV and opened her door, releasing the cuffs and dragging her from the car. His frown marred his handsome face as he glared at her bloody wrists. "Josie," he breathed. "What did you do?"

She tried to tug her hands out of his grasp. "I'd do anything to get away from you, jackass."

He smiled. "I've always liked your spunk."

Two black Escalades approached, halting on either side of Tom's car. Men dressed in black combat gear clomped flak boots onto the cement as they jumped out, machine guns in hand.

Tom glanced at a muscular bald man. "Secure the perimeter of the hangar."

"Yes, sir." The man began barking orders and pointing out positions to the soldiers. They didn't look real. Not one of them even seemed to notice Josie. She counted eight armed soldiers as well as two men dressed in polo shirts and khakis. Must be the pilots.

Turning, Tom dragged her through a small doorway into a wide hangar with two sleek jets parked in the middle. Madison clipped her high heels across the spotless cement behind them. The sharp sound echoed through the vast space. The pilots silently strode toward the two planes, opening hatches and getting to work.

Josie stumbled to keep pace with Tom, her mind whirling. How did she miss the emptiness in him? Even while he threatened her, he only seemed half there. Like he'd enjoy attacking her but could take or leave the possibility. "You know, most people who torture other people need to do it. Like a compulsion."

Tom yanked her into a spacious office, shoving her into a plush leather chair. "Oh?" He reached behind his waist and brought out a large, square handgun to place on the desk.

"Yeah." Josie settled into the seat. Could she get into his head? "I think so. But you, well, you don't seem to really care." She lowered her voice. "What did they do to you?"

His smile chilled the air. "They created me." Both broad hands grasped her armrests, and he leaned down, his face inches from hers. "And you're wrong. The only time I feel alive is when I have someone screaming." Heat flared through his eyes. He inhaled, a dark flush crossing his smooth face. "You smell like softness and purity. Like clouds." His gaze dropped from her eyes to her breasts. "Something tells me you'll be a screamer."

There was the fear. Yet she lifted her chin, waiting until his gaze once again met hers. "If Shane doesn't kill you, I will." She leaned in closer to his face, satisfaction welling when his eyes widened just a fraction in surprise. "I promise you'll die," she whispered.

His teeth flashed in a parody of a smile as he pushed away from her chair. "I adore your confidence." Grabbing his gun, he checked the clip.

Her confidence? Yeah, it was fake. The entire situation sucked. "I stopped being afraid of bullies a long time ago." In kindergarten when she'd smashed Jason Jones in the face with her backpack. Somehow she doubted she could take care of Tom the same way. It didn't mean she wouldn't try, however.

Madison clipped into the room with a diet soda in her hand. "Has the commander checked in yet?"

"No." Tom rolled his shoulders. "I should be there with him."

Josie fought the urge to rub her oozing wrists. "So, Dr. Madison. How did Jory die?"

Madison smiled, closing her eyes to inhale. "My Jory." Her blue eyes flashed open and warmed. "What a smart boy and an even smarter man." She giggled. "He was so small, and then poof, one day he turned into a giant. With *huge* feet."

"How did he die?" Josie eyed the large phone at the edge of the desk.

"He died because he turned against us." Madison formed her lips in a perfect pout. "He turned against the commander." Her head shook. "Terrible decision."

Fire ripped through Josie. "Do you call him *the commander* when you fuck him?" It was a shot in the dark, but instinct took over.

Madison's tongue darted out to lick her glossy lips. "Well, dear, the commander fucks me." She raised an eyebrow. "Surely you understand the difference." Another giggle escaped, and this one ripped through Josie's nerves like a cheese grater. "And no, his name is Franklin."

Tom started, his gaze slashing to Madison.

Josie let a slow smile slide across her face. "Didn't know that now, did you?"

"No." Tom tilted his head to the side. "I didn't know that."

Madison shrugged. "We've been close through the years."

Josie snorted. "I knew his name. Shane told it to me." She crossed her legs, slamming her innocent foster kid mask on her face. "Franklin."

Tom growled. "Shane doesn't know his name. None of us know his name."

Ah, the jerk didn't like that, did he? Josie opened her eyes wider. "Sure Shane did. He told me a long time ago." She lowered her voice. "Maybe Franklin liked the Gray brothers better than you, Tom. I mean, they were his favorites now, weren't they?" Another pure guess, but what the hell.

Tom pushed away from the desk.

Dr. Madison's pale hand on his arm stopped his forward motion. She turned her focus on Josie. "She's quite the little manipulator, isn't she?"

Josie refused to flinch under the hard gaze. "Just like your daughter, am I?"

Madison smiled. "Yes. Although Audrey has a genius IQ." Shiny dark hair flew as Madison shook her head. "Unlike you."

"She was smart enough to get Nathan to fall in love with her—and not with you." Josie let a calculating softness filter into her voice.

Madison giggled again. "Your attempts at digging into my head...I love them. Oh, I wish I could've seen you work on Shane—I'll bet you had my boy so tangled up he couldn't find his way free."

Yet he had now, hadn't he? Besides, she'd never tried to manipulate Shane. She loved him, and she'd given her trust along with love. Josie glanced at the full wall of windows behind her. The sparkling jets waited, silent and watchful in the large space. "I figured you'd have more soldiers here."

"The soldiers are all waiting for your husband," Madison said just as her phone buzzed. She pressed it to her ear, gliding from the office and out of earshot.

Tom followed the doctor with heat in his gaze. "The commander will bring Shane and whoever's with him to the plane, and then we'll get the hell away from this Podunk town." He focused back on Josie. "Not that I didn't enjoy playing the out-of-luck workingman." A Cheshire cat's smile had nothing on Tom's smirk.

She rolled her eyes. "You're such a jackass." The gun waited, heavy and sure, on the large desk. Maybe she should tackle Tom, just lower her head and aim for his gut.

He shook his head, grabbed the gun, and tucked it into his lower back. "Not going to happen, Josie."

That's what he thought. She flexed her fingers. Her wrists nearly bellowed in pain. "So how does this work? I mean, don't you have to file flight plans and everything?" Not that he didn't have government backing anyway.

"No." Tom glanced at his watch. "This is a small airport. We can turn the lights on ourselves, and so long as we appear to be flying by visual, we just take off. Perfectly legal and acceptable." His gaze focused on her, skimming her legs. "Maybe we should come up with something interesting to pass the time."

What an ass. "You're an idiot."

His face darkened with a purpose that chilled her completely through.

Madison clicked her high heels into the room, a frown marring her flawless skin. "We have a problem."

Tom straightened up. "What's the problem?"

Madison glanced at Josie. "Shane hasn't shown up.

Not even a hint of him." She bit her lip. "Maybe we over-estimated his feelings for her."

Josie allowed a small smile to lift the corners of her lips. Adrenaline ripped through her blood. "Maybe you *under*estimated Shane." Oh, yeah. Hope filled her. Her husband was coming.

CHAPTER
31

Shane shot an elbow into Nathan's gut, halting their progress. "Go back to the fucking truck and wait for me."

Nathan dipped a shoulder and rammed solid muscle into Shane's arm. "No." With smooth movements, Nathan yanked open the door to the police station. He'd discarded the bulletproof vest, but in his dark shirt and cargo pants, he still looked more like a soldier than a lawyer. "Detective Malloy has already met me, and there's no reason to do this by yourself. Alone."

A flashback to the military barracks smacked Shane between the eyes. *"Never alone."*

"Never alone." Nathan repeated the mantra they'd coined as scared kids.

Shane followed his brother into the station, their boots clomping in unison on the sparkling wood floors. They should've changed into more casual clothing, but there hadn't been time. "Asking the cop for help might seriously backfire."

"Yep." Nathan plastered on a charming smile for a young blonde behind the bulletproof glass. "Hi, darlin'. We're here to see Detective Malloy."

The woman flushed, her pretty eyes sparkling as she grabbed a phone. Even through the glass, the sound of her breath speeding up forced Shane to bite back a smile.

Seconds later Malloy shoved open the door. He appraised Nathan and then Shane with shrewd, albeit tired eyes. His heartbeat remained steady and calm. "What the hell's going on, gentlemen?"

Shane pivoted, half shielding his brother. "We need to talk. Alone."

Malloy tilted his head. "Are either you or your... lawyer... armed?"

"No." A knife in his boot didn't count. Both Shane and Nathan had left all guns in the truck.

Malloy nodded, stepping back and holding the door open. He led them to the conference room where Shane had first been interviewed. Sitting down, the detective eyed Nathan. "If you're an attorney, I'm a fucking ballet dancer."

Shane leaned over the table, both hands flat. "He's my brother. My wife has been taken by a military group you've never heard of, and if we don't save her, she's dead."

Malloy lifted an eyebrow. "Is that so? She's probably safe without you."

"No. They'll kill her."

"Then why the hell are you here and not going after her?" Malloy's expression gave nothing away.

Shane shoved panic down. "We need you to pull up the new traffic cams all over town so we can see where she is."

Malloy frowned. "Excuse me?"

"We identified her location a short time ago. It's a trap, of course. We need to see where they've taken her after allowing us to trace a cell phone call." Shane tried to keep from grabbing the detective around the neck and shaking him. Time was running out for Josie. Who knew what the commander would do to her? Shane yanked his cell phone from his pocket and played the recorded conversation with the commander.

Malloy paled. "I watched her go with Marsh. Didn't even think to stop her."

"Then this is your fault, too." Shane had no problem using guilt with Malloy. It beat shooting the cop.

The detective hitched out a breath. "Why the hell should I trust you? You've done nothing but lie to me since day one."

"Instincts." Nathan spoke low, calm. A hint of desperation broke through his charm. "You've got them. I can tell. While you might not like what's going on here, you believe us. Now please help us."

Shane stood to his full height. If Malloy refused, he'd go for the traffic cams himself.

Shane twisted the earpiece into his ear, his heartbeat slowing while his mind focused. He lay prone on the pebbled asphalt, his dark clothes blending with the night. Pain echoed through his gut from his surgery. The scent of sage mixed with the wild huckleberries skirting the forest and filled the air. "Do you think Malloy will be safe with Nate?"

"Sure. Stop worrying about Malloy. Cops get kidnapped at gunpoint all the time."

"Funny." Matt was such an asshole.

"I know." Lying next to him, Matt lifted night-scope goggles to his eyes, focusing across the tarmac. The wind lifted his hair. "Besides, I checked out the cop. Combat experience. He might come in handy."

Malloy had surprised the hell out of Shane, leading him right to the cams.

Using the traffic cam recordings, Malloy had zeroed in on Josie's last known location, winding the recording back until two SUVs were seen leaving the area. Heading right for the airport. Once found, Shane had pressed his gun against Malloy's side until they all quietly and serenely walked outside to the truck. Malloy had even chatted with two uniforms on the way. If Shane didn't know better, he'd think the cop had wanted to come on the mission.

At least now, no other cops would show up—well, until all hell broke loose.

Nate and Malloy crab-crawled into place next to them.

Shane eyed Malloy. "I hope this doesn't end your career."

The cop shrugged. "I'm a cop trained to save the victim—Josie needs saving. If it ends my career, I don't want it anymore." He grinned. "Plus, I don't mind having you owe me one."

Nate clapped the cop on the back. "Ready?"

Malloy nodded. "On your mark."

"Now." Nate rolled out of sight and headed around the building, the cop quickly following.

Matt adjusted his goggles with one finger and pressed an earpiece into his ear. "Nathan, set the devices."

Shane flashed back to another mission at a small airport, somewhere in the Middle East. Grisly images whipped through his brain. He shook his head to clear it; now wasn't the time.

"Are you all right?" Matt whispered. "You haven't started bleeding again, have you?"

"No. I'm fine." Those bastards had his wife. No way was he sitting this out. Shane grabbed a thermal-sensing scope out of his bag, focusing on the metal building. "Two guards just inside the door, two working inside the planes, and three people in a room off to the side." His wife. Probably with Tom and Dr. Madison. A chill slashed into his gut, and he tamped down any emotion. Cold focus would win the day, and he was one cold bastard.

"They're waiting for us across town." Satisfaction coated Matt's voice.

"You've been better than the commander for years." Shane shook his head. If not, they'd never have escaped.

"I know." Matt rolled to his feet. "Though he'll figure out our plan soon. We need to get the hell out of here."

Shane jumped up. "Let's do this, then."

"Shane, Dr. Madison is mine." A cautionary tone Shane had never heard before ran through Matt's deep voice. "You save your wife."

Shane bit back a sharp response. His brother was the ultimate protector, had been since Shane's birth. Matt had taught them all, and he'd trained them until they hated him. But he'd been the first through any door and had stood in front of Shane and a bullet more than once. Shane sighed. "You couldn't kill a woman, Matt." Though he wondered. Had Matt been closer to the lunatic doctor than Shane had known?

"She's not a woman. She's a monster." Matt cocked his Beretta and tapped his earpiece. "At your mark, Nate."

The wind picked up and scattered leaves across Shane's boot. He readied his stance, his Glock cocked and ready.

"Fire in the hole," Nathan said through the earpieces.

Two seconds later, the roar of an explosion split the silence into fragments. Fire rolled toward the sky, lifting the metal hangar door. Heat flashed through the air, and they ran toward the blaze.

The sound of fire cutting through oxygen flashed Shane to another time. His hearing fogged. His gut swirled. No. Coldness. He needed to focus. An ember singed his neck. Pain ripped through his skin. He sucked it in, allowing the vibrations to center him. Nothing like pain to sharpen the present reality.

A soldier ran around the building, firing a Colt M16 fully automatic. Shane dropped from a run into a slide that would've made Ty Cobb proud, catching the soldier at the ankles. The man pitched forward. Shane aimed for the jugular and pulled his trigger, rolling to the side and leaping to his feet. The soldier was dead before he slammed to the ground.

Shane leaped through the gaping hole on Matt's heels. Scorched metal scented the air while smoke billowed a haze across his vision. The whirring of jet engines wound through the crackle. The Learjet glided through the open hangar door. He caught a glimpse of dark hair in a side window. Dr. Madison turned her face, a smile lifting her lips. Red nails flashed as she waved. The smacking sound of her pursing her lips and sending him a kiss filled his ears even through the metal and glass.

Anger ripped through him. He ran toward the jet. Was Josie on it? Pausing, trusting his brothers to protect his back, he closed his eyes and listened. Hearts beat all around him, rapidly pumping blood and adrenaline. A soft pitter-patter caught his attention...the heartbeat well known. Josie.

Thank God for super hearing.

He pivoted, running around to the other side of the rumbling Falcon jet. Josie struggled with Tom, who clouted her on the head and threw her in the open hatch.

Shane bunched to leap forward. A soldier rammed a gun barrel into his neck. "Don't move."

The gun ripped away from Shane along with the soldier's body as Matt took him down. The crunch of bones against concrete overwhelmed the sound of fire. Then fire roared louder.

He had to get to Josie. Was she hurt? The Falcon edged toward the opening. Shane jumped forward, loping into a run. Heat whipped around him. Tom smiled, pulling up the stairs. The engine revved louder.

Two soldiers immediately ran around the plane toward him.

Fast as a whip, Malloy appeared from the side and shot the first guy, taking him down. Nate shot the second.

Shane gave a curt nod to Malloy, who nodded back. Yeah, he owed the cop for that one.

Arriving at the plane, Shane reached up, yanking down the ladder. Tom shot a kick into his face, and Shane dodged to the side. Then he dove into the plane, landing on plush carpet and swinging his legs around.

Tom jumped back, levering an M9 pistol between Shane's eyes. Tom retreated another step down the narrow aisle, gesturing for Shane to stand.

Shane rolled to his feet, his gaze slashing to a pale Josie, who sat behind Tom in a cushioned brown seat. Her blue eyes had gone wide. She began to stand, eyeing the gun. Shane gave a slight shake of his head, and she sat back down.

Her shoulders trembled, and Shane felt a fury he'd never imagined. How dare they mess with his wife? He shifted his shoulders, angling his body so Tom couldn't push him out of the plane. The jet picked up speed, rolling toward the open runway. He forced a sarcastic smile on his face. "Why don't you lose the gun and fight me like a man? I mean, you're kind of trained, right?"

Tom returned the smile. And fired.

Josie screamed.

Pain exploded through Shane's chest. The bullet threw him back against the cockpit door. Each rib vibrated as if plucked, and he could actually feel his stitches separating. He slid to the ground and stopped himself at a crouch. "You asshole." The prick had purposefully aimed for the bulletproof vest. "Can't take me at full strength, huh?"

Tom shrugged, tucking his gun at the back of his waist.

The jet turned, gathering speed to roll down the runway, bushes flashing by outside. Josie let out a shriek and jumped at Tom. He pivoted, shoving her up into the air and over two rows of seats. She slammed between the seats and down to the ground with a dull thud.

Fury roared through Shane's body with a heat to match the fire they'd just left. He growled and shot forward to tackle Tom. His shoulders were too wide for the aisle and slammed against chair armrests as the men went down. The bastard shot an elbow into Shane's face. Blood sprayed, but Shane held on to Tom.

The hit to Shane's face destroyed all other pain. He slid into a soldier's state, the place they'd forced him into so many years ago. Pain flowed away. Conscience disappeared. All emotion, all thought...dissipated. Pure instinct took over. He pressed up, levering his forearm against Tom's throat.

The plane tilted, ascending into the dark night. Tom took advantage of the shift, clapping his hands against Shane's ears. Levering his knee up, he shoved into Shane's bleeding belly. Another rib cracked.

Shane sucked in air, loosening his hold. While he could keep pain at bay, his body still reacted to the damage. Tom grappled for position and then tossed Shane over his head.

Rolling, Shane gasped for air, grabbing the nearest armrest to struggle to his feet. The wind whistled outside the still-open hatch. Behind Tom. Out of his peripheral vision, Shane watched his wife yank herself into the seat. "You okay?"

"I'm fine," she hissed. A dark bruise had already begun to form under her right eye. For that alone, Tom would die.

Gears screeched as the wheels were tucked into the plane. Shane settled his stance while the plane ascended at full tilt, swerving side to side as the pilot struggled for control with the hatch open. Air rushed by outside, sucking out papers from the counter near the doorway. Chilly night air filtered through the small cabin.

Tom yanked his gun out. Shane lurched forward, slamming Tom's gun hand against the wall and hooking his arm through Tom's. Shane took a step, twisted his arm, and yanked back, sweeping Tom's knee at the same time. The crack of Tom's arm breaking preceded the thunderous thud of the men hitting the floor, Shane on Tom's back. Tom bellowed in pain.

The plane pitched to the side.

Josie yelped, smacking into the window before grabbing the headrest in front of her with white-knuckled hands.

Tom gave a furious roar, kicking Shane in the back and dislodging him. Both men scrambled to their feet. Shane wiped blood out of his eye, forcing the pain down deeper. It was becoming more persistent.

The plane leveled off, the open hatch a hole of doom. A guarantee someone would plunge through it before the flight ended.

Tom clutched his broken arm, anger etched into the lines of his face.

Shane smiled. The guy lacked Matt's special brand of training to let such emotion show. Good. "Ready to die?"

The cockpit door opened behind Tom, and the pilot stepped out, nine-millimeter pointed at Shane. "Shut the hatch."

Josie gasped. "Who's flying the plane?" The wind whistled an ominous trumpet outside the gaping entry.

The pilot smiled crooked yellowed teeth. A weird light glowed from his eyes, his pupils completely dilated. Was the guy on drugs? "Autopilot." He raised his arm, pointed at Shane, and fired.

Shane jumped in front of Josie, forcing her to the floor. The bullet tore into the wooden paneling at the rear of the aircraft. Dun-colored metal caught his eye. In one fluid movement, he grabbed Tom's dropped gun, slid into the aisle on his knees, and fired at the pilot.

Tom dodged to the side.

The bullet whammed between the pilot's eyes. Gray matter splatted against the cockpit door. Blood cascaded across the front row of seats. The pilot dropped to the ground, his gun clanking on the floor.

Tom reached for the weapon, but Shane leaped forward, his foot pressing down on Tom's hand. Hard. "Not nice, Tommy." If Shane left Tom alive, the man would just keep coming after them, along with the commander. Time to end this—for good.

Tom scooted until his back rested against the far wall, blood dripping down his face, the broken arm dangling uselessly to the side. Fury lit his brown eyes. Hatred curled his lip.

Memories. Flashes of light ripped through Shane's head like sharp knives. Pain coursed until he was sure his ears bled. He couldn't block it. Like a million paparazzi cameras flashing at once, the sight and sounds grew deafening.

Jory.

His brother, shot in the chest, falling to the floor. Eyes open.

Shane's memories poured in like thick concrete. Undercover. He'd found the video, and he'd watched it. Tears had choked him with fury. But then almost two years into his assignment, he'd found the second video. The one where Jory blinked after being shot. Maybe. Maybe it had been a trick of light—the angle of the camera. But...maybe it had been a blink.

Shane gasped, nearly bending over at the memory.

Movement sounded. Josie screamed. Shane turned instinctively toward the sound, the movement saving his life.

Tom tackled him, head into stomach. Shane hit the counter inches from the open hatch. The plane jumped, and then tilted to the left. They were going down.

Shane pivoted, sweeping his leg underneath Tom's. He shoved.

Tom flew out the hatch and into the dark night, his yell echoing behind them to taper into silence.

With a pissed growl, Shane leaned down and yanked the ladder inside before sliding the hatch closed. His ears rang in the sudden silence.

Josie rose from her seat, hurrying toward him. He grabbed and yanked her as close as possible. The scent of wild berries filled his nose. "It's okay, Josie. We're safe."

She lifted her face toward his, tears filling her eyes. "Tell me you know how to fly a plane."

He grinned, lifting her over the dead body of the pilot to sit in the cockpit. Settling his bulk into the pilot's seat, he grabbed the stick and righted the plane. "Of course, sweetheart. I learned how to fly when I was twelve."

"Where are we going?"

"Home."

Whether she liked it or not.

CHAPTER
32

THE PEACEFUL CHIRP of birds filled the early hours of a Montana morning. Shane bit back a wince as Nathan finished taping his ribs. "You have the finesse of a bulldog."

Nate stepped back, a frown on his face. "No training for a week because I'm not stitching you up again." He glanced toward the door as Matt stalked inside, stomping his boots on the stoop first.

Matt tilted his head toward Shane. "Is he all right?"

"Yes." Nate threw bloodied bandages into the trash. "Did you dismantle the plane?"

"Pretty much. We'll use it for parts...can't be traced." Matt yanked open the refrigerator door and grabbed a beer, drinking it in three swallows.

Shane shifted on the wooden chair, his elbows resting on the round table. There was probably a smooth way to say what he needed to say, but he couldn't find it in his head.

Matt grabbed another beer, slamming the door shut. "I can't believe we missed the commander." He dropped into a chair across from Shane. "Though I'm sure we'll see him again soon." His gaze took in Shane's bandages. "Where's your wife?"

"Shower." Shane eyed the long hallway. They'd arrived at the ranch thirty minutes earlier, and she'd headed straight for warm water. "Tell me again about the security on the ranch."

Nate nodded. "Full perimeter. Sensors, cameras, even booby traps I can deploy from here." He leaned against the counter. "The control room is downstairs and has tunnels leading miles away in case we need to escape. I have a helicopter and three land routes out, even without the tunnels."

Impressive. Shane nodded. "Does anyone know where you are?"

"No." Nathan leaned back and grabbed a Guinness from the fridge. "We have office managers in New York and Chicago who report to me, but they don't know where our headquarters is located. Nobody would even guess Rebel, Montana." He swallowed deep and then set his bottle on the table. "Are you and your wife moving in, Shane?"

"Temporarily. Then I'll find her a safe place."

"No. If you're making her family, then she's my family, too." Nate's eyes darkened.

"Never alone," Matt said quietly.

Relief and the sense of home washed through Shane. "I, ah—"

"You're welcome," his brothers both said quietly and in unison.

Nate sighed. "I hope you know what you're doing."

He did. And he knew, without a doubt, that his brother would protect Josie with his life if Shane were off on a mission.

Nathan stretched his arms. "Enough emotion—next we're going to end up hugging and talking about our feelings. I've been monitoring all lines...no record of the explosion or anyone falling out of a plane."

Shane hissed out a breath. Damn government conspirators. He'd even dropped off the body of the dead pilot near the explosion site when he'd fetched his brothers. Apparently the commander had gained some serious clout. "I talked to Malloy. He came up with some story about an anonymous tip that he checked out at the airport...and found the fire and bodies."

"The cop is protecting us?" Matt asked, both eyebrows raised.

"Yes." Shane stretched his hands. "Malloy's a good guy—and he wants Josie to be safe. We're the only ones who can guarantee that."

Matt eyed Shane. "Well?"

"Well what?" He fought the urge to shift his weight under the watchful gaze of his older brother.

"Say what you can't figure out how to say." Matt took another swallow of beer.

"I think maybe Jory is alive."

The world froze. Or maybe only his brothers stopped moving. Stopped breathing.

"What did you say?" Only Nate's lips moved. His body remained still, ready to pounce.

Shane eyed each of his brothers in turn. "I said that maybe Jory is alive. Or rather, maybe he didn't die from those bullet wounds." If his brother was still alive, why hadn't he contacted them? "I saw a second video. He might've blinked." Or it was a trick of the lighting.

"Jesus." Nathan dropped into a vacant chair. "Might

have? Shane, you're dreaming here. I understand it, but you're dreaming."

Matt's expression didn't change. Pure stone. But those eyes. Dark, dangerous, they swirled with enough emotion to make sound. "Tell me you're sure."

"I'm not sure." Shane squared his jaw. "There was a second video, and he may have blinked. That's why I broke cover and headed to Seattle. To see you—see if any of your contacts could get a better image from the video." The video that had disappeared along with his memories—probably in the river.

"What happened after he blinked?" Matt asked.

Shane concentrated on the memory. The camera angle had been toward the floor, where Jory lay. "A pair of shoes, high heels, crossed in front of the camera. Female hands grabbed his shoulders." Doubt filled Shane as the memories tumbled back. He might be giving his brothers false hope. "Then the video went blank."

"Dr. Madison?" Nathan hissed.

"I don't know." Many women wore high heels. God help Jory if it had been the psychotic doctor.

"Where's the video?" Nate asked.

"I don't know," Shane repeated. "Though chances are I had it at the house I stayed in to watch Josie."

Matt jumped to his feet. "We need to search that house and break into the police evidence room to find it. Probably on some sort of flash drive." He glanced at Shane's battered torso. "Good job, Shane."

Shane shrugged. "I wish I could say for sure. Nathan's right. I may be dreaming." But he'd move hell to find out the truth. "I stopped by to get Josie on the way to Seattle, found the bugs, and figured I'd better hang tight to see if the commander found her—hoping I'd find him." And have some answers about Jory.

Matt nodded. "Yeah, I get that. Shane, stay here and monitor the lines for any information on the explosion in Washington while you get your wife settled in. Nate will head back to Snowville to find the flash drive."

Nathan stood. "I put the Texas coordinates in your phone for your next mission."

"Thanks." Matt poured the rest of his beer down the drain of the sink. He turned and strode from the house.

Shane frowned. "What's in Texas?"

Nathan sighed. "Hopefully more intel on the commander and his funding." He set down his beer and eyed the door. "I'll go talk to Mattie before he leaves."

Shane stretched to his feet, careful of the bandages around his torso. Long strides had him pushing open the heavy oak door to the guest room. Josie sat on the bed dressed in a sweat suit, her wet hair wisping around her face. Fragile and soft, she took up a tiny space on the huge bed.

His heart thumped. Hard. "Are you all right?"

She arched an eyebrow. "Of course. I'm not the one covered in bandages."

He smiled, kicking the door shut behind him. Determined steps brought him to the bed. "So."

"So." Her intoxicating scent of wild berries filled the room, filled his heart. "Um. Thanks for my clothes. For having Matt grab them."

"Sure. We'll get the rest this week. In fact, we'll get all your belongings for you." He tucked his hands in his jean pockets to keep from reaching for her. They needed to talk. "First, I just heard from Malloy, and he came up with a pretty creative explanation as to why he was at the airport. But he played dumb as to why there are dead bodies around. Just claimed that he caught the end of the fight."

Relief played across her pretty face. "I'm glad. He wanted to help me."

"He helped us all. We definitely owe Detective Malloy a favor or two." Shane cleared his throat. "Second, I don't want to lie to you." There had to be a smooth way to get her to stay. But all training, all manipulation flew out the window when he dealt with her. She deserved the truth.

"That would be a nice change." A small dimple flirted at the corner of her mouth. The raw bruise on her cheekbone made him hope Tom landed on a spike.

"Do you love me?" He needed to know. He needed to hear her say the words.

Her eyes darkened to nearly purple. "I love you." She plucked at a loose string on the duvet. "I always have."

"You're the only woman I've ever loved." He couldn't live without her. Didn't want to. "I'm selfish, Josie. Life is hard, and I don't want to fight it without you." Sparks flared in her stunning eyes, and he fought a grin. "Because I love you. Because I need you with me. When I stopped by your house on the way to Seattle, I was going to ask you for another chance. Ask you to go with me to meet Matt." Of course, he'd found bugs in her house instead.

He rested one knee on the bed. If he had to get her naked to listen to him, he would. "Now I could lie and say you need to stay here for safety." He shrugged. "But you don't. We could get you a new identity. Lots of money, lots of safety. You don't need my protection."

"I know."

"But I need you. We're family, and I need you in my life more than I need air. Please stay."

Josie eyed her husband. She didn't need his protection, but it was nice that someone finally had her back. The world was scary, and she'd navigated it for so long by herself. "I like your protection." The words hinted at a vulnerability she'd never allowed herself to voice. "I like feeling safe."

While they may only have three months together, she wanted every second. And she'd do whatever she could to make sure they had longer.

His gray eyes warmed to heated silver. Sliding forward onto the bed, he rolled onto his back and lifted her to straddle his groin. She settled herself away from his bandages. "I'll keep you safe, angel."

"Sure." She flashed him a smile that even felt flirty. "We just need to catch the commander, destroy that bitch Dr. Madison, and find the truth about Jory. While remaining safe."

Shane ran his hands down her arms to clasp her hands. "So you'll stay married to me?"

"Yes." Hell yes. He was everything she'd ever wanted. Family. Hers. And even better, he came with brothers.

Sorrow swirled in his eyes. "There's a chance I can't have kids. We don't know if it's possible. They might've goofed up our DNA so much that we can't." Vulnerability twisted his lips.

Her heart warmed, and she reached out to frame his face. "We're going to get past the next three months and make sure that chip is gone. Then, we're in this life together. If we can have kids, and we want to, we will. If not, we'll adopt. Or it'll just be us. Together." Equal partners. "But I want all of you. The good and bad—no more secrets or hiding."

"What about your numbers and accounting? I know how much it means to you."

She shook her head. "Being needed and being counted on matter to me. I can have that without the numbers, without the clients. I have that with you." There was no comparison between a job and the man she loved. He won, hands down.

"I do need you." He smiled. "You have all of me. Forever."

Those were the words she'd needed to hear for so long. Her heart warmed, and peace settled her shoulders. "Good. Since we're here, and I'm a genius with accounting as well as business...how about I help Nate with Sins Security?"

Approval lit Shane's dark eyes. "Excellent idea. The guy could use help."

"And when you need a woman on a mission, I'm your gal. Sometimes men can't go everywhere."

"When I need a woman, you're the only one I'd want." His grin promised he wouldn't be asking.

That's what he thought. "I plan to help."

"You will." His lids lowered to half-mast, his gray gaze darkening. Her thighs softened in response. With a quick movement, he yanked her shirt over her head.

"Hey," she protested. "You're injured."

"So be gentle with me." He reached for the tie on her sweats.

"Why? I don't like gentle any more than you do."

"I like you any way I can get you." He lifted her to tug off her pants. His nimble fingers ran along the outside of her panties. "I love you, Josie Dean."

"I love you, too." Her heart melted while her body quivered. "I'll try to be very gentle with you since you're so obviously injured." She rolled her eyes. "But I wouldn't want to tame you too much, Major Dean."

The world tilted, and she yelped, finding herself under a soldier. He settled his erection between her legs. "I'm not too worried about that."

She grinned, winding both arms around his neck. "Prove it, Major."

Rebecca Zanetti's thrilling,
sexy series continues!

Please turn this page for
a heart-pounding
preview of

Sweet Revenge

CHAPTER
1

S TAB WOUNDS HURT worse than bullet wounds.

Sitting on asphalt in the dark, Matt Dean leaned against the worn brick building and scanned the vacant alley. Garbage cans lined the doorways of the now-closed businesses. The place smelled like honeysuckle.

What kind of an alley smelled like honeysuckle?

He'd been stabbed two days ago, and the staples he'd used had all but fallen out. But he'd had to get as far away as possible from what must now be a bloody crime scene.

Two of the men who'd jumped him would never jump, much less breathe, again. The other two might wish for death when they awoke. How the hell had they found him?

His phone had been damaged in the fight, and he'd had no choice but to continue on his mission, hop on his bike, and ride three states over. Out of their reach.

Time to break into one of the businesses and call his brothers.

He shrugged off his leather jacket and glanced at his destroyed shirt.

A door opened several yards down. He stiffened, reaching

for the knife in his boot. At three a.m., nobody should be in the alley.

"Eugene?" a female voice whispered.

That tone shivered right down his spine. Sexy and frustrated, the tenor promised heated nights. He'd always had a thing for a woman's husky voice.

So he turned his head.

She stood in the moonlight in a compact yoga outfit, her mahogany hair up in one of those clips. Damn, he'd love to let that mass fly.

Maybe blood loss was getting to him.

"Eugene?" the woman called again, holding the door open with her hip. "Your walk should be finished by now, and enough is enough. Your moodiness is getting to me."

Who the hell was Eugene? It was just a matter of seconds before the woman noticed Matt, and he didn't have the energy to fight the mysterious Eugene.

She gasped when she saw him.

Great. Now she'd run inside and call the police.

Except she didn't.

The woman rushed toward him, dropping to her knees. "Oh my God. You're hurt." She swallowed several times and levered away. Her eyes were the color of an emerald he'd stolen from a Colombian drug lord years ago while on a mission. "I'll call an ambulance."

He grabbed her arm, careful not to break the delicate bones. "I'm fine." Pressing his other palm against the brick, he shoved himself up and helped her along. "Though I could use an aspirin."

She stilled and then looked up, way up, toward his face. "Um—"

He tried to smile. "I won't hurt you." Yeah, right. He was at least a foot taller and a hundred pounds heavier than her, found bleeding in her alley. All he needed was duct tape and a ski mask to be a bigger threat to somebody so small.

"Right." She swallowed and shook her arm free. "You're harmless. Anybody could see that." She stepped back.

He grinned. Damn, she was cute. He tilted his head toward his motorcycle. "I'll just get on and leave you alone. Sorry to scare you."

She frowned and rubbed her forehead as she eyed the bike. "Did you fall?"

"Yes," he lied smoothly. "Hit a pothole and basically landed on my head. I was tired and not watching the road."

Indecision crossed her classic face. She leaned forward to eye the tattoo on his arm. "You were in the marines?"

"Yes." Yet another lie. He'd been undercover as a U.S. Marshal, then as a marine, and the tat was temporary.

"Oh." She exhaled. "My brother was a marine."

"Was?"

"Yes. He didn't make it home."

Matt's chest thumped. Hard. "I lost a brother, too." Finally, a truth he could give her. "Hurts like hell and always will." Of course, it was his fault Jory was dead, and he'd been paying for it since. Some souls were meant to be damned.

She sighed. "Well, I can't just leave an ex-marine in the alley. Come in and we can get you cleaned up, but if you're injured too badly, I'm calling an ambulance." She levered under his arm, her slender shoulders straightening to assist him.

Intrigue and an odd irritation filtered through him. "You shouldn't help strange men, sweetheart."

"All men are strange." The grin she flipped him warmed him in places he thought would always be frozen. "Besides, I'm armed."

There wasn't a place for a weapon in her little yoga outfit. But he nodded anyway, happy to be getting indoors. "Okay. Then I'll behave." Then he paused. Perhaps he should let her call for medical help, considering he was in town to find a doctor. The woman he'd been searching for the last five years. But he wanted to be on his game when he found the bitch. "What about Eugene?"

His rescuer bit her lip. "I'm sure he'll be along shortly."

Who the hell was Eugene? Matt tuned in his senses but failed to hear any footsteps. A couple argued several blocks away about who should drive home. They both slurred their words, so neither should drive.

Matt released the woman and forced his feet to move toward his bike. He'd lost too much blood. "Do you mind if I park my bike inside? I'd hate for anybody to steal my baby."

She chuckled. "In Charmed, Idaho? Nobody will take your big motorcycle." Yet she opened the doorway wide. "You can park just inside to the left."

He rolled the bike inside a small storage room holding toiletries and cleaning supplies. "What's your name?"

"Laney." She locked the door and gestured him toward a doorway. "Let's get you that aspirin."

He stalked through another storage room that held all types of alcohol to a bar. A sports bar with widescreens, pool tables, and dartboards. He glanced down at Laney. "You work at a bar?"

He'd figured her for a yoga instructor or a teacher. Not a barmaid.

She gently pushed him onto a wooden chair by a worn

table. "I own a bar." Her pretty pink lips turned down as she glanced at his demolished T-shirt.

"Oh." He frowned. The woman was much too delicate to be closing a bar by herself. Whoever the hell Eugene was, he needed a beating for leaving her alone at night like this. "By yourself?"

She lifted a shoulder while walking behind the bar and returning with a first-aid kit. "My brother and I owned it together." Her eyes remained down.

He understood that kind of sorrow. "I'm sorry, Laney."

She blinked and met his gaze with those amazing green eyes. "Me, too." Taking a deep breath, she straightened. "Let's see what you did to yourself."

He gingerly tugged off his shirt.

Her cheeks slid from rosy to stark white in seconds. Emerald flashed when her eyes opened wide. "You're really bleeding." Then her eyelids fluttered, and she swayed.

He caught her one-handed before she hit the floor.

What the hell?

Easily picking her up, he glanced around the bar. The booths were circular at an odd angle, and the chairs were hard. He could either place her on the bar or on a pool table. Gently, he lay her on a pool table, warmed by how nicely she fit against him. Indulging himself, he removed her hair clip and allowed the curls to tumble free.

He'd been without a woman much too long.

Now was not the time. Yet he couldn't help taking a moment to appreciate her classic features. Delicate and soft women were a mystery to him and something he'd only seen on television. He believed they existed but definitely steered clear.

This one? This one needed protection, and he'd have a nice talk with Eugene when the bastard finally showed up.

For now, he'd lost enough blood. Flipping open the lid of the medicine kit, he frowned. Not what he needed.

Prowling behind the bar, he searched the low shelves. *Ah ha.* A rusty tackle box rested in the back. Inside, he found thick fishing line and flies with hooks. Bending one, he threaded it like a needle after pouring whiskey over it to kill germs. Then he took a swig of the alcohol, allowing the potent brew to slam into his gut and center him.

Minutes later, he'd successfully sutured both wounds. The one on his upper chest took twice as long as the wide gash along his ribs. The guy who'd stabbed him knew how to use a blade.

So did he.

He glanced at the pretty woman on the pool table. How long did a faint last, anyway? Then the phone behind the bar caught his attention. He slapped long pads across his wounds and reached for the phone to dial in a series of numbers.

"Swippy's Pool Hall," a man answered.

"Deranged Duck 27650," Matt said.

Several beeps echoed across the line as it was secured. Finally, silence ensued.

"Where the hell are you?" his brother growled.

Matt wiped a hand down his face. Shane sounded worried. "I'm in place. Had some trouble in Texas, however."

"What kind of trouble?" Shane asked, computer keys clacking across the line.

"Jumped by four men—well trained. They found me in Dallas as I was heading out here." How had the damn commander found him in Texas? He'd only been there a week to gather intel on the woman he'd been searching for.

"No mention of a problem on any police forces or

news outlets." Shane sighed. "They covered the scene up quickly."

Which meant the commander had new resources in the government. Terrific. "Are you sure the woman is here?" Matt asked.

"Yes. We finally traced her to Charmed, but we don't know who she is. I've narrowed it down to a surgeon at the hospital, a veterinarian, or the coroner's assistant." Shane clicked more keys. "My money is on the coroner."

The woman he hunted had been a top-rated surgeon before disappearing and hiding. Chances were she was still cutting into people. Most surgeons couldn't let go of playing God. "I'll boot up my laptop tonight and have you send me the files." His gaze caught on a Help Wanted sign in the window. "I may have just found my cover while in town."

"Good. Stay in touch, Mattie." The line went dead.

Matt rubbed his chin, his gaze on Laney. Pouring a glass of water, he maneuvered over to her. Now all he had to do was get her to hire him.

Laney slowly opened her eyes and tried to ignore the pounding of her temples. What in the world?

A man stood over her, and her memories crashed back.

She shot to sit, her hand going to her aching head. "What happened?"

"You fainted."

The low rumble of his voice matched the battle-scarred chest. Even with two pristine bandages, old wounds lived among the hard ridges and ripped muscles. And the guy was ripped.

A warning flutter rippled through her abdomen. She cleared her throat.

As if he could read her mind, he set a glass of water on the pool table and took several steps back. Giving her space.

"Drink," he said.

Not a man of many words, was he? She took the glass and sipped, allowing the water to cool her heated throat. The pool table was surprisingly comfortable. "Who are you?"

"Matt Dean." He rubbed a hand through his shaggy hair.

He still had dried blood on his impressive abs, and she shoved down panic. The mere sight of blood could make her pass out within seconds. She shook her head. "Why are you in town?"

"After the marines, I decided to tour the country for a while until I run out of money, then I work for a bit, and move on afterwards."

Sad. The guy was obviously running from old horrors. "Is it working? I mean, the traveling?"

"Yes."

The blood disappeared as his physique took center stage. Wow. The new warmth sliding through her veins had nothing to do with caution. Tension emanated around him with the promise of fire and passion.

The kind of guy who'd burn a girl, but it'd be worth it.

He tilted his head toward the sign in the window. "You need help?"

Always, and right now from her own libido. "Have you heard of the Rally in the Mountains?"

He nodded. "The motorcycle rally in southern Oregon? Yeah, I've heard of it."

"Well, the rally is in two weeks, and many of the bikers from the east head through town. We're incredibly busy for those two weeks." She eyed him. At several inches above six feet and broad, he'd be a deterrent to any problems. He'd seen war—the guy was definitely wounded.

And tough. He'd be able to handle any disputes that arose. In fact, with that hard gray gaze taking in the room, maybe the bikers wouldn't mess around. Of course, with that thick black hair and strong-boned face, he'd draw in the women.

The man needed help, and she needed a tough guy in her corner. Plus, he'd served his country and was one of the good guys in a scary world. "I need a bartender/bouncer for two weeks."

He smiled, flashing strong teeth.

She swallowed again. Wounded and scowling, the guy was handsome. Smiling and charming, he was downright devastating. Her heart rate picked up.

His smile widened. Why? It wasn't like he could hear her heart.

Frowning, she scooted to the edge of the pool table. Strong hands instantly banded around her waist to lift.

She gasped, not having seen him move. "You move fast."

He settled her on her feet and waited until she regained her balance.

She tilted her head way back to glance at his face. This close, a strong shadow covered his jaw.

His hands remained at her waist, warm and strong.

"No," she murmured.

His eyelids creased. "Why not?"

"B-Because." She couldn't help but focus on his full lips.

"A woman who ventures into a darkened alley and helps a stranger is brave and likes to take chances." Challenge and something darker lurked in his eyes.

He smelled like the forest; wild and free.

Heat washed down her torso, and she tried to breathe slowly. What in the world was going on? She liked safe, and she liked security. "I hate taking chances."

His mouth pursed as he studied her. "Somehow I don't think so."

A yowling set up outside the entrance door. He pivoted, shielding her.

Her skin chilled from his removed hands, while her heart warmed at how quickly he'd moved into protector mode. "It's all right," she said, stepping around him as relief filled her.

One hand banded around her arm and tugged her back as the yowling increased in volume. "What is that?"

She chuckled. "Let me go."

"No." He released her and moved toward the door, gingerly unlocking it to open a crack. Then he stepped back, surprise lifting his dark eyebrows.

Matted brown fur came into view first before a battered face. Eugene meowed at seeing her. She dropped to her haunches. "There you are." Thank God.

She rubbed his thick fur, careful not to touch his scars. He'd been wounded when she'd found him, and she was the only person he'd allow close. For a brief moment, she'd feared he'd been danger.

"Thank goodness you're all right," she crooned.

Matt locked the door and leaned against it, broad arms crossed. "I take it that's Eugene?"

"Yes." She smiled as Eugene purred like a diesel. "I thought maybe—" Oh. Too much information to the stranger. "Nothing."

Matt frowned. "Maybe what?"

"Nothing." She relaxed. "He's fine."

"Why wouldn't he be?" That gray gaze narrowed on her.

She cleared her throat, feeling suddenly like a specimen on a slide. "Life isn't always smooth, even in a small town." Life was also too short to spend time dumping her problems on a guy who had enough of his own.

"Are you in trouble, sweetheart?" he asked softly, pushing off from the door.

Yes. Definitely. Trouble with all capital letters stood before her like every dangerous fantasy a girl had about tattooed bad boys on motorcycles. "No. By the way, there's a room upstairs you can rent by the week while you're here."

Matt stepped into her space, bringing warmth and the scent of male. One knuckle tipped up her chin. "Sounds perfect. You saved me in the alley, and I owe you. So while I'm here, you're going to let me take care of whatever put that frightened look in your eyes."

The absolute strength and determination across his face should scare her. Yet, lava burned through her veins instead of fear. While she had issues, no doubt the biggest threat stood before her with hard muscles and bloody jeans—because against all caution, she wanted to avoid reality and jump into the heat.

That's how a woman already in danger got burned.

THE DISH

Where Authors Give You the Inside Scoop

♥ ♥ ♥ ♥ ♥ ♥ ♥ ♥ ♥ ♥ ♥ ♥ ♥ ♥ ♥ ♥ ♥

From the desk of Jaime Rush

Dear Reader,

Enemies to lovers is a concept I've always loved. Yes, it's a challenge, and maybe that's what I like most. It's a given that the couple is going to have instant chemistry—it is a romance, after all! But they're going to fight it harder because they have history and a good reason. Each person believes they're in the right.

That's how Kade Kavanaugh feels. Being a member of the Guard, my supernatural world's police force, he has had plenty of run-ins with Violet Castanega's family. They live in the Fringe, a wild and uncivilized community of Dragon shifters who think they are on the fringe of the law as well. And mostly they are, except when their illegal activities threaten to catch the attention of the Muds, the Mundane human police. Because Rule Number One is simple: Never reveal the existence of the Hidden community that has existed amid the glitter and glamour of Miami for over three hundred years. Mundanes would panic if they knew that Crescents—humans who hold the essence of Dragons, sorcerers (like Kade), and fallen angels—lived among them.

Violet is fiercely loyal to her Dragon clan, even if it does sometimes flout the law. But when one of her brothers is murdered by a Dragon bent on firing up the clan wars, she has no choice but to go to the Guard for help. There she encounters Kade, whom she attacked the last time he tried to arrest her brother.

My job as a writer is to throw these two unsuspecting people together in ways that will test their loyalties and their integrity. And definitely test their resolve to resist getting involved with not only a member of another class of Crescent, but a sworn enemy to boot. Juicy conflict, hot passion, and supernatural action—a combination that truly tested my hero and heroine. But their biggest lesson is never to judge someone by their name, their heritage, or their actions. I think that's a good lesson for all of us.

We all have magic in our imaginations. Mine has always contained murder, mayhem, and romance. Feel free to wander through the madness of my mind any time. A good place to start is my website www.jaimerush.com, or that of my romantic suspense alter-ego, www.tinawainscott.com.

Jaime Rush

From the desk of Kristen Ashley

Dear Reader,

While writing MOTORCYCLE MAN I was in a very dark time of my life. An *extended* dark time, which is very rare. Indeed, it's only ever happened that once.

In fact, I wrote nearly an entirely different book for my hero, Tack. He had a different heroine. And it had a different plot. Completely. But it didn't work for me and it has never seen the light of day. I abandoned it totally (something I've never done), gave it time, and started anew.

I had thought it was rubbish. Of course, on going back and reading it later, I realize it wasn't. I actually think it's great. It just wasn't Tack. And the heroine was not right for him. But never fear, I like it enough; when I have time (whenever that is in this decade), I intend to rework it and release it, because that hero and heroine's story really should be told.

Nevertheless, when I finally found the dream woman who would belong to Kane "Tack" Allen in MOTOR-CYCLE MAN, I was still questioning my work because things in life weren't going so great.

You see, sometimes I battle my characters. Sometimes they urge me to take risks I feel I'm not ready to take. Sometimes they encourage me to glide along an edge that's a little scary even as it is thrilling. And when life is also scary, your confidence gets shaken in a way it's tough to bounce back from.

But Kane "Tack" Allen is an edgy, risky guy, so he was pretty adamant (as he can be) that he wanted me to just let go and ride it with him. Not only that, but lift up my hands and enjoy the hell out of that ride.

But as I was writing it, I still fought him. Particularly the scene in Tyra's office early on in the book, where they have a misunderstanding and Tack decides to make his feelings perfectly clear and in order to do that, he gets Tyra's attention in a way that's utterly unacceptable.

I fretted about this scene, but Tack refused to let me soften it. I even sent it to my girl, a girl who knows me and my writing inside and out. If I remember correctly, her response was that it was indeed shocking, but I should go with it.

Ride it out.

In releasing MOTORCYCLE MAN, I was very afraid that my life had negatively affected my writing and the risks Tack urged me to take would not be well received.

As you can imagine, I was absolutely *elated* when I found I'd done the right thing. When Tack and Tyra swiftly became one of my most popular couples. That Tack had rightly encouraged me to trust in myself, my instincts, my writing, and give myself to my characters to let them be precisely what they were, let them shine, not water them down, and last, give my readers the honesty. They could take it. Because it was genuine. It came from the soul.

It was real.

And because of all this, MOTORCYCLE MAN will always hold a firm place in my heart. Because that novel and Kane "Tack" Allen gave me the freedom I was searching for. The freedom to ride this wave. Ride it wild. Ride it free.

Lift up my hands and ride it being nothing but me.

Kristen Ashley

♥ ♥ ♥ ♥ ♥ ♥ ♥ ♥ ♥ ♥ ♥ ♥ ♥ ♥ ♥ ♥

From the desk of Christie Craig

Dear Reader,

Here are two things about love I took from my own life and used in TEXAS HOLD 'EM:

1. Love can make us stupid.

   Sexy PI Austin Brook is a smooth-talking good ol' boy Texan. Where women are concerned, he wings it. Why not? He's got charm to spare. But one glance at Leah Reece and he's a stumbling, bumbling idiot. First he accidentally blows his horn as she's passing in front of his truck, causing her to toss up her arms and drop her groceries. Wanting to help, he snatches up a plastic bag containing a broken bottle of wine and manages to douse Leah with Cabernet from the waist up. And since he likes wine and wet T-shirt contests, it only makes her more appealing and him more nervous.

   For myself? On a first date with a good ol' Texan, we were both jittery. I'd dressed up in a short skirt. The guy, thinking he should be a gentleman, pulled my chair out in the crowded restaurant. I had my bottom almost in the seat when he moved it out. *Way out.* *He* might've looked like a gentleman, but there was nothing ladylike about how I went down. All the way to the floor, legs sprawled out, skirt up to my yin-yang. Laughter filled the room. Snickering in spite of his apologetic look, he added, "Nice legs."

Later when he dropped me off at my apartment, I struggled to get the door of his sports car open. Forever the gentlemen—hey, that's Texans for you—he rushed to open my door, and then shut it. Standing close, he heard my moan, and completely misunderstood. He dipped in for a kiss.

I stopped him. "Can you open the car door?"

"Why?" he asked.

I moaned again. "Because my hand's still in the door."

With a bruised butt, and three busted fingernails, I eventually did let him score a kiss. It's amazing I married that man.

2. Love is scary.

Divorced, and a single mother, I wasn't looking for love when I met Mr. Craig. Life had taught me that love can hurt. And I'm not talking about a sore backside or fingernails. I'm talking about the heart.

Neither Austin nor Leah is open to love. Isn't that what makes it so perfect and yet still so dad-blasted frightening? We don't find love; love finds us. And like me, Leah's and Austin's pasts have left them leery.

At age six, Leah realized her daddy had another family, one he obviously loved better because they had his name and he called that home. Oh, when older, she still gave love a shot, got married, expected the happily-ever-after, and instead got a divorce and a credit card bill for all his phone sex. It's not that Leah doesn't believe in love; she just doesn't trust herself to know the real thing.

Austin, abandoned by his mother at age three, passed from one foster home to another, and learned caring about people gave them power to hurt you. His last and final (he swears) heartache happened when his fiancé dumped him after he got convicted of a murder he didn't commit.

As scary as love is, Leah and Austin give it another shot. Not to give away any spoilers, but I think it'll work out fine for them. I know it has for me. I'll soon be celebrating my thirtieth wedding anniversary. So here's to laughter, good books, and getting knocked on your butt by love.

Happy reading!

Christie Craig

♥ ♥ ♥ ♥ ♥ ♥ ♥ ♥ ♥ ♥ ♥ ♥ ♥ ♥

From the desk of Laura Drake

Dear Reader,

There's just something about the soft side of a hard man that I've never been able to resist—how about you?

Max Jameson looks like a modern-day Marlboro Man. He's a western cattleman, meaning he's stubborn, hard-working, and an eternal optimist. But given his current problems, there's not enough duct tape in all of Colorado to fix them.

To introduce you to the heroine of NOTHING

SWEETER, Aubrey Madison (aka Bree Tanner), I thought I'd share with you her list of life lessons:

1. Nothing is sweeter than freedom.
2. It is impossible to outrun your own conscience.
3. "When you're going through hell, keep going."
   —Winston Churchill
4. There are more kinds of family than blood kin.
5. A stuck-up socialite can make a pretty good friend when the chips are on the table.
6. Real men (and bulls) wear pink.
7. "To forgive is to set a prisoner free, and discover that the prisoner is you." —Louis B. Smede

I hope you'll enjoy NOTHING SWEETER. Keep your eyes open for a cameo of JB and Charla from *The Sweet Spot*, and watch for them all to turn up in *Sweet on You*, the last book in the series!

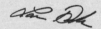

From the desk of Rebecca Zanetti

Dear Reader,

I met my husband camping when we were about eight years old, and he taught me how to play Red Rover so he could hold my hand. He was a sweet, chubby, brown-eyed boy. We lost touch, and years later, I walked into a bar (yeah, a bar), and there he was. Except this time, he was six-foot-five, muscled, with dark hair, a tattoo, a leather jacket, and held a motorcycle helmet under one hand. To put it simply, I was intrigued. He's still the sweet guy but has a bit of an edge. Now we're married and have two kids, two dogs, and a crazy cat.

People change…and often we don't know them as well as we think we do. In fact, I've always been fascinated by the idea that we never truly know what's in the minds or even the pasts of the people around us. What if your best friend worked for the CIA years ago? Or the mild-mannered janitor at your child's elementary school is a retired Marine sniper who didn't like retirement and has found a good way to fill his life with joy? What if your baby sister was a criminal informant in college?

What if the calm and always-in-control man you married is one of the deadliest men alive?

And what if you're now being threatened by an outside source? What happens to that calm control now? That was the main premise for FORGOTTEN SINS. Josie Dean, a woman with a lonely past, married Shane Dean in a whirlwind of passion and energy. Then he disappeared two years ago. The story starts with him back in her life, with danger surrounding him, and with the edge he'd always partially hidden finally exposed.

Of course, Shane has amnesia, and in his discovery of finding himself, he reveals himself to the one woman he ever truly loved. He'd always held back, always treated her with kid gloves.

Now, not knowing his deadly training, there's no holding back. The primal, arousing man she'd believed existed has to take the forefront as he protects them from the danger stalking him from his past. Yeah, he'd always been fun and sexy…with hints of dominance in the bedroom. Now the hints disappear to unveil the true Shane Dean—the man Josie hoped she'd married.

I hope you truly enjoy Shane and Josie's story.

Best,

Rebecca Zanetti

RebeccaZanetti.com
Twitter, @RebeccaZanetti
Facebook.com/RebeccaZanetti.Author.FanPage

From the desk of Kate Meader

Dear Reader,

FEEL THE HEAT is the first in my smokin' Hot in the Kitchen series, about an Italian restaurant–owning family and the sexy, sizzling chefs who love them. And don't we all want a hotter-than-Hades, caring, alpha chef like Jack Kilroy in our lives? A man who cooks, defends his lady, and knows how to treat her right both in the kitchen *and* in the bedroom is worth his weight in focaccia (and the British accent doesn't hurt). But sometimes we've got to work with what the gods have given us. So if you have a husband/boyfriend/sex slave who believes guy cooking = grilling, but outside of the summer months, you won't catch him dead in an apron, read on.

"But he just makes a mess" or "I'm a better cook," I

hear you whine. Who cares? The benefits to encouraging your man to cook are multifold.

1. Guys who cook know how to multitask. If he can watch a couple of bubbling pots, chop those herbs, and pour you a glass of wine, all while *you* put your feet up, it'll eventually translate to other areas. Childcare, taking out the trash, maybe even doing the dishes as he whips up that *coq au vin.*

   Guys who cook know how to get creative. You might ask your man: "Is this made with sour cream, babe?"

   Cue worry crease on guy's brow that looks so adorable. "No, I didn't have any so I used Greek yogurt instead. Does it taste okay?"

   Hold praise for a beat "That's so creative, babe, and less fattening."

   (Positive reinforcement is key during the early training phase.)

2. Guys who cook have a direct correlation to a woman's TBR list. He's brought you that glass of Pinot and he's back in the kitchen where he belongs. Now you can get down to the important stuff—making a dent in your stories about fictional boyfriends who probably cook better than your guy. (In the case of Jack Kilroy, Shane Doyle, and Tad DeLuca, the sexy heroes of the Hot in the Kitchen series, this conclusion is a given.)

3. Guys who cook will evolve into guys who shop for groceries. Nuff said.

4. Guys who cook make better lovers. Chefs have very skillful hands, often callused and scarred from years

of kitchen abuse. Those fast-moving, rough hands are going to take your sexytimes to the next level! As long as your guy is burning himself while he learns, it can only be beneficial to you further down the road.

So get your guy in an apron and let the good times roll. Remember, chefs do it better...

Happy cooking, eating, and reading!

Kate Meader

www.katemeader.com